I0716282

THE PEACE

BOOK FOUR

THE SUFI MYSTERIES QUARTET

LAURY SILVERS

Published by Laury Silvers

This is a work of fiction based on historical places, circumstances, and, in some cases, historical persons as read through the primary sources of the period and the secondary scholarship concerning it. All historical places, persons, and interpretations are ultimately the product of the author's imagination.

Limited selected quotes adapted from secondary and primary sources fall under "Fair Use." Alexander Knysh kindly gave his permission for the use of quotations adapted from his translation of al-Qushayri's *Epistle on Sufism*. Th. Emil Homerin kindly gave his permission for the use of his translation of Aisha Baʿuniyya's poems. al-Kharraz's lines are adapted from the translation of Arin Salamah Qudsi. Ibn Mansur al-Hallaj's lines are adapted from the translations of Carl Ernst and Louis Massignon. Saadia's poem, "Lioness," is attributed to Wallada bint al-Mustakfi (d. 1091), translator unknown. Saadia's poem, "Shall I visit you," is attributed to Hafsa Bint al-Hajjah al-Rakuniya (d. 1185), adapted from translations by Marla Segol and Arie Schippers. Quran and hadith translations are my own adaptations from available online and in print English translations.

Cover by Anthony O'Brien. Copyright, Laury Silvers, 2023.

The Fell Types are digitally reproduced by Igino Marini. www.iginomarini.com

Map of Iraq, Leiden codex Or. 3101, used with the kind permission of Leiden University, and the assistance of Karen Pinto.

ISBN paperback: 978-1-7381013-0-6

ISBN e-book: 978-1-7381013-1-3

❀ Created with Vellum

THE PEACE

BOOK FOUR

THE SUFI MYSTERIES QUARTET

LAURY SILVERS

Published by Laury Silvers

This is a work of fiction based on historical places, circumstances, and, in some cases, historical persons as read through the primary sources of the period and the secondary scholarship concerning it. All historical places, persons, and interpretations are ultimately the product of the author's imagination.

Limited selected quotes adapted from secondary and primary sources fall under "Fair Use." Alexander Knysh kindly gave his permission for the use of quotations adapted from his translation of al-Qushayri's *Epistle on Sufism*. Th. Emil Homerin kindly gave his permission for the use of his translation of Aisha Baʿuniyya's poems. al-Kharraz's lines are adapted from the translation of Arin Salamah Qudsi. Ibn Mansur al-Hallaj's lines are adapted from the translations of Carl Ernst and Louis Massignon. Saadia's poem, "Lioness," is attributed to Wallada bint al-Mustakfi (d. 1091), translator unknown. Saadia's poem, "Shall I visit you," is attributed to Hafsa Bint al-Hajjah al-Rakuniya (d. 1185), adapted from translations by Marla Segol and Arie Schippers. Quran and hadith translations are my own adaptations from available online and in print English translations.

Cover by Anthony O'Brien. Copyright, Laury Silvers, 2023.

The Fell Types are digitally reproduced by Igino Marini. www.iginomarini.com

Map of Iraq, Leiden codex Or. 3101, used with the kind permission of Leiden University, and the assistance of Karen Pinto.

ISBN paperback: 978-1-7381013-0-6

ISBN e-book: 978-1-7381013-1-3

❀ Created with Vellum

To my teachers, all of you.

ACKNOWLEDGMENTS

I thank my partner, Michael, for his ongoing support, and without whom these books would never have been written. Throughout, he has cheered me on, buoyed me in hard days, celebrated my successes, read every page over and over, and wrote all my fight scenes. He is my Kamal Ali.

My account of the period between the two canonizations of the Quran relies primarily on the scholarship of Marijn van Putten and Shady Nasser. Marijn van Putten fact-checked the draft for errors, advised me on the right balance between secular history and tradition for this fictional account, and answered innumerable questions. Links to van Putten and Nasser's work can be found on my website blog. Any errors are my own.

My characterization of Razba, and the early development of type, is taken from Kristina Richardson's work, *Roma in the Medieval Islamic World*. She also kindly read that section and gave me feedback. Any errors are my own.

I would like to thank those who generously sent me published and unpublished works, answered my questions when I got stuck, produced Twitter threads of immense knowledge, or whose scholarship greatly impacted this novel. My sincerest thanks go to Ash Geissinger, Alan Godlas, Hythem Sidky, Antonia Bosanquet, Uwe Bergmann, Behnam Sadeghi, Mohsen Goudarzi, Yasin Dutton, Éléonore Cellard, Sohaib Saeed, Ahab Bdaiwi, Sean Anthony, Emran El-Badawi, Christopher Melchert, Simon Fuchs, Ruth Roded, Sara Abdel Latif, Arin Salamah Qudsi, Peter Groff, Kevin Blankinship, Kenley Borgerson, Mustafa Shah, Stephennie Mulder, Nassima Neggaz, Raha Rafii, Rana Makati,

Amila Buturović, Eric Hanne, Wallied al-Azhari, Arie Schippers, Marla Segol, Marwan al-Asmar, Michael Morony, Karen Pinto, Joshua Mugler, Leila Badawi, Sohaib Sial, @islam_texts, and many others whose names I have lost in my notes, forgive me. Finally, in the scholarly category, my thanks go to several academic podcasts, most especially "Abbasid History," "New Books in Islamic Studies," "Ajam Media Collective," "Bottled Petrichor," "Exploring The Quran and Bible," and "International Quranic Studies Association." And with the culmination of al-Hallaj's story, my thanks go to Carl Ernst and Louis Massignon.

A small group of friends gave me feedback on chapter two: Adnan Mahmutović, Zeshan Akhter, Oonaiza Mirza, Yasser Kassana, Nabilaa Khan, and Abdur-Rahman Syed, especially Mahmutović who generously commented on style. Rose Sutherland gave me feedback on my characterization of Saadia. As always, amina wadud advised me on my characterization of Tein, Zaytuna, and their mother as well as other characters of African descent. For a discussion of my approach to and treatment of racial difference in these novels, please see the blog on my website for an interview led by amina wadud and an essay on the subject. I continue to benefit from the many people who advised me on the characterizations of Baghdadis, and others of Arab, Persian, Turkmen, South Asian, and Chinese descent in earlier novels. Other friends offered writerly companionship and gave me suggestions and feedback, Karen Heenan, Ausma Zehanat Khan, Ahmed Saleh, Rosalinda Wijks, Nakia Jackson, Ali Naqvi, and Yusuf Jones.

I want to thank my early readers, Marian L. Thorpe, who gave the whole novel a much needed developmental read, Tracy Shirvill, and my two editing friends who make me sound better than I am, Karen Heenan and Shaheen Ali. Finally, amina wadud, again, who reads early drafts, comments, believes in my stories, and tells everyone she knows.

All the Muslim creatives on Facebook and Twitter who have built up a beautiful community in which we hold each other through our struggles and hold up each other's successes. And love to #HFChitChat for creating an online community for historical fiction writers.

My love to my family, Michael, Kaya and Ryan, Mishi and Ben,

Eleonore, Tracey, Nancey, Catherine, and Candace and all the Quinseys for their support. And a shout out to Mom. I know you read all the drafts of this book in The Good Place. Thanks to Kathleen Self, always. Thanks to all my neighbours and friends who have given me so much support. A special shout out goes to James Oliver of Oliver Coffee Bar where a heck of lot of this book was edited. And sincere gratitude goes to my teacher, Murat Coskun, for his guidance, and our community for their constant support and companionship.

HISTORY AND FICTION

While the background, some storylines, and even some dialogue are adapted from historical and literary accounts of Abbasid Baghdad and its inhabitants, this is a work of fiction. The book takes up some uncomfortable realities of life at that time. Social norms such as slavery, racism, shadism, gender divisions, marriage, drinking habits, mosque attendance, and class divisions are all grounded in historical sources.

If your interest in reading my novels is to understand present-day Iraq and its people, please close this book and turn to the work of Iraqi writers such as those found in Hassan Blasim's *Iraq + 100* collections, Shakir Mustafa's anthology, or *Baghdad Noir* collections of short stories, and the works of Shahad Al Rawi, Sinan Antoon, Dunya Mikhail, Leilah Nadir, and Ahmed Saadawi. Also see the online journal, "Arab Lit Quarterly." My novels are an exploration of an Abbasid past and, ultimately, how the past is remembered in the Muslim present.

A NOTE ON HISTORY AND IMPORTANT TERMS

A Note on History

MUSLIMS AND NON-MUSLIMS alike may be unfamiliar with the history of the Quran and fear or expect surprises on the scale of Dan Brown's *The DaVinci Code*. Whether it is a relief or a disappointment to the reader, the collection and preservation of the Quran bears little resemblance to that of other sacred texts, each of which has its own particular history and debates. You do not need to read the following to enjoy the mystery, but if you want more depth on the history of the Quran as depicted in this novel, carry on.

———

Recent scholarship demonstrates that the Quran we have today can be traced back to the community of the Prophet Muhammad. To most Muslims, this means that the Quran we have is what Muhammad recited. To others, this means that the Quran we have originated in that period, but no more can be said with certainty.

Traditional accounts report that during Muhammad's day, companions wrote down and memorized the revelation as Muhammad recited it and reviewed those verses over his lifetime. After Muhammad's passing, the first caliph, Abu Bakr (r. 632-634 CE), collected the written materials held by these companions providing the third caliph, Uthman (r. 644-656 CE), the textual basis upon which he would produce an official codex of the revelation itself.

The master codex of the Quran was written based on those collected materials and what was remembered by those who devoted their lives to memorizing it. While some historians continue to debate the existence of the caliph Uthman's collection, other analyses based on the most recent material evidence demonstrate that early Quran manuscripts can be traced back to a single written archetype dated to the caliph Uthman's reign.

A number of accepted "reading traditions," each comprising some small distinctions, were possible based on this master template. Because the written Arabic language had not yet developed markings for some vowels and consonants, some words could be read with a different vowel here or a consonant there. It is said that Muhammad himself allowed for these differences. The possible variations that could make an appreciable difference in meaning amount to less than one percent total of the text, and, as each reading tradition only uses a selection from that one percent, it amounts to even less.

Some three hundred years later, the famed scholar, Ibn Mujahid (859 or 860-936 CE), chose seven reading traditions from that larger number as the only acceptable readings. It may be surprising to Muslims today, but his move to limit the readings was highly controversial and the number would be expanded over the years to a limit of fourteen. The seven to fourteen reading traditions persist to this day. Any good Islamic bookstore should at least have four of them and Quran apps likewise make a number available. The most revered reciters typically have more than one memorized. In Morocco, I had the blessing to sit in the company of a man who had memorized seven.

Still, some Muslims are unfamiliar with this history and may be disturbed. In the present, the reading tradition known by the name of the transmitters, "Hafs from Asim," tends to be most popular. But its popularity is solely due to having been mass produced on an international scale. When Muslims say "not one word" of the Quran has been changed, they may mean the one reading tradition with which they are familiar, such as "Hafs." But the dictum refers to all the preserved words and variations. I have given the shock that some Muslims may feel to the character YingYue. I hope Muslim readers will empathize with her experience and non-Muslims understand what is at stake in our love and commitment to God's words.

———

For readers interested in the secular sources I relied on most, see the work of Marijn van Putten and Shady Nasser. Two pieces of particular significance to the novel will be posted on my blog.

On the differences between the canonization of the Quran and the New Testament, see the podcast of "The International Quranic Studies Association" with Shady Nasser.

For a traditional account that also covers the role of the Quran in the life and culture of Muslims over time, see Ingrid Mattson, *The Story of the Quran*.

If readers want to understand the power of the language and meaning of the Quran for Muslims, there is no better introduction than Michael Sells, *Approaching the Quran*.

Important Terms and People

Quran: Muslims believe the Quran to be the word of God in the Arabic language as revealed to the Prophet Muhammad, mainly through the intermediary of the angel Gabriel and, at other times, directly. Some Muslims believe that the Prophet received the whole of the Quran one night while meditating in a cave above the city of Mecca. From that view, the Quran was like a seed, its full potential revealed verse by verse over the next twenty-three years until the

Prophet's death. As the Quran was being revealed verse by verse, it was committed to memory and to writing.

Uthman's Codex: A master manuscript of the Quran, or, better said, a template representing what early Quran reciters agreed on from what they had memorized, existing written materials, and from the reading traditions of the companions and followers. Some fifteen years after Muhammad died, the caliph Uthman ordered the revealed verses to be compiled from the written materials collected by the first caliph, Abu Bakr. Because Arabic did not have conventions for marking vowels and some consonants at the time, the lettering has been described as "skeletal."

The text accommodated the transmission and preservation of a number of variant readings of the Quran. Because Muhammad is reported to have accepted variant readings of certain verses, saying that the Quran was revealed in seven modes, it may seem as if the script was intentionally ambiguous to accommodate the variations. But this was simply the way Arabic was written in the time of Uthman, no matter the document. Medieval scholars of the Quran would come to believe the lack of markings was intentional. At the time this novel is set, scholars may or may not have held that view, and the novel reflects the views of their day, not later periods, nor ours. No matter the position taken, for all, preserving the variants meant preserving God's word.

Early reciters: a general term for those people who had devoted themselves to memorizing and transmitting the revelation during the time the Prophet was alive and those who came after his passing.

Companion or Follower: Companions were those who were alive when the Prophet was alive. Companionship may refer to someone who spent a great deal of time with Muhammad, or someone who only met him once. A follower is a person from the generation after Muhammad died.

Companion manuscript (or Companion's manuscript): A whole Quran reading tradition representing what a single companion of the Prophet memorized from the Prophet himself, either written down in whole or in part by that companion or their followers. The Uthmanic codex adopted the readings of the companions' manuscripts that were in agreement with the whole and rejected the rest. Most differences were negligible, but some, especially that of Ibn Masud, differed significantly.

Variants: A difference in vowel, consonant, or a recitation choice, such as reading two phrases as dependent or independent clauses, thus potentially changing the meaning. The possible variant choices that would make any appreciable difference in meaning make up less than one percent of the text of the Uthmanic Codex. Muslims and non-Muslim readers alike may be surprised to find that, during the period this novel is set, these variants were subject to vigorous debate.

Modes: What the Prophet meant by "seven revealed modes" was already lost to the early scholars of the Quran. At the time this novel is set, scholars most likely thought it referred to types of variants. Muslims today typically understand it to refer to different Arabic dialects.

Reading: A choice about a single or multiple variants.

Reading tradition: A whole Quran based on reading choices meant to be transmitted widely.

Personal reading tradition: A whole Quran based on personal reading choices, not meant to be transmitted widely. These were typically compiled by Quran scholars or knowledgeable students. Ibn Mujahid refused to compile one and forbade his students from doing the same.

Recitation: The act of vocalizing verses of the Quran.

Ibn Masud: He was a companion of the Prophet who, like others, sat with him regularly, wrote down and memorized the verses of the Quran as they were revealed. He believed the first and last two chapters of the Quran were not revelation, but personal supplications shared by the Prophet. The caliph Uthman wanted to destroy Ibn Masud's personal manuscript of the Quran. Some say he turned it over, others that he ran away with it. A copy survived well into the period this book is set, as well as reports about its contents.

Ibn Mujahid: Ibn Mujahid was a scholar of Quran reading traditions who held that only variant readings that concur with the caliph Uthman's template codex were acceptable. Scholars such as Ibn Mujahid debated these acceptable variants strenuously and even rejected some. The novel includes one of those rejected variants (keep an eye out for *kun fa yakun*) demonstrating how scholars who relied on the Uthmanic Codex alone disagreed strenuously in ways that might surprise Muslims today, and also illustrates that communities outside Quran circles were aware of these debates and had a stake in the outcome.

Not long after this book is set, Ibn Mujahid would publish *The Book of the Seven with respect to Reading Traditions* limiting the number of reading traditions to seven. His position was widely criticized and took several hundred years to be accepted, and then with changes and expansions. One criticism of his project is that the choice of "seven" would ultimately be confused with the "seven revealed modes" mentioned above, and indeed they have been.

Today, his position is considered Sunni orthodoxy. Nevertheless, many Muslims are only familiar with the reading tradition of their region and may be surprised to learn of the seven. Those who are aware of the seven may be unaware that there was a time when the readings were more diverse and that scholars thought it controversial to limit them at all.

In the novel, much is said about Ibn Mujahid's ability to bring men before the High Court for heresy. He would ultimately force Ibn Shanabudh and another scholar before the court to recant their methods. And he was instrumental in convicting al-Hallaj and others, including Ibn Ata, for heresy leading to their executions.

Ibn Shanabudh: Ibn Shanabudh (859-936 CE) was a scholar of Quran reading traditions and plays a role in the novel as a foil for the methods of Ibn Mujahid. Unlike Ibn Mujahid, he prioritized the companion reading traditions, but also used controversial methods of analyses in determining the reliability of those transmissions. He would ultimately be forced to recant his position before the High Court and would live the rest of his life in ignominy. While there were a number of scholars who shared similar methods of debating the reliability of the readings, I only mention Ibn Shanabudh in the novel to keep things simple.

Shia View: While there were Shia who held that Ali ibn Abi Talib's personal manuscript had been commandeered by his political opponents—namely, the caliph Uthman—the majority of Shia scholars accepted Uthman's codex. That said, they accused Ali's political opponents of misinterpreting certain verses of the Quran, stating that the Prophet's family, namely Ali and his sons, were the legitimate inheritors of political and religious authority. Shia doctrine holds that Ali's manuscript has been passed from father to son through all the succeeding Shia imams. This debate is reflected in the novel, with Ammar, in keeping with his character, taking the minority position that Ali's manuscript was commandeered and rejected by his political opponents.

Please see the glossary and character list in the back of the book for more.

The Names of God

Allah

The Peace

The Merciful The Compassionate
The Holy The Unseen The Guardian of Faith The Protector The Firm
The Compeller The Dominating The Creator The Crusher The
Praiseworthy The Forgiver The Evolver The Bestower The Provider
The Dishonouring The Knower The Constrictor The Expander The
Abaser The King The Forbearing The Exalter The Honouring The
Hearing The Seeing The Everlasting Refuge The Opener The Subtle
The Aware The Great The One The Trustee The Grateful The Most
High The Most Great The Preserver The Wise The Restorer The
Embracing The Glorious The Resurrector The Light The Responsive
The Patient The Nourisher The One Who Forms The Revered The
Generous The Watchful The Strong The Mighty The Friend The
Reckoner The Accounter The Originator The Able The Unique The
Life Giver The Slayer The Alive The Equitable The Finder The Noble
The Avenger The Powerful The Expediter The Delayer The Most
Exalted The First The Last The Manifest The Loving The Governor
The Accepter The Pardoner The Clement The Gatherer The Distresser
The Possessor of the Sovereignty The Lord of Majesty and Bounty The
Self-Subsisting The Sufficient The Enricher The Withholder The
Incomparable The Everlasting The Open-Handed The Right Guide The
Supreme Inheritor The Wise The Good The Truth The Judge The Just
The Witness The All Forgiving

"IT'S EASIER TO SOLVE A CRIME THAN SOLVE YOURSELF."

The names of God are the keys to the books. Each name points to the central question addressed by the book through the lives of its characters and the investigation of a crime.

Moreover, each volume represents a successive stage on the Sufi path. In each novel, the famous Sufi guide, Junayd, explains to Zaytuna the work she must do on that part of the path and she cannot solve the crime unless she also works at solving herself. Other characters do this work in their own way.

The Lover is the soul that awakens to its own suffering.

The Jealous, the soul that begins the demanding work of self-awareness and transformation.

The Unseen is the soul that comes alive through dreams and signs that deepen self-awareness and a commitment to the work necessary to arrive at peace.

And last, *The Peace* is the soul that begins the seemingly infinite path to peaceful and complete resolution in God.

DAY ONE
BAGHDAD, 297 HIJRI (909 CE)

1

Zaytuna nudged Kamal Ali, and whispered, "Get up, you idle oaf!"

He snorted, barely containing his laughter.

"Get up, you idle oaf!"

"If you cannot say it exactly as the old woman would, I will not stir."

"An old woman in an old story," she scoffed lightly.

"And when I heard the story, I vowed to be worthy of her."

"I *am* prodding you without relief." She smiled in the darkness and poked his shoulder several times.

"To what, Zaytuna? To what?"

"To be your best. To pray at night with me."

"To do my best to live according to the nobility of the Prophet Muhammad, alayhi salam. And I will not get up until you say it correctly."

She lay back down beside him, settling into his tender embrace, and sighed in mock frustration.

"I will do the words justice, then." But Kamal Ali uttered the old woman's threats with a growl of desire that awakened her own. "Get up you heedless one. Get up, you idle oaf. I swear you will not enter the Fire on account of me. On the piety of your mother, pray that God has mercy on you." He moved his hand to the small of Zaytuna's back, pulling her nightdress up little by little. "Do not slack, for God will decide your case."

As the thought of praying before first light slipped away, Zaytuna suspected that the old woman in the story did not have to contend with the loving attentions of a man like Kamal Ali.

Awakened by the call for the dawn prayer, Zaytuna left their warm bed and lit an oil lamp with an ember from the hearth. Kamal Ali followed her, and they both dressed quickly. He, for work. She, hoping to get to the public baths before Saliha or Yulduz noticed and teased her with sparkling eyes.

Kamal Ali took her in his arms. "I'll be at work by the time you return."

She pushed him back lightly, admiring his face in the warm lamplight: his broad forehead, the wave of his auburn beard, his tender brown eyes, then traced her finger along his aquiline nose and kissed his full lips. "And when will you go to the baths and make up your late prayer?"

"Ah, there is that old woman!" He smiled. "My Nubian queen, I promise I will as soon as I get the men to churning."

With his touch, Zaytuna felt herself to be the great beauty he imagined her to be. A long-faced woman he had seen painted on an ancient Egyptian monument with high cheekbones and wide, dark eyes. A woman who seemed to embody the unattainable beauty of her Nubian mother. No one had her husband's sight. Not even Mustafa. Always and only, she had been the unattractive sister of Tein, a man so handsome he drew the glances of the most cautious women. And what the Arabs admired in her, she despised; reviling the dun-hued skin and straight, black hair of the man who had raped their mother. But from across a square, Kamal Ali had recognized her as his queen and in that single moment had dedicated himself to her happiness, inviting her old sorrows to a welcome rest, finally, leaving her free to love and be loved.

By the time she returned from the baths, only Yulduz and Layla were out in the courtyard, sitting in the shade of the pomegranate tree.

They rested against cushions made from rough linen stuffed with rags, but made beautiful with simple embroidery by Layla's hands. The last of a feast was spread out before them like a sumptuously embellished cloth imported from Sind. Creamy yellow butter, lustrous ochre honey, burnished gold dates, and charcoaled-edged rounds of barley bread were laid out on yellow-clay plates with cracked open pomegranates set among them like rubies in gold. Layla tore off a piece of bread and its earthy scent carried to her, accented by the tang of the buttermilk. Zaytuna's stomach rumbled loud enough that Layla heard, and laughed.

Yulduz greeted her between bites of bread soaked in buttermilk.

"Sabah an-nur," she replied, checking that no wet hair had come loose under her head wrap to give her away. But she could see in the old woman's teasing grin that she knew. Zaytuna blushed, then met her with a smile of her own. In truth, Zaytuna woke every day amazed that her old ascetic self, starving itself and clinging to bitter loneliness, could love the way she loved Kamal Ali.

She gazed at the old woman tearing off bits of bread, then dipping them in buttermilk and handing them to Layla. *Let her tease*, she thought. *Let her tease until the end of our days.*

Kamal Ali had accepted every stipulation in their marriage contract. He would never take another wife. Her comings and goings would be guided by their love, never his rule. The dowry would be paid in full when she asked, not on divorce. Their house would be home to those with whom she shared her life before they met. If little Layla were coming with them to live under their protection, then so would Yulduz and Qambar. And she would not do without her twin brother, Tein, and his wife, Saliha, her dearest friend. None would be left behind in poverty or forced to live at a distance from each other. They had become a family, with Layla a daughter to them all. He even agreed not to move her from Tutha, the neighbourhood where she had always lived, near the Sufi community and the cemetery where her mother and uncle were buried. Beyond their basic needs, his money would be spent on charity, not fine clothes and furnishings, let alone servants.

"Come'n eat woman." Yulduz waved her over. "We've got to keep that fat on you."

Zaytuna touched her soft belly without thinking. "I have to take care of something first," and left them for her room.

The morning light shone through the small, high window, reflecting off the lime-washed walls and illuminating the simple beauty of a space she had come to accept as her sanctuary. She removed her plain wrap and chose the green and pink floral one that Kamal Ali had given her as a promise the day he asked her to marry him. She touched the matted lock she kept threaded with one of her mother's beads and made a prayer for her mother's soul, then unfolded her rug.

The prayer rug, a gift from Kamal Ali at their wedding, prickled under her feet. It was well-worn and unevenly woven. The dye of the green wool did not match from one section to another. Made and repaired by an unskilled hand, it was nevertheless woven with love. When she stood on it, that love spoke to her and held her with its gratitude. She placed her forehead down in prayer, seeking its gratitude for herself.

After her prayer, she held out her hands in supplication for the newly widowed elderly man forced to sell the rug his wife had made for him and for his wife's soul. Kamal Ali had not insulted the widower by offering him alms so he could keep the rug. He haggled badly for it instead, starting too high and settling on a price that would leave the old man with a full pocket. But the old man, wiping his tears with the tail of his faded blue turban, insisted Kamal Ali take the rug as a gift instead. He accepted it and offered him a gift in return, more money than they had agreed on. Kamal Ali declared he had received more than the man. He left not only with the gift for Zaytuna, but also the widower's prayer that Kamal Ali and his wife would know the same affection God had entrusted to them.

The outside door banged.

Layla yelped.

And a jolt of foreboding shattered her peace.

She rushed to the door without folding the rug, her wrap falling to the floor behind her.

Mustafa was in the courtyard.

He pleaded, "Zaytuna, I need you."

Her old anger flared.

Layla's greeting was half out of her mouth until she saw Zaytuna's face and slowly withdrew. Yulduz grabbed Layla's hand and jerked the girl back to stand beside her.

Qambar was out of his room and nodded to Zaytuna, waiting to see if he was needed. The old man, even with his small stature and swollen joints, was there to protect her.

"Zaytuna," he repeated. "A man has gone missing."

"My help?" The question came out as an accusation.

Mustafa's eyes darted among them, then he took a step back.

"My help?" She took two quick steps forward, then another, until he was forced against the door.

"Your help, please." His mouth gaped and his large brown eyes glistened fearfully, but he did not leave. Instead, he softened his shoulders and spread his palms out to her, opening himself to her reproach.

The deferential gesture was sincere and touched her in an old place shared only by the two of them. Suddenly, he was himself again, kind Mustafa, her childhood friend, her first love, not the man who betrayed his wife by revealing his love for Zaytuna at his own wedding.

She gave in, lowering her voice, but unable to hide the disappointment that he would come to her at all rather than keep the necessary distance between them. "What do you want?"

But it came out sounding like a welcome. She realized she stood before him exposed in just her salwar and qamis, and ran back inside for her wrap. Kamal Ali's promise of love lay starkly on the floor abandoned near her prayer rug. She snatched it up, dragging it around her.

Mustafa approached the door, laying a hand on the frame, and looked around the room. His glance fell on her marriage bed and his expression clouded with pain.

"You should not have come," she said.

Then he saw the jug and cup he had made for her placed near her mother's drum and his face cleared. A small smile lifted his pale cheeks, a flush rising with pleasure above the edges of his beard.

Nausea crept up from her toes, heaving her body forward. She clutched at her treasured floral wrap.

"A student has gone missing," he said softly. "He has been gone for over a week. Someone may have abducted him or even killed him. You can find him."

He stared at her in loving desperation and she could not move.

But Qambar arrived at his elbow, saying, "Shame," and drew him back into the courtyard.

Outside, Yulduz was holding Layla close and speaking to her. There was anger in the old woman's voice and in the deep lines of her face, and Zaytuna held onto it for strength, silently begging her to intervene. Qambar led Mustafa to the far side of the courtyard and the door.

"It's been too long, Mustafa," Yulduz said firmly. "Not since you and your wife came to bless this house. We've been hoping you would bring'er back to us. Come back then."

Qambar picked up the thread as he put a hand to the latch. "Yes, please return with YingYue."

The moment broken, Zaytuna found her footing. "You and YingYue are always welcome. Kamal Ali is home every day for afternoon visits." Layla came to her, slipping her hand in hers. She looked down at the girl. "Right? It would be lovely to have them some afternoon."

Wide-eyed and near tears, Layla nodded slowly.

"Thank you for the invitation, yes, of course, inshallah soon," Mustafa answered, stumbling over his words. "My apologies." But he did not leave, instead looking at the ground in awkward silence, fingering the twisted loop of turban wound under his chin.

Out here, away from her room, in her family's protection, she saw him for himself again. Words of assurance were out of her mouth before she could stop them. "The detectives at Grave Crimes will take the case seriously."

Mustafa shifted from one foot to another. "The mother was told there was nothing they could do until there was evidence a grave crime had been committed. A friend came to me knowing that you, Tein, and Ammar had committed yourselves to controversial cases before and found justice where all had feared there would be none."

Qambar tugged at his arm, urging him to leave.

It was a case, only a case. No matter what he felt seeing her again, he was not there for her. "Let him speak." When Qambar shook his head, she added, "Tein and Ammar will want to know."

Mustafa stared expectantly, but Yulduz warned, "Woman, you can't be thinking!"

Of course she was thinking. It was a case. "Take it to Tein and Ammar," Zaytuna repeated.

If there was something for her in this investigation, there would be nothing improper about it. Let him speak through the men and they would give her work to do.

"They are at work," she said, then realized what she had done. Mustafa would be walking into her husband's place of business to ask for them. She could not imagine what Kamal Ali would feel seeing him like that, especially as Mustafa would inevitably say she had sent him.

"I do not know how to find them." He was begging her to come with him, not just give him directions.

Layla pleaded, "Let me go."

The girl missed him, but she could not send Layla; it was only right that she explain to Kamal Ali herself why she sent Mustafa to his doorstep.

"I'll take you." Her empty stomach churned. She held up a hand, rushed back to her room and sat on the bed, her head down, and drew slow breaths until the feeling passed.

Yulduz came in and shut the door behind her. "This isn't wise. Y'know it."

She stood, wiping her mouth with the back of her hand.

"Walking alone with him? And then to your husband's own warehouse?"

Zaytuna changed her wrap for a plain one. "Kamal Ali knows not to suspect me of indecency."

"He mayn't suspect you, but he'll suspect Mustafa. And the gossip, Zaytuna. You care more about a new case than that good man's name."

There was Yulduz again insisting that the small cases that came to her through the neighbourhood: a wayward husband, a stolen heirloom, were somehow an insult to her marriage. The old woman worried over Kamal Ali's displeasure, thinking someday Zaytuna would have them all kicked to the street when she finally went too far. How little she knew him. But this amounted to more, because of Mustafa.

Yulduz took a breath, ready to dig in, but stopped herself, saying only, "And have you no respect for poor YingYue?"

"He'll go there anyway and say I sent him. I have to explain. I'll take Layla."

"Woman!" She huffed, then gave in. "Better, take Qambar."

Yulduz left to get her husband, but Zaytuna called after, "No, I want Layla."

The girl had heard and was standing in the courtyard holding Mustafa's hand when Zaytuna finally emerged. She tried to assure herself that all who knew her and Kamal Ali could have nothing to say with Layla between them and the girl holding his hand.

Qambar whispered something to Mustafa, gripping his elbow. Mustafa's cheeks paled and he nodded quickly.

Zaytuna could not imagine what he threatened. "God cover us," she prayed and hurried to get him away.

Out of their alleys and onto the main road, Layla tugged on Mustafa's hand, pulling him well ahead. Her wrap had fallen back off her head and her braids swung free under her kerchief. The girl seemed carefree, happy to be with her uncle again, until she looked back and Zaytuna saw her strained face. Layla must surely have missed him, but right now she was out in the street to protect their family from Zaytuna's recklessness. She wished she had never left her prayer rug to answer the door.

The road was crowded and noisy with the chatter of people rushing about their business. The wheels of a cart crunched ahead of them while its donkey brayed, complaining to its master. Mustafa slowed, pulling Layla back so he could be nearer to Zaytuna, but a dirty boy with a rough linen sack on his back trudged by, allowing her to get even farther behind. She took the distance to rehearse what she would say to Kamal Ali, but every thought failed her.

The two waited for her by the Hospital Bridge. She glanced through the open doors of the hospital, wondering if Saliha was in the courtyard and could see them. She would demand her own answer for this later, Zaytuna imagined.

Meeting up with them, there was no chance for Zaytuna to hang back as they crossed the bridge. She thought of Yulduz's sharp reminder that she consider YingYue and prayed no one who knew Mustafa's wife or father-in-law would see them together.

Layla walked between them across the bridge, still holding Mustafa's hand but nudging him toward the centre. But it was too crowded; Mustafa had to move closer to avoid the curses of passersby or being hit by a laden camel.

"How are you enjoying your new home?"

It was inevitable that he would try to speak to her, but Zaytuna did not answer.

Several uncomfortable moments passed until Layla answered him, at first formally. "It is very comfortable, Uncle Mustafa." But then it all came tumbling out. "We have all the food we can eat. There are even mattresses stuffed with wool and hearths for fires. Uncle Kamal Ali bought me new clothes. He is so interesting, too. I make him tell me stories of all his adventures when he travelled the world. Did you know he came all the way from Morocco and saw Egypt and Jerusalem, and visited the grave of the Prophet, alayhi salam? I could listen forever…"

The girl spoke sincerely, but wiser than her years from the harshness of life, she was also intentionally reminding Mustafa that Zaytuna was happy, they all were, and that he had lost his place in their lives since the wedding. She could imagine how much it hurt Layla to warn off a man who had become a dear uncle to her, and she knew what it was like for him to hear it. After all, how had she been hurt when she had first observed YingYue gazing at him with blushing cheeks and Mustafa accepting her with joy?

The old jealousy returned, making her want to say to him that this was all his fault for rejecting her when she begged him to consider them one last time before he married YingYue. Her stomach turned again. "There is no god but God," she muttered as they crossed the Ushnan Bridge into Buratha.

The memory of their wedding still shocked her.

One moment YingYue was glancing shyly from under the delicate hammered silver chains hanging from her red bridal cap, the next she was gaping at Mustafa's stricken, tear-stained face as he stared at Zaytuna. But she and YingYue were not the only ones who had witnessed Mustafa grieving the loss of Zaytuna. Kamal Ali, Tein, YingYue's father, and Uncle Abu al-Qasim al-Junayd had seen it all.

The three walked in silence through Buratha, following the donkey carts and camels, down the main road to the market entrance. Talisman writers crowded its edges. A young ghuraba woman, her red scarf tied behind her head such that her ears were exposed, called out promises of love, revenge, and riches. Old women sat on scraps of cloth or reed mats selling pre-soaked beans and fresh herbs tied off with string. Barefoot boys offered their services to carry goods from the market. They crowded in on her. Zaytuna wanted to burst past them all and run through the market to her husband and warn him before Mustafa even set foot in the square.

Once past the gates, Layla slowed and stopped in front of the molded cones of colourful spices, pretending to consider the bright yellow turmeric. The shopkeeper approached, but Zaytuna waved him off, then put a reassuring hand on Layla's shoulder. "All is well." The girl nodded, took her hand and walked on, Mustafa now following just behind.

As they turned the familiar lanes within the market to the small square and the butter house, Zaytuna told herself she would have time to explain and Kamal Ali would understand. Ammar and Tein would be called out to hear Mustafa. She would stand in the background with her husband. If there was something in the case for her, Kamal Ali would encourage her, and she would not compromise his trust nor their love.

The morning light was slanting into the far end of the square. The churning had just begun, but the men were already sweating in their undershirts. Tein, Ammar, and the new men, Ezra and Babak, lifted the staffs with both hands and brought them down into yellow clay jars nearly half their size. Tein stood tall, happy at his work. One would never suspect his leg, injured in battle, had ever bothered him. Ammar, though, appeared grim. She hoped all was well with Nasifa and her pregnancy.

Layla ran to them. Tein put down his staff and lifted her up for a hug while Ammar teased. Ezra nodded to her, but kept churning. Only then did Tein notice her with Mustafa. His smile faded. He put down Layla and went straight to them, Ammar and Layla following closely behind.

"Brother! Back for more of our buttermilk?"

He had been here before. Layla's bright face shadowed with the hurt of a child lied to by one she loved. How could he think they would not find out?

Zaytuna needed to feel her husband's hand in her own, but there was no sign of him in the shop. "Where is Kamal Ali?"

He answered by looking away.

She blushed, but more in pique at herself for asking. He had gone to the baths to wash from their lovemaking as he said he would.

Tein gestured to the table and chairs by the shop, where Kamal Ali had said those first words of love to her. Grabbing Layla's hand, she nearly dragged the girl across the square to sit at the table and wait.

Young Malik came out of the office. "Seyyeda Zaytuna! Layla." He rushed to the far side of the shop to pour them cups of buttermilk. Returning, he served it with a flourish and the sweet, comical gesture reminded her of where she was, assuring her she was safe. But she drank the buttermilk in hurried sips as the men talked.

Layla said, worried, "They are talking about the case."

"I will wait to hear it from Tein and Ammar."

The girl let out a tight sigh of relief, but was still on guard.

Zaytuna watched the men with growing irritation, trying to make out a word here and there but only heard "missing" and "mother," "gambling," and "brothels," but also, strangely, "Quran." Ammar was posturing like he was back in his leather cuirass with his sword at his side.

Mustafa put her in this position. Having to sit with Layla rather than be in the thick of the conversation. Forcing her to go through men to get at a case. Without a second thought, she was on her feet and ready to tell him exactly what harm he had done to her and YingYue because he could not control his feelings.

He whirled to face her and took a step back, his hands out to stop her. The other two followed his movements. Tein grasped Mustafa's shoulder, then walked quickly to meet her, his face begging for calm. Ammar stayed where he was, shaking his head.

She stopped, realizing what she had done before her brother could reach her.

"Sit down and breathe," Tein said through gritted teeth. He motioned for Malik to bring a glass of water. "Once you've had a sip of water, tell me everything."

Zaytuna forced herself to return to the table. Not because he had ordered it, but because she knew this anger, this old, roiling pitch within her, was no longer what she wanted for herself. She sat down hard, watching Ammar and Mustafa. "*You* tell *me* about the case."

Tein followed her stare. Ammar was embracing Mustafa, who, head down, then hurried out of the square and into the market.

When Ammar reached them, he said to Tein, keeping close watch on Zaytuna, "Mustafa will be back in the morning. We have to get back to churning before the day warms up."

But Tein did not move. "I'm going to talk to my sister first."

Ammar shrugged, leaving them to join Ezra and Babak, but that bull-face of his betrayed the thrill of a case set out before him.

"We'll talk later about why you showed up here with Mustafa." Tein sat down across from her.

"He lied…," she started, her anger rising again.

He cut her off. "I'll tell you about the case. But first accept that there's no role in it for you. There may be no role in it for us, either. I'm not interested. And I'm not leaving Kamal Ali for it."

The last words were said as if they were a warning to her. It rankled, but she deserved it.

"A Quran scholar has gone missing. His mother is distraught. She went to the mosque where he studies and asked his colleagues, but no one has seen him for a week. They were desperate for him to return, but unwilling to share any information about him. She had no idea what he does when he is not home other than study and teach and is afraid he has gotten himself into trouble." He paused. "Mustafa got involved, as you know, and spoke to some of the students at the mosque. They all say the man was a gambler and a drunk."

She crossed her arms. "It is obvious his colleagues were too ashamed to tell her that he whores and gambles when not with the Quran."

"Yes, that is most likely, which means he'll show up shamefaced on his mother's doorstep soon enough without our help."

She accepted his account with reluctance. Something in it pricked at her thoughts though, then was lost as she became consumed by the risk she had taken, all because of Mustafa's lie. She would speak to Auntie Hakima about his behaviour. Her face grew hot with resentment and she lifted her hand to her cheek. She would not even be able to attend the evening gatherings for music and remembering the Prophet and God at Junayd's home until it was resolved. Before today, they had kept their distance with only a polite nod, but now even that would be too much.

"Layla! Zaytuna!" Kamal Ali's voice carried across the square.

Zaytuna jumped up and rushed to him, her anger dissolving into tears in his arms.

"My love. My love, what has happened?" He wiped her eyes with the edge of his sleeve.

Kamal Ali guided her back to the shop. His touch drew the confusion and disturbance of Mustafa from her body as a salve draws poison from a wound, leaving her limp in his arms, surprised she was still alive.

As they reached Tein, she answered his question. "Mustafa."

"Has something happened to him or his family?"

"No," Tein answered. "A colleague of his, a Quran student, has gone missing. He hoped Ammar and I could help the family."

Kamal Ali nodded to him, then took Zaytuna's face in one hand. "And you, my dearest, why are you upset?"

"I am fine now that you are here. We can talk when you get home."

"Stay here with me today," he said. "I could use your company."

"I have so much to do at home."

Kamal Ali nodded, then turned to Tein. "Will you come with us tonight to the sama? Or will you be late with Firdaws Ibn Ali and all that talk of philosophy?"

"I'll be with Ibn Ali and the other men."

"They cannot do without you. You must explain what you discuss to me someday," Kamal Ali said, inclining his head.

Do without you. She recovered the lost thought about the case and grasped Kamal Ali's hand.

"What is it?"

Tein gave her a questioning glance.

But Zaytuna held her tongue. She would wait until Ammar was there to say it. Tein did not want the case, but Ammar did. He might find some use for it.

Ammar left his churning and called out a greeting to Kamal Ali, wiping his hands on his apron.

"One thing before I go," Zaytuna said as he approached, then glanced at her husband. "It is something about the case." Kamal Ali raised his eyebrows, encouraging her to go on, but there was concern behind his eyes. She said instead, "Oh, perhaps not."

"My love, what is it?"

"What?" Ammar insisted.

She was near to letting it go, but then Tein grunted in warning, irritating her, so she turned to address Ammar. "Tein said the missing man's colleagues were desperate for him to return, but refused to help his mother."

Ammar replied, "Yes. He claims to have a Quran manuscript that no one's seen since the early days after the Prophet died. Mustafa said they are eager to see the manuscript, but not the man."

"What's the manuscript?" she asked.

"Mustafa didn't know."

There was something, she knew it. "I would ask about that."

Tein interjected forcefully, "There's no case for you. Or us, either."

"Perhaps for the best," Kamal Ali suggested.

As much as the question of the manuscript sparked her interest, she pressed her husband's hand, agreeing. If Mustafa was capable of lying to her the way he did today, there was no telling what else he might do. She prayed the missing man would be home before morning.

2

Mustafa watched from the door as YingYue swayed in prayer, reciting the words of the Quran, *"Which of your Lord's mercies will you and you deny…"*. Illumined by the warmth of a single oil lamp, beads of sweat glistened on her beautiful forehead. Cheeks flushed, her full lips parted in a gasp, he imagined her captured by a desire he would never evoke. She recited the verse again, this time drawing out the last "deny" until he thought she would collapse. The scholars of Quran would be horrified by her heavily accented pronunciation, unwilling to accept that such a voice could be touched by the Source of revelation itself. Yet, the moon gleams with the light of the sun, unaware of disapproval.

He closed the door with the barest click of the latch. But her eyes fluttered into awareness and she left her recitation behind to prostrate again, then finish her prayer, finally giving her greetings to the angels who prayed with her on either side. YingYue faced him on her prayer rug with the beatific smile of a woman who has forgiven her husband so completely that she is no longer concerned with him.

"Assalamu alaykum, husband."

"Wa alaykum assalam." He sat near the cold hearth, slumping back against the pillows.

YingYue folded her prayer mat and adjusted her wrap around her shoulders. Her long, thin braids, always tied off with colourful wool, were twisted into a bun. She no longer wore them loose. He had never got the chance to feel them drape across his body as he had once dreamed. On their wedding night, she lay down and politely asked him to consummate the marriage. Their first and last moment of physical intimacy was cloaked in shame, edged for him with a thread of hope. But the next morning, she pulled that thread through, asking him to leave her to her prayer and marry another wife for his needs, assuring him her father would agree.

"I lost track of time," she said. "How long has it been since the sunset prayer?"

"Not long. I prayed in the mosque and came straight here. But I thought I might see you earlier at Friday prayers with the aunties."

"I prayed here." She approached him, looking him over as if he were her son, not her husband. "Did you eat?"

"I ate alone at a stall."

If she noticed his disappointment that their marriage was defined by these solitary habits, YingYue did not show it. Instead, she removed his turban and set it on the shelf over the pegs in the wall. She returned for the wool wrap thrown over his shoulders, but he shook his head and took her hand instead, inviting her down to the floor. She sat by him comfortably and did not pull her hand away.

They sat in companionable silence for a time. The small room was neat as always. The reed mats and sheepskins were regularly beaten. The walls were freshly lime-washed. His childhood blanket, made by his mother from bits of rag into a Sufi patched cloak, hung reverently on the wall. The brazier was cold, despite the evening chill. They would be warm in bed together soon enough.

As if she knew what he was thinking, she said, "I put down another blanket. We have a sheepskin cover if you like. I do not know your habits in the cold months, but that is what we did in Taraz. Please let me know what you like and I will prepare it."

"All is well."

"Tell me about your day," she asked, as she always did. She would listen attentively as he told her a bit about what he had learned in the mosque and halls of study and she would giggle at the antics of the children he taught.

"A man has gone missing. Nabil ibn al-Qays al-Kufi." He took care not to say that he had sought out Zaytuna. "I do not know him. But he is a student at the Sharqiyya mosque. My friend, Ulgen, is concerned."

"Missing?" YingYue held up her hands in prayer. "God, may he be found safe and relieve his family of their worry."

"Amin." Mustafa gazed at his childhood blanket, each patched edge bound with his mother's love. "His mother is distraught. Ulgen took me to see her yesterday." Mustafa paused before saying, "He wanted me to ask Tein and Ammar for help."

"You can help." She squeezed his hand.

The gesture made him hope for a moment that there might be more than simple warmth in their bed tonight and he lifted her hand to kiss.

She withdrew it before he could, yet smiled sweetly. "As you like, but I would prefer to spend the evening in prayer."

This was always her answer. She opened by acknowledging his right over her. As ever, that led back to the sickening thought of the enslaved girl, Mu'mina, and what she had suffered at the hands of her master. And Mustafa answered, as always, "No, as you like."

"Will Tein and Ammar be able to find him?"

"I will take them to meet Nabil's mother tomorrow."

"Good," she said with a swift tick of her head. "They will know what to do."

"I asked about him at the mosque. Several of the students reported he was a gambler and a drunk." He did not add, "And likely visited brothels."

"A scholar of Quran, gambling?"

"Yes."

"For shame." The flush on her cheeks deepened. "Those scholars must not like him. Why do they not stop him?"

Mustafa sat up and faced her. "I never considered that. The scholars who relayed that information to me are students of Ibn Mujahid, a rival to Nabil's teacher, Ibn Shanabudh."

"They are rivals, but why would their students speak ill of each other?"

She never understood the price he paid among the students and scholars for standing up for Mu'mina. There were loyal friends and a few others who admired the risk he took. But Burhan, preferring Mu'mina be wrongfully convicted of murder than upset the reputation of high-ranking scholars, had turned the rest against him. Reputation was everything for a scholar and he suspected they would protect each other first. Mustafa expected the aunts and uncles to remind him that everything is the will of God, but when he complained to YingYue of their treatment, instead of listening, she had recited *It may be that you hate a thing that is good for you and love a thing that is bad for you.* Now she was interested in understanding when someone other than her husband was involved?

He answered, his voice tinged with resentment. "The two teachers do not respect one another and that lack of respect is passed down to the students. Each has a different approach to deciding which reading of a word in the Quran is reliable and which should be ignored."

"Which readings? Reliable?" Her brow furrowed.

"We have discussed this. Each night, when I share what I have learned with you. And over dinner with your father."

"Forgive me, husband. When you speak of these things, I drift into remembering God."

She did not look sorry and he was hurt. All those nights, thinking she was attending to his conversation. "But I am talking about God's word when I discuss these matters."

"Tell me now. I am listening." Her brow had smoothed and she nodded for him to continue, but her eyes had drifted to that place they went when she was thinking about God.

"No, it is late," he said.

Her eyes came back into focus. "No, husband. I am listening."

All this time he thought she had been learning bit by bit alongside him. Now, where would he begin? He realized he did not even know how much or how little she knew. When she arrived in Baghdad from Marw over a year ago, she had already been studying the meanings of the Quran but had only memorized enough to perform her prayer. She had since been working on the reading tradition popular in Baghdad with an old auntie who was patient with her accent, but she would be unlikely to know the difference if she heard another. After all, it was nothing more than a vowel or a consonant here and there. What would he say? How much? What does it matter, anyway?

He started by recasting a lecture he gave to the children he tutored. "The Prophet Muhammad, alayhi salam, would receive a revelation of verses and recite them to his companions. Those companions would share what they heard. At times, some disagreed about what they had heard and would return to him for correction. This happened throughout the twenty-three years the Quran was revealed, verse by verse."

He paused, wondering if she had heard even that, and nudged her.

"Go on." Her smile was sweetly vacuous, obviously pretending.

"After the Prophet died, the first caliph, Abu Bakr, collected all the written materials on which people had recorded the revelation and asked a companion, Zayd, to transcribe them. The second caliph, Umar, took these pages into his care, then bequeathed them to his daughter, the Prophet's wife, Hafsa, to protect after he died." He raised his voice with parental emphasis as he did for the children, "Women, too, were among those who committed the verses to memory, not only the Prophet's male companions. His wives and other women."

But not even the women's role in the collection of the Quran could rouse her interest.

"Did you hear me?"

"Yes, yes, husband, Lady Hafsa, may God be well-pleased with her, protected the Quran."

He continued with his lecture. "Nearly twenty years after the Prophet died, the third caliph, Uthman, ordered those materials to be used as the basis for a single manuscript. Zayd was asked to lead those who had memorized the Quran most reliably to compose a single manuscript of the Quran. But still not everyone agreed on what the Prophet recited.

"Yes?" She asked, encouraging him politely.

"Some companions had written down the verses they had memorized in personal manuscripts, and these, too, had some differences between them." He emphasized the word "differences," hoping to spark an objection or a question, but there was nothing and his voice drifted toward a conclusion of this embarrassing performance. "So they collected only those verses everyone could agree on, including those verses where Prophet Muhammad allowed for small differences, perhaps in dialect, pronunciation, or in explanation."

But she turned her small face to him, her eyes suddenly bright. Instead of worrying over the disagreements among the companions as she had at first, she recited, "*And We have sent no Messenger except in the language of his people, that he might make it clear to them.*" Then she patted him on his hand. "Tell me then, give me an example I would understand."

Surprised, he said eagerly, "For instance, in prayer you recite from the opening chapter, *Maliki yawm ad-din* with a short vowel 'a'. But another reading tradition has *Maaliki yawm ad-din* with a long vowel 'a'. *King of the day of judgment* or *Possessor of the day of judgment*."

"God is generous." She recited, her voice touched by ecstasy, "*Which of your Lord's mercies will you and you deny?*"

She began to sway under the power of the verse and he took her hand to pull her back before she was lost to him, again. "YingYue. Please, there is more. You wanted to know why the scholars fight. Then hear me."

"Oh, these men," she grumbled. "If they tasted God's word, truly…. Yes, yes husband, why do they fight?"

"By the caliph Uthman's time, there were reports from the furthest cities of grave errors being recited as if they were Quran. Thus the caliph Uthman ordered an official master manuscript to be written, a codex. It was copied and sent where it was needed."

YingYue's brow furrowed again. "Grave errors." She flashed him a suddenly angry look as if he were implicated. "They let it go too long."

He nearly gasped at her finding fault with the Prophet's closest companions, but did not correct her, clinging to her outburst instead. It was not said with Zaytuna's loving fury, but the cutting comment meant she was here, with him, giving him something to hang onto, rather than her ever-artful slipping away.

"And because they waited," she went on, still in a temper, "the scholars have something to fight over?"

Mustafa got up and crossed the room to pour her a cup of water. He thought of Zaytuna. She had kept the jug and cup he made for her with all his love. Was she drinking from it now? He sighed.

"I know that sigh," she said. "You will answer me."

She did not know this sigh, but he returned to her, handing her the cup. "There was no question."

"The scholars, the rivals. This is what they fight over. These vowels."

"And consonants. Sometimes words." He pressed on, relishing her presence, hoping to stir her further. "The caliph's manuscript was completed some twenty years after our beloved Prophet died. It is nearly three hundred years later? We should expect that the transmission of a vowel here or there may be mistaken. I have heard Ibn Mujahid himself say so. No matter a man's devotion and intentions, he is a human being. I will not blame or suspect them." He recited the revealed prayer, *"Our Lord, do not blame us if we have forgotten or erred."*

"And do not lay on us a burden like the burden you laid on those who came before us. I will do as you do," she said, seemingly giving more understanding to the Quran scholars than the caliphs themselves.

"And God cannot err," he stated firmly. "The scholars keep an eye and ear out for any variant that cannot make sense in the Arabic of the Prophet. Likewise, the scholars question if a word has an unacceptable meaning. So they argue. They want to be very careful. They are protecting the inviolability of the Quran as surely as the caliphs did, may God be well-pleased with them."

With each word, Mustafa observed her acceptance. But when she was no longer angry, a veil lowered between them. His eyes pricked with tears. He stood, removed his cloak, and hung it on the peg. YingYue hurried behind him to help him undress and ready his night clothes. He loosened his grasp on the robe and let it fall into her hands. He wanted to carry on speaking, say something edging on scandal, anything to bring her back to him.

Guiltily, he reasoned with himself that it was better if she find out here, with him alone, than hearing about it in the company of the scholars' families she visited. These were well-educated women who not only knew of the study of the readings, but a few of whom were familiar with several reading traditions and had their own preferred ways of reciting certain verses.

YingYue already made little sense to these women. She had reported back how they had laughed at her "quaint Sufi riddles." Her shock over the variant readings would be just another occasion to mock her and, in turn, ridicule him. Whatever made him think that she would have been a better wife than Zaytuna? Because YingYue would be demure among these women, rather than argue? Zaytuna might have argued, but at least somewhat knowledgeably.

YingYue's back was to him as she shook out his robe, then folded it carefully to lie in the chest with their clothes. Reaching out, he began tentatively, "The majority of the scholars agree to the limits of the caliph Uthman's codex. Ibn Mujahid is one of them. But there are others who do not accept the same limits. First and foremost, they prefer to rely on the companions' manuscripts I mentioned, even where they only survive in reports and memory. Ibn Shanabudh is one of these scholars. This is why they are rivals and their students fight."

She returned from the trunk with his night clothes to help him remove his qamis and sirwal. "There is no need to fight over it and none of this you tell me explains why Nabil's fellows would not protect him from his ugly habits or speak ill of him."

Had she not heard him say, "companions' manuscripts"? She must not understand the implication, otherwise she would have reacted. He pushed. "I have not told you everything. Some companions wrote down what they had memorized and learned with the Prophet. Mostly, they were all the same with those small variants I mentioned. But there were some that are considered unacceptable by those with any sense."

Eyes wide, she took a step back.

"These verses were left out of the caliph Uthman's codex." Mustafa reached for her, but she took another step back, then another, until she was at the edge of the bed. He said, almost taunting her. "Ibn Shanabudh will not let those verses go. When I said he prefers to rely on the companions' manuscripts, this is what I meant."

But she was no longer angry; her cheeks had lost their colour, her eyes glistened with tears. "Where have the words of my Beloved gone?"

"They are right here." He gestured to her heart, wanting to touch her.

She shook her head slowly, quiet tears wetting her pale skin. "You do not understand. The unacceptable verses? What happened to them?"

"The caliph ordered the companions' personal manuscripts to be destroyed."

"No," she whimpered. YingYue sat down hard on their bed, seemingly inconsolable. "What if there was disagreement over something that truly was recited but they left it out, only because they disagreed?"

Mustafa sat down next to her and held her hand, feeling each delicate finger, wanting again to kiss them. "Those companions felt the same. Some say one of them, Ibn Masud, ran away with his manuscript rather than allow it to be destroyed. But YingYue, you must understand some of the differences are beyond what anyone should accept. If you relied on Ibn Masud's recitation in ritual prayer, instead of reciting *Maliki* or *Maaliki*, you would not say the opening chapter of the Quran at all. He claimed it was a personal supplication, not God's revelation to be recited in our prayer. You can see the danger in it. The Prophet, alayhi salam, recited these words in every cycle of prayer and we follow him."

She gasped, pulling her hand away. "How could this Ibn Masud be so wrong?"

"I don't know."

"And now his manuscript is gone, and the others, too?"

"No, they are not lost. How would I know about these differences except that men continued to recite them simply to preserve the memory of all that had come before? In fact, a copy of Ibn Masud's manuscript is said to be in Kufa."

"Alhamdulillah. I am glad those readings are not lost forever." She sniffed, holding back tears, then searched his eyes for an answer. "But now I no longer know what it is that I recite in my prayer."

"You recite what the Prophet recited." He held her to him as she wept, settling into the crook of his arm. Mustafa savoured the fleeting moment of intimacy.

She pushed away, got up to find a cloth to wipe her face. After, she remained standing and pulled her wrap close against her as if overcome by a chill. "The scholars argue so we can be certain of what we recite."

"Yes. They are shepherds who guide us to safe pastures in which everything we might graze from is permitted." He offered it as a balm, hoping to pull her back into his embrace, keep her from praying late into the night. But his offered comfort only allowed her more distance. Her expression returned to its placid acceptance of God's will, even in this matter of the Quran.

Mustafa shrunk within himself, left with nothing but the fact that he had gone further than he needed only to please himself, to draw her into his arms, into their bed. It filled him with fear for what he had allowed himself to become.

God, forgive me.

He looked to YingYue to beg her forgiveness, but she had turned her back to him.

"I will take what you have said to Auntie Hakima." She dug out a thick wool wrap from the chest and drew it around her shoulders.

Everywhere he turned, their marriage was a sham. YingYue would not even trust him with this, but had to have it confirmed by another.

"The teachers you mentioned?"

It was a moment before he could face her again. He said, "Ibn Mujahid and Ibn Shanabudh," even though no longer wanted to continue the conversation.

"They fight."

"Isn't it best to leave this alone?"

She pressed him. "This is about the missing man. You said Nabil is the student of one scholar who fights with another."

"Nabil is a student under Ibn Shanabudh," he answered. "It was Ibn Mujahid's students who said he was a gambler."

"It could be slander, then. Not just slander of Nabil, but his teacher."

"I will tell Tein and Ammar tomorrow." The call to the evening prayer echoed in the city. He stood, hoping to end the conversation.

As he laid the prayer rugs out, she said, "Ibn Mujahid fights because he fears we could end up praying so differently from one another that we do not recognize each other as Muslims anymore."

"Yes."

"Who do you think is correct?"

"I prefer Ibn Mujahid," he replied in a strained voice, wishing she would stop.

"I prefer him, too." She stood on her prayer rug, placed just a few fingers behind his. "I prefer safe pastures. The Messenger of God said, 'That which is lawful is clear and that which is unlawful is clear, and between the two of them are doubtful matters about which many people do not know. Thus, he who avoids doubtful matters clears himself in regard to his religion and his honour, but he who falls into doubtful matters falls into that which is unlawful, like the shepherd who pastures around a sanctuary, all but grazing therein. Every king has a sanctuary, and God's sanctuary is His prohibitions. In the body there is a morsel of flesh, which, if it be whole, all the body is whole, and which, if it is diseased, the body is diseased. It is the heart'."

It was the first hadith he had taught her, and he felt a pang for the people they had been, and no longer were.

Their marriage had never known such gentle land. It was his fault for loving two women and marrying only one, leaving him unable to share his life with either. He turned back to look at her, wanting to say that he wished things had been different, that he were different, but YingYue was already in ecstasy, her eyes open but unseeing, her hands over her heart, whispering the opening verses of the second chapter of the Quran, "*Alif, lam, mim. Surely this is the Book in which there is no doubt, a guidance for the godfearing*." Her eyes returned to focus and she smiled at him in perfect peace.

An abyss of hope opened before him and he took her hand, wanting her for himself again, forgetting his guilt of only a moment before.

But she only said, softly, "Go renew your ablution."

Ashamed, he let go of her hand and hurried outside, plunging his head into the basin until he was shivering. He completed his ablution, messily throwing water on his neck, his arms, and feet. Water dripped from his shorn head and thick beard.

Why had he refused Zaytuna that day when she came to him, asking him to reconsider his engagement to YingYue and marry her instead? Hands out, he lifted his head to the heavens and begged God, "Awaken her to my love again."

There was a creak at his father-in-law's door. Caught, he turned around, his heart thumping in his chest until he realized he had not said which woman he hoped God would return to him.

Shouts of men fighting erupted outside, resounding through the streets like an ugly call to prayer. He wanted to offer himself up to them so they might beat him for his wrongs. Instead, he went back inside to his wife.

She rushed to him, taking hold of his soaked sleeve. "What have you done?"

He stood hopeless, his qamis and sirwal clinging to his cold skin, and not knowing what to answer for.

"You look like someone has tried to drown you! Take these off, quickly." She pulled the qamis up and he bent over so she could tug it over his head. "Those, too." She untied his sirwal and they slipped to the floor. His body betrayed him and he was exposed before her. "Put these on." She handed him his night clothes, ignoring what she surely must see, and left their room to hang the wet clothes in the courtyard.

The embarrassment sickened him, chilling his arousal. He dried himself and put on his nightshirt as she instructed.

"There are men fighting out there," she said as she returned. YingYue took his cloak and threw it over his shoulders, then came around to face him. "Those men out there. Maybe Nabil was beaten by

Ibn Mujahid's students. I have seen it myself. In Taraz, then Marw, now here." She took the damp cloth from him. "You scholars, meant to be so wise, yet you cannot help but bring fists to arguments better solved by sincere reflection."

He let go of the cloak and looked toward the bed. "I will tell Tein and Ammar in the morning."

"And Zaytuna, too?" she asked plainly.

He lowered his head to hide his guilt.

"If that is why you are waiting to take a second wife, you must choose another." She touched his chin, raising it so he could not avoid her eyes. "She will not leave her husband."

DAY TWO

3

"LAST ONE, UNCLE!"

Straw pricked at Tein's sandalled feet as he reached down to take the last amphora of butter from Farhad. He lay it carefully in the cart alongside the others, packing the straw around it for safe delivery.

"Good to go!" Tein called out to the driver.

Natar hauled his injured body onto the cart and, with a click of the tongue, took the reins for the donkey just as it lurched forward. They never got more than a craggy frown out of the man. Young Farhad found Natar rude, but the man was a ghazi, like Tein and Ammar, and one who had returned from fighting on the frontier without another word to say. Tein understood him too well.

Each man carried those days at war differently. He had spent his own days and nights drunk within the walls of the cemetery trying to forget until Ammar had brought him to work in Baghdad's Grave Crimes section. Ammar found a place for it within himself and brought home a hard pride in keeping the borders of the empire safe from Byzantine incursion.

But men like Natar just needed decent work and understanding. And the man delivered the butter on time and in perfect condition to the best households in Baghdad, even when he had to cross the Tigris to the palaces of the caliphs' advisors and the great families. That Kamal Ali had a soft spot for the man made Tein love his brother-in-law even more.

Kamal Ali's butter was made from the milk of Awassi sheep chosen from flocks for the shape and fitness of their udders. More, they were not grazed on whatever the shepherds could find, but in fields of barley and wheat stubble set aside for them. A few cheese makers and sellers sought his milk for their own. Instead, he shared with them the secrets of his business and how to build and care for a flock. They sucked their teeth at him and told stories about how he would not speak up for them at the great houses. But Kamal Ali would simply bow his head humbly when falsely accused, saying, "They do not know the worst of me."

Tein loved him. This man of character loved his twin sister, a woman he thought no man would take. Who would love her sharp tongue and clinging sorrow, let alone her bony body fed by worship alone? This surprising man had fallen in love with Zaytuna, given him work that did not force him inevitably to do harm, paid him more than he had ever made in his life, and offered him and Saliha a place in a home bought solely so his own bride would never be without those who mattered most to her. He even brought along Layla and the neighbours because Zaytuna had asked and expanded his business to pay for it all.

If they took the case Mustafa had brought to them, it would mean putting aside the peace he had gained by simply churning butter day in and day out. Kamal Ali would give them the time to investigate. He knew it. But it would not be just this one case. From the moment they quit Grave Crimes, Ammar had plans for them to open a private investigations agency. This could open a door that would lead to another and another.

"No one to answer to but ourselves," Ammar kept arguing, "A chance to think again."

Tein did not want it.

"Come on, you miss having the chance to be right."

He had a point there, but not a point that argued in Ammar's favour.

Tein had resisted him until yesterday.

After Mustafa left, Ammar started in on him. "We will take this case." He pressed Tein as they pounded the cream, nagged him as he loaded the cart, and gave him knowing looks as they clarified the last of the butter for the next day's delivery. Ammar did not seem to care that Kamal Ali might hear or see. Tein ignored him which riled Ammar even more.

After work, Tein had led him to a juice stall where they could talk it over. He tossed back the juice without tasting it, leaning across the table. "I'm not interested. I will not be interested. And I'm not leaving Kamal Ali."

"We can be replaced in a moment. This job takes nothing but muscle."

"You don't even know if there is a case or if the mother is paying."

"I will not churn butter to the end of my days!" Ammar slapped his hand down, rattling the cups. "Up and down and up and down with that cursed staff."

He twitched at Ammar's outburst, then joked, trying to lower the temperature, "Is Nasifa not happy with your arms and chest? Or the money?"

"I'm done coming home at the same time every day to my mother and my wife and my father and my brother and my brother's wife, all expecting more from me. I'm not made for this drudgery. They just informed me that I am to help expand the herd. I come home early enough, I should eat and get out there with the goats. Help them find better markets." He talked like a desperate man. "If I get a case that pays, I'm gone all day. No churning, no nagging, no goats. Walla, Tein, don't try to stop me. If you won't come with me on this case, I'll go alone."

Tein reached out, but Ammar shrank back. Maybe he could help Ammar on this one case, get him a step closer to his own agency. Zaytuna was certainly never short of work. He hedged, "I didn't say I won't take the case, Ammar."

"You're not saying you will."

"Give me tonight." Tein stood and left him to his plans.

Back at work the following day, Ammar said nothing, but he had one eye on the marketplace gates, awaiting Mustafa's return. The morning wore on without him, and Ammar only became more frustrated. Tein did not want to suggest the man had been found, but he hoped Mustafa was late for that very reason. The end of the day came. The clarified butter was being poured into its jars and the men were cleaning up. Ammar was polishing a copper pan dry, still staring across the square. Tein ignored him until an irritated sigh prompted him to look over. He followed Ammar's gaze.

Ammar's wife, Nasifa, was crossing over to them, a shopping basket in one hand, the child in her belly cradled by the other. She smiled, her round face and delicate features lighting up with an invitation for him to come to her. Ammar stood still for a moment too long and her face fell. He rushed to her then, took the basket and whispered in her ear, making her blush. He had always had a short man's sweet tongue with women. Nasifa smiled again, leaning into him as they walked arm in arm.

Malik was already pulling a chair from the table and had a pitcher of buttermilk and a glass ready for her.

She sat gratefully as she returned his greeting. "God bless you."

"How is my nephew?" Tein asked her.

"Or niece," she chided. "Our girl is kicking."

Tein gazed at her belly and longed to touch it and feel the child stretching within her as he had done with Ayzit. Their son, Husayn, had moved inside her as if riding a horse into battle. Ayzit and Husayn were years gone now, slain by Byzantine raiders on the frontier, but he could still conjure out of memory the feeling of his infant son's weight on his chest, his fitful breath, and Ayzit sleeping by his side. He longed for another child, even though Saliha insisted they do what they could to prevent it.

Nasifa gestured to the market gates. "Is that Mustafa?"

A visible thrill ran through Ammar, bringing him to his feet.

Nasifa shot him a fearful look. Tein wanted to reassure her, but he could not. Ammar loved her, but he would never love a steady man's life, and Tein thought he saw in her the recognition of the beginning of the end of their regular days together.

"I have news of the case," Mustafa said breathlessly as he approached.

Ammar pulled out a chair for him. "Tell me!"

Tein looked for Kamal Ali. He had been polite when Mustafa visited once before, ostensibly to buy butter for his wife, but Tein suspected it was only to get a closer look at the man who had married Zaytuna. Yesterday, Kamal Ali's concern focused on Zaytuna. Today, as he came out of the office to greet Mustafa, his expression was welcoming but guarded.

"My wife," he said, sounding guilty, "My wife suggested that the scholars who said he was a gambler must have had a grudge against him. In fact, we wondered if it might have more to do with the tension between the scholars themselves."

"What tension?" Tein asked.

"The two are Quran scholars." He looked directly at Tein, taking a breath as if he were sorting out how to explain. "They are trying to preserve the Quran as the Prophet recited it. This means determining which readings of certain words or verses are most reliably what God revealed. They argue, these men. They argue most strenuously. They differ in their approaches, and, well, it has been contentious at times."

"This is the first I've heard of it." He looked at Kamal Ali with a glint of laughter in his eyes. "Don't tell my sister I don't know enough Quran to hear any differences."

Ammar snorted.

Tein was confused. "Something I said?"

"Something he said." Ammar tipped his chin at Mustafa.

Mustafa seemed uncomfortable. Nasifa was suddenly near tears, pulling her wrap over her face as if to shield herself from the sun.

Ammar took a step toward Mustafa, hands open for attack. "You stand there and admit that the Quran has been altered from what the Prophet, alayhi salam, recited."

Tein stood, ready to intervene, still not understanding. Did Ammar not want the case?

"You Sunnis have made careers debating the alterations, yet you dismiss us Shia when we say that Uthman refused the testimony of Seyyidina Ali's manuscript? Who was there when Gabriel first came with the revelation to the Prophet? It was his wife, Khadija, the mother of his daughter, Lady Fatima, and, the young Ali. They were the first! They were beside him!" He jutted out his chest, challenging Mustafa to battle. "Then after, Khadija's death, God be well-pleased with her, it was our beloved Ali who was there. And it was Seyyidina Ali who was taught the inward meanings of the Book. Ali alone carried the complete recitation in word and meaning!" He shook his head slowly in anger. "So much is lost."

Mustafa moved back a step, while Kamal Ali came around to stand beside him.

"Please. There is no need for such high feeling." Kamal Ali moved so that he was almost standing in front of Ammar to protect Mustafa.

Tein wondered again at his character.

Kamal Ali said, "I, myself, have heard from Shia scholars that the Shia Imams accept the caliph Uthman's codex without criticism. Further, they say the Shia Imams have a copy of Seyyidina Ali's manuscript and have passed it from one to another."

"Liars. Those scholars take their instruction from the caliphate's people."

At this, Nasifa trembled and said, loud enough for them all to hear, "Shame."

Ammar turned his head sharply toward her but swallowed his retort.

In the breach, Mustafa found his voice. "Ibn Abi Layla himself recited from Seyyidina Ali's personal manuscript. The scholars rely on it in their determinations! By God, I swear nothing from Seyyidina Ali's manuscript has been hidden!"

"Do not make oaths on others' promises, Mustafa," Ammar said through gritted teeth. "You could find yourself being held to account on the Last Day for their lies." He turned his back to them all and walked out into the square.

Nasifa got up and followed him.

"I can't see how he'll agree to the case now," Tein said, trying not to sound relieved.

"I'll do it!" Ammar yelled, storming back in their direction. He jabbed his finger at Tein. "Curse your doubt!"

Mustafa raised his hands, entreating, "All that matters is finding a man alive!"

Tein pulled out a chair for Nasifa, who could no longer hide her distress.

"Perhaps," Kamal Ali asked, "Malik could help Lady Nasifa with her shopping and then home?"

The boy jumped forward and gestured toward the market.

"Yes, go with him," Ammar said, then whispered something in her ear. She nodded, leaving with the boy to the market gate. Ammar sat down hard in her chair.

"You say these Quran scholars argue and it may have something to do with the man's disappearance?" Kamal Ali prompted.

Hesitant at first, Mustafa answered, avoiding Ammar's hard gaze, "There, well, there are several camps, but only two seem to matter with respect to the missing man."

Ammar stuck his feet out rudely toward Mustafa, hands clasped across his belly, but he was listening. Any other day, Tein would have laughed at the gesture. Today, he wanted to turn his back on his friend and walk away.

"Nabil is a student of Ibn Shanabudh," Mustafa continued. "For him, it is most prudent to follow the record of the companions' personal readings rather than stay within the bounds of the caliph Uthman's codex. Ibn Mujahid rejects this approach."

Mustafa had found his footing, his language growing high-handed. Tein had to restrain himself from rolling his eyes.

"That would hardly seem so contentious," Mustafa went on, "as, in truth, it does not amount to distinctions that, I would assume, could not be worked out if the men were to work together. But, you see, Ibn

Shanabudh also holds several positions in addition that Ibn Mujahid finds entirely unacceptable, even heretical. And, as Ibn Mujahid has the ear of the High Court, there is always the worry he could make a case against Ibn Shanabudh, and others like him, for heresy."

"Ibn Mujahid's students say Nabil was a gambler, not his own colleagues?" Ammar asked.

"As far as I know."

"So slandering Nabil would slander Ibn Shanabudh?"

"Yes," Mustafa said.

Tein insisted, "Nabil's probably just drying out after a bender."

"Or," Ammar said flatly, "There could have been a fight between the two camps and Nabil was hurt, or even killed, and the students are pointing toward the gambling to avoid suspicion."

"God protect him. Yes." Mustafa's eyes widened. "YingYue suggested as much."

"What about this manuscript that his colleagues all want to see so much?"

"We will have to ask them," Mustafa said.

Tein continued to resist this angle and addressed Ammar, "No more than a day to find him, if he's not already dragging himself home."

"It is fascinating, I must admit. But you must find this man for his mother." Kamal Ali ignored Tein's assertion that there was no case. "I can find men to step in for your work while you pursue it, although, of course, none could replace you. A few days?"

Ammar sat up and gave Kamal Ali respectful attention. "It could be more."

"No matter," Kamal Ali responded, hand over heart, and stood. The men followed him.

Tein sucked his teeth. He had just been signed onto the case and out of his job without having agreed.

"We need to meet Nabil's mother." Ammar addressed Tein. "And we have to look into the gambling and the scholars. I'd rather focus on the gambling first."

Tein nodded reluctantly.

Ammar bowed to Kamal Ali.

"I will meet you at your home in the morning to take you to the mother?" Mustafa asked Tein eagerly.

It was brazen to suggest such a thing, and in front of Kamal Ali. Tein looked quickly at his brother-in-law, but his face betrayed nothing. Mustafa must be mad. Whether he brought them this case in good faith or not, it was certain now that Mustafa was using it to get close to Zaytuna. A curse nearly left his lips. There was nothing he wanted less than to manage Mustafa's lovesickness and Ammar's temper, in addition to being forced back into an investigation.

"Where does the mother live?" Tein asked.

"Near the Sharqiyya mosque."

"Ammar and I will meet you at the main door of the mosque after the afternoon prayer."

Mustafa was unable to hide his disappointment.

Tein wanted to grab the two men and shake some sense into them. The women they married, the gifts the men were given in them. Ammar with a child on the way. How dare they show dissatisfaction?

Mustafa must have seen it on his face. He retreated a step. "I will see you there, God willing."

Tein turned to Kamal Ali. "We will be here first thing in the morning, as usual. After that, I'll come by and train the new men you bring in to cover for us."

"No need. Ezra can do that once the new men are in. But there is one thing." Kamal Ali put his hand on Tein's arm, leading him away so they could speak alone. "Zaytuna. I am concerned she will become involved. Not that I have the right to deny her. God forgive me, it is in our marriage contract that I cannot. And," he emphasized, "I would not. It is only that I worry…"

"I understand." Tein bristled that Zaytuna might cause Kamal Ali any worry on this account and tried to reassure him. She would never betray him by being alone with Mustafa. "There is no need for her. She would not be a help with questioning in gambling houses and not among scholars, either."

Kamal Ali nodded, but seemed uncertain.

"I will keep an eye on her," Tein promised.

4

Mustafa waited outside of the Sharqiyya mosque for Tein and Ammar. The afternoon prayer had long finished and they still had not arrived. Granted, it was a long walk from Buratha and the butter shop, but they knew well how long it took to cross from one side of Karkh to the other. He was growing hot, not sure if it was the warm fall afternoon or frustration of waiting. He tugged at his wrap, loosening it slightly, eager to prove to them there was a case.

While pacing in front of the mosque, Mustafa bumped into a man. Looking up, he was startled to find Burhan with several of his students in tow. Burhan was wrapped in a cloak with richly embroidered edges and a matching, multi-hued turban in shades of red, browns, and greens, so unlike the humble dress of a scholar. Mustafa turned to avoid having to speak to him.

But Burhan would not let the opportunity go. "Assalamu alaykum, ya Mustafa."

"Wa alaykum assalam wa rahmatullah wa barakatuhu, Burhan," Mustafa replied, leaving out Burhan's newly conferred title, "Professor."

Burhan had always taunted him, boasting of his connections

through his father, the judge. While Mustafa had spent his time outside of lessons at the mosque making clay jugs and cups to support himself, Burhan was travelling the empire, the guest of renowned hadith scholars. But then the day had come when Abu Abdurrahman al-Azdi had taken Mustafa under his wing, giving him an enviable education, and making possible his employment as a tutor. There might have been more opportunities had he not gotten involved in Mu'mina's case. Many of those who personally censured Burhan and his father for their involvement had nevertheless closed ranks around the two men and Mustafa found himself unwelcome in some study circles.

Burhan bowed his turbaned head with the same air of superiority he displayed since their early days studying hadith. "I hear you are getting yourself involved in other people's business again. One would have thought you learned your lesson."

Frustration became prickling fear. He opened his mouth to retort that God would be the judge of the lessons they took to heart. Nothing came out and he looked even more the fool.

Raising his eyebrows, Burhan chuckled and the cluster of students followed him into the mosque.

Mustafa did not watch them go or scan the crowd to see who had observed the threat and his humiliation. Instead, he rushed to the intersection of the Basra Gate High Road. Tein and Ammar were coming around the corner just as he got there. He waved them impatiently toward the street curving around the outside of the mosque, walking just ahead of them. "This way!"

"Slow down!" Tein yelled from behind him.

Mustafa stopped short, pulling his wrap from his shoulder, wanting to throw it to the ground, but glared at the men instead.

"Don't worry." Ammar said as they caught up. "If there is something to be found out, we will find it."

Only then did he notice that Ammar was wearing his battle-scarred leather cuirass and sword. Mustafa drew his head back. "You have dressed for a fight to interview the mother of a missing man!"

"Always ready!" Ammar slapped his chest comically.

Tein stifled a laugh, which only made Mustafa feel worse.

Understanding, Tein said, "Brother, we're here," and put his arm around him as they walked toward the mosque.

But Mustafa did not feel reassured. He looked at the students crowded around stalls selling paper ink and pens, prayer beads, incense, perfumed oils, and cloth prayer rugs that could fold into one's pocket and imagined the selfishness of each and every one of those people, unconcerned with what had happened to their colleague and brother.

They came up to the immense blue-tiled arch of the entrance to the Sharqiyya mosque that framed the students and worshippers coming and going. "It's just around the corner, up here. That alley," he gestured, hurrying again.

Mustafa knocked on a small sturdy door in a high wall that curved around a corner just beyond. A young Slav woman opened it enough for them to see the whole of her. He was startled by the beauty of her angular face. Her skin was so pale he could see the blue veins on her temples. Her sapphire eyes were set like jewels within golden lashes and brows, yet there was bitterness in those eyes and the harsh line of her bow-shaped red lips. She wore a rough shift, covered by an old wrap wound under her arms that went just to her knees. Mustafa grew warm at the sight of her smooth, bare legs and perfectly shaped feet, and looked away, his heart wracked by guilt at the pleasure he took from her. "Assalamu alaykum," she said in lightly accented Arabic. He raised his head in time to see her gaze stop appreciatively on Tein, who bowed his head to her, hand over heart. Her expression softened.

Mustafa replied generously, stifling a twinge of jealousy, "Wa alaykum as-salam ar-rahmatullahi wa barakatuhu. I have brought these men to see Umm Nabil."

"Oliga!" a woman's shrill voice called from within. "What are you waiting for? Bring Professor Mustafa in!"

A bit of pride was restored by the use of the unwarranted title as Oliga led the men around the vestibule. The main room was modest but crowded with ornately carved low couches covered with embroidered upholstery, pillows of wool and silk placed along their backs. A carpet of richly coloured motifs he did not recognize covered the entire floor. This was a formerly wealthy family in reduced circumstances. He stole a glance at Oliga as she left them for the courtyard. He supposed she, too, was purchased in better days as a mark of status for this family and, sickened at the thought of his own attraction to her, likely used as more than a servant by the man of the household.

Nabil's mother rushed to them. Her voluminous patterned silk wrap was gathered in her hands, as if red peonies on long leafy stems spilled from her arms. While her bagged eyes were not kohl-stained with tears as the day he saw her at his friend's house, where she had been weeping in the arms of Ulgen's mother, the air of desperation was the same. She let go of her wrap and grasped Mustafa's hands. "God reward Ulgen for bringing you to me! Are these the men who will find my Nabil?"

Mustafa gently pried his hands loose. "Inshallah. This is Ammar ibn at-Tabbani and Tein ibn al-Ashiqa as-Sawda. They are former detectives with the Grave Crimes Section of the Baghdad Police."

"God is the Protector!" She tugged Ammar's sleeve, begging him to sit down, pausing before allowing Tein to do the same. She looked through the courtyard door for Oliga, her eyes narrowed on not finding her immediately nearby. But Oliga returned in a moment carrying a beautifully hammered copper tray with delicate glasses filled with water and an engraved copper plate holding only a small mound of broken walnut pieces.

Ammar began, "May God protect you and your son and forgive us for the delicacy of the questions we must ask."

Mustafa had never heard him speak so formally. It transformed his brutal appearance into that of a noble ghazi here to attend to this wealthy woman's needs, and she responded with gratitude. "Anything, my son, anything."

"Sometimes men run off on their own. No harm has been done to them, only they have tired of their lives, or, if you will forgive me, they have fallen in love with the wrong woman and the two escape to marry. Did he complain? Did he act like a man in love?"

She rubbed the silver talisman case around her neck, murmuring, then let it go, glaring at him for the insult. "I know what love looks like, and my boy was not in love. He declared he would wait until he had succeeded as a scholar to such a position that he could demand a woman who would suit the reputation of this family."

Tein sat forward, but did not speak.

"And complaints?"

"He was held in great respect by his colleagues." Her voice rose. "There is no reason for him to run away."

"When did you begin to worry he was not coming home?" Tein asked.

"The very first night! He has never left his mother alone."

Ammar followed up. "What did you do?"

"I sent Oliga to look for him."

Mustafa was going to ask Oliga about her search, but she had returned to the courtyard. Next to her stretched-out bare legs, he could just see two large dishes of lentils for sorting. He exhaled sharply.

"After two days, I, myself, went to ask his teacher if he had seen him."

"Which teacher?"

The question offended her in some way and she snapped, "Imam Ibn Shanabudh, of course!"

"And what did he tell you?" Ammar asked, unfazed.

"He showed me every grace," she said, as if accusing Ammar of doing the very opposite. "He asked me to sit beside him and called over several of his students."

"And?"

"The men were surprised that he was missing. Not one of them had any idea of where he had gone or what might have happened to him."

"But," Tein said gently, "he must have been friends with some of his colleagues. They knew nothing?"

"I asked about his friends. They explained that he was so serious in his studies, he had little time to spend in leisure."

Mustafa gestured to Ammar to indicate that this could not possibly be true. Study was reliant on such companionship.

Tein asked, "Who brought you in, Mustafa?"

"Ulgen, a student of Ibn Mujahid. He only saw her distress and that no help was coming and so reached out to me," Mustafa explained. "He had heard of my connections to the Baghdad police."

"He has no friends in Baghdad at all?" Tein pressed.

"We were forced to leave our friends behind when we left Kufa," she replied defensively.

"How long ago was this?"

"We have been in Baghdad these past seven months."

That was time enough to make friends at the mosque, Mustafa thought, and certainly so if he were sitting in taverns, but her son would not have brought that up.

Ammar did. "I am sorry to say so, but he is said to have visited taverns and gambling establishments."

Disgusted at the suggestion, but not shocked to hear them, she answered dismissively, "Lies."

He looked to Tein and Ammar, but they seemed not to have noticed. He would be sure to raise this once they left. There was something!

Ammar said, "We can look into your son's disappearance. But you should understand that we are no longer with the police."

"The police!" Her disgust transformed into venom. "I went to them and they turned me away. Horrible man, that Ibn Marwan. Horrible! He told me there was nothing they could do without some evidence of a crime." She reached forward and gripped Ammar's arm. "There is evidence of a crime. My boy is gone!"

Ammar did not pull away, although she was clearly gripping his arm hard enough to be painful. "I am sorry," he said. "We will look into it. But there are things you must understand. We may not find him and while searching for him, we may uncover information about your son that you may find disturbing."

Her eyebrows raised. "And?"

"We will need to be paid. We work independent of the government."

She touched the case containing her talisman again, this time lifting the chain over her head, opening the silver container, and removing the folded paper within. She kissed it and murmured something. As she rubbed the paper talisman itself, an edge of wood-block printed text became visible, revealing a distinctive double-striped red border with black dots. Then, bringing the paper to her heart with one hand, she offered the empty case to him with the other. "Will this be enough?"

Ammar took the case, tossing it once in his hand to feel the weight, then bowed his head in thanks as he slipped it into his sleeve. "What does your son look like?"

"He is your size, but slim and handsome." She sniffed. "He has skin the colour of fresh wheat, chestnut eyes, a distinguished nose, and a luxurious red beard."

That could describe any number of men. Mustafa asked, "No birthmarks or scars, anything that would help us identify him?"

"How does he dress?" Tein followed up.

"To our station, of course."

"How was he dressed when he left the house that day, I mean."

"A quilted washa silk robe in red with a taraz border spelling out our family's name…"

That was distinctive, at least.

"…and a turban to match, red with blue and gold stripes, and plain brown wool wrap so that he might humble himself in the presence of his colleagues of lesser means."

Ammar and Tein stood, and Mustafa followed.

Oliga appeared at the courtyard door to show them out.

"When will you be back?" Umm Nabil followed them to the vestibule.

"As soon as we have any news." Mustafa faced her, hand over his heart.

Oliga followed them out, shutting the door behind her. "Two doors down. Hakan." She gestured to the left. "Nabil sells the household goods to him bit by bit to cover his gambling debts."f

"Thank you." Tein asked gently, "You are in a position to observe him, overhear his conversations. Is there anything that would help us?"

She spat on the ground at their feet. "He's no better than the father.

The two of them were good for nothing more than to fiddle with their cocks. May you find his body washed up on the banks of the Tigris and the birds plucking at his eyes!"

Mustafa gasped at the curse, but understood her anger and uttered the verse insisting on fair treatment of enslaved women, *"God knows the state of your faith and the faith of the woman your right hand owns."*

"God?" She slapped her chest. "Spare me your Quran and buy my freedom if you want justice for the enslaved!"

Shaken, he wanted to take the silver talisman case from Ammar and give it to her, give her everything he had so that she could free herself. Instead, he muttered the verse, *"If any of those your right hand owns want a deed of emancipation, then give them the deed."*

Oliga only looked at him like the fool that he felt and spat on the ground again before turning to go back inside.

"Wait," Tein said.

She stopped with her back to them.

"The talisman Umm Nabil carries. Do you know what is on it?"

Oliga faced him for a moment, sneering. "Justice." Then turned away, slamming the door behind her.

Mustafa looked to Ammar and Tein, but Ammar ignored him and walked ahead. Tein waited a moment, nearly spoke, then thrust Mustafa ahead toward Hakan's door.

"Two doors on the right or left?" Tein called out over Ammar's shoulder.

"Left!" Ammar reached it first and knocked.

A boy opened it and stared at them, wide-eyed. His short blue robe and sirwal were made of good, sturdy linen and his feet were snug in thick leather slippers. An older man with a soft face and grey beard pulled him back with a chuckle and opened the door completely. "Assalamu alaykum, may I help you?"

"Wa alaykum assalam. We would like to speak to Hakan."

He looked them over more closely. "I am his grandfather. You speak to me."

Ammar bowed his head. "Nabil ibn al-Qays al-Kufi has gone missing. His mother has asked us to help find him."

"And who are you that you should be looking for him?" His stance changed, his grip on the door tightening as if he thought they might try to force their way in.

"Just men helping out."

"We don't know anything here."

He started to close the door when a younger male voice whispered behind him, "Ask if they are police."

Mustafa tried to peer past him, but the old man blocked his view.

Hakan's grandfather seemed angry at the interruption, but asked, "Are you police?"

"No." Tein answered.

"I am a scholar of hadith," Mustafa volunteered.

"And you two?"

"We churn butter." Tein smiled.

"It's fine," said the voice within. Hakan's grandfather shook his head and stood back, letting the young man come forward.

"I am Hakan." He leaned against the jamb offering them a cocky smile, but closed the door part way behind him, blocking his grandfather's view.

"We are looking for Nabil ibn al-Qays al-Kufi."

"I heard. But why come to me?"

Ammar matched Hakan's confidence. "You sold his goods for him."

Mustafa shrank back at the directness of the statement.

"No law against a man selling his own possessions."

Tein took a step away from the door and leaned on the wall, watching.

"In Nabil's case, no." Ammar shrugged, then took on a casual but threatening tone. "Look, we're not going to tell the police you peddle stolen goods. We only want to know about Nabil. Tell us what his mother would not know."

"Would not admit is more like it." Unimpressed by Ammar, Hakan leaned in as if he were a gossiping old woman. "Our place opens on a common courtyard with theirs. We've all heard her screaming at him for gambling. Seems he takes after his father, if her taunts are to be believed."

"And you sell the family goods he brings you to cover his debts?"

"I did. Not lately."

"No?" Ammar leaned into the question.

"He complained his mother was sleeping with the valuables they had left."

"Did he play and pay up, or was he in debt?"

"Always running a bit behind."

"And now with nothing to sell, he's more than a bit behind?"

"You'll have to ask the ones who host the games."

"Do you know where?"

Hakan shook his head. "I don't gamble. But I'll take a bite for selling the goods of those who do."

"He must have said something when he complained to you about having nothing to sell."

"Nothing but harsh words about his mother." He smirked. "God forgive him."

"If you could guess, where do you think he is?"

"Kneecapped in an alley somewhere."

Tein grunted in agreement.

Ammar checked with Tein, who nodded, then said to Hakan, "If there is anything else you remember, you can..." He stopped.

"You can find me," Mustafa jumped in. "I am at the Sharqiyya Mosque studying every day."

Tein shook his head at him.

But he gave Hakan his name anyway, "Mustafa ibn Zaytuna."

He laughed. "You take your mother's nasab?"

Ammar quipped, gesturing toward Tein. "You think that's odd, wait until you hear the name of that man there."

Hakan looked at Tein and stopped laughing.

Tein huffed and walked away.

"If he comes back"—he bowed sarcastically as he shut the door—"I will send word to Ibn Zaytuna."

Ammar turned to him, pleased. "Now we have something to go on."

They caught up with Tein, who remained silent as they walked in the direction of the mosque. Ammar let him be, but Mustafa was itching to know their next moves.

"Should we split up the questioning?" he asked eagerly. "I can speak to my fellows at the mosque."

Tein sighed, ignoring him. "We have to go to the hospital and see if he is there. Maybe he was taken in by a local healer or a bonesetter, but that's the place to start."

"Or the police. They might have the body. So," Ammar counted on his fingers, "the hospital. Khalil about his gambling debts. The scholars."

"Should I…" Mustafa ventured again.

"No," Tein said, too sharply, then corrected his tone. "We need to be there for the questioning." He addressed Ammar. "We can stop by the hospital on the way home."

Mustafa raised his head to track the sun in the sky. "It's too late now. The men we want to interview at the mosque will be there tomorrow morning. Can you meet me then?"

"What about tutoring?" Tein asked.

"I have time." He did not, but he would have to make it.

Tein looked unconvinced.

"They have family visiting. The boys will be busy." Mustafa heard himself lying and flushed deeply, muttering, "God forgive me."

"Mustafa," Tein said, "you don't need to come with us."

"I do not have work." He glanced at the sky again, wondering if he still had time to get to Ibn Shahin's home at a decent hour to ask about time off tomorrow.

Tein grunted.

"At least we are getting paid." Ammar removed the silver case from his sleeve.

Tein took it from him and turned it over in his hands, checking the interior, then hefted it for weight and handed it back. "No lead lining. Put it someplace safe. We're not selling it, yet."

"We'll work this case until there's nothing left," Ammar said. "You know, we might have got more out of the mother, even the servant, if Zaytuna were with us."

Mustafa concealed a gasp, his hopes soaring.

5

"WHERE IS MALIK AND HIS BARROW?" Saliha grumbled, shifting her grip on the immense tray of barley smothered with stewed meat and vegetables.

"His mother called for him yesterday," Zaytuna replied. "We'll have him back next week."

Yulduz stopped so they could adjust their grip. A bare-footed boy leading a donkey drew in close and snatched a hunk of meat, nearly causing the tray to lean over and spill out its contents.

"If I had a free hand, boy!" Yulduz shouted. He carried on, his cheek plump with meat, grinning from ear to ear.

Zaytuna snapped, "Steady, Yulduz!"

A cart rumbled by, raising dust that would settle on the food, but there was nothing they could do now. Some people looked hungrily at the food, but kept going, while others responded with gratitude, and said, "May God increase your good deeds."

"Layla should have stayed home to help," Saliha said. "It's too much."

"I won't keep her from schooling," Zaytuna answered.

Qambar was struggling with his side. His swollen fingers were not made for this. He and Yulduz had prepared the stew yesterday. Malik had delivered the large pot to the local bakery to simmer in the hot coals overnight and brought it to their home this morning before he left to visit his mother. Yulduz insisted on making barley at home instead of bringing bread. But the weight it added was making carrying the tray even more difficult.

Another boy was coming with his eye on the food.

"You!" Qambar called out. "If you want to eat, we're on our way to the cemetery. You can eat there."

The boy stopped. "Let me help carry it, Uncle." They paused their shuffling for a moment and the boy, barefoot despite the morning chill, stood next to Yulduz and took the weight she carried. Zaytuna had wished he had relieved Qambar instead. The old woman was like an ox despite her aching bones.

"You could teach your fellows a thing or two," Yulduz said in thanks.

A man in thin sirwal, but no shirt, his turban no more than a scrap of found cloth, rushed to them as if he had heard her wish. "My turn."

Qambar and Yulduz walked beside them on the road, keeping an eye out for trouble. Before they could reach the Shuniziyya cemetery, two other men had come and taken Saliha and Zaytuna's place. Both looked like they had not eaten in days. They would soon have full bellies just like those who lived in makeshift homes on the cemetery grounds and those who had burrowed into its walls to find a safe place to sleep.

She was eager to see the old burrow woman who had taught her so much. If anyone could make sense of Mustafa's intrusion into her peace, she could.

"Carry on through, just over there." Zaytuna indicated a spot just within the walls with plenty of open space.

Families, the old and forgotten, and those who had no other place in the world hurried over. Some came with small pots to fill and eat elsewhere while others waited to squat before the tray and eat as latecomers stood behind them. Other than the boy, those who carried the tray held back, rather than push in with the rest. "Ya Rabb,"

Zaytuna prayed under her breath, "provide for them and keep them safe."

But the old woman in the burrow was not among the crowd. Zaytuna left to find her. Outside the wall, she peered into her woven palm lean-to covering her burrow, but it was empty along with all the others who were now inside, eating. Her few things were still there. Certainly, all was well. But as she searched, she became more concerned. Zaytuna looked up and down the road, then walked back into the cemetery and scanned the rising and falling mounds and headstones for her, but only saw the spot where her mother lay, the two palm trees swaying overhead, and Uncle Nuri's grave.

Zaytuna walked slowly to greet her uncle first. Kneeling beside his grave, she raised her hands to pray for him but did not feel his softness reach her as she always did. She finished her prayer, gathering the blessings in her hands and wiping her face. "Uncle," she asked, "so much has happened. I need you. I need to talk to the auntie. Where did the auntie go?" But there was no answer, no feeling of deep calm telling her all was well.

Then a familiar inkling of sorrow arose within her, as if from within the earth itself, and pulled her down. She tried to turn her head to see her family, to call out to them for help, but she found herself slowly sinking until she lay down beside the grave, her tongue too thick to speak. The warm grit of the earth pressed into her cheek as if someone above were holding her down. Jagged rocks bit into her bones. The sorrow held her tight in its grasp, ushering her into a terrifying emptiness. It was as if she had opened the door to her home expecting the bustling warmth of her family only to find them gone and the house stripped bare as if they had never lived. Terror broke through and she shot up, searching for reassurance from her mother's grave in the distance, but the twin palms stood alone on barren land. She spun around to make sure that Saliha and the rest were still there, but they did not notice her. Turning back to her uncle's grave, she found nothing, again.

The reliable presence of those she loved, living and dead, had withdrawn beyond her reach, leaving her standing in an empty quarter with no escape. Weak kneed, she lost her balance and took several stumbling steps back.

One more step back and she did stumble, but only to be caught.

A woman's voice came from just behind her. "Zaytuna."

The hands restored her footing. She turned to face the woman, but Zaytuna's eyes were still set into the distance and she saw movement among the gravestones. On the far side of the cemetery, a woman in a red gown, her brown wrap trailing behind her, skirted the stones as she walked briskly to the far gate.

The voice called her to attention. "Zaytuna, it is I, Saadia, the sister of Sherwan Ibn Salah."

The scent of jasmine and vanilla awakened her recognition, and she came fully to her senses, horrified. It had been over a year, but she would never forget how this regal woman mocked her poverty when Mustafa took her to her family home. Then, the last time she had seen her was in the courtroom where she stood in defence of Mu'mina. It seemed noble then, but as time wore on, it felt to Zaytuna like no more than the vain largesse of the privileged classes. Why was she here? Why now?

Saadia checked to see if Zaytuna was injured. "You have fallen." She reached out to brush her cheek.

Zaytuna recoiled, pushing her hand away.

But the woman would not leave, instead she retreated a step and flicked her floral silk wrap so it draped perfectly across her shoulder.

"I, I," Zaytuna stammered, wanting nothing but the woman to leave her to find her way out of the emptiness consuming her.

"How is your family?" Saadia asked.

She found her voice in simple politeness. "Alhamdulillah, and yours?"

"Alhamdulillah." Saadia's wide mouth ticked up in a half-smile, as if she knew something Zaytuna did not and was about to tell her.

She looked toward the cemetery entrance and those who were finally getting their chance to eat. Saliha was staring at her. Zaytuna called her inwardly to come and rescue her, but she returned her attention to the people they were feeding. "Alhamdulillah," Zaytuna muttered. "No complaints."

"We see your cousin Mustafa now and again." Saadia carried on as if Zaytuna were not covered in dust, near tears, and unable to carry on the conversation that propriety required. "He has brought his lovely wife YingYue to lunch with us, but we still miss you and ask after you."

All she could think was poor YingYue having to listen to those women asking after Zaytuna's health and felt an even greater desolation. What had YingYue done but love Mustafa? Now he forces her to sit with these elite women and listen to them chattering about nothing when she would no doubt prefer to be left in reflection and prayer? Anger for YingYue's sake brought her back to her senses and she answered coldly, "You honour us with a visit to our humble cemetery."

Saadia gestured in appreciation of the scenery, ignoring Zaytuna's tone. "I walk the city when I am in a mind to write poetry and graveyards are particularly inspiring."

Zaytuna remembered her family teasing her. "You said your family complained that you preferred to write poetry than…." She faltered, suddenly realizing Saadia might have come to meet the woman in red retreating from the cemetery.

"…rather than marry, yes." Her long, oval face opened as if a revelation were arriving from the heavens. "I recited these lines to them when they offered me yet another marriage prospect:

I am a lioness.
No man will make my body his resting place.
And if I were to, would I give it to a dog?
When, O, the lions I have turned away!"

Saadia lifted her sharp chin with pride.

It was as if God had sent Saadia to taunt her from the edges of the abandoned land in which she was trapped. *If she would only leave I could find my way out.* Then thought without thinking, *I could find my husband*. But the face the words conjured belonged to Mustafa not Kamal Ali and a wave of nausea overtook her. She stared at Saadia desperately, swallowing hard.

Saadia looked at her quizzically and became serious. "I mean to say that I have been successful in maintaining my brother's amiable guardianship instead of that of a husband whose demands, shall we say, would not match my desire."

It took a moment before Saadia's admission took shape in her understanding and what it must mean for her, but its meaning turned into her own. She imagined Mustafa searching among the grave stones for a love denied to him. The wind tugged at his wrap, the tail of his turban raised to cover his face from recognition. Taking Saadia's hand, she assured the woman of her understanding and, so, her silence by looking away just a moment too long.

Saadia acknowledged the gesture, but let an awkward silence follow.

"I have married since last I saw you." Zaytuna blurted out to fill the gap, immediately wishing she could take back the words.

"Indeed!" Saadia tucked her head back with a wry expression. "Mustafa did not say. I must scold him next time he visits. But men are like that, always sharing the news no one wants to hear and forgetting what is essential. May God bless your marriage."

Struck by Mustafa's omission, she replied, "Amin," with more feeling than she intended. Then she realized, Saadia suspected that Mustafa still loved her. This was the secret. The woman was no fool and she was probing for more.

"Mustafa mentioned that your mother was an ecstatic poet, al-Ashiqa as-Sawda. He said no one knew her real name, only the sobriquet, 'The Black Lover', and that people still recite her words of love for God."

Is Ying Yue forced to listen to this, too?

Saadia pressed on. "Can you share a few lines with me?"

It was too much. Zaytuna felt dizzy again and looked to the entrance of the cemetery. This time Saliha was walking towards her with a determined gait. It freed her, and Zaytuna tore away from Saadia without a word.

Saadia caught up. "No?"

"You should hear them from another who has the tongue for it," she spat out, facing ahead, driving forward to Saliha.

She asked, undeterred, "Do you follow in al-Ashiqa as-Sawda's path?"

"I do not have her gift. I feed the poor." Zaytuna gestured ahead of her. The last person eating had left. Yulduz saw her and waved her back.

"May God reward you."

All she wanted was to go home to her prayer rug, weep, and pray for understanding.

But Yulduz's face lit up as they drew close. Since that day in court, Yulduz had spoken in admiration of Saadia, often by comparison to Zaytuna, who did not fare as well.

"Is that the Turkmen woman from the courtroom?"

"Yulduz, yes. Her husband, just there, is Qambar."

"And the woman coming to greet us?"

Saliha was nearly to them, close enough to see Zaytuna's expression and was openly worried. She hurried her step. As she walked, her wrap caught around her voluptuous curves, her long black hair was coming loose as always, and her bold face was somehow made more beautiful by dust and perspiration.

"My sister-in-law," Zaytuna explained.

"Your brother is blessed with such a beautiful wife."

Zaytuna did not know how to reply and was grateful when Saliha reached them. She acknowledged Saadia, but took Zaytuna in her arm, pulling her along. "What took you so long, we've been waiting for you. We must leave."

"What a shame," Saadia remarked smoothly.

Yulduz met them.

Saadia grasped the old woman's hands before Yulduz could do the same and kissed them, then held them to her cheek. "It is a blessing to see your honourable face."

The old woman blushed. "It's good to see you again an' in good health." But then she looked Zaytuna up and down. "Covered in dust again, are you?"

"She does this often?" Saadia asked, teasing.

A hand on Zaytuna's arm, Saliha turned on the woman. "And you? You ruined your silk and slippers to wander among our graves?"

With a broad smile, Saadia conceded. "My apologies. Also, my apologies for not introducing myself. I am Saadia bint Salah, an acquaintance of this good woman here," she let go of Yulduz's hand, "and Zaytuna."

"I am Saliha, this good woman's sister-in-law." She turned back to the entrance of the cemetery, taking Zaytuna with her, and forcing the others to follow. She leaned in to Zaytuna. "What's wrong, what did she say?"

"It's not her. Oh, it is her. I just."

"What?"

"I went to Uncle's and he wasn't there for me. I got upset, then turned around and there Saadia was, provoking me."

Saliha put an arm around her waist. "I'll handle her."

Loyal Saliha. Zaytuna leaned into her. "It's fine. This is enough."

"What did she say?"

"Mustafa's been at their home."

"That upset you?"

"It's the way she said it, implying something, like he's revealed to them how he feels."

"Uff. I'd like Mustafa to feel the back of my hand."

Zaytuna touched her arm. "One minute you want me to love him, then next you want to slap him."

"That's not what I said to you," she scolded lightly. "But if you want to go to him, I won't stop you. You're free. No one will tell you that, but you listen to me."

"I don't want to go to him."

She could hear Saadia and Yulduz chatting softly behind them and the pleasure in the old woman's voice.

"You're free. Free to see him or not. Free to work this case or not."

"It's not that simple," she protested, not knowing how to explain.

"It is."

They had reached Qambar, Saliha withdrew her arm from Zaytuna's waist and said to him, "It's time to go."

Saadia and Yulduz caught up, and Zaytuna said, "It was good to see you, Saadia. Inshallah, another time?" But she intoned the inshallah to indicate she did not mean it.

"This must be your husband," Saadia said to Yulduz, ignoring the dismissal.

Saliha started to say something, but Zaytuna held her back.

He bowed with his hand over his heart.

"This is Lady Saadia, the one…"

Saadia cut her off, "Do you bring food here each week?" Then she addressed Zaytuna, "Perhaps I will see you then?"

Yulduz offered eagerly, "Once a week. Zaytuna's Kamal Ali provides for all these good people, and we cook it for them." She looked down the road. "Usually there's a boy." Her face contorted with an apology. "He was busy today. But usually there's a boy who brings the tray balanced on his barrow."

"Let's head home." Qambar put his arm around her.

"May your sacrifice be rewarded a thousand-fold," Saadia said, head bowed.

Saliha left to retrieve the now empty tray, which she righted to its side like a shield.

But Saadia remained where she was, openly taking stock of them. They were exhausted and covered in dust. Zaytuna knew what was coming from a woman such as this.

"I wonder if your Kamal Ali would consider the establishment of a waqf for the people of this graveyard. A business that would dedicate its profits wholly to these people. You would not need to carry food any longer, with or without a boy. A cook-house could be established within its walls. A few people here might be employed running it." She looked at Zaytuna. "It would be easier on your family and friends and continue to give beyond your lives.

"That may be how you people do things," Saliha said, returning with the tray rolling on its side, "but here we give our neighbours food by our own hands."

Yulduz snapped at her. "Woman!"

But Saliha stared back, unashamed.

Saadia took a step back, no doubt unused to dealing with people of their sort who were not servants. She recovered, but her voice had lost its playful, authoritative tone. "Mustafa tells us that you still investigate crimes?"

A lump formed in Zaytuna's throat. Did God send this woman to taunt her? There would be no investigating for her. There would only be Mustafa, calling to her, "I need you."

"She is consulting on a big case." Saliha said.

Her friend was only trying to make her seem important, another act of protection, but this was not the way. And she did not know how much longer she could hold herself together.

Yulduz and Qambar stared at Saliha disapprovingly.

"Oh, do tell!"

"It's nothing." Zaytuna consciously left Mustafa out of it, hurrying the explanation. "I'm not consulting. It is a case involving a missing scholar, led by my brother Tein and his friend Ammar ibn at-Tabbani."

"Ammar, the police investigator at the trial?" Saadia asked.

"Yes, but they are no longer police."

"There is more to this than all of you are saying. You must speak." Saadia smiled, clasping her hands.

Zaytuna took an edge of the tray. "Please."

But this time Saliha did not notice her distress, or was choosing to ignore it, and addressed Yulduz and Qambar directly. "I think Zaytuna should be involved."

Yulduz hardened. "Not if Mustafa is involved. Him, coming to our home like that."

Saadia lit up. "Our dear friend Mustafa is involved! Zaytuna, yes, then you must help." Then to Yulduz, "But why should it be a scandal for your cousin to come to your home?"

Before Yulduz could answer, Zaytuna insisted, "We must go."

Qambar nodded and gestured to Saliha to lift the tray so they could carry it home.

"A scholar, you said?" Saadia addressed Saliha, trying to hold them back. "I may know something about the man."

Zaytuna turned on her. "Your brother is a scholar of law, not Quran." She put her hand on her heart. "I appreciate the offer, but we..."

"These sciences are intertwined," she interjected. "Each relies on the other. My brother must know Quran and hadith to speak to the legal rulings that arise from both. It is a smaller world than you imagine."

Qambar whispered to Saliha, who now finally understood. The three lifted the tray.

"Thank you, lady, for your kind visit." Yulduz eyed the three. "Ignore them, no manners."

Saadia took her hands again and kissed them. "Assalamu alaykum, Auntie." Then to them all. "May God protect you."

Qambar returned the blessing for them.

"If you need me, it would be my pleasure," Saadia offered, as she left. "I gather once a week after the midday meal with some women who might be able to help, scholars of the Quran themselves and the wives of scholars, sometimes others. Come to me first, I will bring you. We meet in three days."

They watched her walk away, straight-backed with a poise unmistakable to her station. Her wrap was finer than anything they could have afforded, even now, and was so long it trailed in the dust, it's edge ruined as if it were no matter to her. Yet, Zaytuna suspected, it was Saadia's attempt at dressing down, worn to fit in among them. She felt the bite of the old resentment toward Saadia and her family from that visit with Mustafa when they presented her with a parting gift of their discarded finery out of pity for Zaytuna's best, an old wrap nearly washed through to rags.

Yulduz, knowing none of this, murmured appreciatively as the woman walked off. Then she turned on Zaytuna. "You'll do no such thing, getting involved. Bring shame upon your husband. God restrain you! It's on your family to control you an' we will!"

"Control her?" Saliha turned on Yulduz, glaring.

"You'd say that!"

Qambar pulled Yulduz back from saying more, but the old woman was right. If this led to her having to be alone with Mustafa, what family would not restrain her, what husband would not abandon her? Kamal Ali's guarantees that she could do as she liked did not assume betraying him by being alone with a man, even in public.

Saliha grabbed her arm. "I see it on your face. Don't you turn away from this case because of them or because of the trouble Mustafa is causing. That woman, whatever she's done to upset you, could help."

A few tears finally broke through. She let go of the tray with one hand to wipe her eyes, knowing she was only smearing the dirt even more.

Qambar balanced her side of the tray for her. "Daughter?"

Even though they were right there with her, the emptiness remained. What had she done to deserve this? Tried to be a help to Mustafa? Walked him to her husband with a chaperone? Agreed to stay away from the case? She needed the old woman's guidance, her uncle's reassurance, her mother's care, and God denied her. All she got was this wealthy woman taunting her with the knowledge that Mustafa still loved her and urging her to take on a case, knowing it would throw the two of them together. The image of Mustafa searching among the gravestones for her returned, bringing with it a stomach turning grief for him. She needed to go home, shut the door behind her, weep into her prayer rug and beg God to return her to herself, to the peace of her home, to her family. What could she answer Qambar?

She took up her side again, saying only, "Don't worry, Uncle."

DAY THREE

6

Zaytuna stood alone on barren red earth, sunken-hearted and trembling. Slivers of cold wind nicked her ankles and cut through her thin wrap. Beside her, a stone wall surrounded a small field of wheat under a deep blue sky.

On the other side of the wall, the stalks, and even the grains themselves, were the creamy yellow of fresh camel's milk and grew so high she could not see over them. A few sheaves of wheat had been gathered and were leaning against the wall, but spilling out of their bindings and near to collapse. Tentatively approaching, she reached over the wall to bind one sheaf back. A single blade of wheat lifted to meet her, touching her fingertip and depositing a grain. The grain increased in weight until she began to perspire under the pressure of holding it. Zaytuna placed the grain on the tip of her tongue and swallowed it. The grain lodged itself in her heart where it became a light within her, illuminating the wall and revealing a gate.

She stepped through the gate. Her burden was lifted. The world within its walls unfurled into an infinite depth of featureless white. A sun shone white light from every direction. She turned around in the field until she was spinning like one of the Sufis caught in ecstasy on a night of music and poetry. She asked, "Is this peace?" The question slowed her to a stop before the open gate. Slashes of red and blue smeared on the cold wind outside, becoming tendrils that wound around each other into a writhing chain and beckoned her to come out into its moaning emptiness. Zaytuna reached out to it and the tendrils turned on her until she was bound in body and sorrow filled her belly.

The bedroom was pitch dark. Kamal Ali snored gently beside her. She got out of bed and her fingers brushed against Mustafa's jug. Half-asleep, she kissed her fingers, then recoiled, fully awake. On hands and knees, she crawled to her prayer rug. Her fingers felt the tenderness woven into the rug's rough wool, her palms its steadiness, and she begged to find her way back within the walls.

Standing in prayer, the verses came to her unbidden, recited in a whisper that felt more like the slow release after a gasp of awareness than the formation of words with tongue, teeth, and lips.

"Wa idh qala Musa li-qawmihi... and when Moses said to his people, 'O my people, remember God blessed you with prophets appointed for you and kings appointed for you, and gave you what He had given to none other. O my people, enter that sacred land God decreed for you and do not turn your backs to it or you turn back as losers'. They answered him, 'O Moses, there are people within of insurmountable power. We cannot enter until they leave.' Among those who were afraid, two men blessed by God spoke up...an'am Allah alayhim..."

Her body moved with the words, one single atom in her heart opening onto another atom and another, expanding out, until her heart opened to the boundless universe above and below, and her voice released, she recited, *"'Go through the gate! Surprise them! When you enter, you will be victors! Trust God, if you are believers!'"*

She bowed before God, prostrated, prostrated again, rose again, recited again, and over and over until the prayer left her kneeling on the rug, offering salutations to the Prophet, his family, and companions. With each movement, a veil was lifted from her consciousness, and then another, until she could no longer avoid seeing the truth.

Zaytuna heard a breath, "Amin," beside her, only then noticing her husband had been following her in prayer. Guilt washed through her, wondering if he had seen the truth, too.

She still loved Mustafa.

Only after she had washed her face in the gathered blessings of her outstretched hands did Kamal Ali take her hand and kiss each of her fingers. She held his hand and they rose and returned to bed together until first light. He fell asleep quickly, his breath soft in her ear, his arm around her, holding her close, and she wept for their marriage.

The first call to prayer came from al-Mansur's mosque in the centre of the round city. The nearest mosques picked up the call, then those beyond, until their voices resounded through the still dark city. Zaytuna had not slept and heard Kamal Ali lumber awake with the call. They got up to dress and met Qambar and Layla in the moonlit courtyard. The two men did their usual dance, each insisting that the other lead. Qambar lost, and stood ahead of them all, reciting softly and restraining grunts as his old joints made it through the prostrations. She wished he would give in and pray seated, but the old man still had some pride left in him.

After the prayer, Kamal Ali kissed her cheek, preparing to leave for the day, but she pulled him into an embrace. Feeling his body against hers, his warmth and protection, Zatyuna did not understand how she could have any feelings for Mustafa other than a cherished memory of their old love. She held him a moment too long and he whispered in her ear, "Come see me today."

"I have to go to see Uncle Abu al-Qasim." The dream. The emptiness she felt at the graveside. She felt as if she were standing on a cliff but could not seem to back away despite the warnings. She pushed him out the door and off to work.

Tein and Saliha were still asleep. Yulduz was mumbling something in her room. Zaytuna retreated to dress, intending to go out for bread and fruit, but when she emerged, Qambar had gone to do it himself. Instead, she took up the leather bucket to fill at the public fountain.

Children and women carrying jugs and buckets stood in line, moving slowly to the front. Her turn came. She placed the bucket in the half-moon basin and caught the water as it flowed from the spout embedded in the tiled wall. Zaytuna examined the tiles as the deep bucket filled. Most were chipped, and some had gone missing entirely, either replaced with mismatched tile or smeared with stucco, yet she became lost in its broken beauty and nearly wept for it.

"Get on with it!" The woman behind pushed her. "Look at the mess you've made for us to stand in!"

Cold water was running over the edge of the bucket and onto her hand, soaking her clothing, and puddling around her now muddied shoes. "I'm sorry, Auntie." She pulled the overful bucket toward her without emptying it a little and spilled even more water. The woman and a child beside her jumped back to avoid being splashed with water and mud.

"Just go!" the woman said, tucking up her wrap so it would not be dirtied.

Zaytuna lugged the bucket past the complaints of those in line and vowed to go to see her uncle, Abu al-Qasim al-Junayd, directly after breakfast rather than wait until later.

He was one of the greatest mystics of Baghdad whose home remained open as a gathering place for those on the path and among those Sufis who had become family, helping raise her and Tein. Just over a year ago, she had asked him to be her guide on the Sufi Path and their relationship had changed. He went from chiding and indulgent to intent correction. She suspected she would not like what he had to say about her dream. What could it mean other than that there was no way to return to the unfettered happiness of her marriage? Was there no way to rebind the sheaves of wheat?

At home, everyone was awake and preparing breakfast. Tein crouched by the reed mat, Yulduz clucking at him for breaking the bread before everyone had seated.

Layla teased, "Auntie, you would complain to the prophet Isa for breaking his loaves!"

"You'd protect that uncle of yours no matter what he did," she retorted with a loving smile.

Saliha noticed her first. "Come and eat, Zay."

Everyone looked up to greet her, but the laughter in their eyes dimmed when they saw her wet clothes and muddy feet.

Tein rose and took the bucket from her. "What happened to you?"

She leaned around him to reassure them all. "I only spilled the water."

"It's still plenty full," he said, walking away to pour it into the basin.

"Go change, you'll catch your death!" Yulduz called out.

Tein returned when she was halfway to her room and stopped her, saying quietly, "Saliha says you plan on working the case."

"I never said a word."

"Why would you do this to Kamal Ali?"

"Do what?" She stared at him, wondering if he could see through to her heart.

"The case, you fool."

"She is the one urging me."

"Uff." He glanced at Saliha. "I told her you might help from home, not out on the street."

"You men!" she burst out. "What makes you think I want any part of it?"

The others looked over.

Tein lowered his voice again. "You seemed like you did that first day. What happened?"

"I cannot escape him," she admitted, her stomach turning.

He crossed his arms. "Tell me what you mean, Zaytuna."

"Old feelings." she hissed, as if her anger could root them out.

"Go see one of the aunties today. This has already gone too far."

"You think I want to feel this way?" She glared, then noticed the others pretending not to listen. Layla, though, watched her with a look of warning and understanding. Zaytuna responded, hoping to reassure them, "All of you. Kamal Ali is my husband and my love."

Layla's expression did not change. She had warned Zaytuna there might come a time when Mustafa was free of YingYue. But he was not free of YingYue, only wishing it to be true. And she did not want it to be true. She only wanted to be free of these feelings. Or did she? Her stomach turned again.

She went to sit with the others despite her soaking clothes, the increasing chill feeling familiar, like the days before Kamal Ali, when she only had one thin blanket and prayed through the night even in the bitter cold. She ate a few hurried bites, tasting nothing.

"Alhamdulillah," she said, ending her meagre meal and standing. "I am going to see my Uncle Abu al-Qasim."

Qambar was visibly relieved, but Yulduz made a face that said she would march her there herself if needed.

Saliha followed her into her room. Once the door had closed behind them, she scoffed, "These men, it's fine for them to want more than one woman. But us?" She put a hand on one hip. "Our wants are untameable and must be disciplined."

"Do I want him?" Zaytuna did not look at her.

Saliha leaned against the closed door and spoke again, ignoring her question. "You shouldn't be made to feel ashamed for still loving Mustafa. They feel no shame. Why should we?"

"Do I love him...that way?"

Saliha gave her a hard look. "Lying to yourself?"

Zaytuna pressed her hand against her stomach.

"You can want both. You can have one."

Want? Love? Maybe it was possible for Saliha to enjoy loving two men, but not her. She pulled some dry clothes from the chest. Then she grasped what Saliha's words might mean and dropped the clothes. She strode to Saliha, grasping her wrist, and whispered, "Are you saying there is another man?"

"Never. I love only Tein." Saliha pulled her hand away sharply. "But I still look and I still want."

"I don't understand you." Zaytuna tugged hard on the door until Saliha stood aside, then pushed her out.

"You are lying to yourself," Saliha said over her shoulder as she left.

She dressed quickly, grabbed her plain, warm wrap, and hurried out. Tein tried to stop her as she was leaving, but she shook off his hand.

"I'm going to see Uncle Abu al-Qasim, Auntie Hakima, too, if she is there. What more do you want?" She was out on the street before he could reply, but he ran after her and she turned to face him.

"Those people in there. Me. I'm worried about you."

"Let me go!" She hurried away, making the turns to her uncle's home without thinking, her mind consumed with Saliha's taunt and Tein's warning. The narrow alleys and streets wide enough only for a laden-donkey to pass were busy. Zaytuna pressed against a mud-brick wall so a woman with laundry on her head could pass, and then the man behind her walked, watching her hips sway. Others pushed past each other with a greeting or curse here and a grumble there.

She searched their faces. People yearned for another just as they did food and a warm bed. And some would take it where they could get it. Wanting another had no limits except those marked by propriety, loyalty, mutual respect, and practicalities. But wanting and love were not bound to one another. Saliha said she wanted other men, yet she only loved Tein.

This was different. There was no denying that she still loved Mustafa, but she did not know if she wanted him. If both, what then? *Do not lie to yourself.* She forced herself to call up his face, his soft brown eyes, begging for her help, and asked her body what it wanted. Feeling no inkling of what she felt with Kamal Ali, she withdrew from the question, pushing him out of mind, commanding herself, *Stay within the walls. Stay within the walls.* Each time she said it, she felt more secure and able to consider that perhaps Saliha was right; perhaps she was making too much of it. It was natural she would still love Mustafa. They had loved each other since childhood, and both had been married to others for only a few months. This will pass, she insisted to herself as she carried on, as if repetition would make it true.

The sun was up as she reached Junayd's door. In her agitation, she knocked louder than she should, but Ziri, tasked with answering the door and keeping order among the visitors, answered the door graciously, as always. "Assalamu alaykum, Zaytuna."

Returning his greeting perfunctorily, she slid past him into the main reception room, then stopped and turned back to greet him properly.

"Good morning, Ziri."

Ziri smiled with his hand over his heart, replying, "May you have a beautiful morning."

He was used to this kind of behaviour from her. Embarrassed, she paused before reaching the great arch leading to the courtyard to force herself into some sense of decorum. There was no point in hurrying. It was too early to find her uncle downstairs. She would sit patiently under the arcaded balcony until he joined them from his family's rooms, recite the name of God until her heart quieted, then be ready when he did come down.

But when she emerged into the courtyard, Zaytuna found him already sitting alone on sheepskins in his usual place. He wore a quilted blue robe and sirwal beneath a thick brown wool cloak with one edge tossed over the other shoulder and a modestly wrapped brown turban.

"Good morning, Uncle." She sat on a sheepskin laid out before him.

As was the custom, he pulled his hand away before she could kiss it and placed it tenderly on her head. The soothing waters of his presence flowed through her, loosening every muscle. She smiled softly, as if awakening into a different world in which there was nothing to fear from love.

"My daughter." His slim, fair face beamed. "You took your time getting here. I told my wife this morning that our Zaytuna was coming. I have been waiting for you since the dawn prayer."

"I had a dream," she said, gratitude spilling from her into his arms.

He took it up. "Tell me."

"I stood outside a field of wheat the colour of milk. The field was bounded by stone walls the same colour. Some of the wheat had been gathered into sheaves, but was spilling open across the wall. I held a grain of wheat that was so heavy I could not bear it. But I ate it and it lodged in my heart. The gate opened and I entered, but when I looked back, I saw colours swirling outside the field. They called me to return." She paused, her shoulders tensing again. She turned her head aside. "What beckoned me, the swirling colours, they were tendrils, turning into chains. I left the field and let them bind me."

"Look at me."

She faced him reluctantly.

"The wheat in sheaves is what you have harvested on the path, yet they are breaking from their bindings. You are not stable enough to hold them. The seed that lodged in your heart is the wrongdoing of Adam, alayhi salam, that which awakened him to his full humanity, his capacity for ugliness as well as beauty, and his taking responsibility for his actions. The wheat left to be shorn is the work that lies ahead of you. The walls are the boundaries within which there is growing certainty of God. Outside there is doubt."

"A warning," she said, dread settling in.

"Yes."

Was she guilty of Adam and Eve's wrongdoing in still loving Mustafa? Brows knitted, she searched her shaykh's eyes. How could love alone, love without wanting, be a sin? *God protect me*, she called out within herself. Folding her hands in her lap, she pinched the flesh between her thumb and forefinger to stop from crying.

"I see talk about certainty has made you doubt. Tell me, daughter, what concerns you."

She hesitated.

"Zaytuna."

"Mustafa." She said it. "I have kept him at a distance since his marriage and mine. But he came to my home, when he knew my husband was not there."

Junayd's soft features hardened.

"He said it was a case to investigate, but it was for me, too. He came for me. And…" She could not say that she loved him. "I fear he is the one who calls to me from beyond the gate."

"It is not Mustafa who calls to you," he said firmly. "It is your own soul's desire."

Horrified that he might have seen traces of unacknowledged

wanting Mustafa in her, she looked over her shoulder for one of the aunts. The courtyard was empty.

"Your soul's desire is your old sorrow," he explained. "You are not free of it, yet."

"But I want to be happy. I have been happy."

"Listen." His voice remained the same, but a tone underneath it, heard only by her heart, increased in intensity until she was held fast and her thoughts stopped their frantic grasping. "Certainty is knowledge that does not come and go with emotional states and the events of your life, rather it is a constant presence in the heart. God has placed you in the arms of love and laid a path out before you, yet you do not entirely trust God's provision. Rather, you trust the familiarity of your sorrow."

Junayd had been telling her this since that first day she went to him as a hopeful student on the path, not as a daughter of this community. What had she known of love as a child? Her mother wandered the empire in the thrall of the divine lover, not the needs of her children. In ecstasy, her mother swayed, her hands raised to the heavens. Zaytuna would huddle in her lap, shaking, as throngs of seekers bore down on them wanting a taste of that ecstasy for themselves. Tein circled, watching for madness or fury; he was no more than a child pulling grown men out from the crowd as they wailed, "Allah, Allah."

Love was dangerous. Safety was unimaginable. And when she died, all hope of a mother's love was lost. The community had taken them in, caring for them as their own. And Mustafa had become like a brother to her, then as they grew, more. But how could they love easily when they had not been suckled on a mother's small loving attentions? How could she have returned Mustafa's love?

Was that not in the past? Zaytuna had undertaken the path under her uncle's guidance and, little by little, she learned to accept the possibility of loving and being loved. She had even come to accept that her mother had loved them, in her way. She had married and found herself basking in Kamal Ali's affection. Perhaps she loved too much? Walla, did she not sit before him a woman in love with two men? Was it sorrow or love? She played with a strand of wool, wrapping it around her finger until it was tight.

Junayd called her attention to him. "Turn away from whatever draws you back to that sadness."

But at the thought of losing Mustafa, her breath became shallow and the tips of her fingers tingled. The tingling turned to numbness and crept up her arms. Light sparked at the edges of her vision.

Her uncle took her hands in his own. The numbness retreated, the tingling folding back in on itself until she could feel his soft, warm hands. Her breaths deepened. The sparks dimmed.

"Is it Mustafa? I must turn him away."

"No. It is you, Zaytuna. Your love of your old pain." He took a moment, considering her. Then he waved his hand dismissively. "Do not worry about Mustafa. He belongs to us."

"He belongs to us," she repeated, the words releasing her. All those years only to be separated these past few months and not able to do more than nod. They missed each other. It was no more than that. Mustafa simply misunderstood what he had lost. Uncle would help him understand.

Fear transformed into incandescent relief. Perhaps they could find a place for their old friendship again? The aunts and uncles would help Mustafa. She did not have to lose him, after all. "I'll stop being so sad, I promise!" In her joy, she took up his hand and kissed it before he could pull it back and pressed it to her forehead.

He frowned, jerking his hand away. "The dream is a warning. It is you. Do not lie to yourself."

Without propriety, she stood in a rush, saying, "Thank you, shaykh, thank you. May God preserve you." She backed away, her hand over her heart, and retreated from the courtyard, wanting nothing more than to run home and tell everyone not to worry.

But just as Ziri opened the door for her, Mustafa's wife walked through it. She smiled at the sight of Zaytuna and pulled her into an embrace. Zaytuna's joy stiffened into guilt as YingYue clung to her like a child. She held herself back from prying her off.

"My sister, what a blessing to find you! You used to come to me to talk." YingYue released her, then took her hands. "Are you busy now? Let me hear your news."

"I must go." No believable excuse followed.

"How can this be?" YingYue searched her face.

Before Zaytuna could respond, Mustafa walked through the door.

Auntie Hakima entered from a small room off of the reception hall, her hands moist from performing ablutions. Her deeply lined brown face was still and she did not speak.

Mustafa's cheeks and forehead turned blotchy red. His eyes darted among the three women, but settled on Zaytuna with a look of apology.

The hope that their friendship could be saved dissolved into anger. He was incapable of it. To offer the apology to her and not to his wife. *God protect us from evil things.*

Auntie Hakima said quietly over Zaytuna's shoulder, "He is in hand, girl." Then she took YingYue's arm. "Come with me. We must talk."

Zaytuna watched as the old woman drew YingYue into the corner of the courtyard near the kitchen where the women typically gathered.

"Zaytuna," Mustafa whispered.

She spun around with a sharp word on her tongue, but there he was, the old Mustafa again. Confused and guilty. She accepted what Uncle Abu al-Qasim and Auntie Hakima said. They had him in hand. He belonged to them. There was no need to be angry. No need to worry.

"I asked at your home," he said. "Layla told me you were here. I can take you to see Nabil's mother." He hesitated, then said insistently, "Now."

7

TEIN AND AMMAR merged with the stream of people on the Basra Gate High Road. The litters of the wealthy swayed on camelback or were carried by servants, while donkey carts and men pushing hand carts went in and out the nearby neighbourhoods. Ammar tugged at his leather cuirass, eager to get to the offices of Grave Crimes and show them what quitting the police looked like. He had a case. A good case, and a case that would pay far more than the pittance he was paid while an investigator. No Ibn Marwan telling him what to do and no politics interfering with justice. He touched the hilt of his sword. They would see.

The towering battlements and ramparts of the Round City of Baghdad stood firm despite being eaten away by flood and years of neglect. Built some one hundred and fifty years earlier by the Caliph Mansur, it had once held the whole of Baghdad. It had been home to rich and poor alike, private and public gardens, markets for those who lived within its walls and without. Now, the city housed mainly barracks, prisons, and administrative offices, including the police. Still the mounted horseman atop the green dome of the abandoned palace could be seen from everywhere; the majesty of the city held sway for Ammar and he missed it.

But Tein mumbled a complaint as they crossed through the Gate House and arches, entrances high and wide enough for men on horses to ride several abreast. As they passed through the Solomon Gates, great iron doors built by jinn for the prophet Solomon himself, Tein held back.

"You coming?"

Tein gave him a hard look, but joined him.

The Grave Crimes Section was set back into arcades just past the gate. Men he recognized wandered in and out of the offices. At the end of the arcade, supplicants waited outside Ibn Marwan's door, hoping the sergeant would accept their plea, move a case forward, or let it go entirely.

At the entrance of their old office, Tein leaned against the jamb rather than going in. Ammar went around him, thumbs in his sword belt, chest out, greeting the men. "Ho! Our brothers!"

The two young men jumped up. Shabib ibn Yunus greeted them with a warm smile, but broad-shouldered Ahab ibn Ishaq betrayed himself, posturing, his wrestler's neck puffed out like a strutting bird. This one could turn out to be trouble.

Shabib joked, "You here for your old job back?"

He grasped Ammar's arm as if they were old friends, but these new investigators were only bright young watchmen whose names Tein and Ammar had sent up to Ibn Marwan to replace them. The men had brass, Ammar had to give them that.

"We are looking into a case you all passed on."

"Which one?" Ahab asked, still posturing, but with less neck.

"Which one?" Tein interjected, with a sharper tone than Ammar would have used. "Ibn Marwan lets you decide what cases you'll take?"

"Ibn Marwan passes on them," Ahab said. "Not us."

"We're asking about a woman who came about her missing son. Nabil Ibn al-Qays al-Kufi."

"Right." Shabib gestured for them to sit down on one of the worn thin couches, but he remained standing. "We asked around before Ibn Marwan made up his mind to shut the case. The son was a drunk and a gambler. We figured either he's on a bender, crossed the wrong man, or went into the river."

"We have more important cases than a drunk doing himself in," Ahab said.

"A lot of cases?" Tein asked from the doorway.

"Always," Ahab said. "Wasn't it like this when you were here?"

"Always."

Ammar asked, "How is Ibn Marwan?"

"He bellows at us that we'll never live up to the two of you, then curses you for leaving." Shabib laughed.

"My apologies."

"He'll forget about you soon enough," Ahab said.

Ammar clapped Ahab on the shoulder. "Let us know if a body turns up?"

Ahab towered over him, letting him know it would come to blows if he did that again, but he betrayed himself. Ammar saw it in his eyes: the man was too kind for the work. He bowed his head, submitting to Ahab's challenge, and said a prayer for him.

"We'll send someone to inform the mother immediately," Shabib answered, getting between the two of them.

"Inform us. Not every man you find might be him. Send a man to Buratha?"

"It's a watchman," Ahab said, "we give the orders."

Ammar told them where he lived, then left the men to chase after Tein, who was walking briskly toward Solomon's Gates. He caught up to him, wondering if Tein's leg was not hurting today or if he could not get away from the office fast enough.

"They'll know soon enough why we quit," Tein said, then asked, "To Khalil? See if Nabil's carrying any gambling debts?"

"The mosque is on the way."

"Mustafa told us to wait for him, but you do what you like," Tein countered.

Ammar let him have his way. There might be a lot of that on this job if he wanted Tein to stick it out to the end.

They left the Round City and walked back by the Basra Gate High

Road, passing the road that led to the Sharqiyya mosque. Not going there first made no sense. Ammar could not help but shake his head. Thankfully, Tein did not catch it. At least Khalil's haunt was on this side of the market.

Tein turned off onto a street bounded by estate walls on either side. Ammar followed as he cut through a network of streets, passing the homes of established scholars and court administrators, their two-storey homes enclosed by high walls and boasting large courtyards within. Finally, they came to a small market gate.

The entrance led them through a narrow alley banked by small stores selling dried goods and wares for the neighbourhood. It let out onto a road of furniture makers, then the sellers of cloth for upholstery, and after that the wool for stuffing.

"He's usually around Abu Sa'id's office." Tein gestured to an alley just after the wool shops.

The reed awning over the alley was shabbier than those covering the streets they had just left. Broken slats let in more light, but they would also let in rain when it came. The walls were in good repair, though, not worn away by damp. Ammar supposed the purpose was to make passersby avoid this market alley, thinking nothing of value lay down it, but two men dressed for close fighting standing on either side of a door were enough to keep the curious away.

Tein took the lead, ready to answer their questions to get an invitation to see the boss. But there were no questions and no trouble. One man nodded at Tein with a glimmer of recognition, then ducked his head through the door. Ammar heard him say, "Police." He waved them inside.

The office was modest. Reed mats covered the floor. There was only one couch, the rough mattress covered by sheepskins. A door led to another room where a scribe sat at a low desk. He glanced at them before dipping his pen and continued writing in a large volume.

Sitting on a low couch, prayer beads in hand, Abu Sa'id watched them expectantly. He did not rise. The boss was dressed like the men guarding the door, in a trim turban of simple cloth and the short tunic and robe of a fighting man with a dagger at his belt. He was old, but only a fool would challenge him.

Hand over his heart and head bowed, Tein said, "Assalamu alaykum, Abu Saʿid, sir."

"Police? Here? I pay my tax to the marketplace inspector. Did he not pass on your cut?"

"We're not police," Tein said.

"Forgetting your black turbans is no trick."

"Not police anymore."

"I'm not hiring."

"We're not looking," Ammar said.

"What then?"

"We came to see Khalil."

Abu Saʿid bristled. "Khalil told you to meet him here?" He glanced at the two men just outside the door. "He'll see what a man gets for that."

Tein shook his head. "Khalil brought me here over a year ago. On your ask."

"Aha!" The man's eyes widened with recognition. "You're the Nubian he fought with on the frontier. He said you could crush a man's skull with your bare hands."

It was an exaggeration of Tein's skills, but not his brutality. Things had changed, but Ammar knew there would never be enough distance between the man Tein was once and the man he was now. Ammar could not see Tein's face, but the boss caught his reaction.

"Ashamed of yourself, are you? Being police is better?"

"I'm not police." Tein growled, taking a step closer.

One of the men moved into the doorway. The scribe stared from the other room, reed pen in the air. Ammar did not think it would go any further, but readied himself to get his friend out of the room without any trouble if it came to it.

"Fine, fine." Abu Saʿid waved his hand. "You are here to see Khalil. He's not here."

Tein grimaced and moved back against the wall where he could watch the men at the door and the scribe. He indicated that Ammar should take over.

Abu Saʿid raised an eyebrow at the move.

"Where can we find him?" Ammar asked.

But Abu Saʿid addressed them both. "This sounds like more than a social call."

"We're searching for a missing man," Ammar explained. "He got behind in his gambling debts."

"We do not make men go missing over debts. We are not among the inheritors of the estate."

"Not even to hold the man hostage until his family pays out?"

"The cheek!" He chuckled, but it was an ugly sound. "Don't press me."

"Don't you want to know the man's name? The one we are after?"

"Go on, then."

"Nabil ibn al-Qays al-Kufi. He has been missing for over a week now."

The boss leaned back. "If he had debts, they never came to us."

"You remember all the names in your head?"

He called into the next room. "Butrus, check our records for Nabil ibn al-Qays al-Kufi."

The scribe turned back page after page, finally calling, "No."

Abu Saʿid shrugged. "You see?"

"Have you heard the name?"

"No."

"Let's go," Tein barked, and walked out.

But Ammar had more questions. If this was how Tein was going to behave, maybe he should tell him to go back to churning and he would handle it himself. Abu Saʿid could be an important contact in future cases.

"You heard your friend." Abu Saʿid gestured toward the door with finality.

"Thank you," Ammar said, frustrated. With his hand over his heart, he bowed his head to Abu Saʿid, then to the men standing at attention as he left. Tein had not waited and Ammar went back the way they came to find him standing in the middle of the busy market street, towering over passersby who gave him a wide berth.

When he reached him, Ammar did not bother asking about his mood. He did not want to know. He started right in on the case. "So he was only in debt to the gambling house. He was able to sell off enough household goods to keep the debt collector away. That angle doesn't look so good anymore."

A voice called out over the crowd. "Tein!"

Ammar followed the sound. The kohl-eyed Arab nearly was as tall and solidly built as Tein, and handsome enough to turn women's glances away from his friend. Smiling, the man swept his wool cloak over one shoulder at the last moment to more easily embrace Tein, but all was done with an eye on Ammar and one hand ready to grasp the dagger at his belt. Khalil obviously did not remember him. Or maybe he did. Ammar smiled to himself.

"We were just looking for you." Tein slapped him on the arm.

Khalil looked at Ammar more closely. Recognition finally hit him and he grinned. "The little Shia boy in hiding! I wanted to give you a beat down for all the attitude you gave."

Ammar remembered it differently. If he had not acted tough, Khalil would have beaten him for being weak. At fifteen, Khalil was already a thug, so eager to kill that their sergeant did not trust him not to hurt one of their own during the relentless days of walking, waiting, setting up and breaking down camp along the frontier. He lasted only a few months before the inevitable fight happened. The sergeant had him shipped off to border skirmishes where the killing would be more regular. But those were the days when Tein, too, was eager for battle and the two had become fast friends.

"A bit taller," Ammar remarked, "but you haven't changed."

"No taller for you."

Ammar laughed. He had asked for it.

"Tein never said you were working with him." He slapped Ammar's shoulder, but not hard enough that he had to brace against it. "The three of us here. Like old times."

"We're not police anymore," Tein said.

Ammar followed up. "We're investigating on our own now. We need a little help."

Khalil led them to a space in-between two wool shops.

"A man has been missing for over a week now," Ammar explained. "Nabil Ibn al-Qays al-Kufi. A young man about my size. Light-skinned, brown eyes. Beard has a lot of red in it. He's a scholar studying Quran at the Sharqiyya Mosque. Comes from old money and dresses like it, right down to the taraz. He's a gambler and was selling off the family treasures to pay his debts, but the mother's hiding it all now and he probably owes. We thought maybe you knew if he'd been approached for collection."

"The family have connections?"

"Not in Baghdad. They've lost everything. They're nobody here. As far as I can see, they're on their own."

"You say he's been gone about a week?" Khalil became serious. "Not us. I send the men out for shakedowns now. No one like that this week or further back."

"I'm not looking forward to going door-to-door at all the gambling houses," Tein said.

Khalil mocked their task. "There are how many in the Karkh marketplace alone?"

So it would be on him, then. It would mean a lot of time away from home. Ammar suppressed a smile. "I'll take on the door-to-door. No trouble."

"And hope they tell you the truth." Khalil's eyes lit up. "I know. You could go to each of them asking if he is there gambling and tell them his mother wants him home."

Ammar exclaimed, "Who could deny a mother!"

"For a mother, they'll empty the fool's pockets and hand him over. But if he's a nobody, then they'd give him up if they suspect he won't pay."

The two men laughed.

Tein said, "He's always been able to keep up, until now."

"Maybe he's on a winning streak?" Khalil speculated, still grinning. "They might give him more time. That could explain why he hasn't been turned over to us. Naw, he's probably scrounging for something to steal or borrow to get himself out of trouble. Maybe selling those fine clothes."

"But not dead." Ammar said.

"Dead?" Khalil looked at him like he was stupid. "Not by their hands. None of the gambling houses are going to kill a man. It would be the end of them, you know that. Even if they could deliver a killer to the police when they came calling, without well-placed friends and hefty bribes, the marketplace inspector would shut them down. It's not worth it."

Ammar looked knowingly at Tein. They had seen it themselves.

"They'd give him to us to get the money out of him," Khalil said, hand out. "You know how this works. So let that be."

"What about being held hostage for payment?" Ammar asked.

"Has the family been contacted?"

"Not yet."

"Why are you going so far with this, Ammar? Talking like he's dead, kidnapped, after only a week?"

Tein asked, "If he couldn't pay up at one gambling house, how fast would word spread about him?"

"Here, he'd be barred by all of them within a week. But he could cross the river to Rusafa."

"Or leave Baghdad altogether." Tein sounded hopeful. "If he is still around, we should assume he's gambling or in a brothel somewhere. Maybe he had some money we don't know about and he's been enjoying himself for the week."

The suggestion irritated Ammar, though. It made the most sense, but it meant the case would be cleared up quickly and he would be back to churning and the threat of herding goats.

"If he's dead," Tein said, "then I'd suppose he did it himself. I'd not want to bring my humiliation home to that mother. His body will turn up, then, as long as he didn't walk off the bridge into the middle of the Tigris."

"Swift waters," Ammar said, "but bodies come up sometimes." He liked this option. If this angle turned out to be true, they could keep investigating right up until they found the body or too much time had passed for his safe return to be likely. That, and his share of the silver talisman case, would give Ammar the time and money to tell his family he would be opening his own investigations office.

Tein asked, "Khalil, will you keep an eye out for him?"

"Nabil ibn al-Qays al-Kufi," Ammar repeated.

"Got it." The three moved out to the edge of the street. Khalil took Tein by the arm. "Where are you living these days? I'll visit."

Tein evaded him. "If you think I'm putting your handsome face in front of the women of the household, you are out of your mind."

"Wise, my friend. Wise." He turned to Ammar. "Good to see you again."

"And you!"

Khalil stepped out into the busy street as if he expected everyone to get out of his way. They did.

Ammar snorted as they moved off into the crowd.

"Jealous?" Tein taunted.

Ammar ignored him. "At least he's not churning butter. Gambling houses next?"

Without another word, Tein walked away, but he turned in the direction opposite to the nearest nahariyya offering gambling and women for a daytime marriage. Ammar hurried after him.

8

ZAYTUNA WALKED past Mustafa without a word, slamming their uncle's door behind her so he could not follow.

He ran after her anyway. "No one will know I took you."

She strode in the direction of home.

"Nabil's mother did not speak openly with Tein and Ammar." Mustafa caught up again. "You need to speak to her."

"And YingYue?" she asked, still walking.

"She told me to come to you."

Zaytuna stopped and looked around, worried someone might see them together. "I don't believe you."

"You must understand, our marriage." He blinked several times, fighting tears. "It is not what you think."

"Oh, Mustafa, what have you done?"

So YingYue was no wife to him. It explained her friendliness. And his need, coming to her the way he did. If he had not betrayed himself at the wedding, things would have been different. He would have settled down with his wife and put Zaytuna in his past. That's all this was. His mistakes. His loneliness. Now, here he was before her, having ruined everything, fighting back tears. Needing her again.

She walked away from him, circling around herself in thought.

Go with him. He's not the one calling to you in your dream.

Her aunt and uncle had assured her they had him in hand.

Comfort him. Let him know he's not lost everything.

But then, her uncle's warning. And Saliha's warning not to lie to herself.

What is it that you want, woman?

He watched her, letting her think. She turned away from him, from those eyes.

Do not lie.

Fine. Then, I want our old days back. And I want in on the case. What harm is there?

Her aunt and uncle had told her not to worry about him. Tein told her she could investigate where women were involved. But not with Mustafa leading her there. To many, just walking alone with a man was as good as being in his bed. She thought of Kamal Ali being told that his wife had been seen in the street with another man. He would trust her, brush off their gossip. But she knew how she would feel, and she could not let it rest so easily.

You cannot go with Mustafa, neither to comfort him nor to ask the mother questions.

She returned to him, saying, with regret, "No."

"Come, please."

The innocence and the hurt in his voice called to her.

What harm is there in him allowing him to lead me to Nabil's mother? It would give him some solace. I would interview her alone. He could leave me there.

Mustafa stood perfectly still, waiting.

If he walks ahead of me and we don't speak closely for more than a moment, we can manage it without gossip. I'll only go as long as I do nothing I would want to hide from Kamal Ali. I can go.

"Walk ahead of me," she said, her decision made. "No tempting gossip."

Mustafa blanched. "Yes, of course."

She waited until he was two or three paces ahead, then set out behind him.

Every so often, he looked over his shoulder, smiling tenderly when he saw she was still there. His smile brought back their childhood days when she was new to Baghdad and he had led her through the streets when every corner had threatened and confused. Each time he turned back now, her heart broke open to him a bit more until it was as if they were walking side by side.

Finally, he stopped and turned, waiting for her. His eyes were warm, his forehead clear of worry. He too had felt their companionship in this strange way. Only then did she realize that they were in sight of the Sharqiyya mosque. So lost had she been in tasting their old days together that she did not know what streets they had travelled to get here.

"This way."

She followed again, a few paces behind. Mustafa walked slowly, and she expected him to knock at every door until he finally stopped before one and waited for her to catch up. Once there, they were able to be side by side and there was no harm in it. They had regained something of who they had been for each other in the walk. It was good. He would leave her here. All was well.

"Ready?"

She nodded and he knocked.

The door was opened by a servant. Zaytuna clapped her hand to her chest in surprise. Not because of the woman's unusual beauty, but because of the rage that marred it.

"Assalamu alaykum, Oliga." Mustafa bowed his head slightly.

"What happened to you? Happy today? Did you find him?" she asked insultingly. Mustafa only lowered his eyes, blushing. She caught it and frowned at Zaytuna. "Over this woman?"

Zaytuna did not care that the servant mocked her, but not Mustafa, not in his state. But what could she say in his defence that would not make things worse? She quickly directed the conversation back to the reason for their visit. "Our friend, Mustafa, felt that it might help if I spoke to Umm Nabil."

Still appraising Zaytuna, she said to Mustafa, "So you are not stupid. You brought a woman."

"I'll leave now," he mumbled to Zaytuna. His tone no longer held the sweet reassurance they had gained on their walk together.

"No," she said. "Wait for me."

An emptiness crept in, opening into her gut. She should not have said it. But he blushed more deeply and fell over himself in response, making it impossible to correct her mistake, so she left him outside, waiting.

Oliga led her into a shabby room overstuffed with luxurious furniture and announced her visit. The mother did not rise from the richly embroidered cushions that surrounded her. A moist kerchief lay over her eyes. She let out a mournful cry. "My son." The woman was distraught, as she should be, but something else was there that Zaytuna did not trust. Zaytuna glanced at Oliga and saw her smirk at her mistress before disappearing into the side room.

She struggled to pull herself away from the trouble of Mustafa waiting outside to make sense of this strange scene. "Assalamu alaykum," she began, hand over her heart. "I am Zaytuna bint al-Ashiqa as-Sawda. I am working with the men who visited you earlier."

"Wa alaykum assalam." Umm Nabil lifted the edge of the kerchief, revealing one red-rimmed eye. "You share the mother's laqab with the other, but you are not black. I see God blessed you with your father's seed."

Zaytuna bit back angry words, but she could not control her expression.

The woman sniggered. "Imagine being bothered that you are not black."

"I came here to help find your son. But perhaps you would prefer someone else."

Umm Nabil dropped her handkerchief and sat up. Her eyes were red, but the rest of her face did not show the marks of prolonged weeping. Zaytuna suspected her of a performance, but then doubted herself, having let her anger get the better of her. It could be that the mother's distress was sincere, but also that she was enjoying the attention. A wealthy woman like this was used to being at the centre of things.

Oliga returned with a gleaming copper pitcher and two glasses.

Zaytuna turned to go.

"Do not leave!" Umm Nabil thrust forward. "I need you! Those men have done nothing. Let us see if you can help." Her hand went to her throat for a moment as if to touch something that was not there. She waved her hand impatiently at Oliga. "Pour the water!

"My brother said Nabil simply didn't return home." Zaytuna remained standing. "No message or reason?"

"And not for any of the reasons they think, either!" Umm Nabil looked her up and down. "Oh, come and sit. I should mind my tongue."

Oliga's eyes widened. She left them for the courtyard.

Zaytuna sat on the end of the couch nearest the door.

"I know those men. I know what they think." Umm Nabil's eyes flashed. "He did not run off with a woman. He was not in love. He did not abandon me. My only son. My only child." She pressed the damp kerchief to her eyes.

"What do you think happened?"

"He rubbed those scholars the wrong way." She dabbed at her eyes. "They bore a grudge against him. Especially one named Bahr. Bahr ibn Abi Shuayb. You look for him."

"What did Bahr do?"

"Am I to investigate for you? My Nabil did not tell me anything except that they accused him of going too far and they intended to ruin him." She sucked her teeth. "Ruin our name? As if it had not been ruined enough already." Before Zaytuna could ask how, the woman waved her arm and burst into what could only be true sobs. "Look at us! Look at what we have been reduced to!"

Propriety and simple kindness required that she touch the woman, console her somehow, but Zaytuna could not bring herself to do it. Instead, she stared out the window at Oliga chatting with three other women. Only one of them was dressed adequately. They noticed Umm Nabil shuddering in tears and did not bother to stifle their laughter.

"You see how we are treated!" Umm Nabil stifled a sob. "Even my slave laughs at me."

Her slave. Zaytuna felt Oliga's bitter anger and gladly provoked the old woman further, hoping to get the woman to say more than she wished. "Perhaps he abandoned you to your poverty because he could not bear it?"

The shock of recognition was there for only a moment before she leapt to deny it. "Not my son." She pointed insultingly at her. "Not my son!"

Zaytuna bowed her head in apology. "Forgive me. We must ask questions that are uncomfortable, even offensive. I have become too much like the men. I know better. I know just by looking at you that this son of yours would never leave you."

"Never! If he had any regret, it was only that he could not protect me as his father had done. We have had to sell most of our valuable things to live." She looked out the window. "All our slaves are gone, all but that one out there whom no one will buy because of the mouth on her."

The women outside laughed again.

"He knows what this has done to me and would never abandon me to it."

The woman had to know that her son was gambling. Zaytuna wished she could have talked to Mustafa or Tein first about what they had discovered when they were here.

"He was moving up as a scholar. My boy has been promised a teaching position. Not at the mosque, not yet, but to the children of a grand family." She raised her chin proudly, as if her son were not lost and his colleagues had not threatened to ruin him. "We will soon rely on his income alone."

"I see." But a typical tutor's position paid mainly in respect, certainly nothing that would cover this woman's needs. Mustafa's work teaching children would allow for no more than a simple room and simple food. He and YingYue relied on her father's generosity and shared his home. Nabil must have lied to her about what he would make, that is, unless he did have some recognition and the promise of work in one of the great homes. But if Nabil's colleagues had it in for him, any job he might have held could be lost already. Baghdad was filled with scholars vying for private teaching positions. These families could fire and hire at will.

The mother reached out to her. "You understand the gravity of these scholars' threats, then."

"May I ask what caused this change in circumstances?"

"My husband was a gambler. God forgive him." Her face flushed, perhaps with embarrassment, perhaps anger. "He drove us into great debt. We never knew until he had passed and the family assembled to divide the property."

Zaytuna wanted to ask how her husband had been able to protect the family while he was alive, as she claimed, but said the required prayer instead. "May God have mercy on his soul."

"Amin." She held her hands out and gathered the prayer to her heart.

"What happened when the debt collectors arrived?"

"No, you do not understand," she said impatiently. "He sold our vineyard, all our holdings, to a man whose land adjoined ours. The sale met my husband's debts and the land continued to provide us day to day with the wealth we had always known."

"If he sold the land, how could the family continue to live on it and take a living from it?"

"You are not listening! The agreement was that this man would only take possession of the property on my husband's death." She brought the kerchief to her eyes again and sniffled. "The moment he died, I ordered our cook to stop preparing our dinner, as it no longer belonged to us, but must be divided among the inheritors. His family, myself, our son."

What a grand protestation of piety, refusing to eat the dinner before her as it no longer belonged to her and her son alone. This woman, with her love of wealth and no kindness for the one whom her right hand possessed, would have eaten the whole pot.

But maybe she would have ordered her cook to stop? Maybe it was part of what it meant to be a woman of standing? What did Zaytuna understand about the wealthy or what they would be like when they lost everything? If she took a wrong step with Mustafa, she would lose everything, too. Not only a marriage fed by a stream of unencumbered love, but her family, the home, the stability that Kamal Ali provided to them all. What piety would she pretend to for a shred of dignity?

The woman was speaking, but Zaytuna could not hear her over her own thoughts.

If you took a wrong step? Mustafa is outside waiting for you. Her stomach turned, wishing she had not come at all. *Do not lie. You wanted to be with him. You wanted this case.*

She had to leave, now, and took a breath of finality before standing.

"You want to leave me? Empty promises from every one of you. Bring back my silver case if my boy's life means so little to you!"

"I am here," she said, forcing herself to remain. "Where is your husband's family? Your family?"

Umm Nabil's face turned red. Sputtering, she protested, "None would take us into their home!"

Nabil had no one except for this mother who held onto her son as her only salvation. Perhaps it had been too much for him. The river was never far away. "It must have been very hard on Nabil, knowing what was now on his shoulders."

"He suffered under the burden, but he is a good son and he met it with a smile. I know." She glared. "I am his mother."

Zaytuna involuntarily glanced toward the door, imagining Mustafa waiting for her. "The scholars said he had gone too far." She returned her attention to the mother. "He had a manuscript they wanted to see."

"Ask them, I tell you. Ask Bahr. He is behind it all."

She stood, not able to keep herself there any longer.

"My God, you are just like the men. Why will you not address what has truly happened here?"

"What then! What do you believe has happened?"

"Bahr! Bahr has attacked my dear boy!"

"I assure you, we will find out." Zaytuna backed up slowly toward the door, not sure if she cared about the case anymore and not knowing if she wanted Mustafa to still be outside or not.

"Girl!" Umm Nabil struggled to stand.

At the call, Oliga glanced up but did not move, returning to her conversation.

Now upright, Umm Nabil's jaw was set. "Enough! You go speak to those scholars. Find Bahr Ibn Abi Shuayb. He has done something to my faultless boy!" With those last words, she fell back onto the couch, heaving.

This was no performance. The woman could not conceive that their losses and her demands had driven Nabil, likely spoiled from the start, to abandon her one way or another. Zaytuna faulted her, but tried to sound reassuring. "I promise you the men will pursue it."

She meant it when she said "the men." After today, for her sake and Mustafa's, she could not be involved if there was a chance she would see him. She finally turned toward the vestibule and threw the bolt hard, now praying Mustafa had not waited, not knowing what she would say if he had. She needed to think about how she would explain everything to Kamal Ali.

Outside, the street was empty. But instead of the relief she expected, she heard herself cry in a whisper, "Mustafa, where are you?" He emerged from an alleyway across the street and she hurried to him. "I was afraid you left."

"Come. We can talk safely here." Mustafa turned down one street, then another, drawing her into an unfamiliar neighbourhood. She turned the last corner to find him standing in an alcove doorway, beckoning her. "My love."

Zaytuna stopped just out of reach. She had been holding the edge of her wrap to cover her face from him, but she let it fall away.

"I can divorce YingYue," he insisted. "You can leave Kamal Ali. We can be together. We must! Our whole lives there has only been you and…"

"No!" Thoughts that had been hiding under thoughts slipped out. "We lost our chance."

"Never." His voice deepened and he held his hand out to her. "Come to me, now."

She did not move.

"People will see you. Come here to talk. Only to talk."

Everything that had passed between them was in her grasp. She opened her hands and held them up to keep him at bay and herself where she stood.

"It is my fault, my love." He checked up and down the alley. "I should have come to you when you asked. I should never have married her. I thought I wanted... I was wrong."

"No. My fault," she admitted. "I pushed you away until you pushed me away." The ugly way she had spoken to him through the years. Inviting him in, then rejecting him because she was too hurt to be loved. How much was he meant to take? By the time she began to trust, he had found YingYue. She tried to pull him back and he rightly turned her away. Yet here they were again. What between them had ever gone right? They were wrong for each other and it would always be like this. "There can be no regrets."

"I regret..."

"Layla warned me this would happen."

"What do you mean?"

"She asked me once how I would feel if once I married Kamal Ali, you and YingYue were to divorce. If I would regret it." She remembered the rest of the conversation, too. She had told Layla that Mustafa had never found her beautiful. That he never made her feel beautiful. Worse, that he was embarrassed by her. She could never follow him into the houses of scholars and the wealthy. She could never be the woman he needed her to be.

"Do you regret it?"

She meant to simply say "No," but answered instead with her own questions, finding the old hurt still fresh. "Does YingYue accompany you to the homes of your colleagues? Is she polite? All the things you needed in a companion?"

Guilt altered his features. "She is gracious, but they mock her simple piety. They ask about fashion. She answers that 'God is beautiful and loves beauty'."

"No better than me, then."

"I love... I love you, Zaytuna."

"Love is not enough."

"I love the intelligence of your face. The cleverness in your eyes. That you keep that one lock in honour of your mother, threaded through her bead."

"The cleverness of my eyes? My mother? You never made me feel beautiful."

"Zaytuna, how could you doubt me?"

Mustafa's passion was plain on his face, softly wanting, but not like an animal. His wanting her came from a deeper place than mere desire, and she understood it as she now understood herself. He was not whole without her. The world slowed around them and, for the first time, she knew how Saliha and Tein had ended in these places, when love drew you beyond all boundaries. She saw herself as in her dream, watching the colours turn into beckoning tendrils. For a fleeting moment, her body moved with its wanting toward the doorway. But she took hold of herself, lowered her eyes and took two steps back. "I must leave." But she did not move any further. "I won't give you what you need."

He stepped out of the doorway.

"What you need, too. I saw it on your face."

"No." She grasped her wrap and drew it across her cheek. "I love my husband. Please stop."

"Not in the way you love me."

She had no answer to that and grieved for them; the sorrow pulled her in, entwining itself around her. Even loving Kamal Ali, wanting Kamal Ali, this grief would always be there, haunting her. Is this not what she was made for? Loss, and ever more loss. Uncle Abu al-Qasim said to turn away from her love of her own sorrow. But she did not understand. How, when every choice, every turning away, would lead to it?

A horrible silence settled between them. Neither moved toward the other, neither left. Then a child ran between them to get past, startling Zaytuna out of her madness.

"Enough."

"The case," he said, his voice cracking. "Tell me what she said about the case."

"The case was only an excuse for this."

"For us."

"Never again."

She left him in the alley, but found herself turned around, not knowing the way back. There was a tavern on the corner, just a table and three stools. The owner leaned in the doorway.

"I'm lost," she said.

"Please sit." He removed a jug of wine near the door and put it inside. "No one is here. If they come, I'll send them away."

He retreated to the back, then returned with a glass of water for her. She sat on the stool, grateful for a moment to collect herself and try to understand what had happened. The tavern owner stood close to the street in a stance of protection as people passed, staring openly at her. How different he was from Salman, she thought, who was probably sitting in front of his tavern right now as if he owned the whole of Baghdad. He would have tried to pry out what had led her to his table, then he would have mocked her for her past pretence to piety.

She sought the calming waters she felt in the presence of the aunts and uncles and in those moments when she forgot about herself, waters that released every muscle, that rooted her to the depth of her being so she could take more careful steps ahead. But nothing reached her. Only emptiness. She would return to Kamal Ali, unsure of what she would say, and prayed he would accept her.

But Mustafa? What would he do now that he had been rejected by both of the women he loved?

The tavern owner tapped her table with his finger and gestured toward the alley to her left. Mustafa was there. He had said her name, but she had not heard.

"Zaytuna," he said again.

She felt nothing. No desire for him. No anger, either. Not even anger that he had involved himself in a family's tragedy and offered to help find their son only for this, to have a chance to bind her to him completely. If it had been only a few months earlier, before meeting Kamal Ali, she would have gone to him willingly. But she had made a different choice, and she chose Kamal Ali again.

She stood, thanked the owner, and went to Mustafa.

His eyes were distant. His wrap hung messily over his shoulders and his arms were slack, but volatile in their stillness. She hesitated to come closer, but feared more that he would not hear her in his state and drew in, just beyond arms' reach. "You will always be my Mustafa, my first love, my friend, but not my husband." Then she took a few quick steps back.

Just behind her, the tavern owner said, "I'm here."

Mustafa did not lash out. Instead, he crumpled to the ground as if she had taken life itself from his hands. A woman gasped and a man nearby expressed concern. There were whispers and the shuffling of feet. Unable to go to him, Zaytuna wanted to cry out. Was there no way to console him? She begged the tavern owner, "Please."

He went to him, speaking quietly in Mustafa's ear, and helped him to stand.

Mustafa broke his long stare, put a hand on the man's arm and thanked him. Then, head down, he walked away.

She imagined him wandering the streets in confusion, pickpockets and thugs taking advantage and ran after him, stopping just close enough for him to hear, no longer caring who saw her. "Let me guide you home."

"No. Take me to Uncle's, please. I cannot find it without you."

9

"I'm heading to Abu YingYue to ask about that talisman."

"YingYue's father? He doesn't buy silver," Ammar caught up, noticing that Tein was dragging his bad leg.

"Not the case. The talisman itself."

"I don't understand."

"It's a hunch." He stopped, gesturing behind them. "Don't come with me. You go door-to-door. The nahariyyas and the gambling houses are back that way."

Was Tein going to be like this the whole case? Deadening the bit of life he'd been able to claw back?

The midday call to prayer sounded, saving them from an argument. "There's a prayer hall up there. Wait for me. Then we'll get some food."

He went ahead of Tein and through a nondescript door nestled between two shops. Rugs that had seen better days were laid out end to end. The hall was small, windowless, and already crowded with men. There was no place left but the near corner of the last line. Ammar was glad. His distinct prayer movements would not give him away, forcing him to endure directions to the nearest Shia prayer hall for the next time.

The man next to him reeked of damp wool. When Ammar prostrated, the space was so cramped that he had to twist his body to keep from hitting the heels of the man ahead of him. Instead of saying the prescribed words in every bow and prostration, he ended up praying the case would open a different life for him and that Tein would help even if he did not want to follow him there.

Outside, Tein waited for him, popping nuts into his mouth from a sack. Tein offered it to him as he approached. "To Abu YingYue."

Without another word, Ammar grabbed the sack and followed him deeper into the market. They wound through streets and alleys, some busy, others with just a few shoppers being hawked at by men from their stalls. Two women, arm in arm, looked over dishes and bowls glazed a creamy white with touches of black or splashes of blue and green. The scent of their rose perfume reached him. He wondered if Nasifa would find the dishes beautiful, too, and thought for a moment to stop. She deserved pretty things. He could buy a small bowl to hold her earrings. Maybe she deserved more. But she was stuck with what he could give, and he was not sure if it would be enough.

In the paper seller's street, customers gathered at counters or sat on stools in front of the shops. Some sold ink and paper of all qualities, while others also had shelves of scholarly manuscripts available to be copied at a price. Men sat in the back of these narrow shops at writing desks, pen in hand, labouring for a buyer. Tein was a regular on this street, but he walked with purpose past each of the sellers, acknowledging none of them. He finally gestured to a man in an undyed linen turban, his back to them, leaning against the street-front counter of a large shop more than double the size of the rest.

"Ya Abu YingYue!"

A Chinese man turned to face them, his gentle smile widening in recognition.

From Tein's stories, Ammar knew him to be a fair but firm businessman. Abu YingYue would do no harm, but he would do no business with anyone who was not scrupulously honest. He made no excuses for anyone's behaviour and certainly not his own. Ammar had imagined him to be stern, not a man with good humour etched onto his craggy face. Mustafa was lucky to have this man as his father-in-law, instead of one like his own who managed to match his father in ignorance.

"Tein, my son, how are you? How is your family?" He waved over a boy in the street and threw him a coin with four fingers in the air.

Three men were at the rear of the store, but Ammar guessed who the fourth would be. Two were printing on paper using a wooden block, one preparing the ink, while the other pressed evenly onto small squares of paper weighted flat. The third sat on a bench near the shelves of manuscripts, one leg oddly thrown over the other, surreptitiously sizing them up. His garments were deceptively simple. Dark brown wool was sewn to resemble the robes worn by hawkers, yet a glimpse of the lining revealed thickly quilted silk in a pattern of gold and red stripes. Ammar pegged him as Ghuraba, a traveller and seller of talismans, and a wealthy one at that.

Tein politely refused Abu YingYue's offer of refreshments. "You mustn't. We'll only be a moment."

"Tein, how can you come and not stop for a visit?"

"I see you each week on my way to sit with Firdaws ibn Ali!"

"I am only jealous of Baraqan"—he ticked his head further down the street—"that his shop should host such stimulating conversation."

Baraqan, Ibn Ali and other men gathered to read philosophical works or review debates they had heard in salons where philosophy, poetry, and literature were discussed. Ammar had sat with them once, bored out of his mind while Ibn Ali, the pharmacist at the Barmakid hospital, shared the philosophical questions he had discussed that day with the great Dr. ar-Razi, philosopher and medical man. Never again.

"You are welcome to join us," Tein said.

Abu YingYue declined. "But that would mean missing the sama, and I cannot."

There was a hint of scolding that Tein should miss the Sufi gathering in remembrance of God and the Prophet for such talk and Ammar got his first taste of the firmness of the man's character. But Tein did not seem hurt. Rather, he took Abu YingYue's hand across the counter, kissed it out of respect, and tried to bring it to his forehead before Abu YingYue drew it back in an irritated flush of humility.

Abu YingYue waved over the man on the bench who unfolded himself to stand. He smiled easily as he approached, but there was an acute intelligence there masked as welcome interest.

Tein noticed, too, and murmured, "That one's already surmised the name of my maternal grandmother."

Ammar grinned. It sounded like Tein might be enjoying being back in the game rather than letting his mind slip into those pots of milk fat.

"This is my friend and former partner, Ammar ibn at-Tabbani." Tein put a hand on his back. "Ammar, please meet Abu YingYue at-Tarazi."

"He has mentioned you many times!" Abu YingYue opened a door inset into the counter and came around front, pulling up stools, saying, "I have scolded him for never bringing you to me."

The boy returned with a copper tray holding four glasses of pomegranate juice and a plate of flaky cookies shaped into rings.

The man followed Abu YingYue around and took a stool.

"Tein ibn al-Ashiqa as-Sawda, Ammar at-Tabbani, please meet my friend," Abu YingYue nodded to the stranger, "Razba ibn Salim."

Razba. So the man is Ghuraba. Why would Abu YingYue keep company with one of their beggar kings? Good thing for them, though. This one could help find Nabil. Future cases, too. Their people were everywhere selling talismans, performing small plays or dancing in the streets, ballad-singers and the pickpockets who followed them from tavern to tavern. And certainly, there was no one better placed to get Tein to drop his hunch about the talisman so they could get onto a real search. He smiled and grasped the man's arm. "Well met."

Razba returned Ammar's goodwill, but his expression remained inquisitive.

Abu YingYue murmured, "Bismillah," as the men took their first sip.

The juice was sweet and tart and not watered down. It brought Ammar back to the good days of life on the road to the frontier, stealing pomegranates off trees and carving out a full-mouth of seeds with his teeth.

"You are here about Mustafa's case?" Abu YingYue drew back, addressing Razba. "A young Quran scholar has gone missing. His mother has asked for help finding him."

"You police?" Razba asked.

"We were police."

Suspicion flickered across Razba's face.

Tein saw it, too. "We work churning butter now. Just helping out Mustafa."

Razba's reply was no more than a puzzled expression.

"There is so little to go on," Ammar said. "We came to follow up one of Tein's hunches."

"Please share it," Abu YingYue said eagerly. "I am at your service."

"The missing man's mother wore a talisman case around her neck," Tein said. "She kept touching it as we spoke. It struck me as odd at the time, although it shouldn't have. Her son's missing. She would rub a talisman."

"Did you see what was written on it?"

"I only saw that it was block printed and had a distinctive red border. Do you know where that would have been done?"

"Not here. I do not print talismans, only prayers."

Razba lightly scoffed, "Prayers that people use as talismans."

Abu YingYue put his hand over his heart. "I cannot control what people do with the prayers I print. I only want to put the prayers in their hands."

"Maybe your Sufis do not use talismans, but outside of Baghdad, to the east, mystics sew talismans into their clothes!" He addressed Ammar and Tein with a genuinely open smile this time. "The Ghuraba are my people. We block print talismans to sell. I will brook no insult to the practice."

"Just so, just so." YingYue bent his head in apology.

Razba got up and went back into the store, taking a large leather shoulder bag off a peg at the rear. Returning, he held out a piece of paper to Tein with densely printed text surrounded by a double-striped red border. "Did it look like this?"

Tein was already off his stool. "Yes! That exact edging. The black dots, too. That doesn't look like Arabic, though. I saw Arabic lettering."

"This is the advantage of printing," Razba told him. "We can produce talismans for whomever asks, whatever their religion or language. Whatever we need, we can produce them in great numbers, quick to sale, yet seeming to be custom made for each buyer. If it had this border, it was ours." He paused, looking pleased with himself. "Stopping in Baghdad this past year, we have flooded the market with our product."

"Is there anything special about it?" Tein asked.

He winked. "Other than that our talismans have a reputation for efficacy?"

"The blocks you carve for printing, other than different languages, do the talismans all say the same thing?" Ammar shrugged. "Some of your customers can't read. They would never know."

"I can see what you think of us." Razba frowned at him. "No, we have numerous blocks carved for distinct needs: love, protection, curses, wealth. And for the special customer, we will hand write one particular to their situation."

"I meant no insult," Ammar said, hand on his heart.

"A misunderstanding, then." Razba did not mean it.

Ammar didn't mind; he had not meant the apology. He had been inside one of their mastabas on an old case for Grave Crimes. Grifters, every last one of them. If he was to approach Razba in the future, then the Gharib would have to know that Ammar could not be fooled.

"Her servant bought it for her," Tein said to Razba. "A Slav woman with nearly white hair and large blue eyes? Do you know her?"

"You hope to trace down the person who sold it to her and find out what the talisman said? Her son is lost. She touches her talisman. It is obviously a talisman for protection." He waved his hand in dismissal. "Or perhaps it is new and a charm for God to return what has been lost?"

That made sense, given the wealth that had been stripped from them. He hoped Tein would accept it. "How many people do you have out selling them? She lives near Sharqiyya Mosque. Do you have people near there?"

"You sound like police now."

"Forgive my friend," Tein said. "Old habits. But would it be possible for you to ask whoever sells in the neighbourhood if the Slav asked for one and what it was for?"

He nodded to Tein. "For you, I will ask."

Ammar snorted, shifting in his seat to indicate they needed to leave.

"You have been a great help, sir," Tein said to Razba. "If you have any news about the talisman, would you tell Abu YingYue? He will get it to us."

But Abu YingYue tried to hold them back. "You must not leave until you hear about what Razba and I have been discussing." He invited Razba to speak.

Ammar stood, but Tein stayed put.

"Please," Abu YingYue said to Ammar. "I have been waiting to tell Tein. It is a fascinating conversation I hoped to bring to Baraqan and the other men."

He sat again, and Razba let out a pleased grunt.

Addressing Tein, he said, "I had heard of Abu YingYue's reputation and approached him to discuss the possibilities of different methods of printing."

"You see," Abu YingYue said, "Razba works seasonally at the mint, creating die punches to produce caliphal coins."

"We create punches for words and phrases, but also individual letters. We make letters according to their place in the word. Initial, medial, or final forms. Then we position them to spell out what we like and press the coins."

"Imagine," Abu YingYue said, "if we did the same for the books we presently hand copy? One would have the flexibility of arranging the letters page after page as one likes."

Tein sat up, interested. "I've seen what goes into carving the blocks to print those small prayers. But die? How many of each letter and position would you need? Pressing the paper to it? How would that even work?"

"Razba came to me because block printing long documents has been done in China for centuries. He thought I would be interested in his thoughts about using die to do the same." Abu YingYue tugged on his sparse beard, smiling. "I am! And I am intrigued by the very difficulties it poses."

"It's got to be faster to hand copy," Tein said.

Ammar tapped his foot, impatient for the conversation to end.

"When it comes to book length documents, hand copying is more practical at the moment. Even block printing presents a problem," Razba said. "Abu YingYue told me that in China, blocks are carved only for the most essential documents because of the sheer scale of storing them."

"Tell them," Abu YingYue urged.

Razba's eyes sparkled. "But some of us Ghuraba etch on tin instead of blocks to print multiple talismans and save the etched sheets to use again. Tin would be more compact, obviously, to store. We've also discussed pressing the die on tin, then running paper on the inked tin sheets as needed." He sat up with a sigh. "Sadly, the size and cost of such an operation is not practical for Abu YingYue and I at the moment, but we enjoy making impossible plans."

"Baraqan and the rest would very much like to hear about this," Tein said. "Firdaws Ibn Ali would jump at the chance to print his medicinal formulae and share them widely. I can only imagine what Dr. ar-Razi would think. I am sure we could meet on another day so you would not have to miss the sama."

Abu YingYue nodded, adding, "It is not only the possibility that is interesting, but it also raises certain ethical questions that I did not consider until recently." He lowered his voice. "Just the other day, a young man came to me asking us if I could block print his manuscript of the Quran. I refused, of course. But can you imagine?"

Ammar tensed, grasping the implications. "Was it based on Uthman's codex?"

"No." Razba addressed Ammar this time, his eyes alight with mischief. "He announced it was a fully marked companion's reading tradition, consonants and vowels. One reading only."

Ammar tapped his leg. "He did not say whose?"

Abu YingYue ignored the question and carried on. "Can you imagine if one reading tradition of the divine revelation became universally accepted by mere virtue of being widely accessible in print? It would be impossible to print all the other reading traditions to complement it, even if we limited ourselves to those that accord with the manuscript of the caliph Uthman. And what about a companion's manuscript like this fellow had or the preferred reading of an individual scholar?"

"What was it?" Ammar demanded, cursed-well knowing it was not Seyyidina Ali's.

"Neither one of us were in a position to know what we were looking at. But imagine, a companion's reading tradition becoming the only Quran people know!"

"Nabil?" Tein looked at Ammar. "Is this the manuscript his colleagues want to see?"

Ammar started. "It may just be."

"God protect us, the controversy this would bring down on our heads, not to mention the harm done to the Muslim community." Abu YingYue continued. "Who are we to make these decisions?"

"The young man, what did he look like?" Ammar asked.

"About your height, Ammar, but with a red beard. He wore a modest scholar's turban, but his clothes promised he could afford the work. Red silk!"

"That sounds like the man we are searching for." Tein said.

"My!" Abu YingYue shot up, nearly knocking his stool back.

Razba leaned against the counter wall with the satisfaction of a man enjoying a particularly good storyteller spin his yarn.

"I suppose he did not give his name?"

"No," Abu YingYue answered. "I did not press him. I was polite, but clear that we would not undertake this work and I wanted him to leave immediately."

"Is there anyone else who could?"

"There is only one other who employs artisans that could make block prints of the quality and quantity necessary for such a job, and he is in Rusafa. But, like me, I do not believe he could or would take on the job. I know him well. He is a pious man. Imam Hossam ibn Yusuf is a master of Baghdad's reading tradition and leads daily prayers in the hall near his shop."

"We have to check." A walk to the great market in Rusafa simply to ask would take most of a day, and Ammar was eager at the thought of it. Things were looking up.

Abu YingYue said, "Yes. If the young man had been there, Imam Hossam would perhaps recognize the reading tradition."

"You said the talisman was in a case?" Razba asked.

"Yes," Ammar replied. "A silver case the length of a woman's thumb and beautifully etched. Heavy to hand, yet not lead-lined."

Razba whistled. "I cannot imagine the servant bringing an object of such value out with her. But a Slav would stand out. Perhaps someone will remember."

Ammar did not see the talisman angle going anywhere other than leading them, by blessed coincidence, to find out Nabil was trying to get a manuscript of the Quran printed. That was worth tracking to Rusafa but also to the scholars at the Sharqiyya mosque. If they knew about Nabil trying to get that manuscript printed—and they would surely grasp the threat of distributing it throughout the empire—they may have tried to stop him in any way they could.

"Perhaps the man was beaten or killed for trying to print it," Razba suggested.

Ammar smirked. "They're not above violent correction."

Abu YingYue looked stricken.

"You sent him away. None of this is your fault," Tein assured him, then stood, glancing at Ammar. "All we know now is that he is missing."

But Abu YingYue was still upset. Tein embraced him and said something Ammar could not hear. Abu YingYue's face softened.

After they left the shop, Ammar asked, "What did you say to Abu YingYue?"

"That Shaykh Abu al-Qasim would protect him."

"Will he?"

"Yes, if God answers his prayers and the men in the courts are sympathetic."

Entering the thick of the main market street, Ammar felt free. Every passerby, the children, men, and women, servants with sacks on their backs or bags in their hands brimmed with life. He and Tein had work to do. Gambling halls. A Quran manuscript begging to be printed. Scholars with a grudge. The case was on. Butter and goats receded further and further into the distance.

He looked up at Tein with a grin. "Quran scholars tomorrow with Mustafa?"

10

It had been a long day. Tein wanted to pull Saliha to him, smell the rosewater in her hair and the clean scent of camphor on her hands. But when he opened the outer door, Kamal Ali and Zaytuna were sitting on the reed mat chatting with Qambar. Her head was on her husband's shoulder; his arm was around her. Kamal Ali greeted Tein as usual, but Zaytuna was tense. Something had gone wrong.

Zaytuna whispered to her husband, who withdrew his arm so she could stand. Saliha, having heard him come in, was already out of their room and had taken his hand, tugging on him to go with her before Zaytuna could reach him.

Qambar called out a teasing warning. "Go say your marriage vows for tonight first."

"Oh, you!" Saliha replied lightly, but there was a touch of irritation in her voice and also a particular heaviness in her features that Tein knew well. She must have washed a child for burial today. He promised himself to speak again to Qambar about the teasing.

The old man was only trying to protect her. He loved Saliha like a daughter. It was down to Qambar that they were married at all, even this temporary marriage, one night at a time, rather than a proper ceremony and marriage like Tein had wanted. Knowing Saliha would not marry and the two would find their way to each other, married or not, Qambar had proposed that a temporary marriage would save them. And it had. Saliha remained a free woman by day and his wife by night, but only when she agreed.

"Where are Layla and Yulduz?" Tein asked.

"They went out for food," Saliha answered with an edge to her voice.

This was something else other than washing a child.

As Zaytuna stepped away, Kamal Ali touched the hem of her long qamis. It had been months and the man was still besotted with her. Tein had expected that Kamal Ali's affection would wane in the face of his sister's inconstant moods, but it had not.

"First," she said, coming to them, hands out, forestalling any questions. "I won't see Mustafa again."

"Again? You saw him?" he whispered, incredulous and becoming angry with himself more than her. "I should have stopped you."

"This shouldn't be her problem," Saliha interjected harshly, not caring if Kamal Ali heard.

Here was the irritation. Saliha was anticipating this conversation.

Zaytuna carried on, ignoring her. "He took me to see Umm Nabil today, but I did not get much from her. Probably no more than you did."

They had been alone.

"Why was Mustafa involved?" He glanced at Kamal Ali, wondering if he could hear their conversation, but he seemed busy with Qambar. "Does Kamal Ali know?"

"Yes, I told him."

The man was reaching for her hem even after knowing she was with Mustafa today.

"I shouldn't have gone with him, but I did."

"What aren't you telling me?"

"Why does she have to tell you anything?" Saliha snapped.

"I want to tell him." She put a hand on Saliha's arm, but Saliha snatched it away.

"I ran into him at Uncle's. Uncle Abu al-Qasim and Auntie Hakima told me not to worry about him, that they have him under control. So when he told me he could take me to Umm Nabil, I followed. At a distance."

"Even that, Zaytuna."

She stared at him, not answering the charge.

"Fine. What did you get?"

"Nabil's father gambled all their wealth away, their land, the house, everything. He sold it to a neighbour with the condition that it would only come into the neighbour's possession once the father died."

She seemed on surer ground here. Whatever she was not saying had to be about that walk with Mustafa.

"The family didn't know about the sale?"

"No. At least she says they didn't."

"But now the son is gambling like the father," he said. "She's lost her husband, her wealth, her standing, now perhaps her son. But we looked into the gambling. It didn't go anywhere. Not yet, anyway."

"She insists we look at scholars."

Tein cocked his head. "We?"

"I did not say I was going."

Saliha rolled her eyes. "She's promised to be a proper lady."

The comment was directed at him, but he saw that it pained Zaytuna, who turned her face away. He knew better than to intervene between the two and he continued to wonder how they stayed friends at all. But her reaction reminded him of what it cost her to stay out of the case. He would tell his sister whatever he found out from now on and ask her advice. But he would also ask Saliha why she did not want to protect her friend from the danger of being alone with Mustafa.

The outer door pushed against his back. He stepped aside for Layla and Yulduz, who came in carrying the food.

His stomach grumbled at the warm scent of fresh bread and fatty roast chicken.

Tein took the clay pot of chicken from the girl. Having gotten used to having a steady family, Layla no longer rushed over for hugs held too long whenever one of them entered, but her eyes still lit up hungry for love. He leaned down and kissed her head, then gave his sister an understanding smile.

Qambar fussed over the cloth laid out. Saliha took the bread from Yulduz and tore the loaves into pieces and he set the pot down in the centre. Tein gazed on his newfound family as if the world and all its riches had been given to him. Zaytuna followed them, bringing a large jug of water. Her husband did the honours, lifting the lid off the pot, revealing two fat, browned chickens resting in their drippings.

Layla told them about her day, and Tein watched their faces as they dabbed the bread into the pot. He suddenly feared losing it all. The conversation faded as his ears thumped and his chest tightened. He reached for a cup of water, feeling foolish. Hiding behind the cup as much as drinking from it, he sipped slowly, focusing on steadying his breath. There was still a fist-sized lump pressing on him, but the pounding was fading and Layla's voice came back into focus.

"Rana and Sara did not!"

"Old Lady Manar saw them." Yulduz sounded serious, but Tein saw a twinkle in her eye.

Whatever Layla had gotten up to with the girls who lived next door, it was not any real trouble in Yulduz's estimation. One more deep breath and the fist pressing into his chest eased.

Saliha elbowed him, a hunk of thigh meat in her fingers. "Get in there, or there'll be nothing left."

He pulled off a leg for himself and ate.

"We were only playing kharaj," Layla whined, sounding like a girl much younger in years.

"Since when is kharaj played by hiding objects in other people's courtyards?" Yulduz opened her hand, palm out, then folded it shut. "You hide it in your hand."

"The ball was too big," Layla offered in weak defence.

"Just stay out of the old hag's way," Saliha said.

Yulduz stifled a laugh and Qambar looked away, the back of his hand over his mouth. Having had his own run in with Old Lady Manar, Tein was inclined to laugh, too, but kept it to himself.

Layla muttered, "May her goat's milk curdle."

Tein burst out laughing, releasing the last of the pressure. "She doesn't have a goat!"

Qambar and Kamal Ali looked sadly at the girl for cursing, so he stifled his laughter, but Saliha chuckled beside him without minding.

Zaytuna waved at Layla to come and sit beside her. She moved, nestling in between Zaytuna and Kamal Ali. Zaytuna whispered something in her ear. Layla nodded, frowning, then reached and dejectedly took another bite of chicken.

"Invite them here, my daughter." Kamal Ali patted her hand.

The girl's frown softened enough to signal that her hard feelings were passing. Then she took another bite with a larger piece of bread this time, filling her mouth until she could not close it to chew politely. He stifled another laugh.

Tein went from holding in his laughter to silent tears, not knowing that he was weeping until Saliha touched his cheek. All he could see and feel was the beauty of Layla playing with girls in the neighbourhood, their heads together sharing some secret or chasing each other around corners. The harshness of her early life behind her, she had become a child for the first time and not one of them begrudged her. It was a childhood he and Zaytuna had not had themselves, a precious childhood he hoped to give to his own child someday. He only wished his sister could feel the same, rest in the certain love of this family, let the bond of this household be enough to forgo whatever she still held in her heart for Mustafa.

Saliha pulled off a piece of chicken with a bit of bread and held it out to him. He allowed her to feed him, then he fed her in thanks, and they all returned to their meal.

Afterwards, when all was cleaned up, he touched Saliha's shoulder lightly, hoping the two of them could retreat to their room and rest in each other's arms. She smiled and went in to wait for him, closing the door behind her. But before he could go to her, Kamal Ali and Zaytuna stopped him.

She spoke first. "I didn't finish telling you what the mother had to say."

"Tell me, then," he said wearily, checking on Kamal Ali to see how he was faring. He saw nothing but a man standing by his wife and admired him.

Yulduz was nearby and said, "Oh tell us all, please," and joined them.

He wished Zaytuna had not spoken when the others could hear, but if Yulduz gossiped with the neighbours, it could hardly affect the case. Thankfully, Qambar had sent Layla off to go to sleep, so he did not have to explain anything to her. He wanted the girl's mind on her few chores and her friends, not a missing man.

"There is not much else to say," she said in apology to Yulduz. "He was promised a position teaching. Umm Nabil thought her son would save them with his tutor's salary. We all know how little they make." Zaytuna glanced guiltily at Kamal Ali, but he gestured for her to continue. "She insists the scholars were trying to ruin him, especially this Bahr."

"Did you find out why she named him?"

"No. But what struck me was that she refused to consider his gambling, or that he had failed her and may have run away, or worse— more reasonable explanations—and blamed the scholars instead."

Yulduz piped up, "If something shameful's happened, better it the fault of someone else."

"You have a point." Tein said. "As for him ending his own life, Grave Crimes will send us a message if a likely body shows up. Saliha said she would speak to the corpse washer for men each day, too. We're checking up on it."

"You said scholars?" Yulduz asked.

"Just a piece of a puzzle," Tein replied, not wanting to offer more.

But Zaytuna answered, "She only said that the scholars wanted to ruin him, but not why. Tein, I asked about the manuscript but got nowhere."

"Manuscript? What d'you mean?" Yulduz poked Zaytuna's arm.

It seemed to him that the manuscript was their best bet right now, but it was late and he did not want to explain to Yulduz about a Quran manuscript everyone wanted to see, a man wanting to print it, and scholars who could be at each other's throats over disagreements. Tein gestured in invitation to Zaytuna to field the question, having brought it on herself.

"We're not sure, Yulduz. A Quran manuscript that the scholars wanted to see."

"Ammar and I are following that up tomorrow. And you, Zaytuna," he said reassuringly, "the mother revealed more to you than us. Good work."

"I am good at talking to women." She checked with Kamal Ali. "On my own."

Her husband took her hand and kissed it.

"Will you trust me that if we need you to interview a woman, we will ask?"

She agreed, but he did not believe that she would not go looking for opportunities.

The call for the nighttime prayer came just in time to put a stop to the conversation.

Zaytuna and Kamal Ali left to spread out the rugs they used for prayer outside.

Layla came out with her night clothes on, her long hair in a thick braid, and a warm wrap draped over her head. She tugged at Tein's hand. "Watch over Auntie Zaytuna," she said, no longer sounding like a child.

Of course, she had heard. He shook her hand lightly. "Don't you worry about a thing."

"May God accept your prayers," Tein said to them all, restraining a glare at Zaytuna for worrying Layla and left them for his room.

Saliha was hanging her clothes on the peg, already in her soft wool nightdress with her hair in its loose nighttime braid.

"How was work today?" He said softly. "You've got that look like there was a child."

"No, not that." Her back was still to him as she brushed her hand along her clothes.

Her mood seemed like more than annoyance on Zaytuna's behalf, but he took her at her word. Embracing her from behind, he felt the curve of her body against him and the day's troubles fell away. In a voice thick with desire, he asked, "Will you marry me?"

"I offer you my body according to the Quran and the Sunna for whatever chink of coin you've got in your pocket and without either of us inheriting from the other from right now until we leave for work tomorrow. But," she said, turning around and pushing him away, "only for sleep tonight, my love."

Despite wanting her, he answered, "I accept," from a tight throat, and pulled three fals from his pocket. "Your dowry, my love, for sleep."

She took the change, placed it on the chest of clothes, and got into bed.

Tein turned away, trying to think of something else other than her body, and undressed. *The manuscript*, he asked himself, *why did Nabil want to print it?* He hung up his belt and dagger on a peg, then his wrap, his quilted qamis, and undershirt. *What is in it?* He dropped his sirwal. She sighed appreciatively from the bed and he was fully aroused again, but he dutifully pulled a nightshirt over his head before facing her, joking, "Look what you've done."

"Come to bed." Her tone suggested there might still be a chance, but then she added, "to sleep."

Tein lay down, turning his back to her.

She curled up behind him, her breasts pressing against him.

If she wanted to sleep, she should sleep. He rolled on his back to push her off.

"I was comfortable," she complained, moving away.

"I wasn't."

She chuckled, realizing what he meant.

But her good humour only annoyed him. He sat up. "Tell me. Why do you make Zaytuna feel bad about letting go of this case? You know how hard this is for her."

"Mustafa is the problem, not her," she said, meeting his pique with her own. "I told Zaytuna he should be careful not to walk too close to my hand."

He crossed his arms over his chest. Mustafa was a problem and if slapping him would solve it, he would. But Saliha did not seem to understand the depth of Zaytuna's attachment to Mustafa like he did, and like it or not, he was on the case. "If we could do this without him, we would. Kamal Ali won't ask her to stop, so the risks she's taking come down to me."

"Uff. You want to protect her? Get rid of Mustafa." she objected and turned over, this time giving him her back.

Maybe she was right. Mustafa had brought the case to them, but they did not need him now he had introduced them to the mother. Did they need him to approach the scholars at the mosque? He and Ammar had interviewed in mosques before. They no longer had the threat of the name "police," but they knew how to talk and get answers. They needed Mustafa to explain what was at stake when it came to what mattered to these scholars, though. But none of that required him to be out with them every day.

Saliha interrupted his thoughts. "Remember the woman who stood for Mu'mina in court?"

He did. You would think the woman had stood up to the tyrant Yazid himself from the way Yulduz told it.

"She was in the Shuniziyya cemetery yesterday," Saliha said, rolling over to face him.

"That's a long way from across the river in Rusafa."

"I think she had a tryst there with another woman."

"Truly?" Then he remembered Zaytuna saying she refused to marry.

"She claimed she was there because the cemetery offered inspiration to write poetry."

"Using the graveyard of the poorest of the poor." The woman had stood for Mu'mina, but Yulduz's stories made it sound like she thought herself the girl's saviour. It was always like this for the elite of the city, the poor existed to serve their every need. Now their graveyard for assignations.

"When Saadia noticed us, the woman ran off to the far gate and Saadia strode to meet us."

"I hope you haven't shared that with Yulduz."

"Oh, the piety," she joked. "Yulduz was there."

"What made you think of her?"

"The case. She encouraged Zaytuna to take it and offered her help getting into women's scholarly circles if she needed it."

"Why was Zaytuna talking about the case with her?"

"I brought it up, not Zaytuna," Saliha answered defensively.

"No, it's good." Tein let it go and kissed her on the forehead. "That could be useful. And no Mustafa. Why didn't Zay tell me?"

"You made her feel like she needs your permission."

Saliha was right, but look what happened when Zaytuna went out on her own. She went straight to Mustafa. There was something about that meeting she hadn't told him.

"Mustafa visits Saadia's brother often. But if she went, it would just be with women."

But Zaytuna might run into him, even if she was only sitting with the women and he with the men. It was still compromising. Tein did not understand why Saliha could not grasp the risk. He clamped his mouth shut. If he said anything, they would end up in a fully-fledged argument.

Saliha asked, "How do you like being back on a case?"

"I don't like it. Look at all this trouble it's causing."

"What will you do?"

"I'll see it through, for Ammar's sake. He wants back to working cases."

"This is his chance to start that private investigation agency. No compromises?"

"That's how he sees it."

"And you don't think that will work?"

"Once you are in a case, the case calls the shots."

"What do you want?"

He touched her cheek. "I want to churn butter and come home to my family."

Saliha took his hand and they remained in silence for a few moments.

Then she said, "I washed a woman who died in childbirth today. The baby died within her."

He pulled her close. It was the death of a child, after all. She took several long, shuddering breaths and he waited for her to say or not say what she needed. Then tears came, surprising him. Never before had she wept for the death of children. Always, even with the worst cases, children beaten to death, she had not cried, only held him as long as she needed. When it was over, they would make love to grab hold of life again.

Now she trembled in his arms. It was more than a child dying. More than her defence of Zaytuna. It was a mother and child who had died. *It's about her*, he thought. She feared this would happen to her.

His heart expanded until he could no longer bear it. He had finally discovered the reason for her refusal to have a child with him. There was a chance. They could have a family. They would have only the most experienced midwife. She could talk to Ibn Ali for reassurance. Dr. ar-Razi himself if need be.

Tein took deep breaths along with her, finding within himself a place of sweet hope as she found her way back from grief. After a time, she moved against him, asking playfully, "Where is that butter staff I disappointed earlier?"

Instead of answering her by tracing his finger along the curves of her body as he knew she liked, the thought that it was only fear keeping her from having children held him fast. He spoke without considering her reaction. "Are you afraid of dying in childbirth or of the child dying?"

She tensed.

He braced himself.

Saliha sat up, pulling the blanket up to her chin. "I will never be made to be a mother."

The fist that had been pressing up against his heart came back around for another go at him. Tein reached out to her desperately, not knowing how to make it right. But she threw his hand off and lay down again, giving him her back.

DAY FOUR

11

"SHARAFUDDIN SAID YOU WERE OUTSIDE."

Mustafa flinched at the voice behind him.

"Why so jumpy?" Abdulmalik came up beside him.

"It was only a surprise."

Abdulmalik put his hand on Mustafa's shoulder, urging him to come inside.

Mustafa shook him off and continued looking down the road for Tein and Ammar.

"You going to avoid your old hadith circle again to sit with Ibn Mujahid's students?" Abdulmalik said it lightly, but the hurt was clear.

"I'm watching for my cousin and his friend. They are meeting me here."

"Come back when you are finished with whatever you are doing, Mustafa."

He ignored the meaning behind it. "It could be awhile. We are searching for Nabil ibn al-Qays al-Kufi."

"God give his mother ease." Abdulmalik paused. "'We'? Do you mean your cousin? Tein? The one who quit the police?"

"Yes, and his old partner," Mustafa said distractedly, as he watched the road for any sign of them.

"The partner, he is the one who spoke for Mu'mina in court?"

"Yes."

"What could Nabil's mother tell them? She did not know his habits."

"No." He faced Abdulmalik impatiently. "Tein and Ammar are coming here, to the mosque, to talk to the Quran students."

He took hold of Mustafa's sleeve. "Are you sure you want to do that? Your reputation is not strong enough to withstand the gossip."

"Gossip about trying to help a mother find her son!"

"Help find a son that is no longer welcome here?"

"God forgive them."

"Mustafa, you know Burhan looks for any error of yours. He has never forgiven you for Imam Abu Abdurrahman's favour toward you and then his and his father's humiliation in court. It was your cousin's partner, this Ammar, who spoke against him."

Abdulmalik was right. He recklessly attached himself to the fate of Nabil. But there was no other way to reach Zaytuna. So be it.

When Zaytuna left him at the door, Uncle Abu al-Qasim had not been home. Ziri took him in hand and sat with him, arm around his shoulder, and let him weep. Abu Muhammad arrived and spoke to him soothingly. Other men gathered around, raising their hands in prayer for him, despite not knowing the source of his distress. The boy, Abdulghafur, brought him water and sat with them. An old uncle joined them and put his hand on Mustafa's knee. Auntie Hakima came, clucking in sympathy. She murmured prayers with her hand on his head and he felt his torn self being mended, thread by thread.

She left them and Abu Muhammad asked him to listen. "You do not need to forget her, but you must give her up." Then he addressed the surrounding men. "Who here has forgotten their first love?"

Now understanding his distress, the men sighed, some in pain, others with pleasure, but each mentioning a name as if they might conjure the woman into their arms.

"Fatima."

"Azadeh."

"Maha."

Abdulghafur rasped, "Zaynab," then buried his face in his sleeve.

But Mustafa would not say her name. He would not give her up.

Now, today, in front of the mosque, standing beside Abdulmalik, he could only follow his love's example. Zaytuna would expect him to carry on despite further risk to his reputation. The risk itself would only drive her deeper into the fight. No matter what Nabil had done, the man's life had value. Everyone must see that. He could not turn away now. He replied to Abdulmalik with a verse from the Quran. "*If God helps you, none can overcome you. If God forsakes you, who could help you after Him? Let the believers put all their trust in Him.*"

"Surely God speaks the truth, but God's help may be to remove you from this mosque, your studies, and your future in Baghdad as a scholar."

"I must."

"Watch yourself," Abdulmalik said, then left him standing on his own.

Young students and those, like Mustafa, whose careers had just begun, were streaming through the wide arched entrance to the mosque. They would gather to chat and debate ideas before the great scholars arrived and their classes began. Each dreamed of having their own designated teaching spot by a pillar someday. Their reputations solidified, they would be ones whose works would be copied, not the ones who copied the works of others.

But Mustafa could no longer hope.

It was not just Burhan and the influence he wielded through his father. Mustafa did not have the wealth to travel for months or years on end, even though YingYue's father was willing to take over his daughter's care completely. And without travel to hear hadith directly from those who had the shortest lines of transmission between themselves and the Prophet Muhammad, he would never have the breadth of knowledge to do more than teach children.

Sherwan Ibn Salah had advised him to branch out, encouraging him to sit with scholars from other fields of study that would not require him to leave Baghdad. Mustafa was young enough to change specializations, Ibn Salah argued. Study of the law was a good path for a man with his knowledge of hadith. He spoke well of Mustafa among his own, and Mustafa loved him for his efforts to raise his reputation. But after Mu'mina's case, after he had debased himself making legal excuses for her suffering, he could not bear the law. So he had drifted from the community of hadith scholars to the edges of Ibn Mujahid's circles of Quran recitation, only to feel even more hopeless as he learned how much he did not know and despaired of ever fully understanding.

Tein and Ammar finally turned the corner from the Basra Gate High Road. Mustafa weakened as they approached, afraid of what would happen when they interviewed the scholars and students, but stood firm for Zaytuna.

"Assalamu alaykum, Tein, Ammar."

"Wa alaykum assalam. Ready?" Ammar asked.

"Anything we need to know before we go in?"

"We will be meeting with Ibn Mujahid's students first. Nabil is the student of his rival, Ibn Shanabudh. There is real hatred between the two. Each thinks the other is compromising the preservation of God's revelation."

Tein asked, "Bahr Ibn Abi Shuayb is one of Ibn Mujahid's students?"

"Bahr?" Mustafa asked.

"Zaytuna got the name." Tein eyed him, seeming to expect a reaction, then said, "Nabil's mother blames Bahr. Says he was trying to ruin Nabil."

Mustafa prickled under his stare, fearing she had told him more than that.

"Then we're looking at a scholarly rivalry," said Ammar.

"And what the manuscript means to them." Tein finally broke his stare and turned to Ammar. "If there's nothing else, then?"

Mustafa stopped them. "Please probe carefully. There may be no involvement at all. These are not the typical men you interviewed when you were police. I will bring you to the circle I frequent. I think it is best to start there. Be careful not to expose one of them, a Turkmen student, Ulgen. It was he who brought me to Nabil's mother."

"And this Bahr?"

"I do not know him."

"Don't worry." Ammar clapped him on the shoulder, an encouragement that did nothing to put him at ease.

"Also, too," he stammered. "Burhan, the son of Qadi Abu Burhan, the man who represented Ibn Hisham in court. He is in the mosque. He will recognize you, Ammar."

Ammar raised his eyebrows. "Then very much like the men we interviewed when we were police."

"All I am saying, brothers, is please take care. I am also a student."

Tein said, "We don't need you."

Mustafa stepped back, shame rising again from all that Tein implied, then he steadied himself. He must do this. He repeated to himself the verse, *If God helps you, none can overcome you.* "No, I will come. You do need me."

They slipped off their boots and shoes and followed Mustafa inside. Students clad in wraps thrown over their shoulders sat on the mosque carpets or sheepskins near pillars, reading, waiting, talking, debating.

Ibn Shanabudh's students were on the far side of the mosque. His circles were small by comparison to Ibn Mujahid and those studying hadith and law, but impressive all the same.

Abdulmalik and Mustafa's colleagues studying hadith were on the same side, but closer to the entrance to the imam's quarters, near the mihrab facing Mecca. His friends had their backs to the entrance. Thankfully, Burhan, with his small group of four students, was seated behind a pillar and could not see him.

Nearest to the mosque entrance, Ibn Mujahid's students, some three hundred or more, gathered around scores of his teaching assistants, taking up nearly one quarter of the mosque space. Low writing desks were set out around some; for others, reading stands; for others, nothing at all. The teaching assistants were distinguished by scholars' turbans. Mustafa looked among them for Ibn Hammad.

"This way."

Abdulkhabir ibn Hammad had already begun the lecture. He

listened to a student reading from a manuscript laid open on a stand, then stopped him, correcting him forcefully. Although he had turned out to be even-handed with his students as Ulgen promised, Ibn Hammad's stark face and brusque manner had made him seem frightening at first. One student, the fawning Kadan, was nodding eagerly at Ibn Hammad's comment and, as always, touching his ear as if tapping a drum. But another noticed the three men approaching and signalled to his teacher. The students whispered to each other as Ibn Hammad stood to greet them.

"Assalamu alaykum, Teacher." Mustafa bowed his head, hand over his heart.

"Wa alaykum assalam..." He paused, seemingly searching for Mustafa's name. "Have you brought us new companions?"

"This is Tein ibn al-Ashiqa as-Sawda and Ammar at-Tabbani. They were investigators for Grave Crimes with the Baghdad Police, but are now looking into private matters. Umm Nabil has asked them to investigate her son's disappearance."

"May you have success in finding him." He gazed at them expectantly.

Tein answered his unspoken question. "Mustafa suggested you could help. If we could ask you a few questions."

"What can we do? He was not one of us. He was one of Ibn Shanabudh's students." He gestured across the mosque where a group among them was watching the conversation unfold.

"We will be speaking to them, too," Ammar said. "Do you remember anything from the day he disappeared?"

The teacher responded with a gracious, yet empty, expression.

Kadan stood strong, while other students struggled to hold their tongues. He prayed one of them would break with propriety and say something, even though their teacher had instructed them not to through his own silence.

Ulgen tipped his chin to Mustafa. He wanted to say something, but not now, not in front of the others.

Mustafa gestured subtly that he understood.

"All the same, did you see him leave with anyone?" Ammar asked.

No one gave in immediately. But Tein and Ammar did not give in to the discomfort of silence.

The standoff lasted only a few moments longer, until the student who had been reading from the manuscript spoke, but only to reiterate his teacher's refusal to give them anything. "He was not with us. As we said, he was not one of our colleagues."

Ibn Hammad shook his head at his students to refrain them from speaking any further.

Tein said, "Now that, there, you don't want them to speak. If he has nothing to do with you, why would you be worried about what your students might say?"

Mustafa was shocked at this provocation and wanted to apologize to his teacher.

But the question did not fluster Ibn Hammad. On the contrary, he replied firmly, "We do not take part in the spread of gossip."

"Helping us find a man who may have come to some harm by sharing what you know is not gossip."

"Maybe you can help us with another matter?" Ammar asked. "We visited a paper shop in the Karkh Great Market that provides block printed prayers and is experimenting with printing short volumes."

"Abu YingYue," Ibn Hammad said, without glancing at Mustafa. "A fine man."

His father-in-law had informed him last night about Nabil's visit to the paper shop. The implications for his family could not be overstated. Mustafa put a hand on Ammar's arm, hoping he would rethink what he was about to say and that his father-in-law would be protected.

But Ammar did not acknowledge the touch. "Abu YingYue reported that Nabil had approached him to block print a manuscript of the Quran."

To a man, they gasped. Some students exclaimed, "God protect us from evil things!" Others cursed Nabil under their breath. All stood and joined their teacher, crowding Mustafa, Tein, and Ammar for answers. Ibn Hammad gestured for them to stop, and they stepped back.

"Abu YingYue confirmed he had a manuscript in hand?" Ibn Hammad asked.

"Yes," Tein replied.

"Was it a copy of the caliph Uthman's codex or a reading tradition in keeping with it?" Ibn Hammad was unable to hide his concern and Kadan moved in close behind him.

"Let me be clear," Tein started. "Abu YingYue refused his request. Not only because block printing even the caliph Uthman's codex has not been done and could not be done without consultation of the scholars, perhaps not even without the permission of the caliph himself, but specifically because Nabil wanted all the markings of only one specific reading tradition included."

"This is just like Nabil." Ibn Hammad had lost patience. "Ya Rabb! The trouble he stirs!"

"Perhaps it was for personal copies of his own preferred reading of the Quran in keeping with the codex?" one student suggested. "For his family?"

"Uff!" another exclaimed. "He is Ibn Shanabudh's student. Why would he accept a reading tradition that respected the blessed boundaries of the caliph Uthman's codex?"

A third student said bitterly, "Perhaps Ibn Shanabudh requested it."

Mustafa thought of YingYue's observation that all of this might be about slandering Ibn Shanabudh and glanced over at them. The attention of one circle of students among them had not wavered. They would need to be questioned next.

A student turned on his fellow, his face red with distress. "You fool, Ibn Shanabudh would never. The point here is that Nabil wanted it printed!"

Another finished for him. "It could be reprinted how many times over, sent out to the people, mosques, put in caravans, sent to the far ends of the empire where people may not know better. It could be seen as the decided reading! And what reading?"

The bitter student spoke again. "If Ibn Shanabudh has done this, he should be brought before the Mazalim High Court. Imam Ibn Mujahid should be told..."

But Ibn Hammad cut him off. "Ibn Shanabudh would do no such a thing. It is directly opposed to his teaching. He does not want to limit the readings. He would be pleased to expand them well beyond what is reliable, simply to satisfy his own arrogance. God protect us from evil things. Perhaps you should sit with him and understand."

The red-faced student, astonished, exclaimed, "God has put Nabil in harm's way to protect the Quran itself."

Ibn Hammad ignored him, but his expression revealed that he wished to shut the conversation down. Still he asked, "Abu YingYue refused, you are certain?"

"Yes," Tein replied. "Absolutely."

Mustafa prayed for his father-in-law's safety and that this conversation would end.

"Nabil is not fit to be a scholar," a student said. "He imagines himself to be a latter day Ibn Masud, escaping Uthman's clutches with his personal copy, claiming it, and only it, is correct!"

Ibn Hammad stared at him coldly and the student retreated behind another man.

Tein stepped in close to Ibn Hammad. "What about that did you not like?"

"It is only the shock of the insult to a companion of the Prophet, Ibn Masud, may God be well pleased with him. Ibn Masud mistook the Prophet's direction to use certain chapters as prayers to mean that the chapters themselves were prayers and not Quran at all. He left with his personal manuscript in full sincerity."

Mustafa nodded vigorously, wishing he had known this when YingYue questioned him.

"Nabil claimed to have a manuscript and refused to present it." Ibn Hammad sighed with resignation. "He said he feared us taking it from him and destroying it as the Caliph Uthman sought to destroy Ibn Masud's manuscript."

The other man put his hand over his heart and apologized. "We mean to say that Nabil only sought attention."

"None of you knew what was in his manuscript?" Ammar asked.

"No." Ibn Hammad answered for them. "We assumed it was an empty boast."

Ammar asked, "And this matter never came to blows?"

The teacher forced a chuckle. Kadan and the others followed him, cracking smiles. Ibn Hammad said, "If we had known he was trying to print it, perhaps. But more likely we would have taken it to Ibn Mujahid. It might even be a matter for the High Court, although that would have to be determined with due process."

Another said, "Walla, I assure you we did not know he intended to print it."

Mustafa wished he could make them say "walla" to the rest, to vow that what they had said was true. Ulgen had given him no details other than that Nabil claimed to have a manuscript, but from the way they talked, he felt in his heart that these men were lying. How could he return to sit with them again? Then again, he suspected they would not wish him to return either.

The teacher gestured again to Ibn Shanabudh's students. One was still watching and Mustafa noticed with dread that Burhan was watching, too, from a pillar nearby. "As I said, he is Ibn Shanabudh's student and it is on him to control his own students. But Ibn Shanabudh, for all his wrongs, would never agree to printing any copy of the Quran."

Tein and Ammar seemed to accept it, bowing their heads in farewell, and Ammar saying, "We'll speak to them now."

Mustafa turned, vowing to tell them exactly what he thought once they were outside.

But Ibn Hammad held him back. With the exception of Ulgen, they all turned on him.

"We thank you for having studied with us, brother," Ibn Hammad began. "But it is time you returned to hadith study. There is nothing more we can offer you at your level of competence."

He bit his tongue from rejoining that he could no longer sit with liars who claimed devotion to God's revelation but would hide information that might mean the salvation of a man's life. Instead, his eyes pricked with tears. His reputation was once and for all ruined.

Wordless, he fled them to join Tein and Ammar, who had not yet reached Ibn Shanabudh's students at the far side of the mosque.

They were in mid-conversation, Ammar saying, "These men are too easy to trip up."

"We'll have it out of them in no time," Tein responded.

Burhan was still standing by a pillar close enough to hear whatever they said to Ibn Shanabudh's students. And anything said in Burhan's hearing would be repeated. While there was no hope for Mustafa, he did not want his father-in-law's name mentioned.

Mustafa tugged at Tein's sleeve. "Come outside, please, for a moment."

They shrugged and followed him.

At the entrance, he begged, "Please do not mention Abu YingYue again. He will be implicated in some men's minds."

Tein apologized sincerely. "Of course. We should have spoken to you first."

Ammar agreed, but Mustafa could tell he did not regret it.

"Mustafa." Ulgen called them quietly from around the corner, gesturing for them to follow him. "Come, come!"

They hurried over to find Ulgen standing with another man, his hood pulled over his face.

"I could not speak in front of them, you must understand," Ulgen said breathlessly.

"Tell us." Ammar said.

Ulgen put his hand on the man's shoulder. "You must hear what Bahr has to say."

Tein shot Ammar a look.

Bahr was broad-shouldered, built like a man who could carry a sheep on his shoulders, yet he was fidgeting nervously. His thick auburn beard grew high on his cheeks, which were visibly flushed. "Nabil." He tugged his hood down further. "He and I are from the same town."

Ammar took a step forward, saying again, "Tell us."

"His father was a gambler, a drunkard. He lost everything, brought shame down on his own family. Left them penniless when he died. You will hear about this. So I must explain."

Tein and Ammar did not seem surprised. Zaytuna must have discovered it in her interview with Umm Nabil. *My love*, he thought, *we could find this man together if only they would allow us.*

"We fought, and it came to blows."

"The fight. What was it about?"

"He believed I would expose him. I had been in Baghdad for years before he and his mother arrived, but of course I already knew about his father." He paused. "And Nabil's habits."

"How did he respond?" Tein asked.

"Nabil threatened he would kill me, or worse."

"Worse?"

"Destroy my reputation." He glanced at Ulgen and Mustafa. "Future generations will make decisions about our reliability, the reliability of our contributions, based on reputation. Just as we consider the reliability of men in the past. Even rumours might be reported when my name comes up. I might no longer be considered reliable. All these years, ruined."

Mustafa chilled, knowing this end had already come for him.

"I told him I had no interest in such a fight, but I would not give into threats. He was ruining his own reputation."

"What happened?"

"He pushed me and we fought. We grew up on farms, scrapping with the other boys. We know how to fight and when to retreat, but he kept going." He paused. "I grabbed hold of his throat to show him he had gone far enough, but he pried a finger off, from my writing hand you understand, and tried to break it. I gave up."

"What happened after?"

"He walked away victorious. Prancing like a horse delighting in its finery."

"Did others at the mosque see him walk away?"

"Several did. As I said, I wanted you to hear about the fight from me first. Know, too, that I never exposed him. I do not want the sin of shaming him on my soul."

"And the attitude of them in there?" Tein gestured to the mosque.

Bahr frowned disdainfully. "He had not one friend. I do not understand why Ibn Shanabudh let him continue to join his circle. Very much like Ibn Shanabudh, to go against all that is settled to allow a man like Nabil to sit with him."

"Oh?" Ammar asked.

His cheeks flushed again, this time in anger. "Nabil is a symptom of Ibn Shanabudh's disease."

Perhaps YingYue was right, Mustafa thought.

Tein interrupted as if he could hear Mustafa's thoughts, "So you would prefer that Nabil be exposed and bring down Ibn Shanabudh with him?"

Bahr was surprised by the accusation. "Ibn Shanabudh is already counted among the blameworthy, an innovator, by some of our greatest Quran scholars. He does not need one such as Nabil to do the work for him. Ibn Shanabudh will never be revered by future generations. But if he is not careful, he may find that Imam Ibn Mujahid has him brought before the court."

"That's the second time today we've heard about Ibn Mujahid's powers to bring a man before the Mazalim High Court," Tein remarked.

"I can see you do not have the requisite knowledge to understand what is at stake."

Ammar sniggered.

Mustafa did not condone Bahr's high-handedness, but he wanted to intervene and explain—Muslims far and wide must have safe pastures, certainty rather than confusion—but he held back. Not now, and not in front of Ammar.

"All to say, sirs, while none of us would mind if we were to hear Nabil's body had been dragged from the river, we had no need to put him there ourselves."

Ammar smiled slowly, saying, "No one here mentioned that Nabil might have been murdered."

Bahr faltered only for a moment. "If something has happened to him, look to Ibn Shanabudh's men. I would not put it past anyone who insists on preserving these unacceptable readings as equally reliable to the caliph Uthman's codex. As for us, when his mother came to the mosque begging for help, we stood with her, and one of our men even walked her to the police."

Ulgen turned his head sharply and stared. "That man was me. I walked her to the police because no one else would, not even Ibn Shanabudh's people. Nabil's sins should not stain his mother." He put his hand on Mustafa's shoulder. "Nor a scholar's reputation because he does what is right."

Mustafa felt Ulgen's defence, and wanted to embrace him.

"And, so you know," Ulgen continued, "the police would not help."

Bahr seemed chastened. "May God reward you, Ulgen." But then he raised his eyebrows in Tein and Ammar's direction. "Yet that does not explain their involvement."

"A mother's son is lost." Mustafa declared, "There is no end to the means we will use to find him."

"You may wish there were," Bahr replied ominously. He bowed his head and left.

Tein loosened his body to fight and went to go after him, but Mustafa grasped his sleeve. "No, please."

Ulgen took a wide berth around Tein and followed Bahr back to the mosque.

Ammar said, as if he had not understood what had befallen Mustafa, "We have to go back in there and question Ibn Shanabudh's students."

"You cannot. Please."

Ammar said, "We'll go in without you."

"They already saw me with you," he pleaded.

Ammar shrugged. "Then the damage has been done."

"I am ruined," he cried.

Tein put his hand on his arm. "No man is ruined for doing the right thing. We can walk away from this case now. You can tell people you convinced us to drop it."

Ammar huffed.

But Ammar was right, Mustafa knew. It was too late. Too late for his reputation. Too late for Zaytuna. All he had left to his name was his own conscience. He thought of YingYue at home, soft and delicate YingYue. What would she say in this moment? Mustafa imagined her tilting her head and replying, "As you like," then returning to her prayer. And Zaytuna? He did what he knew Zaytuna would want him to do. "Yes, yes. We must all go in and continue."

"Good, because there are a lot of people in there who would be glad to see this man dead." Ammar gestured behind them. "Including that one right there."

12

Tein led Mustafa and Ammar back into the mosque, but he wished he were walking away instead. He felt no obligation toward the mother or the son. If the world eats up people like this, then there is some justice. Who was he to stop it? He had lost himself for a moment when Bahr first approached, feeling obligated to stay and listen to a man he already disliked just by the way he held his body and tugged at the hood of his cloak. Nothing the man had said dissuaded him that his initial judgment was wrong. But the threats to Mustafa made his hands twitch to find their way around Bahr's throat. A few days back into a case and the killer in him had reappeared

How could Mustafa sacrifice himself this way for Nabil? For these people? Men who walked in the way of the Prophet embodied the principle of ithar, it is true. But Uncle Nuri cannot have meant sacrificing oneself to protect oppressors. He tried to conjure Uncle Nuri's voice within him for guidance.

A clear memory inhabited his inward vision. His uncle was telling him that he had once smashed wine jars as they passed by him in a cart bound for the palace. Not because it was wine—his uncle walked by taverns every day and never did a thing—but because the wine jars were a manifest sign of the caliph's corruption.

A hand grasped his shoulder, a finger pressing up under his chin. Tein stopped, unable to take another step. A melodious yet firm voice spoke, the words washing through him rather than heard. "Support your fellow, whether he is oppressing others or oppressed." Tein balked inwardly, but the voice answered, "By stopping him."

"What's wrong?" Ammar whispered over his shoulder. "Your head thrown back like that?"

His head dropped forward with the shock of Ammar's voice, but the words he had heard settled deeply within him. Tein did not know what had happened, but he knew what his mother and sister looked like when they fell into ecstasy.

For the first time in a long while, he wanted a drink.

Despite his resistance and his desire to run to the nearest tavern and pour a jug of wine into him until his head never tipped up like that again, he could not wrest free of the feeling that he must go ahead. He tried turning away, but his feet drove him forward, Ammar striding beside him, Mustafa hiding behind.

To a one, Ibn Shanabudh's men watched them approach, backs straight, ready to resist.

From beside his pillar, Burhan tracked them across the mosque.

Hand to his heart, Tein bowed his head to Ibn Shanabudh's students. "Assalamu alaykum."

The men returned his greeting and waited expectantly, giving nothing and not inviting them to sit.

Tein sat anyway, legs tucked underneath him, impossibly so given his old injury, but his thigh was warm and gave no trouble. Mustafa came out from behind and sat beside him, nearly touching. Ammar remained on his feet, taking a threatening stance in his leather cuirass, one hand on his sword. No doubt he was drawing even more attention to them from other parts of the mosque, but there was nothing he could do about it.

"One of your men is missing," Tein said. "Nabil ibn al-Qays al-Kufi. His mother asked us to find him. The police will not act. We hope you will help us."

A man in a deep blue turban spoke with a half-cocked smile. "You want us to go looking for him with you?"

"Fan out across the city, peering in every doorway and shuttered building?" another asked.

A man in an undyed cloak and narrowly wrapped turban pointed to Mustafa. "That one has drawn unwanted attention to this mosque."

Mustafa said under his breath, "God protect me."

But Tein surprised himself. He did not lash out for Mustafa's sake, but let them carry on, revealing themselves.

The man in the blue turban followed up. "Leave it and let Nabil take the consequences of his own actions without our aid."

"And if he is dead?" Tein asked.

"Then he is dead. May God forgive his sins."

"What consequences does Nabil need to face?" Tein continued.

No one seemed interested in answering the question, and not, he sensed, because it was a secret.

Ammar spoke. "We are not letting this case go. The mother has hired us to look for her son. As long as that money lasts, we're going to continue. And she gave us a great deal of money."

"The woman has no money. Nabil has no money." The man in the blue turban waved his hand. "Leave us."

Ammar took a step toward them. "You think I am trying to find this piece of shit..."

The men gasped at his use of language in the mosque.

"... and help that harridan of a mother out of my warm feeling for humankind?"

Tein felt eyes upon him, and turned to find that Burhan had taken a closer position, leaning on a nearby pillar and watching the scene unfold. He addressed Burhan directly. "Come and take a seat if you want to listen. I am sure these men do not mind. They have nothing to hide."

Burhan responded with a smug smile, then walked away.

Behind him, Mustafa whimpered.

"So Nabil is one of you," Tein said.

"If by that you mean that Nabil sits at the edge of our circle and Ibn Shanabudh has not asked him to leave, then yes."

"He makes trouble?"

A man from the back answered with an air of wanting it to be over, "He spoke out of turn. Made claims with no evidence. He had inadequate knowledge of grammar and poetry and was barely acquainted with the companions' reading traditions. He was familiar with the reading tradition of Hamza ibn Habib, but would often err even in what he did know." But as he listed Nabil's weaknesses, his voice rose, becoming incensed. "Despite his profound ignorance! Despite that, he would declare a vowel here, a word there, a phrase, a phrase should be changed! All without any evidence from any transmitted reading nor on the basis of language!"

A man glared at him to be quiet.

He became only more shrill. "And when asked where he got it, he claimed…," but then he did not finish the sentence. Instead, his eyes widened and he shut his mouth.

The man in the blue turban rolled his eyes at the display of emotion. "He claimed to have a copy of Ibn Masud's personal manuscript."

The others looked at him and shook their heads, except for the one in the undyed cloak.

"Subhanallah!" Mustafa exclaimed. "Ibn Masud's personal copy of the Quran? The one he wrote out himself sitting alongside the prophet all those years?"

"No, no, a copy. I said, 'a copy'."

Ammar asked, "And he claimed the differences he shared in class were from that text?"

"Yes," he said. "But you must understand, there is a copy of Ibn Masud's reading tradition in Kufa. There is no mystery to any of this. Nabil's claims did not always match that reading, nor any of the accounts we have of Ibn Masud's reading. Nabil lied."

"What did Ibn Shanabudh say?" Tein asked.

"He was patient with him."

"Perhaps he was more open to Nabil than you think?" Mustafa

asked tentatively. "Everyone recites from Ibn Masud where it is in agreement with the caliph Uthman's codex, but I understand that Ibn Shanabudh accepts even those parts where it does not."

The man in the undyed cloak glanced at him sideways, but his words were measured. "Yes. We prefer the reading traditions of the companions, the ones who were closest to the Prophet, alayhi salam. Further, we use our knowledge of Arabic grammar and language to determine what expressions might be most reliably Quran. Consider that if the Quran's language is inimitable, then surely our approach would be most effective at determining which of these differences in language among the transmitted recitations fits that criterion." He gestured in the direction of Ibn Mujahid's students. "What is their criterion? A template that allows for readings that, in some cases, stress the credulity of the Quran's exquisite Arabic expression?"

Beside Tein, Mustafa was trembling and muttering to himself. "Stresses credulity. God protect us from evil things and keep us in safe pastures." Tein could tell he was near tears and put a hand on his back to steady him.

"I don't buy any of this," Tein said. "Ibn Shanabudh kept this man around despite his ignorance. He must have had something Ibn Shanabudh wanted."

The man in the undyed cloak closed his eyes for a moment, then conceded. "The copy. He claimed to have an autographed copy."

Under Tein's hand, Mustafa became perfectly still.

Tein said, "You'll have to explain that."

"It is a copy, but he claims it was signed by Ibn Masud himself, verifying its accuracy."

"An artifact, a valuable one at that," the man in the blue turban said. "Ibn Shanabudh wanted to see it. Everyone wanted to see it."

And that everyone, Tein thought, included Ibn Mujahid's men.

"Wait, where would Nabil, a man like that, have gotten it?" Ammar asked.

"He would not tell us," another man in the group answered.

"How could he?" another said, exasperated. "It does not exist."

The men were silent, but there was more. Tein allowed his attention to move slowly from one man to another until they were so uncomfortable, one would inevitably give in. "We are not leaving until you tell us."

The man in the blue turban checked with the others. One shrugged, starting to sweat, but the rest remained quiet.

Tein addressed him pointedly. "Where is Ibn Shanabudh? Maybe we should ask him whether you should help?"

"He is in Kufa," one said boldly. "Will you go there to threaten him?"

"Tell me what would threaten you." Tein put his hand on his dagger. "I'll make that work."

The man stammered, "Nabil...he claimed that Ibn Masud declared in his own writing that he had read his copy back to the Prophet, may God bless him and peace, and that the Prophet had approved it. All of it. Even those parts that the caliph Uthman's men, the community of reciters, declared were in error."

His colleagues glared at him. The man shut his mouth hard.

Tein knew somehow it was not true, that no such manuscript existed. But Mustafa grew more distressed. He leaned in and whispered in Mustafa's ear, "This is a lie."

Ammar broke in. "Isn't the story that Uthman went to Ibn Masud and asked for his copy? Uthman wanted to destroy it, so Ibn Masud ran away with it instead?"

The man in the undyed cloak nodded slowly. "Others say he handed it over. No one has the original. The copy in Kufa is not an autograph. Valuable to Quran scholars, but we cannot be certain the reading in its entirety goes back to Ibn Masud. Which of us would not want to see a copy that Ibn Masud himself approved?"

"The claim that the Prophet himself approved it, that would be valuable to you," Tein said.

"Well, yes, to us. I do not suspect that Ibn Mujahid would welcome it so readily. It would call into question the soundness of the caliph Uthman's collection."

Ammar laughed with satisfaction.

"That is not so!" Mustafa objected. He got to his knees and it appeared as though he might attack the man for saying it. "Which among the companions accepted Ibn Masud's rejection of the first and last two chapters of the Quran? He was mistaken. God forgive him."

Tein wondered if this was the motive for Nabil's disappearance. "Are you claiming this manuscript implies that the caliph Uthman, friend and companion to the Prophet, gathered a false Quran?"

"No! Not a false Quran." The man in the undyed cloak sighed. "Uthman, may God be well-pleased with him, collected what everyone remembered to be true and excised that upon which they disagreed. You must understand no personal manuscript had power over this agreement among the early reciters. The community's reliability was held to be greater than any one claim."

"Safe pastures," Mustafa whispered through his tears.

There was something more to be probed in what the man had said, but the divisions between the two groups were becoming clearer. Ibn Mujahid only accepted variant readings that were bounded by the caliph Uthman's codex while Ibn Shanabudh preferred variant readings that could be traced back to the personal manuscripts of individual companions. If Ibn Mujahid's people thought this manuscript existed, what would they do to prevent it from being exposed?

Ammar said, "It sounds like you believe the manuscript is not a fake."

"How would we know unless we saw it?"

The one in the blue turban spoke up. "Ibn Shanabudh did not believe he had it. People have made such claims about different companions in the past." He looked directly at Ammar. "Charlatans, every one of them. Ibn Shanabudh expected he would demand money up front for an unseen manuscript, then disappear. He was waiting for Nabil to show his hand, at which point we were to take hold of him and make an example of him."

Ammar responded with bravado. "If it were real, it would expose the caliph Uthman as a liar and the whole early community as liars, preferring themselves over the truth. Seyyidina Ali..."

The man cut him off harshly. "I suspected! You are one of those Shia who believe that the caliph Ali's personal manuscript is the true

Quran. Do you not even follow your own Shia Imams? Your own Imams have a copy of the caliph Ali's manuscript themselves and they accept the caliph Uthman's codex."

The man in the blue turban countered. "Is that why you all are here?"

Tein held his hands out. "No. Please. But Ibn Mujahid and his people could not have been eager for that manuscript to be exposed."

Ammar pushed through. "They would want to destroy it, to finish what Uthman started."

Tein grumbled, wishing Ammar would stay out of it.

"Again, Ibn Shanabudh wanted to see it before making any judgment," the man in the undyed cloak said, eying Ammar with irritation. "Its existence was no threat to us. Ibn Shanabudh would not even have accepted it on the basis of the signature alone. He would have put it to the same test of language as we do every other reading."

Tein asked again, gesturing to the students on the other side of the mosque. "Did Ibn Mujahid know?"

"Well, that is just the thing." The man paused. "He did."

"My God," exclaimed Mustafa.

Tein remembered how the students had looked at each other when one of them brought up Ibn Masud's manuscript. He turned toward Ibn Mujahid's group and was not surprised to find them staring. Bahr was standing further off by a pillar but watching, too. The manuscript did not exist. He knew it in his gut as surely as he knew he was sitting before these men in the mosque. But if Ibn Mujahid's people thought it did, who knows what they would do to protect the reading traditions that come through the caliph Uthman's codex?

"Ibn Mujahid demanded that he produce the manuscript," the man in the undyed cloak continued. "But Nabil announced that Ibn Mujahid's own student Bahr had seen it and could vouch for it."

"And Bahr?"

"He denied having seen it, of course."

"Right then and there, Ibn Mujahid had Bahr pulled out of the crowd and demanded that he take an oath that the only true recitation would be that in accordance with the Uthman's codex, warning him of the tortures in the next world."

"When did this happen?"

The man in the blue turban lifted his eyebrows. "The day Nabil went missing."

Tein jumped to his feet, but Ammar was already running to the side of the mosque where Ibn Mujahid's people were seated. Mustafa followed, passing Tein, as Bahr sprinted for the door and escaped through the entrance with Ammar not far behind. Hundreds of men in the mosque, seated or standing, watched in shock. By the time Tein reached the entrance, only Mustafa was in sight.

"He is gone."

"Let's hope Ammar got hold of him."

Within minutes, Ammar came back, breathing hard. "If he's smart, he'll be headed out of Baghdad," he said angrily.

Mustafa gasped. "Bahr killed him over the manuscript."

Tein heard himself say, again not knowing where the certainty came from, "There is no manuscript."

Ammar snapped, "You don't know that."

Tein shrugged. But Uncle Nuri would demand that he stay on the job to prove it.

13

The house was quiet except for muffled noise from their alley. The call of the oil salesman and the sound of children running past drifted over the wall. Zaytuna stood over a basket of wet laundry, the line stretched overhead. Layla was under the pomegranate tree jumping at a branch, trying to grasp one of the ripe fruits.

"Layla, please. Your hands will get stained. Wait until after we finish the laundry."

She gave Zaytuna a long face, moped over to the basket, and pulled out a vibrantly coloured wrap. Zaytuna took the wrap from the girl, shook it out, then folded it so it would fit on the line with the other clothes. The two had washed clothes for countless houses back in the days when they were glad to have thickly calloused hands and lived with the worry of critical inspections by housekeepers eager to dock them the bit of coin they had earned. Now, because of Kamal Ali, their hands were softening, she had only herself to please, and Layla was free to complain.

Zaytuna lifted her face to the sun, enjoying the morning's peace. Yulduz and Qambar would be gone most of the day, having made the long walk across the pontoon bridge to visit her friend Marta for a family feast day. Saliha was at work. Tein and Ammar had gone to meet Mustafa at the mosque.

Mustafa.

She returned her attention to the wrap on the line, tugging it straight more than was necessary. At the thought of Mustafa, her stomach began to nag her again, fearing that yesterday was not the end of it. She had left him at Uncle Abd al-Qasim's home. Ziri, who saw everything from his post at the door, understood immediately and led him inside, but she feared he would be back for her.

The sun and quiet of the morning suddenly became oppressive. Where a moment ago, Layla's silence had been sweet, now it had become a concern. The girl should have been nattering away in the background about all the little things in her day. The long face she gave earlier now seemed to be more than a childish complaint.

The laundry hung, Zaytuna retreated to the dappled shade of the tree, resting on pillows, while Layla resumed her efforts to grasp one of the last of the season's pomegranates. The girl circled the tree, making plans to climb it. Zaytuna breathed deeply, and took small sips of water to settle her nagging stomach.

Having found a foothold, Layla was up in the tree, legs hanging down, the pomegranate she sought in one hand. Eyes on the fruit, she asked guardedly, "How is the case, Auntie?"

There it was. She had not imagined it. Despite her assurances yesterday, the girl was still worried that she would leave Kamal Ali and their family and this life they shared now would be broken apart. Zaytuna could not blame her.

"Do you remember the woman from the graveyard, Saadia? I'm going to see her today. I'll leave once you are off to Rana and Sara's mother."

"I could come with you."

"You already promised your friends. I'm going to sit with some wealthy women and listen to their gossip."

After a moment, Layla asked what she really wanted to know. "Alone?"

"Yes." Zaytuna answered. "Remember when you asked me, just

after I agreed to marry Kamal Ali, whether I would be sorry if Mustafa and YingYue divorced and I could have him back?"

Layla did not answer, but leaned into the trunk of the tree, wrapping one arm around it, the pomegranate in the other hand.

"That time has come. Mustafa and YingYue's marriage isn't what they hoped it would be. But you need to know that this marriage of mine is more than I could have imagined. I love Kamal Ali. I love our life together. I love this life with you all."

The girl let out a small cry. The pomegranate fell from her hand and exploded, a few seeds spattering the clean laundry. Zaytuna sprang up and stood under the tree, holding out her arms. "Come, girl."

Layla slipped down out of the tree and into her embrace. "You promise you won't meet with Mustafa?"

"I want to do what I can without him, that's all." She wiped Layla's tears away with the edge of her wrap. "You go get ready to leave."

Layla let go and stood back. "What do I tell Uncle Kamal Ali when he gets back from work?"

"I am going to see him as soon as I send you off." She took the girl's chin in her hand. "No matter what, that's not for you to do. It's never for you to protect us. It's for us to protect you."

Layla threw her arms around Zaytuna's waist, then ran to her room.

Every choice she made hurt someone, but hurting Layla felt as bad as hurting Kamal Ali, maybe worse. Who was this girl who had found her way into her heart? The old dream returned. A fawn came to her, nosing through tall grasses in a meadow, and curled up against her to sleep. She had awakened to find Layla there, snuggled in her arms. Zaytuna wanted to hold Layla like that now, assuring her that she would give up anything for her. She asked herself if that was what it meant to be a mother.

Her own mother had given over the protection of her children to God, letting go of Zaytuna, her hands raised in the throes of ecstasy as the crowds crushed in on them. How could she be sure she would not abandon this girl, like her mother had her, now she fell into ecstatic states herself? She answered with a whispered prayer, "God protect her from me."

There were fewer pomegranate stains on the laundry than she expected. Zaytuna wet them before the flecks dried and set in for good, then arranged the worst out of sight. After, she set about cleaning up the fruit scattered on the ground.

Layla came out into the courtyard. Her face was bright, the worry allayed for now. Red-rimmed eyes were the only mark she had been upset. She stared at the clean courtyard, then at Zaytuna, and came close to tears again. "I should've cleaned it."

"It was nothing. Go." Zaytuna turned Layla's shoulders to face the door, kissed her on the head, and sent the girl off to her friends before she could object.

Zaytuna shut the door, then returned to the laundry to see if she could get out those stains. She gauged the time by the shadows in the courtyard. Getting out the stains and rehanging the laundry was going to make her late to see Saadia. Zaytuna pulled down the stained pieces from the line and hastily spot-cleaned each one and rehung them, tugging them straight again, this time with less care.

It would be a long walk to the pontoon bridge, then across the Tigris to Rusafa, and her visit had to be well-timed. She had to catch Saadia just after their midday meal and rest, but before she would leave for her afternoon visit with the women. But Kamal Ali's butter shop was in the opposite direction. Going there first would surely make her late.

She pulled her best wrap around her, the one Kamal Ali had given to her as a promise of their love, admiring, even in her rush, the abundance of pink flowers and green vines that surrounded her, and stepped out into the alley. The door shut behind her. She looked left, then right. To Saadia or Kamal Ali? She needed to speak to Kamal Ali first and if it made her late, so be it.

The roads and bridges to Buratha were busy with traffic. She looked over the side of the hospital bridge. Men with sacks on their backs trudged back and forth from the canal landings, while others steered basket boats along the water to the next landing for delivery. She strode across the bridge, weaving around the workers and walkers, and onto the next bridge until she was slowed behind two men who had dropped the load they were carrying between them.

For a moment she thought of turning back, but stayed where she was, allowing herself an exasperated sigh. A young woman carrying a heavy load scowled. Zaytuna saw her old self in her and wanted to assure her that all would be well, but did not know if it would be a lie or not. They filed past slowly, then she broke free wanting only to see her husband and feel his steady love.

At the market arch, she held back for a moment to enjoy the sight of him with his men from across the square. Kamal Ali looked pleased as he inspected the butter, put a hand on Malik's head, and hailed the delivery men as they prepared the carts to accept the amphoras of butter and jars of buttermilk. The donkeys twitched their ears and snorted. One brayed as she approached. Kamal Ali lifted his head and smiled at the sight of her. Zaytuna held out her hands as she hurried to him.

He met her halfway, but the gamey scent of fermented butter forced her to take a step back as her stomach turned again.

"My love, what's wrong?" He tried to come closer, but she took another step back.

She laughed, swallowing hard. "Who ordered fermented samn?"

"One of the jars was cracked, and I'm afraid it must have touched my clothes." He objected playfully, "But you have always loved my samn."

"A small spoon of it in a large pot of stew." She took his hands quickly, then stepped back again. "I wanted you to know that I am on an errand about the case today."

His face tensed.

She continued with emphasis, "I will not see Mustafa. I am visiting …"

"You do not need to tell me any of this," he interrupted, but the tension on his face was still there. "I trust you."

It made no sense. She had already betrayed him by being alone with Mustafa. That day, she had come home and told him that Mustafa had offered himself to her and she had rejected him. She shared how

Mustafa had broken down and how she had led him back to her uncle's so they could care for him, but she had not revealed how close she had come to joining him in that one terrible moment.

Instead of anger, he had expressed his sympathy for Mustafa, imagining the pain of losing her and understanding that too much had gone unsaid after the weddings.

"Why?" Zaytuna asked plaintively.

"Why do I trust you?"

"Yes."

"I trust our love."

She wanted to argue with him, warn him about the nagging feeling in her gut, urge him to save himself, to accept that she was not worthy of him.

"My husband." Her voice caught in her throat. "I never want to lose you."

His expression eased. "What will you be investigating today, habibti?"

"Saadia invited me to join a circle of her friends. The women may know some of the men involved or have heard gossip about the case."

"Only you can meet with these women, Zaytuna."

She grasped his hands again, not caring about the scent until it became too much, and sent her stomach reeling. Backing away, she said, "I must leave now if I am to get to Rusafa before Saadia leaves without me."

He looked up at the sky. "If you would prefer, stay for lunch with us, then take a skiff from the Isa Canal up the Tigris to Rusafa."

A skiff. She had never travelled on the river; river travel was for those who had more money than washing clothes could provide. She balked, feeling such kindnesses were not for her. Then, taking in her husband's open and generous face, she told herself, *Maybe good things are for you.*

Malik came out of the market with lunch for the men.

"Come and eat with us."

They walked together to the table where Malik was laying out long loaves of seeded bread, grapes, nuts, fried pastries stuffed with meat, and dried sausages. Kamal Ali pulled out a chair for her, a bit away from everyone else. Malik gave a questioning look, but she answered him with a crinkled nose. "You all smell like samn."

The boy made her a plate and brought it to her with his usual flourish and a "Ya bismillah," but her stomach turned, and the sight and scent of the food was too much for her.

Only then did she see Tein was there. He came out of the back of the warehouse, where they stored the clean amphoras and buried the butter to ferment. He stopped at the sight of her, then smiled, and came to greet her.

She would have held her hand out to stop him, but with all the men now milling around the table, tearing off bread, popping nuts into their mouths, and biting into sausages, there was no escaping his embrace.

"Ugh, you all stink." She pushed him off. "I thought you were with Ammar at the mosque."

"I just got here, and I'm headed back to Ammar soon." He glanced at Kamal Ali and said loudly, "I could not keep from the churn."

Kamal Ali bowed his head in thanks and went back to eating.

"You prefer this to investigating?"

He did not answer, but she knew he would gladly never work a case again while she knew she could not live without it.

"I came to let Kamal Ali know I was going to visit Saadia and meet her friends."

Tein picked up a pastry, giving her a wary look. "Did you mention that the family is close with Mustafa?"

Kamal Ali's face tensed again. She did not understand why Tein would bring that up when she was doing all she could today to set things right. But, the truth was, it had not occurred to her that Mustafa might be eating lunch with Saadia's brother, Ibn Salah. Was there no escaping him? She reached out to touch Kamal Ali. "I forgot. I won't go, then."

Tein stroked the sparse beard on his chin. "When the servant comes to the door, can you say it is private? Ask to have them bring you to Saadia without mentioning it to the men?"

"If he was there, he would have left already. I'll be there after their midday rest." But then she realized that Saadia would relish putting them together, and expecting her arrival, might keep him from leaving. She answered herself as much as them, "I won't go."

Kamal Ali stood. "This matter is between the two of you. But I believe you should go."

When Kamal Ali was in the warehouse and out of earshot, Tein sighed, then said, "I trust you."

She pressed her hand against her pained stomach. "Can I trust myself?"

"Show yourself that you can." He half-joked, "I can't be everywhere."

Not long ago, the old Tein, stuck in taverns and misery, would have agreed with her, bitterly grumbling that neither of them had a right to trust anyone, let alone themselves. She took strength from him. "I will show myself I can."

"Eat." Tein gestured to the food.

"You sound like Yulduz." She took a tentative bite of bread. But the touch of hope had settled her gut. The calming waters approached, although still at a distance. Her appetite leapt at them and she hungrily cleared her plate.

"Now," Tein said, "let me tell you what we found out at the mosque."

14

After lunch, Kamal Ali escorted Zaytuna to a landing on the Isa canal to catch a skiff. He helped her in, then paid the man. More money was in her pocket, so much she could hire a litter to return home. The skiff pushed away and she murmured, "Trust yourself."

Never had Zaytuna seen the city traveling by boat within its great canals. The walls of estates, homes, and small markets swept by above the grassy banks until a landing appeared. Workers loaded and unloaded skiffs and round basket boats. She strained to see past the ruined walls of Birkat Zalzal just coming into view. As children, she and Tein had cooled their feet in its pool and played among its trees. People were strolling the grounds and she saw a child being chased by another and wished she could slow the boat to touch that memory a moment longer.

A skiff with a small covered cabin passed them. The boatman had already raised the sail, rather than steering by the current alone. The wind blew away the gauzy curtains, revealing a couple sitting stiffly, looking away from one another. She vowed to hold on to the happiness she had in hand. Soon Zaytuna's boatman had raised the sail and they were out onto the Tigris. She gripped the seat, expecting a turbulent fight against the river's swift current, but it went smoothly and the boatman chuckled at her fear. She laughed with him, releasing herself into the glittering sunlight and the bite of the wind off the water.

Too soon, the skiff thudded alongside the sandy bank of the landing nearest the pontoon bridge connecting east and west Baghdad. Two boys tugged it in. She climbed out onto the dry bank to walk up the steep path to the road into Rusafa, leaving behind the exultation of the river for growing unease of the task ahead.

The last time she walked to their home, Saadia's brother, Ibn Salah, had disinterestedly argued with her about the legalities of using enslaved women for sex. Angry, Zaytuna had countered, ruthlessly exposing the grim experiences of the women his hypothetical reasoning was meant to govern. Embarrassed, Mustafa had made excuses for her. By the time they reached the house and she was shuttled off to sit with women who gaped at the sight of her poverty at their table, Zaytuna had enough of these classes and Mustafa's fine feeling for them.

Today, despite wearing clothes fine enough to go through the front door, part of her wanted to go around to the servants' entrance. But she knocked on the outer gate used by guests, reminding herself she was there for a case, not to be heartsore for how she had been treated nearly a year ago.

A sweet-faced boy in a jaunty uniform of quilted blue wool opened the door.

"I am here to see Saadia bint Salah. I am Zaytuna bint al-Ashiqa as-Sawda."

If the boy was surprised at the oddness of her name or that she was too late for lunch and too early for visitors, he did not show it. He invited her in with a genuine welcome. His easy manner could only mean a housekeeper with a good heart and a family who did not abuse their servants. She reluctantly chose to give Saadia another chance.

The boy did not leave her in the outer courtyard, but brought her directly into the reception room. She slipped off her shoes and he placed a beautiful pair of red shearling slippers before her. The thick wool lining cradled her stockinged feet, every little bone settling into the softness of them.

The room was brightly decorated in jewel tones and hues of gold. Thickly cushioned low couches were strewn with striped silk pillows tied off with gold-threaded tassels. Five small hammered copper trays resting on carved wooden stands were set out so no guest would have to stretch their hand for refreshments. The ashes in the hearth were banked and nearly burnt down, but the early afternoon sun warmed the floors and the room.

Before Zaytuna could sit, she heard the scuff of slippers and within a moment Saadia stood in an inner door.

"Ahlan!" Saadia embraced her warmly, then stepped back. She touched her cheek with one finger. The voluminous sleeve of her green velvet house robe slipped back elegantly.

Under Saadia's discerning eye, Zaytuna's precious wrap suddenly seemed dingy. She felt as she did before, pitied for her poverty, and nearly turned around to leave.

But Saadia clapped her hands, commanding, "Come with me! I have taken the liberty of laying out some clothes that will make you feel more comfortable."

Zaytuna followed her through the courtyard to the stairs. The first and second floor arcades were built of stuccoed brick and decorated with carved vegetal and geometric repeating patterns. Upstairs, they passed by arched windows and doors inset around the walkway. Saadia's room was on the far side, out of the sun. The painted door was wide open, but a beautiful curtain of Turkmen bound-dyed cream and purple silk covered the doorway and moved with the breeze. Saadia held it open for her. Inside, oil lamps set into niches lit the room. Thick carpets were laid end to end. A beautifully carved wood cabinet stood on one side, a trunk on the other. Low couches were set into one corner, with two small copper tray tables in front. The bed was raised off the floor and big enough for a family to sleep on. The blankets and pillows could not be seen for the number of clothes laid out across it.

Saadia put out her hand to invite her to choose, but Zaytuna hung back.

Imagining the most luxurious clothes she had seen in the marketplace, she thought she knew what to expect, but she was overwhelmed. Gowns, robes, and wraps of sumptuous fabric were tossed on the bed as if they were nothing. One was printed with strange birds floating through forests of tiny pale green leaves and pink flowers. Others were embroidered or cut with sleeves so long it seemed they might reach the floor. Dense beading sparkled like jewels in the lamplight. All were embellished with piping and embroidery in such tiny stitches it would have taken months upon months to produce.

"Thank goodness! We have just enough time to dress you and style your hair."

Zaytuna touched her faded head cloth, tied back in a bun. Through the cloth, she felt her mother's bead threaded through her one matted lock. A flash of anger tore through her, but a voice informed her temper with perfect clarity. *No one will touch any part of you.*

A maid, older, heavy bodied and soft-faced, entered and took Zaytuna's wrap off her shoulders before she realized what was happening. She flinched, jerking forward and nearly released biting words on the elder, but trapped them at the last second, unwilling to hurt a servant for what her mistress had instructed her to do. The maid stepped back, giving Zaytuna room.

"Shaheen, let's start with her hair."

"No," Zaytuna said.

"But we remove our head coverings in each other's presence, do you… "

"You do. I will not." She said it easily, without emotion, and wondered at herself.

Saadia made a face as if she were in the presence of a stubborn child.

"Then at least you must change the head wrap." She leaned over the bed, picking through the scarves and placing them next to the gowns.

Shaheen remained at a distance, waiting.

She would not change herself for these people, nor should she. "I will not wear them. But understand, as far as what you want, you may dress me in these clothes, but I cannot wear them."

Saadia understood. "They would know you for your station."

"Will they accept me as I am, if I say I am there about the case?"

"It is best not to begin with that. Although once the conversation begins, they may become intrigued." She gave her an encouraging half-smile. "Intriguing these women is the way."

"I need a story about why I am there."

Saadia considered. "Your mother."

"Excuse me?"

"I mentioned that Mustafa had recited her poetry to us."

"Not my mother. You won't use her."

"Shush. I will simply explain that, as your mother's daughter, you are also a lover of poetry and mysticism."

"You said these women are scholars of the Quran or married to them."

"They are, but also lovers of poetry and mysticism." She raised her eyebrows. "Well, with one exception, but they will welcome you. Trust me."

If that was all, Zaytuna felt she could manage it.

"Shaheen, tell Yasmin to bring us some of those gazelle horn cookies that Mustafa loves so much." She faced Zaytuna, bright eyed. "He was here for lunch today. It is a shame you were not with us."

Without being invited, Zaytuna sought out a couch in the corner and sat heavily. Before she could stop herself, she asked, "How did he seem?"

"Seem?" The woman could barely hide her curiosity.

"Nothing." She recovered. "Tein said Mustafa had not been feeling well."

"Hmm," Saadia said slowly. "Yes, he was not in good spirits."

"May God heal him."

"Amin." Saadia held up her hands in prayer, but had her eye on Zaytuna. She stared a moment too long, but if she expected that Zaytuna would say more under her gaze, she was mistaken.

Shaheen returned, and Saadia stripped to her underclothes. Saadia explained as Shaheen dressed her, "We are going to the home of Sayyida Farhana bint ibn Abdulrazzaq. Her father is administrator of the caliphal coffers and her husband works in the same echelons..."

She struggled to follow Saadia's description of the guests she would meet today. The sound of a plate being laid on the copper table next to her jarred her to attention. The gazelle horn cookies were before her. She shrank from them as if Mustafa were standing in a doorway supplicating her for just one touch. In her heart, she begged the girl to take the cookies away, but the servant was already gone. Zaytuna stood, picked up her own wrap where Shaheen had laid it, and waited for Saadia by the door.

Soon, they were out into the street. Servants and masters alike reacted to the sight of them, a grand lady such as Sayyida Saadia bint Salah walking with a servant as if they were equals. Saadia seemed to enjoy the scandal of the moment, releasing a laughing sigh. Zaytuna kept her focus straight ahead, praying the visit would be worth it.

They slowed before the long walls of a great estate. Palm trees clustered in threes towered over the high walls, casting shadows across the monumental face of the upper floors. Several wide and intricately carved clay grills were inset into the walls, letting in light, yet screening the view of family rooms within. Only at the last moment did she notice a narrow, turreted guard house. The man within had come out to speak to another on the ground.

"Allow me to draw them out," Saadia said. "When the conversation opens to you, only give them what they need to keep talking. It will not take much."

The advice was needed. Zaytuna did not know where she would begin with women like this.

Saadia strode ahead to the double gates. A door within one gate opened without her knocking. A servant dressed in matching embroidered lavender silk sirwal and robe, with a red sash and matching turban, pulled the door wider with a bow. "Assalamu alaykum."

"Wa alaykum assalam. Sayyida Farhana is expecting us."

The outer courtyard was as Zaytuna expected, larger than Saadia's entire home and grounds, and designed for repose. Fruit trees, rosemary shrubs, vines climbing trellises, and pots of blooming flowers were arranged around a quiet pool of water. She imagined this must have been what Birkat Zalzal was like before its ruins were abandoned to the people of Karkh and braced herself for what was to come.

The servant led them up the broad path through a tiled entrance and into a reception room with upholstered couches and gleaming tray tables along the walls. There were two sets of large arched double-doors, carved and painted with geometric designs at opposite ends. One would be for the men of the family and their guests, the other for women. The servant opened a door for them and they passed through.

The sound of women in conversation came through a doorway to their right. Saadia was already hailing her friends with "Assalamu alaykum" and stringing their names together in a pearly sing-song voice. Zaytuna stood in the doorway, watching.

A group of women in finery so rich she could not tell if one was greater than the other lounged on low couches, a foot draped here, an arm across a pillow there. Their long hair was braided artfully around their heads or lay in silken curls across their shoulders. The scent of their perfumes was overwhelming, rose mixed with musk and vanilla, cut only by pungent citrus. She thought she might be sick from it. Only one surprised her, a young woman with a wide, open face, yet hard, unsmiling eyes. Her cream-coloured caftan was unadorned wool, yet it seemed finer than anything worn by the other women in the room.

"He would never!" one of the women objected.

Another, her hand fluttering over her mouth, nodded, giggling.

How could these women be scholars, the wives of scholars? They sounded no better than Yulduz when Marta visited, as the two turned over and enjoyed every morsel of scavenged suspicion and heartbreak. Saadia was right. It would not take much to get them talking.

Saadia gestured for her to approach as she introduced her first to Lady Farhana, mentioning her mother's name, "She was known as al-Ashiqa as-Sawda, a great ecstatic and poet belonging to the folk of God."

If not for the wrinkles around her eyes, Zaytuna would have thought Farhana was younger than herself. With head bowed and hand over her heart, she returned the lady's greetings. "Wa alaykum assalam wa rahmatullahi wa barakatuhu."

"Ahlan! Ahlan!" Farhana stood and took her hands with a sincere welcome, drawing Zaytuna to sit beside her. "I do not need to be introduced to your mother's name or her poetry. My father was devoted to her. He told me he followed your mother for weeks until she disappeared. He was bereft and repeated her words to us often to console himself." She paused, searching her memory, then recited,

"He who tastes the love of God vanishes
from his selfish soul and its cares to abide in Him,
Annihilated without an eye or trace remaining,
rapt in witnessing the awesome beauty of his love."

Farhana said her mother's words as if they were her own, not at all what her mother meant by them—a meaning beyond the measure of those in this room—yet true to this woman's heart. It was as if Zaytuna heard her mother's poetry for the first time, without any of the old resentment and longing for a mother she could never have. Inexplicably, she heard the words of a woman, not a mystic, and held onto them as if she were a child, grasping at her mother's hem.

"May God have mercy on her soul." Farhana took her hand. "I know my father would have been honoured to meet you and share stories of your mother with you."

The room had gone quiet and the women held out their hands in prayer for her mother's soul, but the young one with the hard eyes watched her with an expression she could not read. A servant brought a handkerchief on a small tray. Zaytuna only noticed then she had wept and blotted away her tears, mumbling, "Amin."

After a moment, one of the women across the room asked, "Perhaps you might share some more of your mother's poetry with us?"

Before meeting Farhana, she would have refused to allow women such as this to sully her mother's memory by reciting her words for the mere pleasure of it. Still, she refused, but only because she could not afford to lose her composure further.

There was silence again, lasting just a moment too long. Saadia ended it. "Zaytuna has come to us for another reason."

She turned to Saadia, unsure she could speak.

But Farhana was already prompting her. "Yes?"

Taking a moment, even though it was not enough, she smoothed her wrap, then began. "I am grateful for your appreciation of my mother and your prayers for her. I wish I were here to share her poetry with you all. But Lady Saadia brought me to you today to ask about a missing man."

One by one, their expressions transformed from sisterly consolation to sober interest, revealing the faces of the intelligent women she had expected.

"No need to say 'Lady' among us," Farhana interposed. "We are all sisters. What can we do?"

"He is a scholar of Quran. A student."

A woman sitting at the far end of the group in a deep blue caftan with gold embroidery at the neckline sat up, saying severely, "Nabil ibn al-Qays al-Kufi."

"Yes. You know him?"

"My student mentioned him to me. Nabil is in grave trouble with both Ibn Mujahid and his own teacher, Ibn Shanabudh. It would be best if he does not return."

"His life…," Zaytuna began, wanting to say that he might be in danger, that it was not just a matter of having angered his teachers.

But next to her, a woman in a floral gown interrupted. "Amat, you do not know." She patted her hand. "That fool and his manuscript is not the half of it."

Amat turned her hand up in a demanding gesture. "What then, Atika?"

Another woman in a silk gown with a deeply cut, beaded neckline blurted, "My dear, they say this Nabil is in league with Mansur!"

"Mansur?" Zaytuna looked among them, praying they did not mean al-Hallaj.

"Mansur al-Hallaj, of course," Atika replied

Zaytuna's heart clenched, not knowing what this could mean, not just for the case, but for her family, the Sufis of Baghdad who would bear the brunt of his ecstatic sayings and erratic behaviour, as they had once before.

"If only we could hear Mansur recite his delightful verses of love again," the woman sighed.

Amat frowned. "Ghada, this is a serious matter."

"A few of us were visiting the Queen Mother at the palace and he arrived," Farhana explained. "Mansur remains the talk of our sisters here."

The woman beside Ghada pinched her playfully. "You are forever misunderstanding his verses. They are about God."

Ghada laughed it off. "I can make them mean what I like after looking into those eyes."

Zaytuna held out a hand to stop them. "What do you mean 'in league' with Mansur al-Hallaj?"

Atika tugged at the sleeve of her floral gown. "Mansur recites verses that were not revealed, as well. Ibn Shanabudh may invite this sort of thing, but Ibn Mujahid will want to see the back of them."

"Verses not revealed?" Saadia asked, taking the words from Zaytuna's mouth.

"Mansur inserts 'God of gods,' and 'Lord of lords', I hear," Atika said.

Zaytuna was about to ask what she meant by that, inserted where and how, when Amat said through gritted teeth, "I have never heard a reading of the Quran that uses those phrases. I have never heard an account of those phrases in any reading, even those accepted by the likes of Ibn Shanabudh."

"Amat, the Queen Mother informed me that he is writing a Quran tafsir and he does not purport these words to be revelation, but rather commentary on the revelation," Farhana assured her, but eyed them all to draw a line over the point.

"Why assume that?" She retorted, her hand at the neck of her blue caftan.

Ghada put on a serious face. "Perhaps he has maintained a variant reading that preserves those verses abrogated by God, like the readings of al-lat and al-uzza?"

Amat's response was cold. "If you are unwilling to listen to your husband when he talks to you about Quran readings, do not speak of them."

"Why would I bore myself?" Ghada giggled and pulled at her heavily beaded neckline, drawing her finger down between her breasts. "I make sure there is no talk when we are together and we are both happier for it."

The women laughed. Even the hard-eyed one, who struggled not to, gave in.

But Zaytuna did not, waiting until they quieted. "Atika, excuse me, why did you say Nabil and al-Hallaj were in league?"

The young woman with the hard eyes bit her tongue in an expression of disgust.

Atika said, "I heard that Nabil sought out Mansur to inform him that he had an autographed copy of Ibn Masud's manuscript. He thought al-Hallaj would be sympathetic. Ibn Masud's claims for the revelation were dismissed just as al-Hallaj's should be. So you see the young man and he are in league."

The logic was so absurd that Zaytuna was not sure she believed that Nabil had sought out al-Hallaj at all. But one thing she knew now: the news that Nabil claimed to have an autographed copy of Ibn Masud's personal manuscript of the Quran was widespread. She returned to an earlier comment. "I can understand Ibn Mujahid being concerned. But why Ibn Shanabudh? He himself does not adhere to the caliph Uthman's codex."

"If this story about al-Hallaj and Nabil is true, both Ibn Shanabudh and al-Hallaj should take care. Ibn Mujahid is closer to the court than either of them, but," Saadia emphasized, "he would not act without proof."

And how easily al-Hallaj would give him proof. Just standing on street corners, perched on mosque steps, in private meetings— wherever he preached, al-Hallaj managed to incite ecstasy, devotion, frenzied hopes of divine acceptance, but also fear and aggression with language about God the populace could barely understand.

"Closer to the court than the Queen Mother?" Ghada scoffed.

"The Queen Mother Shaghab protects al-Hallaj from accusations of heresy as well as from those Shia viziers who wish Mansur might meet with an accident. But she may not always be able to do so."

"Does Ibn Mujahid know what al-Hallaj has been saying?" Zaytuna asked.

"Know?" Amat said. "He has his eye on him. Ibn Mujahid brooks nothing that has the scent of heresy and al-Hallaj, well..."

Saadia insisted, "Ibn Mujahid would not and cannot act on simple disagreement no matter the strength of his feeling. He would take it to the court, laying out a case to convince the judge, the vizier, and legal scholars."

Zaytuna looked at her anew. She seemed to know this personally, not based on reputation.

"He sounds like a Qarmati at times," a grey-haired woman said. "I would not put it past al-Hallaj to be in league with those revolutionaries."

Ghada responded plaintively, "Don't speak ill of my Mansur."

"The Queen Mother excuses him," Farhana explained to Zaytuna. "He is only preaching to the people of the countryside in language they understand. They favour the Qarmatis, you know."

The grey-haired woman objected. "Are you mad? The language is one of revolution. He preaches against social inequities and injustice. The people will rise up against the caliph. What happens to us, then?"

Zaytuna held back, despite wanting to ask the woman if she thought standing up for the poor was a threat or if she feared it could not be done without revolution. But she knew the answer. It served women like this for women like Zaytuna, and those she loved, to stay in their place no matter what they suffered.

The woman continued, "The caliph should not let that fester. God protect us from evil things."

Atika waved her hand dismissively. "You know that boy caliph could not care less about politics. His mother and the viziers fight amongst themselves to run the empire."

"Take care speaking of the Queen Mother and her son in my home," Farhana warned.

The young woman with the hard eyes glared, nodding her head sharply.

"Cousin, please," Atika said. "No one is speaking ill of her. A woman in her position must fight for her son's security. Who waits in the wings to take his place? But the Qarmatis! One word to those peasants and they will be burning down Baghdad before long!"

"Yes." Saadia sat forward. "Remember when the military had to go into the streets to protect us from those Shia mobs who thought the caliph had one of their own ritually killed? It was…"

Zaytuna clamped her hand over Saadia's to keep her from speaking about their last big case. Did Mustafa tell this family everything? She turned the conversation back to this case, insisting, "But how do you know Nabil is associated with al-Hallaj?"

Amat sat back, eyebrows raised, as if waiting for one of the women to produce any proof.

The young woman looked as if she wanted to speak, but crossed her arms instead.

"Know?" Ghada smiled. "We don't seem to know. But if we gossip long enough, we will come up with something!"

"With respect, why are you asking about Nabil at all?" Amat asked Zaytuna with an expression of having wished she had asked this before speaking in the first place.

"I, along with my brother and his partner, have been hired by his mother to find him."

"I see," she said, casting her eye at Saadia, not hiding her disapproval.

"I know this woman and her family." Saadia grasped her hand. "Do not be humble, dear."

It was not humility; she did not want the conversation sidetracked.

"It was she who helped bring to an end the political unrest recently by finding those responsible for the death of the Shia boy."

"Not me alone. My brother and his partner," she tried to explain, but the women were already murmuring to one another, not listening.

Farhana called them to her attention. "And we are grateful for her service. Please, sisters, help her however you can. Think of Nabil's mother, at least. She must be suffering terribly, God help her."

Amat said in a tone that implied it was not a request, "If we are to help, then you must tell us what you know."

"Yes!" Ghada clapped gleefully.

Zaytuna repeated only what they already must know. "Nabil is a gambler. At first, we assumed he was off indulging himself or had been injured due to his debts. This may still be the case. But then his claims to have an autographed copy of Ibn Masud's manuscript came to light, along with the tension surrounding it, and we are following that up." She left out the part about Nabil wanting to print the Quran. "No one has any respect for him, but another student seems involved. He ran from our questioning. Bahr ibn Abi Shuayb."

"I cannot see how we might help," Amat said.

But they had confirmed that everyone knew about Nabil and his manuscript and the concern was greater than they had realized. She hoped the gossip about Nabil and al-Hallaj was just that, but even as gossip, it affected their investigation. At least now she knew to warn the aunts and uncles. Hand over heart, she said, "If you can think of anything else, please share it with Saadia."

They fell quiet until a small cough broke the silence. The young woman with the hard eyes finally said her piece. "First, I want you to know that while these women here indulge in talk of ecstasy with God, it is a grave error of the soul and all will be judged who indulge in it. I will not speak ill of your mother, May God forgive her. I pray you will not follow the error of her path."

Zaytuna gripped the edge of her seat, praying that whatever the young woman had to say would be worth enduring this insult.

"Qadira!" Farhana corrected. "We know you indulge us and we, in turn, indulge you, but this woman is my guest."

Qadira did not apologize, not even with the acknowledgement of a bow of the head. Rather, she finished what she had begun to say. "I believe I saw this young man, Nabil, speaking to Mansur al-Hallaj in the marketplace this morning. He seemed desperate, standing before him as a student would a master. Mansur al-Hallaj was advising him."

Saadia pressed Zaytuna's hand. "In the Rusafa Market?"

"Yes. Mansur and his supplicants were seated listening to a storyteller, one of those scourges who weave fancies about the lives of the prophets out of the myths told by the Christians and Jews. May God protect our prophets from their lies." She sat up, back straight, hand raised like a blade. "God's revelation came to wash these stories from our minds and souls, yet these storytellers repeat them! And, of course, Mansur is among those gladly drinking their poison."

Zaytuna interjected, barely hiding her derision. "And how would you know it was Nabil?"

"I did not at the time," she replied, unperturbed by Zaytuna's tone. "It was only now that we are speaking of him that I thought of it."

"What did he look like?"

"He was an Arab and wore his cloak after the fashion of the Kufans. He was slim, not short, not tall, quite average looking, except for his beard, which was auburn, nearly red."

"Fashion of the Kufans?"

"Only certain young men do this." She flicked her hand over her shoulder, creating an image of a gesture rather than a style.

"You seemed to have taken a second look,." Ghada teased.

Qadira scowled at her.

"Ghada," scolded Amat. "You see your own sin in others who are innocent of it."

The woman tittered, but the point had been made, and Ghada leaned back into the pillows.

"Did anything else happen?" Zaytuna asked Qadira.

"He ran off while Mansur was still speaking to him." Qadira sat forward, straightening a fold in her cream caftan, before demanding. "What will you do about this? Will you stop this young man and Mansur? Will you rid us of their heresy like you did the Shia who wanted to kill us all?"

Zaytuna gasped at her venom. Amat crossed the room to stand

between her and Qadira, her blue caftan blocking their view of each other. "Forgive our sister."

God protect us. The case was taking a turn that had suddenly become dangerous to everyone she loved. Qadira was not alone in these sentiments about al-Hallaj. There could be no worrying about running into Mustafa to clear this case, too much was at stake. She readied herself to leave and inform Tein, doubting he would put in any days at the butter shop when he heard what she had to say.

DAY FIVE

15

"Tein, we have to talk."

Worrying over the risk that al-Hallaj posed to her Sufi family, Zaytuna had gone back to the butter shop to look for Tein. But of course, the shop was closed and he had gone to meet Ammar. She waited for him at home, but he came back late and she missed his arrival while she was in prayer. So this morning, since long before first light, Zaytuna positioned herself in the courtyard, eyes on his door.

"I just woke up."

Saliha came out of their room behind him, rubbing her eyes, her hair a mess.

"You're going to be late for work," Zaytuna chided.

"So early with that mouth?" She put her hand on Tein's shoulder and handed him a cloth. "Wet this for me?" She returned to their room.

Zaytuna followed Tein to the water basin. "It's the case."

"Then it can wait." He reached down to the basin.

"No. It's al-Hallaj."

He straightened abruptly.

"One of the women says she saw Nabil, or a person she thinks is Nabil, with al-Hallaj."

"Where were they?"

"The market in Rusafa."

Bleary-eyed, he ran his hand over his bare head. "Uff, and Ammar has been doing nothing but making the rounds of Karkh. Maybe Nabil is staying in Rusafa?"

"Are you listening? I said al-Hallaj is involved."

"Tell me what they said about Nabil," he said harshly.

She nearly grabbed him by his nightshirt, but he swung around, feeling it coming. His face was raw with emotion: anger, fear, disgust, and unmistakable sadness.

"Speak," he hissed.

"I, I," she stammered. "I didn't have to tell those women a thing. Nabil has made a lot of trouble. Everyone is aware of the manuscript. He cannot be staying with a fellow student. Who would stand by him or offer him a bed?"

"He's in a hostel, then."

"It's worth a try."

Saliha called his name from within their room.

Tein bent down to pour water over the cloth. "I have to go get Ammar," he said, standing up slowly. "We'll start canvassing Rusafa today."

"Ibn Mujahid is after al-Hallaj."

He wrung the cloth until she thought he would rip it in two.

"We must protect them." She put a hand over his.

Tein's grip relaxed, but it seemed like from sheer force of will.

She took the cloth from him and went to answer Saliha's call.

Standing just inside the door, Zaytuna handed her the cloth.

"Where's Tein?" she asked, braiding her hair over her shoulder.

"The case has taken a dangerous turn."

Saliha dropped the braid, snatched the damp cloth out of Zaytuna's hands, and burst into the courtyard. Zaytuna was right behind her. "Tell me."

He was still by the basin, bent over it and pouring cups of water over his head, but straightened at the sound of her voice.

Ashen with fear, Saliha held her hands out, demanding an answer.

Water dripping down his face, he took her hand. "It's the aunts and uncles. Not us."

She stared at Zaytuna. "That's no good, either!"

"No, it is not."

"Well?"

"It's a lot to explain right now," Zaytuna answered. "It's best if we just go straight to see our uncle."

"Right," agreed Tein. "We'll go see Uncle Abu al-Qasim first, then I'll go to Rusafa."

Layla came in the front gate, bucket of water in hand, and stopped short. "What's wrong?"

"It's just the case." Tein took the bucket from her.

"They aren't saying what." Saliha held the cloth like she was willing to use it as a weapon. "Not even to me. But your uncle told me not to worry and I trust him." She eyed Tein with an expression that said her trust was conditional.

"There's no need for any of us to worry," Tein said, pouring the water into the deep basin. "In fact, I have a job for you."

"Tein …," Zaytuna objected.

But the girl leapt on it. "Yes!"

"I need you to go to Uncle Ammar's house and let him know we are going to check hostels in Rusafa today. Otherwise, he'll continue on in Karkh."

She looked disappointed.

"This is very important, Layla," he stressed. "I'm going to rely on you to give him this message. I won't be able to meet him right away, so he needs to go without me. There's a kebab shop we ate at before. He knows it. I'll be there just before the midday prayer. This is important. Tell him Nabil was seen in the market in Rusafa."

"I can do it."

Yulduz and Qambar came into the courtyard, bread and fresh cheese in hand. She demanded, "What are you having that girl do!"

But Layla was already rushing into their room, Zaytuna on her heels. She tied her good kerchief around the back of her head, making sure her braid was in place, then took her warm wrap down from a peg and wound it around her body under her arms, drawing the loose edge over her head.

"Thank you for doing this for us. It's important. But don't forget you have your Quran lesson at Uncle Abu al-Qasim's."

"There's plenty of time." Layla grinned, flushed with pride, and hurried past her.

"Get something to eat at Uncle Kamal Ali's on your way back," she called after her. But the outer door had slammed shut before Zaytuna had finished speaking.

The cloth had been laid out on the reed mats for their meal and two disks of fresh bread were stacked on it. Qambar had settled his old bones down on the mat, tore off a hunk of bread and held it out to Saliha. "Stay, daughter. You must eat."

Taking the bread, she said, "I wish I could." She turned to Tein. "Are you leaving now?"

"I'm hungry." He kissed her forehead, but his mood was no better.

"I'm late," she grumbled and left.

Yulduz glared at Tein from the covered kitchen. "You never should have sent her."

He sat down next to Qambar.

"She's going to see Kamal Ali on her return, then from there, her lessons," Zaytuna assured her.

Yulduz nodded, but was still irritated. When she came out balancing a large plate of dates and walnuts, she said to no one in particular, "Get the jug of buttermilk, will'ya?"

Zaytuna ducked into the kitchen for the jug, but the fresh tang of the buttermilk hit her in a sickening way and her stomach turned. "What is this case doing to me?" She held her breath as she took the jug out to the rest.

"Cups?" Yulduz looked at her like a fool.

Glad to put the jug down and get away from the scent, she went back for the cups. Short a cup for herself, she put them in front of Yulduz, then stood up, taking short breaths, and wiped her mouth with the back of her hand.

Yulduz opened her mouth to speak, then looked at her quizzically.

Her eyes sparkled for just a moment, and she shut her mouth with a small smile. No doubt a tease was on the old goat's tongue, but Zaytuna was not equal to it and she returned to her room to get her wrap.

Back outside, she said, "Hurry up and eat, Tein. We're wasting time."

Tein grabbed a handful of walnuts and got up.

"Give this to her for the road," Yulduz had torn off the charcoal-dark edge of the bread and held it out to him. He jammed the walnuts into his mouth and took it from her.

Zaytuna opened the outer door.

Tein handed her the bread, mumbling with a full mouth, "Wait."

In the street, she sniffed the bread. Her stomach approved and she tore off a small piece of the burnt crust and let it sit on her tongue for a moment. The taste of charcoal and burnt nuttiness of the wheat seemed to relieve her queasiness and soon she had picked away at the crust of bread completely.

"Why aren't you eating?" Tein asked, joining her.

"The case is a worry, that's all."

"The last time I saw you pick at a piece of bread, you were in your ascetic days, loving Mustafa with all the misery you could manage."

One moment he is telling her to trust herself to turn away from Mustafa, the next he is criticizing her for what the struggle was costing her body. She strode ahead of him faster than she knew he could walk early in the morning. At the next corner, she tired of making her point and waited for him to catch up.

"If you're done punishing me," Tein said, "tell me what I need to know."

It was one word too far. "This situation is more important than what is happening with Mustafa and Kamal Ali. Maybe you could keep your mind on it?"

He raised an eyebrow at her and walked on ahead.

"The women think there is some connection between Nabil and al-Hallaj," she said, catching up. "Both claim to have readings of the Quran that Ibn Mujahid does not accept. In al-Hallaj's case, readings that no one would accept. They suspect Ibn Mujahid is after them both now."

"So the fear is that Ibn Mujahid would make a broad sweep, getting the court to come after the Sufis on the idea that the aunts and uncles have made the same mistake as al-Hallaj?"

"They did not say that. But it happened before, with Ghulam Khalil leading the way. If it had not been for Uncle Nuri, how many of them would have been executed?"

"I hope this is just the gossip of rich women."

"Saadia didn't believe it of Ibn Mujahid, though. She insisted to the other woman that he would be fair, that he would not bring anyone before the court without proof. I suspect she was speaking from experience."

"You have to go back and see Saadia."

"Why? I got what I could from them."

"Did you ask if Nabil is staying with any of her friends?"

Ghada would protect Nabil if al-Hallaj asked, but Zaytuna doubted the woman's husband, a wealthy and important Quran scholar, would permit it or react well if he found out she was hiding him. All the same, Zaytuna scolded herself for not prodding.

———

Uncle Abu al-Qasim's door came into view. Tein hurried ahead, pulling his leg painfully along, then knocked harder than he should once there.

Ziri answered his knock with a concerned face. "Assalamu alaykum."

Tein said, "Wa alaykum assalam. My apologies, brother. We know it is early but we must speak to Shaykh Abu al-Qasim."

Ziri ushered them in, then turned at the stairs to go up to the family quarters.

Tein went into the courtyard to wait, but Zaytuna remained behind, standing near the bottom of the stairs and staring at the space underneath. As a girl, she would play at mystical retreat, counting out "There is no god but God" on her fingers, inhaling when she should be exhaling, trying to push herself into an ecstatic state, but only becoming out of breath and dizzy.

Her uncle's voice reached her before she heard his soft footfall on the stairs. "My daughter."

There was a gentle smile on his fair face and his brown eyes shone. Dressed simply, as always, he felt like nothing more than an uncle in whose presence a child is safe. She had not always felt this way, neither as an angry child nor in later years when she avoided him to keep from having to address her troubles. But she felt secure with him now.

He took her hand as he stepped down to the main floor. His skin soft and warm, his grip steady, he soothed her and his greeting became an embrace that would carry her to the farthest distance.

"I hear you have news."

"Tein is waiting in the courtyard."

"My friend Imam Abu Abdurrahman al-Azdi is staying with me. He is probably with Tein now. May he join us? I trust him."

The imam who had been so good to Mustafa. Certainty gave way to guilt. There would always be something reminding her of him. Fearing failure, she glanced in the direction of the stairs, wanting to hide away from it all, but said to her uncle, "I trust whom you trust."

Tein and Imam Abu Abdurrahman were seated on sheepskins, chatting warmly. Her brother's worry about al-Hallaj had seemingly disappeared as he spoke with pleasure about the work of churning butter.

"It is not as simple as thrusting a staff up and down or the use of the best milk that makes good butter," Tein was saying. "There must be a loving and gentle intention, like approaching one's bride…"

The imam raised his hand to his mouth, chortling.

Zaytuna's cheeks grew hot, and she nearly scolded him.

"Ah! I did not mean that!" Tein protested, realizing what he had said. "I only meant that all matters should be entered into with reverence, even churning butter."

"Including meeting one's friends." Junayd let go of her hand and settled comfortably with the men on the sheepskins. "Now tell us,"

Junayd said, gesturing to Zaytuna, as she seated herself on a sheepskin next to Tein.

But she did not know where to begin, and said, "Mustafa has asked us…"

"Yes, Mustafa." The imam perked up. He turned to Junayd. "Will we see him?"

Junayd nodded briskly, but to end that line of conversation.

Zaytuna found herself unable to speak.

Tein stepped in. "Mustafa has asked us to help a mother find her son who has gone missing. The police cannot help, so we offered. The young man, Nabil ibn al-Qays al-Kufi, is a student of Ibn Shanabudh. It's a strange case, disturbing as he claims to have an autographed copy of Ibn Masud's manuscript. There are many reasons he might be missing, but he seems to be at the centre of tension in the study circles of Ibn Shanabudh and Ibn Mujahid."

The scholar sat back sharply, eyes wide.

Junayd's expression became deadly serious.

"There is no evidence this manuscript exists." Tein put a hand out. "Everyone, even his colleagues, says the claim is simply Nabil seeking attention. It wouldn't be out of character given what we know about him. He and his mother were wealthy once, now orphaned and impoverished. It may have been a way to seem important. Although, if that was his reason, it did not work for him as he hoped. They all seem to despise him."

"He must produce the manuscript!" the scholar exclaimed.

"He refuses. But he claims to have shown it to one other person, Bahr, a student of Ibn Mujahid's, whom he has asked to vouch for him."

"And what does that man, Bahr, say?"

"He ran when we went after him."

"What could that mean?" the imam asked them all.

That he's involved, Zaytuna thought.

"Imam," Tein asked, "what do you think would happen if this young man were to bring the manuscript into the open?"

"The scholars would welcome it. Of course, Ibn Mujahid's people would reject those parts that do not accord with the caliph Uthman's codex, use it to affirm the recitations that do, and examine the rest with great interest."

"Ibn Shanabudh's students talked like it would stir controversy among Ibn Mujahid's circles, challenging the orthodoxy of the caliph Uthman's codex."

"Then Ibn Shanabudh's men do not understand the methods of their rivals!"

"You are certain that no one would see the existence of the manuscript as a threat."

"Not unless they were fools or madmen. But why does the young man not produce it?"

Junayd asked Tein, "What do you think?"

"The autographed manuscript does not exist," Tein said forcefully, then backed up, measuring his words. "He's exploiting the tension between Ibn Mujahid and Ibn Shanabudh for a reason we do not yet understand. Maybe Nabil thought he could get some power or respect from the claim? Or maybe he thought he could get them to buy it from him without seeing it first?"

The imam leaned in. "The library at the Sharqiyya Mosque would purchase it. If not them, a private buyer would step forward without question."

"The autographed manuscript does not exist," Tein repeated.

Junayd nodded in agreement, but the scholar was skeptical. "What evidence do you have?"

Tein faltered.

"What did Ibn Mujahid say?" Junayd prompted.

Tein gestured in the direction of the Tigris. "In more polite language, he told Nabil to fish or cut bait."

"Indeed," Junayd said. "I am inclined to agree with you and Ibn Mujahid."

"And Ibn Shanabudh?" the imam asked.

"The same." Tein's face lit up, remembering. "Ibn Shanabudh's students said that Nabil was unfamiliar with the reading tradition of Ibn Masud held in Kufa. That would imply he did not have a copy himself to work with. I mean," Tein faltered, "otherwise he would know."

Zaytuna added, "His mother has pointed to the young man, Bahr."

"The one who ran?" The imam tugged his beard. "Has this Bahr harmed Nabil?"

"It may be that Nabil has only abandoned his mother," she said. "They are in reduced circumstances as the father left them with nothing. Nabil gambles and had sold off most of the wealth they had left."

"He may have been hurt by an enforcer for the gambling establishments," Tein added. "Ammar and I visited the ones we know about in Karkh and no one is admitting to anything. Of course, he may just be drunk somewhere, or with a woman, and we just haven't found him yet."

Junayd said, "Son, I am not sure why you brought this to us, other than, I confess, it being a matter of great interest."

"I'm sorry," Zaytuna jumped in. "I should have said first."

"We should have said," Tein corrected.

"As part of the investigation, I went to a gathering of wealthy women. Some were wives of scholars, while one was a Quran scholar herself. They believe Nabil is associated with al-Hallaj."

Junayd was perfectly still, but Imam Abu Abdurrahman's cheeks reddened with anger.

"One claimed Nabil sought out al-Hallaj," she continued, "because he's been adding his own words to the Quran, beyond any of the known recitations, either those accepted by Ibn Shanabudh or those that agree with Uthman's codex."

"God protect us from evil things," exclaimed the imam.

"Others disagreed, saying it is only tafsir, clarification of the meanings of a few words. But the others claimed he does not say that, instead he recites it as if it were Quran. They have no evidence for it," Zaytuna said. "But I'm not sure that the truth matters. If they are discussing it, that means others believe it, too."

"Exactly what Ibn Masud is accused of doing out of

misunderstanding!" Imam Abu Abdurrahman asserted. "But I doubt anyone will give al-Hallaj that benefit of the doubt."

"No." Junayd was grim. "Some say he believes what he receives in private unveiling from God is Quran itself. But we have been assured this is not true. He does not claim it is Quran, nor does he recite it in prayer. But he makes confusion all too easy."

"The women said that Ibn Mujahid has close relationships in the High Court. They warned that he wants to make a case against al-Hallaj."

The imam addressed Junayd. "Ibn Mujahid is a steadfast man. Of course, we all agree on the boundaries Uthman's codex places on the readings, but I understand he finds the number of those within its limits is becoming too many and wants to limit them even further."

"That is an unusual position for the scholars of Quran."

"A student of mine sat in his circle once and asked him about certain readings of Qunbul and Ibn Amir and he slapped his hand on his thigh and listed those he thought were wrong. After each, he said most strenuously, 'Wrong!' 'Wrong!' 'Wrong!' And Qunbul was his own teacher. If that is how he feels about widely accepted readings that accord with the caliph Uthman's codex, you can only imagine how he feels about those which are not."

"What were his complaints about Ibn Amir? Our companion Adnan is from Damascus, so he has been teaching Ibn Amir's reading tradition to our children's circle rather than Baghdad's reading, Duri."

"For one, *Kun fa yakuna.* But you yourself disagree with this reading, accepting only *Kun fa yakunu.*"

"They make their decisions based on scholarly judgment alone. *Yakuna* is, we agree, grammatically improbable. But we make our decisions from a higher awareness."

"Do not say that in his company," the imam said with a joking smile.

But Junayd did not find it funny and only inclined his head. "I believe Ibn Mujahid will have Ibn Shanabudh in court one day."

Tein asked, "And al-Hallaj?"

"Yes."

"Ibn Mujahid shares a similar concern with the Caliph Uthman, may God be well-pleased with him," Junayd said. "The average believer needs stability. Most especially where our prayers are concerned. Even if only the accepted readings proliferate, the people lose their certainty. He is not wrong to want to limit them."

"Just so," the imam answered.

Junayd continued, "I do not send letters with mystical secrets in them for fear they will be opened and read by the wrong person, thus putting the reader at risk, putting us all at risk."

"I don't understand," Zaytuna said.

"Just as Ibn Mujahid wants to limit the people's exposure to too many readings and the confusion that arises, it is wrong to teach a mystical secret to someone who is not ready to understand it. The person may be led astray in their belief, and lead others astray. It is dangerous to all."

"Which is why al-Hallaj is such a danger," Tein said.

"Yes, he exposes the mystical secrets and uses language that seems intended to inflame."

"And he gets involved in politics," the imam said.

"He preaches against injustice," Zaytuna countered, remembering the women's dislike of him for simply standing up for the vulnerable.

"No one faults him for caring for the poor," Junayd responded. "It is the way of the Prophet, and a way we all follow."

"He is at fault for fomenting revolution in the language of the Qarmatis," the imam said. "They have declared that there is no longer a need for our religion."

Junayd's lips tightened at the imam's statement, and Zaytuna wondered why.

"The women said al-Hallaj is friendly with the Queen Mother," she said.

"Yes, and these associations may keep him protected for now. But there will be a time when not even the Queen Mother can save him. In fact, association with these classes of people only taints him further." Junayd acknowledged Tein and Zaytuna. "Thank you for bringing us this news. We will warn our brothers and sisters to be more circumspect."

But that warning would not stop those whose ecstasy overflowed in public and had the love of the people. Their mother would not have been stopped from preaching in the graveyards, just as Uncle Nuri could not be stopped. And, despite everything, al-Hallaj's friends among the Sufis would not abandon him. It was likely they would be swept up in his guilt before the courts.

Junayd's expression had changed from concern to seeming as if he were looking within himself, or listening to information from a source other than himself. Then, he returned to them and said firmly, "This young man, Nabil, must be found and at least this association with al-Hallaj brought to a close."

"We are looking, Uncle," Tein assured him.

"He is alive. I can share that much. He is alive, but uncomfortable, perhaps cold."

Tein asked insistently, "Was he in the river?"

"I do not know more. May what I see at least help to invigorate your search in knowing he has not died. But my son, no matter what happens, do what you can to sever this young man's problems from our own."

"I will."

"Daughter, would you visit those women again and insist that we have nothing to do with Nabil or al-Hallaj?" Junayd asked. "They may have some influence."

"I will get them the message, inshallah." She turned to the imam. "Do you still think that Ibn Mujahid would not be angry about this manuscript, now people believe Nabil is involved with al-Hallaj and false revelations?"

"The manuscript, no. The young man behind it, yes. He would be angry."

Zaytuna stood, hand over her heart.

Tein stood with her. "We are at your service."

Ziri walked with Tein and Zaytuna coming out of the courtyard to open the door, but as he did, Auntie Hakima arrived.

Her face lit up, and the old woman, half their size, embraced Tein as if he were a little boy still in her care. "Is that wife of yours feeding you? Those cheekbones are beautiful, my son, but I do not like the hollows."

"Yulduz, our auntie who lives with us, feeds us as if we had never eaten before."

"Then it is that job of yours. Eat some of that butter when the boss is not looking!"

Auntie Hakima turned her attention to Zaytuna, tugging her sleeve and drawing her back into the courtyard. "Well met. I want to talk to this one."

She greeted Junayd and the imam, then walked Zaytuna to her spot by the kitchen, Tein following behind.

"I'll catch up with Hilal while you two chat," Tein said.

But it was Abdulghafur who came from the kitchen to greet him, not the cook. The boy grew taller and broader each time Zaytuna saw him, what with hauling sacks of grain and beans, not to mention the large copper cooking pots. But it was his smile, his peace at being in place, that made her happy. He and Tein ducked into the kitchen and she could hear Hilal's loud greeting.

"Sit." Auntie Hakima's tone turned suddenly harsh.

"Auntie, what's wrong?" Zaytuna sat down next to her and the certainty that all would be well abandoned her completely.

"What are you doing with Mustafa?"

"Nothing!"

"Tell me what happened. He was here, the men were consoling him. You two were together."

"I brought him here that day." She scrambled within, wondering if she could hide how close they had come to a grave betrayal. "I had rejected him."

"I heard, but not before he took you to see that lost man's mother. You foolish girl, what were you thinking?"

She shrank under the woman's glare.

"You a married woman. Him a married man and married to *your* sister on this path. And what did you find out by risking so much?"

Auntie Hakima meant if what she had found out on the case was worth it. The answer would always be that the case was not worth losing Kamal Ali. "I found out…" She paused to collect her thoughts and say what she wanted to say, but nothing more. "I found out that I want to be right where I am, with my husband."

"Oh, did you? Because that's not what I see from here." Auntie Hakima reached out and tapped two fingers over Zaytuna's heart.

The shock of her momentary touch wrested away every restraint. Zaytuna covered her face with the edge of her wrap and burst into tears. "We've loved each other for so long."

Auntie Hakima took her hand, giving her time to compose herself.

"You know their marriage is not what he hoped?" The old woman asked plainly.

"Or what YingYue hoped?"

"No, not what she hoped, either." Auntie Hakima stared across the courtyard at Junayd. "I warned the old man and he brushed me off. But God knows those two would not be dissuaded from marrying even if we tried to stop them."

"What happened?"

"You know what happened." She let go of Zaytuna's hand. "One look at you and his wedding became his funeral. She saw it."

"What do I do, Auntie? I don't want to love him."

"Stay away from him. Let YingYue sort out what she wants to do with him without you influencing him, making him think…"

"Nothing," Zaytuna said. "There is nothing for him to think."

"Oh, there is plenty for him to think. You say you are where you should be with your husband, you don't want to love Mustafa, but what lurks in that heart of yours? The wrong circumstances, you could be swayed." She pressed a finger into Zaytuna's thigh. "Women can love more than one man just as men can love more than one woman. But women, we cannot have them."

Saliha had said the same, but it was not what they assumed. "It's not like that."

"What, then?"

She felt her uncle's presence as if he were beside her, urging her to speak from some place else within her, an overlook onto the raw emotion, the wound of her love for Mustafa. "I don't want him, but I don't want to let him go."

"You don't love him at all, then."

"If I truly loved him," she said with sickening clarity, "I would free him."

Auntie Hakima got up suddenly, standing with an ease Zaytuna had never seen before. Once up, she commanded, "You. Do not move," then she hurried to the reception area, her staff thumping.

Only then did she notice that no one was talking in the kitchen. Tein had to have been listening. She pulled her wrap over her face, this time to hide from her brother, knowing he would come at her, too, saying she had no right to trust herself.

"Sister."

But it was not Tein. It was the gentle voice of YingYue. She was trapped. Tein in the kitchen, YingYue beside her, Auntie Hakima behind her. Whether or not she had no escape from them, she had no escape from herself. Zaytuna commanded herself to admit the part she played in their tragedy.

She pulled her wrap away and faced YingYue. She would hear what YingYue needed to say. She would accept it. She would apologize. She would promise to never see Mustafa again. And she would keep that promise.

YingYue sat before her, seeming troubled, but not angry. Zaytuna could not understand it.

"I am ashamed," Zaytuna admitted.

YingYue took Zaytuna's hands in her own. "Come, we are sisters in our love of a good man. This love bonds us to each other."

Zaytuna itched to pull her hands away, but she forced them to be still while YingYue spoke.

"Stop fretting, poor thing." She let go of Zaytuna's hands, lightly slapping one. "You showed me what a foolish girl I had been. Since an infant, my heart has only desired God. I spent my youth writing letters to my Beloved and casting them into rivers and streams for Him to find. Yet, here, where I was instructed to come find my teacher to complete my path, I was drawn away from God by a man. I yearned for Mustafa, not seeing he was an idol I had placed between me and my love." She recited, *"Decked out fair to men is the love of lusts—women, children, heaped-up heaps of gold and silver, horses of mark, cattle and tillage. That is the enjoyment of the present life; but God—with Him is the fairest resort."*

"I don't understand."

"That verse and the others like it, God is warning the men, yes, but it is a warning to women that they get caught up in all that is fair, too. We get caught in lust, wealth, status, and children. I nearly lost myself." Her expression opened with wonder. "I would have lost God. If not for you, Zaytuna! If not for you!"

Zaytuna shrank back.

"I told Mustafa he could have you, but you were engaged to Kamal Ali. He would not go to you. Then you were married and it was impossible. Now, he comes to you when it is too late. I told him you would never be Zaynab to his Prophet."

The outrage of what YingYue suggested shook her body. "Does he think he can ask Kamal Ali to have me as the Prophet asked Zayd to divorce Zaynab!"

"I told him you would not," she said matter-of-factly.

She nearly screamed. "My God! Is he going to Kamal Ali?" She reached out, gripping YingYue's hand so tightly she snatched it away.

"He wants you to ask Kamal Ali to release you and come to him freely." YingYue paused, touching her hand. "And then you will be my sister in marriage."

"Lord protect me!"

But YingYue carried on as if all this were some kind of blessing bestowed on them both. "I will retire to worship. You will not be a second wife, except in name."

Zaytuna stood in a shot. A hand fell on her shoulder and she swung around. Auntie Hakima stood firm, leaning on her staff. YingYue rose gracefully and stood next to the old woman as if she were her ally in this horror.

"You two have my happiness sorted out to suit yourselves!"

"You love him!" YingYue reached out, but Zaytuna drew away, repulsed.

"What did you say to her?" Auntie Hakima demanded of YingYue.

Zaytuna ignored the old woman, turning on YingYue. "Ask him to release you if you want to be alone with God. Do not involve me."

"But poor Mustafa, what will become of him?" YingYue pleaded.

"Walla! He is not a child!"

She ran from them all. There was no chance that her uncle and the imam did not witness the conversation and that Tein heard it, too. Angry and confused, now she was the object of a humiliating spectacle. Looking only at the ground ahead of her, she pushed past Ziri and into the street. The door shut behind her and she stood frozen in place, not knowing where to go.

16

Tein had overheard everything. Zaytuna's admission of love for Mustafa. YingYue's plan for her. And Auntie Hakima's anger. Having held his finger up to his lips to Abdulghafur and sent him back to work with Hilal, picking grit from the lentils, he positioned himself as close to the door as he could without being seen, then hurried after Zaytuna when she ran. Auntie Hakima yelped as he burst out of the kitchen and slapped him on the arm as he passed, crying, "Comfort her!"

He was relieved to find her still outside and said her name before approaching. She may have waited for him, but that did not mean she would not lash out if surprised, given what those women had put her through. He strained to understand why Auntie Hakima would push her to admit she still wanted Mustafa, then make her sit and listen to YingYue beg her to be a second wife.

"Comfort her." There would be no need if they had not been so cruel.

Zaytuna faced him, arms crossed, her skin mottled with humiliation.

"I know you love Kamal Ali."

"I do." Tears welled in her eyes.

"Tell me. What do you love about him?"

"I..."

Tein stopped her. "Every day I see my sister happier than she's ever been. But one morning with Mustafa and you're in tears, angry and bitter again."

She lowered her head.

"Mustafa is a brother to me, but he's not worthy of you, and you are not worthy of him." He drew closer and touched her cheek. "You two, always pulling each other to this awful state. It's been like this since you were children."

"I know."

"Kamal Ali has his faults like any man. But his worst fault is not telling you how he feels, letting you find your own way without having to take him into account." Tein told her the truth. "Your husband is in knots over the possibility of losing you."

"God forgive me." She pressed a hand against her forehead.

"Come." He pulled her hand away. "Let's get you some water, a bite to eat. We have work to do. I won't leave you to it alone. Any of it."

Zaytuna embraced him, her hands clutching his robe, and took shuddering breaths. When she finally let go, she dried her eyes and straightened her wrap.

"We're going to have to disturb your rich friend since our only lead right now is that Nabil was seen with al-Hallaj. Ammar should be at the hostels in Rusafa. So our next stop is Saadia. And you need to insist that al-Hallaj has nothing to do with the Sufis."

"To the river?" She sniffed, then checked her sleeve pocket. "Yesterday, Kamal Ali sent me to Rusafa in a skiff. I left the money he gave me at home."

"You and I are going to have to walk."

They found their way onto the Basra Gate High Road and began the long walk to the pontoon bridge spanning the breadth of the Tigris, connecting its east and west sides. Zaytuna trudged beside him, arm in arm, exhausted by emotion, her eyes on the ground. The wide road was busy as always and they kept close to the bordering estate walls, broken only by arched entrances leading to narrow side streets and great homes beyond.

A man in a fine black turban, leather cuirass, and a sword at his side came out from one of those archways just a few paces ahead of them and turned up the High Road in the direction they were walking. A watchman followed a few steps behind like a beaten dog, dragging his staff. Tein wanted to pull the man aside and tell him no job was worth his dignity, but he knew what the bit of coin he got meant to him and his family. Men like this were stuck until they could find a way out. Some took to the job, enjoying having a bit of power for once and using it as it had been used against them. Not this one; he knew the type. Incapable of the violence required, they were failures to a one. The man who led him was police but Tein did not recognize him. He was a man of rank. The cloth and wrap of his turban gave him away. His boots alone cost him more than a watchman would make in years.

The watchman stumbled. With a sharp turn of his shoulder, the officer spat at the distressed man, "A full dish in front of you, but you won't touch it!"

To call a man in that state ungrateful. And for what, not taking a bribe? Not going along with whatever was put before him? Tein reared up, the old anger surging. He let Zaytuna go as each muscle fell into place, his gait shifting to attack from behind, his hand on the hilt of his dagger.

Zaytuna stopped, knowing better than to touch him in that state. *Knowing better.*

The thought hit him flat-handed to the chest. He fell to one knee. But just as being pushed off a woman before the first thrust did not stop a man from wanting her, every bit of him surged to take the man down. Tein groaned in pain, mouth open, face twisted to the heavens, flesh and soul laid bare, then gasped, falling to all fours, panting.

Through his breaths, he heard Zaytuna telling passersby to keep going. They asked if he needed help. He felt them staring. She did not touch him yet, still knowing better. Bile burning, hand on knee, he forced himself to stand. The man he wanted to kill and the watchman he wanted to protect were long gone.

"Come," she said, getting him walking, not asking what had happened. Not yet, anyway. But her shoulders were thrown back now. The exhaustion gone. Her face was stern and alert. He needed her, and she knew it. He cursed the case and what it had dredged up in them both.

"If it weren't for the aunts and uncles, I'd quit."

"Go back to Tutha, then, if you are so afraid of becoming like you were before. But if that is all it takes to set you on fire, what good are you hiding away churning butter?" She stopped at the turn onto the road to the Sharqiyya Mosque. "You think I don't know what this is like?"

"To want to kill?" He scoffed. As if her feeling for Mustafa could compare to taking a life.

She replied plainly, gesturing toward the mosque. "I understood in an alley down there how you and Saliha ended up meeting in ruined buildings."

Tein had not imagined it had gone that far. The anger rose again, Mustafa now taking the form of the man in the black turban, but he did not let it pass further than the growl in his throat. "How much do you understand?"

"He invited me in and I did not join him."

Mustafa had tried to draw her into an irrevocable betrayal.

Reading his face, she said, "There's no need to beat him. He's destroying himself." The sadness in her voice returned. "I rejected him, but he knew before I did that I didn't mean it. Auntie Hakima showed me I didn't mean it, either."

"What does that mean!"

"Not what you think. I don't want him the way I want Kamal Ali."

Maybe it was like wanting to crush a man's throat to banish his own pain. An animal wanting, always lurking, waiting to overtake him. He hoped this was the end of it, but he knew his sister well enough to know that she was going to have to burn her hand to know the fire was hot. It was not enough to tell her. Not enough for her to admit it. Mustafa. Tied up in her every which way. His empathy for his brother overtook his anger, but not his resolve that Mustafa would never see Zaytuna alone again on his watch.

The pontoon bridge was up ahead. Something was blocking the way and people shuffled in place, muttering complaints. Workers stood still, their burdens on their backs. One man bent over with his hands on his knees rather than put the sack down. Tein understood. What was the point of releasing a burden only to have to put yourself back under it again?

The call came to cross. A donkey cart rumbled by, but it did not stop the complaints from a few who gestured at the driver for holding them up. Tein winced at the thought of Natar having to take the butter cart across this bridge twice a day. A man like him, having suffered so much, now having to withstand such insults.

The bridge withstood the swift current of the Tigris, but still moved underneath them as they crossed. Women with tiered trays of goods on their heads swayed for only a moment, getting their footing, then carried on. A girl held tightly onto her mother's wrap, staring out at the water, but her mother put an arm around her and directed her to keep her eyes forward.

"If Nabil went into this water," Zaytuna said, "he would have died."

"He could be cold like uncle said for other reasons, but if he went in on the bank of a canal, he could have got out."

"It's got to be something else."

"How do you feel about this woman, Saadia?"

"I don't know if I can trust her."

"Why?"

"I feel like she is helping us only to entertain herself."

"We'll see how entertained she is when we show up unexpectedly so early in the day."

The bridge road spilled out onto a wide gap between walls. Palm trees swayed in the wind, and the mosque rose high in the distance. Its arched façade was tiled in blues and greens and stood three times as high as the mosque building itself. Intricate calligraphy and repeating vegetal designs had been carved into the stucco. Zaytuna gestured to the left, where a wide street broke off from the main road leading to the mosque.

The power and wealth of Baghdad had truly crossed the river when the caliph abandoned the Round City. Great estate walls lined the street, protecting and insulating the wealthy, rivalling anything in Karkh. They walked around a gentle curve east and the long walls became shorter, revealing several smaller estates. Stopping before one of these, Zaytuna knocked on the outer gate.

An older male servant opened the inner door of the gate and looked at them both with suspicion.

"Please tell Lady Saadia that Zaytuna bint al-Ashiqa as-Sawda is here with her brother."

The servant stood still for a moment too long, wanting to refuse them, then shut the gate door, leaving them in the street.

Zaytuna widened her eyes in mock surprise.

"The only surprise here is that we weren't shown to the servant's entrance."

"Saadia was expecting me last time, so I had no trouble."

A woman's scolding voice came over the wall, a man's followed, and in a moment the door opened. A tall woman, equaling Zaytuna in height and, by her eyes, equalling her also in intelligence. But unlike his sister, this woman had never doubted herself and her confidence made an otherwise plain face beautiful. A man hurried behind her, placing a skullcap on his head, clearly irritated that Saadia had opened the door on her own. He wanted to commiserate with the man, that he loved two just like her, his sister and his wife, and lived under the thumb of a third, Yulduz.

"Assalamu alaykum! Zaytuna! Ahlan!" She appraised Tein with interest. "And this is your brother, Tein. Come in!"

As she opened the door wide, the man stepped out in front of her. "Assalamu alaykum. It is good to see you again, Zaytuna." He bowed his head with a hand over his heart. "You must be Tein. Your cousin Mustafa has spoken of you often. I am Abu Mubarak Sherwan Ibn Salah. Please, our home is your home. Ahlan wa sahlan."

The servant, seemingly unchastened, ushered them through a

narrow courtyard and into a reception room. Wide couches in expensive fabric lined the walls. Pillows, inexplicably tied off with gold-threaded tassels, were strewn against the back cushions. A boy was before the hearth, hastily lighting a clean-burning thorn bush fire. They slipped off their shoes. Zaytuna put on a pair of red shearling slippers and he took a large pair from the array left out for guests.

"We apologize for bothering you so early. It's the case."

"Sit, sit." Saadia nodded eagerly. "I hoped it was you when I heard the door."

Her brother took a spot far from the hearth, inviting them to sit in its warmth instead, and draped his wrap around his knees. His expression was less welcoming. Without looking at his sister, he asked, "Case?"

"Sherwan, I have not yet had the time to explain," Saadia said.

"Now may be a good time." But he inclined his head to Zaytuna. "I understand you continue to undertake small investigations for local women, but had no idea my sister was involved."

Tein glanced at Zaytuna. She did not betray herself to this man who had belittled her work. Everything she had been through this morning, yet she did not come back with sharp words, not even a bitter eye.

But then it came, subtly cutting. She ignored Ibn Salah as if he had not spoken to her, addressing Saadia alone. "At the gathering, one of the women said she had seen Nabil with al-Hallaj."

"Nabil ibn al-Qays al-Kufi?" Ibn Salah asked.

Tein started at him knowing the name.

Saadia ignored her brother, likewise. "Yes, Qadira mentioned she had seen them. I wanted to tell you, she is entirely reliable, an intelligent young woman and a Quran reciter of extraordinary grace. She married well below her station to a Quran scholar of little means." Saadia glanced at her brother. "Qadira is married to Ibn Rafi."

Her brother's expression became gravely serious. "I know who she is. Why are you interested in this Nabil?"

"If he is a student of al-Hallaj, perhaps one of the women among your friends may support him," Zaytuna said to Saadia, "or a woman they know might be protecting him. Ghada perhaps?"

Saadia shook her head. "Unless she paid for Nabil to be in a hostel. Her husband would never permit it and she would be unable to hide it from him. Her maids, let alone the housekeeper, the men who work in the house and grounds, they would know and word would get to him."

"Maybe she knows someone who might?"

"Qadira would be the one to ask."

The servant approached the door with a large tray holding two pitchers, glasses, and small plates of food. But Ibn Salah, red-faced, finally burst out, "Saadia! You know what is going on here! What are you doing?"

The servant took several slow steps backwards.

He continued in the strongest terms. "Mansur al-Hallaj has the Queen Mother's attention now, so she can protect him, but what about when that is no longer possible? Then everyone who has spent time with him will become suspect. The viziers still want him dead. Think of our family! We would be ruined."

"I do not see him," she said. "The other women do. Calm yourself."

"You will be caught up in it." He stood, cheeks bright red, then sat back down, defeated.

Saadia dismissed him with a glance and returned her attention to Zaytuna. "Qadira is a child of the last caliph's harem. One of his many daughters. She was not born for a life at court. Her only interest was God's words. Thus, the Queen Mother married her to the Quran teacher." She widened her eyes with delight. "From behind a screen they fell in love and the Queen Mother sent them off with a private stipend."

"Qadira visits her often?"

"My dear, she is how we even find ourselves in the company of the Queen Mother."

Tein understood. "The Queen Mother would know if anyone was protecting Nabil."

"Yes, brother of Zaytuna, yes. She has spies."

Zaytuna asked, "If Qadira is so close to the Queen Mother, then why did she expose al-Hallaj by suggesting Nabil was with him?"

Saadia smiled broadly. "You heard her. She despises him."

"Walla! At least one of you women has some sense." Ibn Salah addressed Tein, "Do you know what this man has been up to? Do you understand the threat?"

"I assure you we do."

"But do you know the extent of it?" Ibn Salah did not wait for an answer and listed the risks in a pedantic tone. "He sounds like the Qarmatis. They control Bahrain. They control the Hajj roads. They want to dismantle the Kaaba. Because the Qarmatis have blocked the Hajj road, al-Hallaj has been preaching that those who cannot travel to Mecca should do the pilgrimage at home. What he intends by this is meaningless. But it appears he is undermining the ritual of Hajj as part of the Qarmati plan."

Tein had not heard this before. It was the exact sort of thing that would irrevocably stain the reputation of the Sufi aunts and uncles, and they would find themselves in court for heresy along with him, executed because al-Hallaj would not control himself. He said through barely controlled fury, "He begs for death. What comes to that man will be deserved. But he'll take good people down with him."

Zaytuna pleaded, "Saadia, please don't let the women confuse al-Hallaj with the Sufis..."

He barely heard his sister's voice. His legs had gone cold, then numb, and the numbness was spreading. Now in his gut. He pressed his hands against it and it felt like someone else's flesh. Now reaching his heart. Tein clawed at his chest, gasping. Zaytuna was before him, speaking, but he could not hear her. The others held him steady with hands he could not feel.

Then, a voice was in his ear. "Beg for forgiveness!" An unseen hand gripped him by the back of the neck and yanked him back from the edge of death.

Forgive me!

The numbness retreated.

Forgive me!

His body prickled, free of it.

Forgive me!

Breath came slowly, each a newly formed regret for having wished punishment on al-Hallaj.

Ibn Salah handed him a glass of water and he batted it away, afraid he would choke.

"What happened?" Zaytuna asked.

"It's passed," he managed.

But she sat closer to him, her leg touching his.

Ibn Salah was still stiff with anger, as if Tein's attack had underlined the risk posed by al-Hallaj. "This man will bring us all down."

Tein listened, gripped by the fear he would be reprimanded for their anger at al-Hallaj, not simply his own curses.

"We only want Nabil," Zaytuna repeated.

"Do not downplay the risk." He gestured to Saadia. "And my sister plays with this fire."

"Brother, please."

"I forbid you from visiting those women again, Saadia."

"You forbid me?" She faced him. "You have no right to forbid me."

"Up until this moment, I have never had the need to exercise it."

"We will have this conversation, later." She smiled thinly. "Imagine what our guests must think of us."

His red cheeks blanched. "I apologize. You must understand."

"We do." Tein measured his words. "More than you may imagine. Our own community is threatened by association with him." He felt no reprisal for saying this much, but wished they could leave, so there was no risk of saying more.

"Is this true?" Ibn Salah asked.

"There are some who mistake al-Hallaj for one of the Sufis and blame us all." Zaytuna insisted to Saadia, "You must tell the women, tell them that he has no connection to our community."

She nodded. "By God, I will."

Ibn Salah sighed, nodded, and folded his hands on his lap and asked Tein, "Why, then, are you searching for Nabil?"

Saadia rolled her eyes.

He took a breath to answer, but Zaytuna spoke first, giving him more time to recover. "We are helping a friend investigate his disappearance. We don't know why yet, but too much points to his claim to have an autographed copy of Ibn Masud's personal manuscript. He's been missing for over a week."

"al-Hallaj would get himself mixed up in that." Ibn Salah slapped his knee. "A good friend is a colleague of Ibn Mujahid and told me all about this Nabil. Ibn Mujahid does not believe the manuscript exists and he is merely angry with the young man's behaviour. These are serious matters, and Nabil trivializes their work. al-Hallaj could make it all much worse. I told this to your cousin only yesterday."

Tein repeated the same contention he had to Imam Abu Abdurrahman, that Ibn Shanabudh's students thought the autographed manuscript would challenge the caliph Uthman's codex, then added, "True or not, the students at the Sharqiyya Mosque act like it exists, and there is more to it than Nabil trivializing these scholars' work."

"Absurd. The only people who love gossip more than women are students. They're more back-biting and malevolent than goats in a pen."

Saadia looked at him sideways.

He said, "I can assure you Ibn Mujahid is not overly angry at this young man."

"What does he get angry about, then?" Tein asked.

"Ibn Shanabudh and his like!"

"And those who recite the Quran in Persian." The sister gave him a knowing glance.

"Excuse me?" Zaytuna asked.

Tein had heard it before on the frontier, new Muslims reciting the Quran in prayer in their own languages. The Arabs would laugh at them as if the few necessary lines were so difficult as to require this concession.

"We legal scholars who follow the school of Abu Hanifa have argued that those unfamiliar with Arabic who have just entered Islam may recite the Quran in their own language as they learn. But Ibn Mujahid would never equate these matters with Ibn Shanabudh's methods. These differences of legal opinion are acceptable, even if he prefers one over another."

This must be what Zaytuna had meant when she said Saadia spoke from experience. They themselves had a run-in with Ibn Mujahid over this very question, and he had been reasonable with Ibn Salah.

"But what if Nabil had made inquiries to block print the manuscript?" Tein asked.

"Explain yourself."

"Nabil approached a printer in the Karkh Market."

"A printed book of one reading tradition of the Quran available to anyone who wants it!" Ibn Salah slapped his thigh. "By mere ubiquity it would at least supersede more marginal readings, more likely even those with repute. God protect us from evil things, we would lose all our reading traditions. We would lose God's words! Did the printer say if he had the text with him?"

"A manuscript they did not recognize. It could have been anything." Tein leaned forward, finally grasping Nabil's intent and feeling the fool for it having taken him so long. "Nabil doesn't need a manuscript, only the rumour of one. This is why he made a point of saying exactly what it was he wanted printed. The threat of printing is enough."

The servant took another chance. Ibn Salah stared him down and he retreated again.

Saadia got up and spoke to the man in the courtyard and he left with the tray.

"This makes no sense," Saadia said, returning to her place. "If no one believes the manuscript exists, then how would the threat of having it printed cause any trouble?"

Ibn Salah said, "Because he has inserted doubt into the conversation."

Tein nodded. "Without the threat of printing, I would not have given it a second thought. What could come of it? Either the manuscript exists, and the scholars make use of it, or it does not exist and the young man has been a fool. But this. If it exists, and if he is successful in printing it, it is a great threat. Doubt becomes an obligation. Something must be done."

"I see. It is imperative you find him," Saadia said to Tein and Zaytuna.

Tein asked Saadia, "You see why we need you to ask if anyone is hiding Nabil."

"Of course," she replied.

Ibn Salah turned to her. "You must take care that none of this comes back to us."

"I will ask Qadira discreetly, and if she does not know, I will ask further afield, then send a messenger to you. Where should I send him?"

"What about Kamal Ali?" Zaytuna asked. "If we are not home, better the messenger gives it to him than Yulduz."

"Will your messenger go as far as the Buratha market?" Tein asked.

"He will go where I command."

"Send it to Kamal Ali ibn Abdussalam al-Fassi's butter shop in the Buratha Market."

As they were changing back into their boots, a smiling boy arrived to show them out. Zaytuna thanked him as she stepped through the door. Saadia and Ibn Salah remained within. There was something triumphant in Saadia's expression, and he felt for her brother, who watched them go with a frown.

17

"Let's go through the market to find Ammar," Tein said to Zaytuna. "If I were him, I would start searching in the hostels first and those nearest to the road leading to the bridge."

If Tein had his bearings, they could continue on this road east and it would lead them to Abd al-Muttalib Square and onto Jasmine Vine Road, a place he knew too well, and from there into the market. After Saadia and Ibn Salah's stretch of road, the estate walls grew in height and length again. The gates to the homes were broad enough for ten men and had guards stationed in front. The wide streets were not as busy as in Karkh. Mainly, men walked along in clusters; some were obviously servants, but others wore fine cloaks, their turbaned heads inclining to their companions. A well-dressed man rode by on horseback while a boy led a camel laden with goods. A lone dung collector had stopped by the side of the road to rest.

The estate of the vizier Ibn al-Furat was coming up on their right. Abd al-Muttalib Square opened up beyond it. The house at the centre of their last big case was on the corner, and he was thankful that Zaytuna did not mention it as they passed. Once through the market arch at the end of the road, it became more crowded, not just servants and porters, but also wealthy women in trailing robes and men with wool cloaks thrown over their shoulders and turbans in multi-hued fabrics.

He led her down a busy side street and was hit by the scent of meat on a grill. The best kabab he had ever eaten in Baghdad was just down a cul-de-sac. It was early yet, but a line of men and boys trailed around the corner. He wanted to join them. The call for the midday prayer was a way off, and he did not want to wait to find Ammar before eating. Eat first, he decided, then look for Ammar, and double back here later if they could not find him. Tein fell into the back of the line.

But Zaytuna objected, perspiration dotted her forehead. "I feel sick."

"You looked off this morning, too."

"This case is burning a hole in me."

He looked longingly at the line of men waiting for food. "We're going to have to walk by it."

She went on ahead. All he could do was drink in the scent of fat blistering on the coals and fresh bread coming off the tannur as they hurried past. But a wall of food and juice stalls were coming up across from several hostels. The savoury tang of vinegar and stewed meat at the stall serving tharid was not as overpowering and he hoped she could hold on long enough for them to question the hostel proprietors.

"Right there." He led her through an arcade to the first hostel. There were stools and a table out front. "Do you want to come in with me?"

"No." She sat down on one of the stools, bent over, taking small breaths.

"What about some water?"

She shook her head and he went inside.

A short man sat alone on a low couch, eyes closed and cross-legged, counting prayers on his knuckles.

"Assalamu alaykum," Tein said quietly, wishing he did not have to disturb him.

The hostel keeper opened his eyes slowly. "Wa alaykum assalam!" Still serene from his prayers, the man's calm reached out and held him, smoothing the edges of his own disturbed state. Tein felt as if he were in the embrace of a beloved uncle.

"I'm sorry to bother you. I'm looking for my partner. He would've asked about a missing man."

"No bother at all." The hostel keeper stood. "You are always welcome. A stocky man with the bearing of a ghazi came by earlier. He visited all the hostels in this arcade."

"That's him. I suppose the one we are searching for is not here?"

"It seems not. I am sorry for his mother. Any man who abandons his mother has abandoned paradise. May he come to his senses, and return to her."

"Inshallah, we hope to bring him back."

He held his hands out in prayer, "May God open the road before you and reveal his location." He mumbled prayers on the prophet, then wiped his face.

"Amin." Tein hoped his prayers worked.

The man pulled a leather thong at his neck, and a triangular leather talisman pouch popped out. He kissed it, then raised the pouch to his forehead before tucking it back inside his robe.

Of course! The man Abu YingYue said was the only maker of block printed prayers was in the Rusafa market. Why hadn't he thought to go there first? Maybe Nabil had been. Tein said, "I'm looking to buy a block printed prayer. Anyone around here?"

His eyes lit up. "Imam Hossam. His paper shop is not far from here. Continue past the food stalls to your left when you leave. Take a right and you will be on a main road. The paper shops are not far. His prayers are powerful. Verses from the Quran, names of God, and numbers positioned just so." He nodded enthusiastically. "Imam Hossam can print one for you immediately."

"You have been a great help." Tein bowed his head and left.

The man followed him out. "I told your partner to ask for one to find the man."

Tein thanked him again, then smiled eagerly at Zaytuna.

Her colour had returned. "You look as though you found him."

"A lead."

She stood, one hand on the table to steady herself. He put a hand out to help her; she took it gratefully.

Tein gestured to the hostel. "He reminded me of the print maker here in Rusafa when he pulled his own talisman pouch from around his neck. Better, he told me Ammar had been by these hostels already and that he advised him to get a talisman to find Nabil."

"Inshallah!"

They had just got around the corner to the paper shops when they saw Ammar leaning on a narrow counter, sipping from a delicate glass.

Seeing them, Ammar put down his glass, and spoke to someone in the shop they could not see. He waved them over, calling out, "Well met!"

The paper shop was twice as large as Abu YingYue's but set up similarly. Three men in the back were copying manuscripts on desks set against a long wall of shelves. There must have been one hundred manuscripts tucked into thin slots as wide as an arm. On the opposite side, all types and qualities of paper were on shelves and there was a section for reed pens in boxes and bottles of ink in every hue. In the centre was a long table. A manuscript lay open, a ruler and pen as well as small pieces of paper, small enough for the average sized talisman, were laid out. Tein could just see the squares laid out in a grid and words taking shape around its border. In the rear, a large frame drum hung on the wall.

A tall Turkmen with a gentle face greeted them with a hand over his heart. "Assalamu alaykum wa rahmatullahi wa barakatuhu."

"This is Imam Hossam ibn Yusuf, a colleague of Abu YingYue."

"Wa alaykum assalam, I am Tein ibn al-Ashiqa as-Sawda and this is my sister, Zaytuna."

"Our brother here has explained. I hope I have been of some help."

Ammar nodded with satisfaction. "Nabil has been here several times."

Tein silently thanked the hostel keeper for his prayers.

"And he is staying in Rusafa."

"Sir, did he mention a hostel or that he was staying with someone?" Zaytuna asked.

"I believe he was staying with friends. There was no reason to ask for his address, but as we chatted, he mentioned his hosts."

"What did he say?"

"Only that it was at a great estate, and that while his every need was cared for, he had not seen his hosts since the day he had moved in."

Tein whispered to Zaytuna, "How would he be cold?"

"I don't know. But I trust Uncle."

"When was he here last?" Tein asked Imam Hossam.

"Two days ago. He stopped by quickly and ordered a ream of paper, pens, and ink. It took two men a day to rule that much paper, but he has not returned for it."

Ammar said, "The first time he came here, he asked about block printing the manuscript."

"God protect us from evil things," said Imam Hossam.

"Abu YingYue said you would refuse."

"Indeed. But once I refused, he did not task me about it further. He stopped by to chat, asking about the cost of a copyist, then ordered the ruled paper and pens."

"He planned to copy it himself," Ammar said.

"Yes, it seems so. But I found it odd that he proposed block printing, which would require great funds, then balked at the relatively inexpensive cost of hand copying the manuscript himself."

It was another gambit. Maybe he was planning on creating a manuscript, not copying one. Ibn Shanabudh and Ibn Mujahid's demand to see the manuscript had driven Nabil into a corner. But why had he not come back for his order?

"Did he show you the manuscript he wanted printed?" Zaytuna asked.

"No," Imam Hossam answered, carefully. "And I did not press him."

"Where is he?" Zaytuna turned to Tein.

"My guess is not in someone's great estate anymore."

"Why's that?" Ammar asked.

"He's moved on, or he would have been back for the paper."

"It's only been two days, Tein," Ammar objected.

That made sense, but Tein trusted his uncle that he was cold and uncomfortable.

"So you visited Saadia?"

He had no intention of bringing up the conversation about al-Hallaj and risking Ammar cursing the man and said only, "She's going to ask the women in her social circle if anyone is hiding him."

"I'm going to wait here with Imam Hossam for Nabil," Ammar said. "He'll be back."

"Out in the open like this?" Zaytuna asked.

He gestured across the street where a few small tables and stools were set out. "I'll wait there."

"What's next?" Tein turned to Zaytuna. "We should check the market. He might be out. Look in hostels as we come across them."

She gave him a worried look. "Let's head home for today."

"I'm keeping up the search." His attack had long passed and he did not need her fussing over him. "You can stay or go."

But she followed him, and he led her deeper into the market. Zaytuna did not complain or question as he scoured the passersby, looking in shops with fabrics piled high, scrutinizing those waiting at apothecary counters, even checking the small prayer halls tucked in-between shops. Through it all, she did not say a word until they hit a street lined with dried fruit and nut shops and she tugged his sleeve. "Eat."

The cadence of her voice came from their distant past, after their mother died and before he had left for the frontier. They had been sharing a small plate of stew with one hunk of mutton at the centre. Barely in his teens, he was already taller and broader than most men and there was never enough food for him. She picked out the meat and placed it before him.

"Eat," she said again.

Customers pressed around each stall. Sturdy old housekeepers with their long apron wraps draped around and over their heads gestured at what they wanted and chided the shopkeepers to give them the best. Boys stood nearby to carry the burdens, one sneaking food from a basket at his feet. Well-dressed servants and fine men bought snacks for the women they accompanied in the market, who waited at an appropriate distance from the crush of people. Tein made his way in as customers left until he was standing before the baskets and barrels of nuts and dried fruits from across the empire.

Glancing back at his sister, he pressed his hand to his chest again, but for a different pain, the exquisite love that fed them through all they had endured together and how far they had come. The shopkeeper called him to attention and Tein gave him the order, each choice what love would have paid for, had it coin to give. The shopkeeper handed him a full sack of the most expensive fruits, requiring nearly everything he had in his pocket.

Zaytuna took the sack from him and peered inside. Pulling out a long piece of pale green dried melon, she declared, "You spoil me!"

They found a bit of wall to lean against a way down from the shop, and ate.

"The shopkeeper said that melon is from Marw. Something of our Uncle Abu Bakr."

She held up her hands in prayer for their uncle, who had so gruffly taught them about God before leaving Baghdad, and now lived so far away in Turkmen lands.

Tein watched her tear off a large piece of the prized melon with her back teeth and chew, mouth full, relaxing into the joy of childlike gluttony.

Digging in the sack, he pulled out a thin slice of fruit the colour of a red sunset alight with fiery orange blazes. "These are from China."

Zaytuna snatched the red fruit from him with a laugh.

From a second sack, he pulled out a handful of walnuts, lifted his head to pour them into his mouth from his fist and chewed, enjoying the sweetness of the woody meat cut by the pucker of new wine.

Then the cold came, rising up from his feet and finding its way into his fingers, shoulders and head, but strangely leaving his heart warm and beating. al-Hallaj was here. The nuts turned to grit in his mouth.

"One of the aunts or uncles is here," Zaytuna said, craning her head to see. "I can feel it."

"It's al-Hallaj."

"What?" She faced him. "I don't see him."

"He'll be here soon."

"Ya Rabb!" She put a hand on his arm. "How could you feel it? You never have."

"I did not ask for it."

She took him in with wonder and kinship. "Tell me."

"During the last case, al-Hallaj did something to me. I've been like this since."

Her confused features fell into place. "That explains…"

"Fine," he stopped her and brushed her hand off.

Uncle Nuri's patient guidance had brought him out of taverns, unclenched his fists and loosened his hold on his dagger, and made him worthy of Saliha. All the aunts and uncles had done their part. But none of them had pushed him to be like his sister, let alone his mother, not even Uncle Abu al-Qasim. Then al-Hallaj came and broke Tein open, not caring that Tein hated him, or that he barely thought of God. It left him fearing al-Hallaj's power even more.

He had forced Tein to sip from the well in which his mother had drowned. With that one sip, he felt safe for the first time in his life. More than that, he was filled with the sense that whatever came, it would find its place, and he would find his place within it. He put his hand to the butter churn instead of his dagger. How could he explain that churning butter built a wall around him, widening his world with its limited terrain? The man forced an impossible peace on him, yet threatened the lives of everyone he loved. How could he welcome him? Only curses suited his arrival, and now those had been taken from him.

"Assalamu alaykum, my children." The voice of al-Hallaj cut through the noise of the market.

They watched him approach, winding his way through the crowd. Zaytuna took Tein's trembling hand and he did not let go.

"You. I have not seen you since you were a child," he said to Zaytuna. "But this one, we seem to find each other."

As he cast his eyes on Tein, a tether of light resolved into existence and bound them to him. The marketplace seemingly emptied and silence fell like a gentle rain.

"Wa alaykum assalam, uncle," Zaytuna said, without fear, as if this person were not holding her in an inescapable grasp.

Tein opened his mouth to ask him to remember the safety of the Sufi community, but every word curdled on his tongue. Instead, he felt their rejection of al-Hallaj as if it had been he who had been cast out for breaking rules that none had the right to make, and said aloud, as if al-Hallaj were speaking through him, "For speaking the truth of God to the estranged? For this I was estranged?"

"I am the bush through which God informed Moses," al-Hallaj answered, whispering into the emptiness of the marketplace. He stared into their eyes and addressed God. "I have embraced, with my whole being, all Your love, O my Holiness. You have manifested Yourself so totally that it seems to me there is only You in me. I examine my heart amidst all that is not You. I do not see any estrangement between them and me, and only familiarity between You and me. Alas. Here am I, in the prison of life, reunited with the whole human race. Take me with You, outside of this prison."

Zaytuna clenched Tein's hand.

"Your sister understands the bindings of the soul. Why have you returned to this world?"

"I...," Tein began.

"Shh. You have warned your aunts and uncles of me. What else can you do to protect them but take my life? I would lay my head in your hands if you were the one." He looked into the distance as if he were seeing something, then sighed, returning his attention to Tein. "You complain of me, but have you ever complained of your uncle Nuri?"

Tein slowly shook his head.

"You do not rail against him, he who smashed the wine jars of the caliphs. He who spoke the truth of God and was cast to the dunghills. Nearly executed. Exiled instead. How am I different?" He leaned in. "And your mother?"

Zaytuna's hand loosened in his. She swayed.

"Do not speak of my mother." His anger wrestled with the bonds of light.

"Do not condemn God's friends," al-Hallaj countered.

Sparks of light danced at the edges of his vision and his ears filled with a deafening hum. He wanted to escape, but could not find a way. The sparks closed in, occluding his sight, the empty market, his sister. Then al-Hallaj disappeared and a patch of tall swaying grass came into view. Hundreds of birds burst from the grasses into the bright sky, revealing his uncle Nuri just as he was that day on the canal bed, holding out his arms and saying the same words, "My son, you've come to visit me."

Tein fell into his arms, but heard al-Hallaj speaking in his ear.

"You will never taste what your mother did. Your sister, though, *wa zaytun*, her mother's black light courses through her."

The tender world of his uncle and the canal fell away. He found himself being held in al-Hallaj's arms and pushed him off, furious, reaching for Zaytuna to wrest her free. She was fixed, watching al-Hallaj, her face bearing the traces of ecstasy.

al-Hallaj addressed her. "This begins your first true steps on the path, my daughter."

Tein tried to get in between them but could not move and listened helplessly as al-Hallaj instructed his sister with words he did not understand.

"The path of innumerable steps in the white light of *the soul at peace with God*. Will you make short work of it? Will you leave the grasp of your old days for good and find yourself in a stream of light, each drop a yellow, burning sun, and *return to your Lord content*, accepting the travails of being satisfied with God? Will God accept you into the deepening purple waters of unbounded faith *for being pleased with you*? And, then, perhaps God will have *perfected your religion for you*, and you will enter the black waters of the ocean without shore, accepting all light and rejecting none." His voice turned to warning. "Be careful, there is no guarantee. To your last, you will beg forgiveness."

Zaytuna's eyes closed as she collapsed. Tein dropped down and held her in his arms. She was perfectly still except for the long, smooth breaths of deep sleep.

"Yet you, Tein, taste the love of your family and wonder how you will breathe without their presence. You breathe the sour air of other people, not the sweet scent of divine union. Your beloveds are idols and mine is God. When you have embraced God's love such that God has erased you, there is only God in you. How could you stand to return, cast into the teeming square of this life, reunited with the whole human race? You will beg God, like I, to pull you out. I only complain of this!"

Tein trembled, terrified that Saliha would be ripped from his arms, his sister gone, his family deserted, and he, back within the walls of the cemetery, tasting the dust of graves, barred even from his mother's bones. His mother, who had chewed dates in her own mouth before placing them in his infant mouth, now drew their taste from his tongue.

"You fool." al-Hallaj sighed with irritation. "I am saying that you do not need to protect this community. But hear this: the day when I redden the gibbet with my blood, the Sufis will don the coat of literalism. They will join the scholars, seeking to share this world's square with them, while we will be outside its open gates, calling them to free themselves." He threw his head back. "That is how they hide!" Then, al-Hallaj bent over until his face was a hand's span from Tein's own. "They hide in the open, with their enemies." He straightened. "Call your sister. She's passed away into God."

But Tein remained fixated on the intensity of al-Hallaj, fearing what he would do next. Zaytuna's breathing changed on its own and she reached out and took hold of him. He faced her unwillingly. Her expression was soft, each line carved by hardship released. Her eyes were clear, nearly black glittering pools.

"Help me up," she said, "before someone interrupts us."

Suddenly, he heard the noise of the market again and felt the brush of robes against him. He lifted her, knowing those around them were watching.

Ignoring the crowds, she faced al-Hallaj.

"I've been sharing secrets with your brother. I have urged him to love divine, eternal life."

She put her arm through Tein's, but it was she who was supporting him.

"I have one last secret to share." He stared straight at Tein. "Soon you will know the greatest idolatry. A woman you love is with child."

He bowed deeply and left before they could respond.

Saliha is pregnant.

Violent joy ripped him open, taking his mind with it.

He was doomed to sacrifice himself before the idol of loving his family and he keened with gratitude to be ruined so. But his mind, unbound and reeling, led him to the memory of his late wife, Ayzit, and his infant child, Husayn, slaughtered, lying in a bloody embrace. His joy fell to its knees before their bodies and he vowed to protect Saliha and their child.

This is what al-Hallaj meant.

Tein gazed at his hands. He would become a watcher again. A killer in waiting. For Saliha and their child. He looked desperately at Zaytuna. This is exactly what their mother had not done. She had put her children in danger when she fell into ecstasy, refusing this worldly love of her children for God alone. He vowed he would love his child the way he had not been loved. He would protect his child the way he had not been protected. If giving them up to danger was the price of the peace he had felt with that one sip al-Hallaj had forced down his throat before, he would never know peace again.

Zaytuna held him for only a moment, not understanding, then put her hand on his shoulder. "There's more to this than you right now. We must ask him about Nabil." She turned back in the direction al-Hallaj had gone and found him stopped at the same shop, waiting his turn.

Tein knew it had to be done, but he no longer cared about the case. He only wanted to find Saliha and place one hand where their baby was growing within her and the other on his dagger. But he joined his sister, watching, and listened.

"Uncle."

He faced her just as the shopkeeper asked al-Hallaj for his order. "What is good here?"

"The dried melon from Marw," she said easily and Tein had no idea how she was even speaking after all that had just happened.

"You heard her," he said to the shopkeeper, "give me a mix of your finest and most rare and do not stint on the melon from Marw."

"Uncle," she pulled him back. "We are searching for a man and some say you may be hiding him."

"Where?" He held open his cloak, winking. "'There is only God under this cloak'."

Zaytuna chuckled and touched his arm. "Please. His name is Nabil."

He shrugged, and Tein wanted to grasp him with both hands and shake an answer from him.

"He claims to have a copy of Ibn Masud's codex."

Recognition lit up his face. "Yes! I was sitting with my friends listening to tales of the prophets and he insisted on my attention. The storyteller had only just got to the part when the Seven Sleepers had awakened when he pulled me away. I will never hear that story again, just that way. Alas, what is this world if not that? These passing moments. The ass tried to flatter me with a warning that Ibn Mujahid would come for me and that I should be careful." He glanced around him as if his companions were there with them. "My friends laughed at the man and I gently asked him to leave. Then he declared that he had an autographed manuscript and would I not like to see it? Would I not like to use it against the man who would bring me to the gibbet? I told him I would embrace the man who brought me to such an end." He threw his shoulders back and spread out his arms in welcome. "'Then come!' I called to him, 'We shall embrace him now'. Instead, he ran off."

"When was this?"

"Yesterday."

"Did he show you the manuscript?"

Tein knew the answer before he said it.

"There is no manuscript. The boy is a troublemaker."

Zaytuna gave him a crooked smile. "Not like you."

"Not like me." He laughed and said loudly enough for all to hear, "My daughter," and embraced her in the street. People looked askance, but there were no whispers.

Tein stared as his sister teased this man as if he were one of their beloved uncles.

Sack of dried fruit in hand, the shopkeeper called to al-Hallaj. Acting as if he were a loving grandfather surrounded by pestering children, al-Hallaj shooed Tein and Zaytuna off with a scolding look, and gave his coin to the man.

Tein eagerly walked away, pulling Zaytuna along.

"Tein, stop," she said, catching up. "You will be a father."

He kept walking, still unsteady from the news. "Don't tell Saliha."

"Yes. It's better not to say anything." She took his arm. "But it would've been better if you hadn't known."

Not knowing be better? The news of the culmination of his every want, a family again, a tiny hand gripping his finger, his arms full of life.

But Zaytuna went on, "You remember what Auntie Amina said when that old woman came around telling fortunes. The problem with knowing means you have no time to grow into what will come. Knowing makes you look around every corner and miss what you needed before it happens."

The shock found an easy path to resentment. "You think I'm not ready to be a father?"

"I think you are not ready for Saliha finding out she is going to be a mother." She returned her hand to his arm. "You will be a wonderful father."

He accepted her clarification and let it go. "Home?"

"We need to tell Ammar what al-Hallaj said, and I need to find Bahr."

"You?" He would not let her go unprotected. "You go home and leave it to us."

"No," she said. "I'll go to his house to question the servants. We may get all we need that way. If he's there, God willing, he will speak to me."

Fearing her answer, he asked, "How will you know where to go?"

"I'll ask Mustafa."

Only a moment ago, his sister had collapsed into an ecstatic state and now she wakes wanting to see Mustafa, not her own husband.

"I am going to ask Mustafa," she repeated firmly.

"I am coming with you."

She gazed at him strangely. "To my last, I will beg forgiveness."

"What's that supposed to mean?"

"That I cannot return to Kamal Ali without seeing Mustafa again."

"I'm to be a father. Saliha a mother. You love Kamal Ali. Our home. Our people. You will throw all that away because"—he stopped, a curse against al-Hallaj nearly out of his mouth—"because this man...?"

"Because this man led me into a moment of passing away from this world, from myself?" She looked down, guiltily. "I don't know how to explain."

"Did this happen when Uncle Abu al-Qasim did the same to you before?"

"Exactly the same. I left that state of passing away in God only to run directly into myself, my worst inclinations." She turned back sharply. "You don't understand. Exactly because of what just happened, I must face it. Retreating to Kamal Ali will not make my feelings for Mustafa go away. I must end it once and for all."

"Are you sure it is an ending?"

"I'll know when I get there."

"You'll what?" He stared. "Would Uncle Abu al-Qasim tell you do to what you are planning?"

Zaytuna crossed her arms.

"Exactly what I thought. I am coming with you."

"You cannot save me from myself."

"I could lock you up. Any man in any other family would do so."

She scoffed. "I am not under your protection."

"If you will not think of yourself, think of us," he insisted.

"Go home and hold your wife and your tongue. I am stopping back at the paper shop to see Ammar." She pulled another fiery dried red fruit from the sack, then turned her back on him, cutting through the crowd.

He nearly went home, leaving her to destroy her life, all their lives, but she was under his watch whether she accepted it or not. Tein hurried after her, coming close to cursing her for her recklessness. By the time he caught up to her at the paper shop, she was deep in conversation with Ammar.

"That did not deter one of the women from hiding Nabil." Ammar smiled with satisfaction.

"How do you know?" Tein demanded, walking up.

Zaytuna answered for him. "Just after we left, a boy came to pay for the paper."

"Nabil sent him? Did you follow the boy back?"

"No, no," Ammar said. "Not like that. I questioned him. He said that his master's household would not allow a guest's debt to go unpaid."

"Who is he staying with?"

"Was he staying with, more like. You were right. The boy told me that the housekeeper was angry because Nabil was acting like a little caliph, demanding food and drink to be brought to his room at all hours. She had to keep it secret because the woman of the house had not informed her husband."

"Ghada," Zaytuna said.

"What happened?"

"The housekeeper told the boy that no whore of a wife would ruin her good name. She told the husband."

Tein had to hold back from staring at Zaytuna.

"Do not cross a housekeeper," Ammar said in a sage tone. "The lady is banished to her wing. Bad for us. Nabil was out on his ear and no one knows where he went."

"Two days ago, then. Did he have anything with him?"

"He did. A leather sack. I asked them how big it was or if they knew what was in it. It was big enough for a manuscript and some clothes.”

“He could go home if he liked, but he prefers to stir up trouble. Let’s just go tell his mother and be done with it.” And, he wanted to add, be done with Zaytuna running after Mustafa.

“No. We’re still on the case.” Ammar was firm. “We have to know who is after him and why. We need to talk to Bahr.”

Zaytuna interjected, “What we know is that the existence of the manuscript would be welcome. They are afraid of his threat to block print it.”

“So whatever he is after, he can’t get it without printing it,” Ammar reasoned.

“You are talking again like the manuscript exists!”

“Fine, Tein. The threat of printing it is enough. Or maybe forging one. Maybe that is why he wanted the lined paper.”

“We need Bahr,” Ammar said. “I’m going to stay in Rusafa and keep tracking Nabil down. I was only waiting for you, hoping you’d come back this way.”

“I am going after Bahr tomorrow.” Zaytuna said.

Tein kept his mouth shut.

Ammar put a hand on his shoulder. “Stay here with me. All night! Just like old times.”

He shrugged him off angrily, lying, “I promised Saliha.”

“You see how it is?”

“What!”

“These women are in the way of the case.” He tipped his head at Zaytuna. “Present company excluded.”

She sucked her teeth at them. “The two of you. I’m leaving.”

Tein watched her disappear into the crowd, set on destroying their lives. Something else he would have to clean up because there was no one but him to protect them all. “You got it backwards.” He gestured at Zaytuna’s back as she left. “She’s the problem.”

“What?”

“Nothing.” Tein regretted saying it, not wanting to explain. “The case is the problem.”

Ammar placed his hand on the hilt of his sword. "Go home to your wife, then."

"I saw you the other day," Tein accused him. "Your wife carrying your child and you were unhappy to see her. She saw it, too. You love this case more than your own wife and child."

"I wasn't made for this," Ammar spat out. "I wasn't made for being at home. I was made for the battlefield. She's only known me while I churned butter. She doesn't know how to be my wife."

"Nasifa fell in love with you on our last case. She fought on that case, for your sake." He lowered his voice. "Talk to her."

"You talk to your wife."

"If you aren't careful, she'll be no more to you than the mother of your son."

Ammar lifted his sword slightly from its sheath, but Tein had seen the alarm in his eyes. He did not want to be an indifferent husband. He only wanted more.

"Stay out all night, then," he said. "But send a messenger saying where you are so she doesn't worry."

Ammar shook his head slowly. "Go home."

Tein left, vowing to send his own message to Nasifa.

DAY SIX

18

IBN SHAHIN'S boys were chattering excitedly upstairs as Mustafa placed that day's portion of Abu Umar ad-Duri's reading tradition on the low desk. They were coming up to the verses about the young prophet Yusuf cast into the well and he had promised to fill in the rest of the story. He enjoyed animating it for them, telling it as he had learned, listening to storytellers in the marketplace. He and Zaytuna had sat at his mother's feet, holding hands with worry, waiting for Yusuf to be saved by his brothers, only for him to be sold into slavery. After the story, he planned to send the little ones off to practice their recitation of the first and last two chapters of the Quran and instruct the eldest with a discussion of grammar in the verses they would read that day.

"There is a lady outside asking for you." The servant boy appeared as if out of nowhere, making him jump.

Please God, not YingYue.

She had come twice before about something trivial, never understanding that he should not be disturbed at work except in an emergency. He had already twisted the truth for excuses to meet Tein and Ammar, and could not imagine Ibn Shahin would accept anymore from him.

The children's footsteps were on the stairs.

He hurriedly followed the servant through the kitchen to the rear courtyard. The cook glanced at them as she positioned loaves of bread within the hot tannur with a long curved stick and flicked out those that were done into her rag-covered hand. The boy opened the rear gate for Mustafa, but no one was there. He clicked his tongue with frustration, then stepped out and looked down the alley.

In the distance, a tall woman leaned against the wall, her back to him. Her wrap blew out behind her in the breeze. Deep red, pink, and green contrasted beautifully with the yellow clay of the bricks on the wall. Dust rising from the street transformed her into a long-stemmed rose growing miraculously in the desert. Even if not for her slim frame and height, her shoulders were thrown back in a way he knew all too well.

Zaytuna had come for him.

She did not come to his home shared with YingYue and YingYue's father, as she should, with a companion, or, even more in keeping with propriety, send a message. Zaytuna had only been to his place of work once before, to declare her love, to promise that she could be a wife to him, to reach him before he married YingYue. He let her go that day. Never again. The men at his uncle's encouraged him to mourn her as if his own wife had died in his arms. Yet here she was, as if by a miracle, returned to him. She had come to him. For him.

The children were forgotten. Mustafa did not run to her but slowed, every muscle in his body anticipating her love. He called her name from that place of desire, his voice thick with emotion. "Zaytuna."

She turned as if out of time. "I need your help."

It was like that first day when he had come to her saying the same, but unlike her, he answered, "Anything."

"I need to find Bahr, to speak to him, or at least his servants. I don't know where he lives."

She is here. For me. Not this. For me.

"I could have sent a message." She looked up and down the street as if someone were listening. "I hoped you might do more than tell me how to find him."

"Yes." He held his breath.

"Could you come with me? I can't go into the mosque by myself to ask his colleagues." She became more serious, her eyes worried. "We also need to talk about the other day. About our old days."

"I'll come now." He started to leave with her, nearly reaching for her hand to lead her away, but pulled back before he erred again and frightened her off. The mosque was not far; he could make some excuse to accompany her to Bahr's home as well.

"Don't you need to tell them you are leaving?"

Shocked into awareness, he turned sharply toward the open gate door. He would have to go back. The children would be waiting, having been informed he was speaking to someone and would return. If he left with her, he may not be welcome back. But if he went back into Ibn Shahin's house and put off the class, telling them he would return tomorrow, he would asking, not telling, and Ibn Shahin would refuse. He had already begrudged Mustafa the bit of freedom he needed for the case. Mustafa held up his hand, asking her to wait while he ran to shut the gate door. "They were not expecting me today. I only came because I had some free time."

When he returned, she asked, "To the mosque first?"

"Yes. Tein and Ammar acted so much like police when they were there. Of course Bahr ran. God willing, we will do better."

"Is there a chance he will be there?"

"God knows."

They walked side by side with an appropriate distance between them, but he found himself swaying towards her and having to correct. Still, she did not lurch away from him, a clear sign of her acceptance.

As they turned the corner onto a narrow street of shops, the crowd caused them to walk more closely. Mustafa noticed a woman haggling with the greengrocer next to them. She and the grocer gestured energetically over the quality of the onions. There was a man beside her. He leaned in, his body and hand open to hers. He loved her. The haggling completed, she passed the onions back to the man and her face came alive with desire. Mustafa came alive with her. His hand reached out past any restraint and brushed against Zaytuna's fingers.

She jerked her hand away, pulling her wrap over her face, and moved into the crowd away from him.

He went after her, raising curses. Desperate not to lose her in the busy street, he nearly shoved a woman aside until finally he caught up with her and whispered behind her ear, "My love." She did not reply, but took two quick steps to put more distance between them. Mustafa hoped she would be willing to speak to him by the time they reached the mosque. It was only a fright, he told himself. Nothing could change the fact that she had come for him, that she loved him. He wished he could see her face, but she kept the wrap drawn over it, only one eye exposed to see the road ahead.

A few more turns and they were at the Basra Gate High Road, not far from the road leading to the Sharqiyya mosque. She hurried across it without him, then waited on the other side. After, they walked in charged silence until they reached the mosque. He tugged his long robe straight, threw his wrap over his shoulder, and touched his turban. But at the great doors into the mosque, she held back.

"Would you like to talk?" he ventured.

"No," she said. "Not now." She turned her face aside, still veiling herself from him.

It was a promise for later. "Would you like to come in with me?"

"No," she snapped.

Mustafa drew back at her tone.

She cleared her throat and said more evenly, "I'll wait for you here."

"If he is there, I will draw him outside to speak with both of us. Otherwise, I will find out where he lives and we can go there next."

But the sharp change in her tone worried him; he feared he had gone too far. A knot tightened within him and he chastised himself as he went into the mosque.

Within, there was the usual scene of hadith students at the far corner near the imam's private entrance. Ibn Shanabudh's circles were straight ahead on the other side while Ibn Mujahid's students gathered nearest the entrance. Some three hundred or more were clustered in small groups around his teaching assistants. Ibn Mujahid himself was further in, sitting near a pillar, with a small group around him and a manuscript open before him. Mustafa walked slowly towards them, his eye out for Bahr. But circle after circle, he was not there.

"Mustafa." Sharafuddin came up beside him. "Come!"

Only then did Mustafa notice that there was a sea of turbans where Sharafuddin's father usually sat. The imam should have been teaching his daily lessons in hadith in which they learned the names of the transmitters, their biographies, and were taught the means to judge the men's reliability and the reliability of the chain of transmission. Instead, nearly a hundred men were crowded around a scholar, some at the edges, standing and chatting. Several women, their faces veiled, sat within the door to the imam's home. Mustafa craned his head and saw him. It was Imam Abu Abdurrahman al-Azdi. He was back in Baghdad, from Medina, the city of the Prophet and peace.

Imam Abu Abdurrahman had taken him under his wing, permitting him to receive the Hadith of the Golden Chain, reports of what Muhammad said and did with the fewest transmitters between them and the Prophet himself. He, Mustafa, was permitted to hear these reports from Imam Abu Abdurrahman al-Azdi, who heard it from Abu Ali al-Yamani, who heard it from Imam Malik, who heard it from an-Nafi, who heard it from Ibn Umar, who heard it from the Prophet himself. The certificate he gained allowed him to teach, transforming him from impoverished, unmarried Mustafa the potter, to Mustafa the scholar and husband to YingYue. He shivered.

"Are you sick?"

"No, just thinking of that day we sat with him and how it changed my life."

Sharafuddin placed a hand on his back. "You look pale."

Mustafa brought his hand to his forehead. It was clammy.

"I should go greet him, but then I would be obligated to sit and I cannot." He looked longingly at the group as he asked, "Do you know Bahr ibn Abi Shuayb? A student of Ibn Mujahid."

Sharafuddin scoffed, half turning to get back. "Know one of them? There are hundreds of his students."

"Go back to the imam," Mustafa urged. "You should not miss anything. Besides, you must teach me what you learned later."

"Come with me."

But Zaytuna was waiting outside. He needed to bring her something—anything—lay it at her feet, and so hear her disclose her love.

"Why do you sit with Ibn Mujahid?"

"Is it wrong to expand my knowledge beyond hadith?" He did not want to say that he had already been expelled from their circles. "It is not that. I am sorry. It makes me a more valuable tutor. I am married now and rely on my wife's father to support us. My pay at the moment would not be enough to rent our room."

"The difficulty in spreading yourself over several specializations is that you may find yourself master of none." Sharafuddin put his hand on Mustafa's shoulder. "We are still students of hadith. If you do not advance, what are you expecting?"

"Who will ever sit at a pillar to learn with me?" he asked harshly. "My reputation is stained. My only chance now is to make myself a more valuable tutor."

Sharafuddin's eyes softened with understanding. He did not object, even if only to be polite.

Ibn Mujahid's teaching circles were breaking up. Mustafa said, "I must go. I am sorry to miss the class, but I must take care of an important matter." He walked away, saying, "assalamu alaykum," over his shoulder.

A teaching assistant he had sat with once before was standing by a pillar with a man he did not recognize. Unlike the teaching assistant, who dressed more plainly in a scholar's turban and stood with his hands clasped over the sash at his waist, this man leaned casually against a pillar, wearing a bright red turban and his wrap thrown carelessly over his shoulder.

Mustafa did not intrude, but hovered nearby, listening for a break in their conversation. But before he could greet them, the man leaning on the pillar noticed him. "Assalamu alaykum."

"Wa alaykum assalam. I am sorry to bother you." He nodded to the teaching assistant. "I sat in on one of your classes. I am a hadith student but have been enjoying learning more about Quran readings."

"Of course, welcome." It was obvious the man did not recognize him.

"I was looking for one of your students, Bahr ibn Abi Shuayb."

"I know you, now." His stance became defensive. "You were with those two men who questioned him outside the mosque. What is your business?"

Mustafa did not balk at his tone. "Your informant must have told you that we are looking for Nabil ibn al-Qays al-Kufi. His mother reported that he and Bahr had fought."

The one in the red turban stood straight. "Bahr is a good man. That Nabil, on the other hand."

"We cannot help you," the teacher said, attempting to cut off his colleague from continuing. "I only hope that Nabil has left the city, although I do not wish him on another."

"Not even Ibn Shanabudh," the one in the red turban replied wryly.

"Whatever Nabil's qualities, he is still the son of a mother who grieves and worries."

The teaching assistant gave in. "Bahr and Nabil did seem to know each other well. But while Nabil was eager, Bahr wanted nothing to do with him."

"Yes," the one in the red turban added, "he wanted nothing to do with him once Nabil accused him of having seen the mysterious manuscript of Ibn Masud."

"When did this happen?"

"Right before Nabil disappeared. Nabil asked Ibn Hammad to bring him before Ibn Mujahid himself."

"Ibn Hammad?" Mustafa asked. "Ibn Mujahid's teaching assistant?"

"Who else? We were all there. It was extraordinary. Nabil insisted he had the manuscript but was unwilling…"

"Unable," the teaching assistant corrected.

"Yes, unable to produce it. Ibn Mujahid said the existence of such a manuscript would be valuable to their study and he would like to see it. But Nabil refused."

"Ibn Mujahid wanted to know why he was speaking of it if he were not in a position to produce it," the teaching assistant clarified.

"Ibn Mujahid never lost his patience," the man in the red turban said, enjoying the feel of the story. "Before us all, Nabil pointed at Bahr and said Bahr had seen it. In fact, he insisted that the two of them had been studying it together and Bahr was convinced that the Prophet approved Ibn Masud's reading."

"We were aghast," the teaching assistant assured Mustafa. "And Bahr denied it all."

The one in the red turban added, "Then Nabil angrily declared that Bahr secretly sided with Ibn Shanabudh and rejected the boundaries set by the caliph Uthman's codex."

Why would Bahr hide this? He must have known they would find out.

"It was a grave accusation," the one in the red turban said. "Ibn Shanabudh even recited rejected verses from Ibn Masud's reading tradition while leading the prayer one day, in public, in the mihrab of the mosque. I heard there was nearly a riot that day. He should be barred."

"I knew he had done so, but I had no idea it was here!" Mustafa said. "And a riot?"

"I do not know the details, but everyone has heard about it." He leaned in like an old woman sharing gossip in the market.

"We do not know what happened or where," the teaching assistant insisted. "It could be the gossip of his enemies. Or he could have been reciting accepted readings, only the congregants were unfamiliar with them." He brushed off the accusation as foolishness. "The people are unaccustomed to any reading other than what they have been taught." He scolded his companion. "We have no idea what he was reciting."

"I would not put it past him," the man in the red turban said, then slipped into a righteous tone. "He should be disallowed a pillar to teach."

"There is no reason to bar him. Surely it was unthinking of him to recite accepted but unfamiliar verses. We discuss them, but we do not recite them so as not to upset the people at a moment in which their minds should be on God."

"Unthinking?" the man in the red turban said. "No, he was selfish. He should only recite from ad-Duri's reading when leading the people of Baghdad. Ibn Mujahid is correct. We should not confuse the masses."

Mustafa found himself nodding vigorously, wanting to jump in with his own thoughts, but looked reflexively toward the entrance. Zaytuna was waiting outside. "What happened after that? I mean, to Bahr?"

"Like we said, Ibn Mujahid himself barred Nabil from approaching our circles."

The one in the red turban said, "In no uncertain terms, he told Nabil to bring the manuscript to him or never return."

"And Bahr?"

"He denied it all," the teaching assistant repeated. "But Ibn Mujahid no longer trusts him. He is under our watch for any signs that what Nabil said is true."

"But we have not seen him for a couple of days," said the one in the red turban.

"Perhaps when we find Nabil, we can clear Bahr's name," Mustafa offered. "If you could tell me where Bahr lives, I could find him and, inshallah, resolve this matter quickly."

The teaching assistant looked around the mosque, then gestured at a young black man in a green turban just joining a group of students. "Himmat ibn Isiib may know where he lives."

"The man in the green turban?"

"Precisely. I have seen them come and go together."

"Thank you for your help." He placed his hand over his heart to leave, but the one who was his teaching assistant stopped him.

"Take care with your involvement," he said. "You may find yourself unwelcome not only in our circles of learning"—he tipped his head toward the corner of the mosque where the Imam Abu Abdurrahman was teaching—"but others."

He did not know his warning was too late.

Himmat noticed Mustafa's approach and left his colleagues to meet him halfway. His expression was stern and Mustafa expected to be turned away.

"Assalamu alaykum. I was hoping you might help me find a friend."

"Wa alaykum assalam. I know you are looking for Nabil," Himmat said impatiently.

"I understand you are a friend of Bahr," he spoke quickly. "I hoped you could help me find him so his name can be cleared."

Himmat crossed his arms and looked back at his colleagues, some of whom were watching him. He gave them an irritated shake of the head.

"Would you mind coming outside? My cousin is waiting for me."

Despite his reticence, Himmat said, "I will speak outside."

"I…"

"Outside," Himmat repeated. He turned to his colleagues, giving them a beleaguered look and indicated he would return quickly.

Mustafa hurried to the entrance, but Zaytuna was no longer there. As he leaned against the great archway to put on his boots, he searched for her among those coming and going from the mosque.

"Where is your cousin?"

Then he saw her beside the mosque, standing perfectly straight. Her face was unveiled and her expression inscrutable. The knot within him tightened. "This way." He led Himmat to her, hoping he was bringing her the answer she needed and he would be forgiven.

When Zaytuna saw Himmat, her face softened into curiosity and, without realizing, Mustafa squeezed Himmat's hand.

Himmat snatched his hand away, but asked Mustafa warmly, "Your cousin is Nubian?"

"Yes, her mother was a famed Nubian mystic."

"Like Dhu'l Nun al-Misri?"

"She was known as al-Ashiqa as-Sawda. I always imagined Auntie was Dhu'l Nun's daughter."

"Was she?" Himmat asked, fascinated.

They reached her before he could say he had only imagined it.

Himmat did not wait to be introduced. "My sister, daughter of al-Ashiqa as-Sawda, it is a pleasure to meet you."

Hand over heart, she bowed her head to him as he did to her.

"This is Himmat ibn Isiib. A friend of Bahr."

"I would not call him my friend," Himmat said smoothly, addressing Zaytuna only.

"No?" She asked.

"He liked to confide in me." He gave her a knowing look. "I like to gather confidences."

Despite being useful in the moment, Mustafa was taken aback by such an unseemly trait in a scholar of Quran.

But Zaytuna smiled. "Fine weapons."

"Just so!" Himmat clapped his hands with pleasure. "How can I help?"

Mustafa asked, "I heard some of your colleagues say just now that Nabil singled Bahr out in front of Ibn Mujahid. Do you know why?"

Himmat looked quickly around him before speaking. "Nabil was drowning before Ibn Mujahid's demands. Perhaps he hoped to take Bahr with him? But none of us would have held out a hand to save the man."

"I don't understand," Zaytuna said.

"Nabil was arrogant. Bahr was arrogant. They were childhood friends, both raised in wealth and privilege." He rubbed his two forefingers together. "The same."

"Are they friends, still?" Mustafa asked.

"Not according to Bahr," Himmat said. "He left the village over ten years ago. As he tells the tale of his youthful success, he had a great facility in memorizing and reciting the Quran, and despite being ungainly, he had the pure voice of a prepubescent boy. Men arrived in throngs to the mosque to listen to him and weep. Women would sit outside rending their garments as his voice reached them in the courtyard. A visiting scholar convinced his parents that he should study formally with him. By the age of eleven, he had two reading traditions through Asim memorized. When it came time for the scholar to move on to Baghdad, he brought Bahr with him."

"Subhanallah!" Mustafa gaped. "How many does he have memorized now?"

"Five. He added a third reading through Asim and two through Abu Amr ibn al-Ala. Until Nabil trotted Bahr out before Ibn Mujahid to be questioned about his manuscript, he was a well-respected student and teacher. Ibn Mujahid would ask him to produce a variant reading on the spot and he would."

"No one inside mentioned this."

"They are distancing themselves from him as we speak," Himmat confided.

Zaytuna said, "When the men spoke to Bahr, he said nothing about his reputation being ruined."

"Why would he?" He leaned in. "The shame."

"But he must have said something to you about Nabil's claim," she said.

"Only that Nabil boasted but would not produce it. Then, after Ibn Mujahid put him on the spot, that Nabil had ruined him."

"Before the manuscript came up, were they friendly?"

"Bahr tried to make things right between them when Nabil arrived in Baghdad, but Nabil used him, then finally scorned him. It was after that Nabil implicated him in the controversy over Ibn Masud's manuscript."

"Make things right?" Mustafa asked.

"As I understand, Bahr's father had loaned Nabil's father enough money to pay off his gambling debts, using his home as collateral. Bahr's father loaned him far more than the home and land was worth, but requested only the home and land be turned over should he not be able to pay." He tapped the fingers of one hand against the palm of the other, eyes wide as if he doubted the tale. "The father kept to God's injunction and charged him nothing for the loan."

"Then Nabil's father died," Mustafa said.

"Yes, and the land and house came into Bahr's father's hands."

"Why did Bahr's father not just forgive the loan? If he could afford to lend it, he must be able to afford to lose it."

"Bahr would not elaborate, but the father was a businessman, not a friend of God."

"So Nabil blames Bahr for his father's actions?" Mustafa asked.

"That is it, exactly. Even though Bahr had nothing to do with it. These wealthy people love their grievances."

Mustafa was as wary of the rich as any of their like, but the poor held onto grievances, too.

"So Nabil wanted revenge on Bahr for his father." Zaytuna said.

"Oh, my dear. He got his revenge. Nabil would come to Bahr for money. I was with him once and Bahr gave the money to him, saying, 'This belongs to you more than me'. He admitted that such demands happened regularly and complained that Nabil took pleasure in taking the money from him. It seemed that way to me. Indeed, Nabil took the money and mocked Bahr for it."

"Could this business about the manuscript be only to ruin Bahr's reputation?" Zaytuna asked.

"That seems logical."

"We heard that Bahr and Nabil had a physical altercation?"

"It was bound to come to blows. But Bahr walked away despite having the capacity to unman him."

"Where does Bahr live?" Mustafa asked. "Have you been to see him?"

"In a rooming house. I did go there to check on him, but his neighbours have not seen him."

"Tell us where it is."

"Not far from here." He turned and gestured to a side street just before the Basra Gate High Road. "Go down that last street, turn left, then right again at a small square bordered by grocers and food stalls. Ask for Umm Jarir."

"If he returns before we find him, will you tell him that he can trust us?" Mustafa asked. "We do not wish him any harm. We only want to find Nabil."

"Do not try to fool me. You suspect he is involved in Nabil's disappearance. Bahr is a man of great strength," he warned. "A wrestler. I would not challenge him, physically, that is."

"There won't be any need," Zaytuna said. "We're only being paid to find Nabil."

"But consider that Bahr may not want you to find him." Himmat bowed to her. "I will return to my studies. But first, is it true what Mustafa says, that you are the granddaughter of Dhu'l Nun?"

She glanced at Mustafa and smiled fondly at him, then said to Himmat. "I do not know my mother's people."

"You know me. I hail from your mother's land. I am your brother and forever at your service." He bowed his head, and left them without giving Zaytuna his back until he was near the mosque entrance, when he turned and went inside.

"A brother." Mustafa said. "Tein will want to meet him."

She did not reply, but offered him an open expression and he took a chance. "I will accompany you to Bahr's home."

"No," she replied, but her expression was still tender towards him and he did not understand.

"Why?"

"I needed your help in this instance, no more."

He refused to believe it. "That's all this was? You coming to me?"

"I did say we needed to talk. I wanted…"

"You wanted," he cut her off. "But not now?"

"You touched me, and…" Her voice trailed off.

He reached out again recklessly, wanting again to ask her to marry him. "My love. I…"

Instead of waiting for him to apologize, to insist he knew she still loved him, she stepped quickly out of his reach and hurried off toward the Basra Gate High Road.

Stunned, he watched her go, not understanding why she came to him in the first place or what she could be doing. His rashness in touching her was not enough to explain this behaviour. She was forever leading him on, then pulling away. He wanted to rush after her and lash out, but he turned it on himself. Head down, he stomped off, each foot's hard landing a jolting comment on his stupidity for believing there had been any hope. "Fool, fool, fool."

A stick tapped his leg and he swung his head up to warn whoever had touched him.

"Take care, boy!"

Mustafa faltered. Auntie Hakima stood before him, eyes blazing, her stick raised, ready to beat him if he made one word of reproach.

"Auntie," he said, regaining his balance. "Auntie, what are you doing here?"

"Looking for you! This is where you study, is it not?"

"Yes, Auntie." He reached for her hand and kissed it. "Is everything all right?"

"YingYue has told me everything. I have spoken to Zaytuna." She looked behind her angrily. "I saw her leaving, but she did not see me. She was weeping, trying to hide it under her wrap. What happened?"

He stared in the direction Zaytuna had walked. *She was weeping. She still wants me. It was only that I touched her. Too soon.*

"I had to get to you first. Look at me, boy!"

Mustafa reluctantly faced her.

"Those men have plans for you!"

"Not here," he said. He led her to a juice shop nearby, but it meant walking through the street where he had taken Zaytuna, past the alcove where he tried to kiss her. The tables were full, but two young men saw them coming and stood so the old woman could sit. But she waved at them not to bother.

"Auntie…"

"This is good enough, or perhaps we should stand in that alcove back there?"

Horrified, he choked back an objection she would never accept.

"You have a responsibility to YingYue, Mustafa. You cannot divorce her."

This. This is what this was. The old woman was there on YingYue's behalf. "If you have spoken to her, you know what our marriage is like."

"Yes, yes. But what does she want other than to be an absent wife, unbothered by men? You'll take a new wife. She will remain with her father. Leave her free to worship!"

"I only love one other…" his voice trailed off.

"Take your responsibility," she said without a trace of sympathy.

"And Zaytuna?" he countered, not caring how he sounded. "What if she wants me? She could divorce Kamal Ali."

"Oh, you child!" She smacked his leg with her stick, harder this time and he jumped. "This is not about wants! Zaytuna will not be a second wife to you. So you would abandon your responsibility toward YingYue because of this childhood attachment?"

"It's more than that!"

"It had better not be." She tipped her head up at him in warning.

"No!" He put out his hands. "I mean, we love each other."

She looked at him harshly. "I overheard that hadith scholar you admire so much saying to your uncle that you should divorce YingYue."

Embarrassment burned through him that Imam Abu Abdurrahman knew his secrets. He raised a hand to his hot cheek, but then he understood. His mouth fell open, and he grasped her hands. "This is their plan!" he said excitedly. "They are arranging my marriage to Zaytuna! They will intervene with Kamal Ali." He glanced up. "Oh God! You have answered my prayers!"

"What? You men! Children, every one of you!" She shook her stick at him and strode off.

19

Ammar found Tein waiting for him against a wall on the Karkh side of the pontoon bridge.

"Unless Nabil is being protected by another one of Saadia's friends, I cannot see how he is still in Rusafa.

Tein asked, "You search all night?"

"Brothels and gambling establishments part of the night. Hostels and marketplaces today." Ammar tried to prod him into feeling guilty. "I got a room to sleep a few hours and paid two watchmen to carry on, gave them more money than they earn in a week."

"That's still not much."

"What do you have from Zaytuna? Did she find Bahr?" he asked, giving his aching back a good stretch.

"If she came back already, I missed her. But I saw Kamal Ali last night. Saadia sent a message saying her friends denied hiding him. If she asked Ghada, we know she lied. Maybe Ghada had paid for Nabil in a hostel somewhere? Not in Rusafa where there might be gossip? It's all we've got from that angle."

Ammar wanted to offer a comparison between Tein's commitment to this case and his sister, who was doing more under unusual constraints, but he held back. Maybe in the end, he would invite

Zaytuna to be his partner in opening an investigations agency. Her husband did not seem to mind. Leave Tein to his churning.

"Where to?" Tein asked.

"If we assume he has left Rusafa, where else would he go in Baghdad?"

"Everything Nabil is trying to do demands the threat of block printing a manuscript, so let's check back in with Abu YingYue."

"I checked with Imam Hossam before I left. He hasn't been back."

Ammar placed the sun in the sky. It was still early afternoon. "Does he take a long midday break?"

"The shop might be open by the time we get there."

They joined the stream of people on the road leading off the bridge to Rusafa and into Karkh.

Tein said, "I sent your Nasifa a note yesterday, telling her not to worry."

"My woman!" Ammar's fury came at him so fast he did not know he had grabbed fistfuls of Tein's robe and pushed him until Tein was falling.

Tein did not fight back. There was no knee to the gut or elbow to the head. He just brought Ammar down with him. Ammar rolled to his side before hitting the ground and was up again in a moment, hand on his sword.

A woman screamed and scrambled out of their way. Two men came forward to intervene. Tein righted himself, but stayed on the ground, waving off the men, who reluctantly retreated.

"How dare you get in between my wife and me!"

"Is she your wife? You don't act like it."

His foot itched, wanting to kick Tein in his injured thigh; instead he went for his manhood. "That's bold talk from one who has to renew his own marriage every night."

"Can I get up?" Tein's face was hard as stone, but he did not come for him.

"You are not the protector of my family. Attend to your own. Maybe there is business there you are missing because your eye is on my wife."

"You're right." Tein said from his place on the ground.

The man would not give into a fight. Ammar still wanted to kick him.

"Nasifa is like a sister to me."

"That's not why you did it." Ammar stared down at him. "Say it, you've resented being on this job and think I should resent it, too."

Tein said something under his breath.

"What's that?"

"Yes." But he looked away as he said it, and that wasn't what he had said.

Ammar held back for a moment, deciding whether to kick Tein or help him up. Eventually, he held out a hand and Tein grasped it, but Tein was mistaken if he thought this was over.

Wisely, Tein kept his tongue on the walk to the Karkh market.

Not that Ammar would have heard him had he spoken. He was walking the streets as if he were going into battle, charged for a fight, but knowing if he acted he would be the one cut by his own sword. Tein had stepped into a breach that he himself had created. He had left his wife for other men to console. Ammar did not notice how long they had walked or even that they had arrived at the paper sellers until Tein finally spoke.

"Still closed."

Ammar brought himself around. All the paper shops were shuttered but one. He was not interested in waiting silently with Tein, the fact of the fight hanging over them.

Tein walked a bit further down the street. "Baraqan is not back yet, either."

A voice from behind them called out, "Abu YingYue won't be in for a long time yet! I have everything he has." They turned. A shopkeeper was leaning across his counter, waving them over.

Tein started toward him, and Ammar followed. "Assalamu alaykum!"

"Wa alaykum assalam. Now, how can I help you?" He gestured to paper of every quality and kind, as well as books waiting to be read or copied. His shop was much smaller than Abu YingYue's and there was room only for one copyist in the back, but like all the shops, there was always steady trade in a city of scholars, writers, and readers like Baghdad.

Ammar leaned on the counter, but it was Tein who spoke first. "We came to ask Abu YingYue questions as part of an investigation to find a missing man."

The man's expression changed. "If you are not here for trade…"

Tein touched his blue turban where, if he were still police, it would be black. "We are not police. We're searching for a missing son. He is said to have come around the paper shops."

"I don't know this man."

"We haven't even described him!" Tein laughed, but took a step back from the counter to give him more space. "He has been approaching paper shops about having a Quran manuscript copied. He wants many copies, not just one. Has he been here?"

"Go, if you are not interested in buying." The man was firm. "This is not a tavern."

Ammar wanted to step in and press him further, but Tein put his hand over his heart and thanked the man for his time. They returned to Abu YingYue's shop and Tein leaned against the shutters. Ammar kept trying to say something, anything, but nothing would come other than the urge to fight himself by lashing out at another.

"There he is." Tein tipped his head for Ammar to look down the road.

"Good," Ammar said harshly. "I want to know why that man was so afraid of us."

"Maybe he's no fan of police."

"We're not police."

"Doesn't mean we are not like police."

Ammar thumped his cuirass. "What is that supposed to mean?"

"Just what it says. People may fear us like they fear police."

"This again? Then I'll say it again, that's why you interfered in my marriage. Not about protecting your like-a-sister-to-you, Nasifa. About you thinking we'd all be better off at the churns." Ammar did not wait for a response and left him to greet Abu YingYue. "Assalamu alaykum!"

"Wa alaykum assalam." Abu YingYue seemed uneasy. "Do you have any news?"

"He's alive and about his own business. We saw Imam Hossam. Nabil tried to get the manuscript printed there, too."

"Did he show the manuscript to Imam Hossam? He could identify it with a glance."

"No, he didn't bring it with him," Ammar said. "When he showed you the manuscript, what did he do?"

Abu YingYue's eyes widened, understanding the question. "He opened it for a moment, long enough for me to see it had been marked, but no more. Still, I would not have known it unless I had seen the opening chapter, *alhamdulillahi rabbil al-amin*. His manuscript could have been anything at all! You may want to inform Ibn Mujahid's people."

"Why is that?"

"Excuse me." Abu YingYue hailed a boy who was walking by. He could not have been more than ten years old and was barefoot and in clothes that would barely keep out the chill that would descend on the city in just a few hours. He threw him a coin to bring cups of juice and plates of nuts, then returned his attention to them, unease clear on his face. "Two of Ibn Mujahid's men came by yesterday to warn me against copying any text he may bring to me, not simply printing, but copying. They went up and down this road, telling each of the paper shops that Ibn Mujahid would not allow it."

Ammar glared at Tein. "That's why the paper seller down there was afraid to speak to us."

Tein ignored him, reaching out protectively to Abu YingYue. "They threatened you."

"I told them that he had inquired about block printing the Quran, the cost of carving the blocks as well as printing and binding," Abu YingYue said. "They became agitated. That is when they threatened me."

"What did you say?"

"I explained that few could afford such work, but that I would not do it even if he had the funds. I assured them I understood the implications of mass printing one reading tradition of the Quran."

"Did they say what they would do if they suspected you of printing it?"

"No." He gestured up and down the street. "They had no need to explain. With or without the attention of Ibn Mujahid, we would be brought before the High Court to answer for it."

"This fool," Tein spat out, "putting everyone in danger."

Ammar asked, "They think the manuscript exists, or why would they be here? What did they look like?"

"Arab, Persian, I do not know. They did not share their names. Both had brown eyes, dark brown beards, wearing similar clothing. One had a stark face and wore a scholar's turban. He frightened me. The other was clearly a follower, taking his lead. That one touched his ear nervously."

The scholar had to be Ibn Hammad, the teaching assistant of Ibn Mujahid they had spoken to first and the other a student of his.

The boy returned with a tray holding large cups of what could only be nabidh and a small plate of broken nuts from the bottom of the barrel, then slid the tray onto the counter.

Abu YingYue asked him, "Where did you get the nabidh?"

The scruffy boy stammered, "Not the tavern, Uncle."

"Come inside," he invited with a smile.

But the boy took several steps back and ran.

"I scared him," he said sadly. "I have a basket of old shoes for children like him. At least he was sharp enough to get nabidh and the worst nuts. The change will buy his family a good meal. May it be a blessing for them."

Tein left his nabidh on the tray, but Ammar drank deeply. It was only lightly fermented and the sour tang and sweetness of the apple cut through a thirst he did not know he had, slaking his temper. Then he drank the cup intended for Tein.

His old friend would not touch even this, so lightly fermented that it would not even get a child tipsy. The memory of how far Tein had fallen when he had brought him into Grave Crimes softened him. Ammar took a breath and forced himself to accept that for Tein, a life investigating was no good. His friend was walking Baghdad as if the Byzantine soldiers were nearing their camps.

Not good for Tein, but good for him. And Ammar vowed to find a way to do it so that no man has the opportunity to judge his treatment of his wife.

"I'll speak to them about you," Tein tried to reassure Abu YingYue.

Abu YingYue did not seem not assured, but placed his hand over his heart in thanks. He asked Tein, "How is your family?"

"Everyone is happy at our home," Tein said. "We are blessed."

There was some kind of meaning behind his words. Abu YingYue seemed relieved.

"And you?" he asked Ammar.

"Alhamdulillah," Ammar answered, not understanding what had passed between the two men.

"We need to return to the mosque."

They left Abu YingYue murmuring a prayer, no doubt to protect not just himself, but also the people of this street.

Backtracking north through the market, they found the small market gate they had come through, leading to a neighbourhood that would let out onto the Basra High Road. Once across the busy road, the mosque's great façade loomed at the end of the street, Ammar stopped him.

"I can go to the mosque if you want to head home."

But Tein took it the wrong way, snapping, "There's work left to do."

The man was inexplicable. Did he want to go home to churn butter and keep an eye on his family or not? Ammar tried again. "How is Kamal Ali doing without us?"

"Fine. He only needs men who want to be regular at the work. There was no trouble finding replacements for us given how much he pays."

"When the case is over," Ammar declared. "I'll use the money to open an investigations agency. I know you won't come with me."

He did not respond, only hurried along, dragging his bad leg slightly.

"For God's sake, man!"

Tein stopped. "It's your family, not my business. It's only that this case has caused trouble in my family. It's good I'm here to protect my community from Nabil. The Sufis, Abu YingYue..." He nearly said something else but stopped himself.

Ammar did not understand what he was getting at. "I'm opening the agency alone."

"What if Saliha were to become pregnant?"

"Your face! You suspect it!" Ammar pulled him into an embrace, then held him off at a distance. "Our boys will be cousins. They'll run off and make trouble just as we did!"

"God forbid," Tein's voice dropped, and he escaped his hold. "I want a different life for my child."

The comment struck hard.

"No. I mean..."

Ammar waited to see what he did mean.

"I don't want our children to want to run away from us."

Tein as good as hit him, and there was no fighting back. With the hours needed to investigate cases, he would be leaving his son to be raised by the very father he himself had run from. But it would not be the same, he reasoned. It had to be different. They all had each other.

"Saliha and Nasifa must spend more time together," he insisted. "They will be sisters. It will be different. Our children will be cousins. My mother will take your child as a grandchild of her own." He pushed Tein lightly. "May I tell her?"

"No! Saliha has not said yet. It's only that I suspect."

"I understand. My mother saw the change in Nasifa before she saw it herself. Not a word." He touched Tein's arm, not bringing up again the complication of their temporary marriage. He could not imagine Saliha being happy when she found out being pregnant meant their nightly marriages reverted to a permanent one until after the baby was born and became a legitimate heir. Instead, he reassured him. "All will be well."

Tein looked at him as if he were some kind of fool and started walking again. Ammar let it go.

They stopped at the entrance of the mosque to remove their boots.

"You lead," Ammar said, hoping it would shift his mood, but Tein pushed on, not acknowledging him.

Inside, the classes had broken up. Ammar looked for Ibn Hammad and the hulking body of Bahr among the thinning clusters of students. Neither were there, but he recognized one man from Ibn Shanabudh's circle whom they had spoken to on that first day.

Tein scanned the crowd. "Ibn Hammad isn't here."

"Bahr neither."

"I guess we can't go person to person and tell them to leave the paper shops alone."

Ammar gestured toward the man in the blue turban in Ibn Shanabudh's circle. "He liked to talk. Maybe he's got something on Bahr."

"Just tell him about the paper shops. See what that does. Then let's go."

But Ibn Shanabudh's men were not involved in threatening the paper sellers. It would be better if Tein left the questioning to him, if this was how it was going to be. He was going to ask about Bahr, instead.

Ibn Shanabudh's student with the blue turban was seated before a bookstand holding an open manuscript. Another man was beside him, looking over his shoulder, the two chatting quietly. It was not until Ammar and Tein were nearly on top of them that they noticed. The one sitting in front of the manuscript jumped. The other leaned back, hands on his knees, and greeted them before they had a chance. "Assalamu alaykum. No one is here, as you can see. You will have to come back in the morning when classes resume."

Ammar started to speak, but Tein interrupted, not leaving the questioning to him after all. "Nabil is still out there pretending to have Ibn Masud's manuscript and trying to get it printed."

"Do you see him here? There is nothing we can do."

"Even if he had it. Even if it were real. No one will print it. No one," he emphasized. "No one wants anything to do with him. If you hear any gossip otherwise, correct them."

"Is that why you are here, to protect the paper sellers?"

"In part."

The one in the deep blue turban said, "Mustafa should have thought of that before he got involved in this case and put his father-in-law under suspicion."

The men saw Tein's anger surge. They scrambled up, moving the manuscript out of the way, then stood near the pillar for protection.

"The manuscript does not exist," Tein said forcefully. "There is no evidence it does."

The man put his hands out. "We don't believe it, either."

"The paper sellers say Ibn Mujahid's men are threatening them not to print it."

The one in the blue turban seemed confused. "So it does exist?"

Ammar jumped in. "They seem to think it does."

The two looked at each other, then the one in the blue turban said, "They must know something we do not. I cannot see Ibn Mujahid sending his men out unless there was something to it."

The other man whispered something in his ear.

"What?" Tein took a step forward.

He looked angrily toward the other side of the mosque. "Ibn Mujahid must want to control the manuscript."

"Why?" Tein asked.

Ammar did not need the answer, because these sorts of men were always trying to control the revelation. From the beginning, they rejected Seyyidina Ali's reading, taking only what suited them, what suited a caliphate in which the Prophet's family would be sidelined from their rightful authority over the people. He did not care that even the Shia Imams said Ali's manuscript was safe with them and that they accepted the caliph Uthman's codex. He refused to believe it and he was not alone.

"We have been trying to explain. The act of preserving the Quran is in debating which style of recitation, which vowel or consonant, which grammatical ending, is correct. There should be no end to our efforts."

"But Ibn Mujahid wants to shut down that debate," the other man continued, "not just with us, but within his own circles, as well."

"We fear one day he will. He sees himself like a latter-day Caliph Uthman!" the man with the blue turban said with disgust. "It is on his shoulders to control the readings, to protect the people."

The other man snapped, "Who gave him this power?"

Ammar burst out, "Enough!"

Several people nearby turned and looked.

Tein objected, "If this is about controlling the manuscript, then why would Bahr run?"

"Because Bahr must have seen the manuscript, after all."

The one in the blue turban said, "Ibn Mujahid's men are after them both!"

Tein put his hand out. "There is no manuscript. But maybe they believe there is. There's a difference. All Nabil wants is for you people to fear it exists. To fear that he will have it printed or copied and sent across the empire. It's chaos! All Nabil wants is chaos!" He faced Ammar, saying, "This speculation is getting us nowhere," and walked away from the men without another word.

Ammar started after him, but the one in the blue turban pulled him back. "There," he said, pointing insultingly at a black man watching them from a nearby pillar. "That one hears everything."

He hurried to catch up with Tein and direct him back to question the black man, when the man overtook Tein, reaching him before Ammar could.

"Tein Ibn al-Ashiqa as-Sawda!" The man smiled warmly.

Tein shook his head, still angry and confused.

"I met your sister and cousin yesterday." His eyes sparkled mischievously.

There was more about that the man wanted to say, and Tein suddenly looked like he was going to get it out of him. Ammar stepped in before he could act, but the man realized he had erred and stepped back, bowing his head submissively.

"My apologies," he said. "I am Himmat ibn Isiib. A friend of Bahr.

I informed them where they could find my friend. I hope they were successful."

Tein's temper was near to coming loose and Himmat was realizing it too late for his own good. Ammar took hold of him, walking him out of Tein's reach. When they turned around, Tein was gone, pulling his boots on at the door of the mosque. Ammar went after Tein, leaving Himmat standing there.

"I'll handle Zaytuna." Tein pounded his heel down into the boot and left without looking back.

Ammar watched him go, understanding that there was more to what Tein was carrying than worry about his community, Saliha, or whether or not Ammar was home enough for his wife's sake. Something was going on between Zaytuna and Mustafa and he finally grasped that was why Mustafa had brought the case to them at all.

DAY SEVEN

20

Tein came awake with a start. After leaving Ammar at the mosque, he had walked the city until his anger was spent so he would not confront Zaytuna and say what he could not take back. But there was not far enough to walk. Eventually, his thigh throbbed with pain and his foot dragged, so he made his way home.

It was dark when he arrived. He could hear Zaytuna and Kamal Ali quietly chatting. Kamal Ali sounded happy, and it raised his ire that his sister could betray him so flagrantly and then come home to him. That man at the mosque, Himmat, his eyes had let on that something was going on between her and Mustafa. If Ammar had not got in between them, Tein would have found out what the man knew. He would never have believed Zaytuna capable of this kind of manipulation, yet here she was, turned into a woman he barely recognized. He had crawled into bed with Saliha, who felt his anger and turned from him.

But he was still angry when he awoke in an empty bed. It was light enough that breakfast might have already come and gone. Saliha had got up without waking him. He could still hear her. At least she had not left without a word. But he heard Kamal Ali, too, still happy, and Zaytuna's lightly teasing replies. He dragged a wrap on over his nightshirt and opened the door.

Saliha looked up, scowled, then ignored him

Kamal Ali hailed him, kindly, but wary. Qambar, too. Yulduz kept her mouth shut. Only Layla got up and came to him with a cup of water, holding it out, with a worried expression. He took it from her and his anger dissolved into shame. The rest saw the change in his expression, but did not remark on it, only returning to their conversation while Layla filled the basin with water and kept an eye on him.

Kamal Ali said something he could not hear and raised Zaytuna's hand to his lips.

Saliha teased him for being late to work. "I've never known you to be a lazy man, Kamal Ali."

"Is it lazy to take the day to please one's wife?"

His temper flared again and he wanted to demand if his sister understood what this man was giving of himself for her sake. His restraint was more than Tein thought he could bear in similar circumstances.

In a rush, Ammar's warning about Saliha came back for him.

Look at the woman you marry each night. When she leaves for work each day you are no longer married and she carries nothing with her but love's obligation.

Unable to control his emotions, he stormed back into the room, shutting the door and leaning against it.

If she wants another man, she would take him and hide nothing from you.

But her honest freedom only led to other suspicions.

If she's pregnant, she'll end it. No more nighttime marriages. No more freedom. No more work that she loves. You are fooling yourself if you think she'll keep your child.

He swung the door back open, wanting to examine her expression for withheld intentions, but she had gone. "Where is she?"

Yulduz said, "Gone for bread."

"I'll go find her." Tein walked to the door bare-headed and bare-footed in his nightshirt, his wrap hanging off him. But as he opened it,

Saliha came through. Seeing the plain displeasure on her face, he shrunk back.

She pushed past him, whispering, "Dress and walk me to work."

Tein retreated to their room and did as he was told. He came out, tugging his robe straight under his cinched belt, knowing he still looked like a wild man. Saliha handed him a piece of bread and some dates. What could he say to her? Zaytuna had betrayed Kamal Ali, and was willing to live with this lie between them, and he did not know what to do with it? Worse, that it made him doubt her in ways that could ruin them?

"Are you going out on the case?" Zaytuna asked tentatively.

Unbelievably, after everything, she still asked about the case. Tein decided he was through and she would be, too, if he could help it. "I'm going to see Nabil's mother. I'll tell her he is alive. After that, I'll go to Uncle Abu al-Qasim to update him. The investigation is over."

"Should you not keep searching?" Kamal Ali asked.

"Ammar will keep going." Zaytuna watched Tein carefully.

"You won't? But why?" Kamal Ali asked.

"We've done enough," he said. "Never home. Putting our families at risk." His voice rose. "Who knows what we'll become if we keep on at this!" Tein stopped himself from saying more, afraid the truth would come tumbling out. Instead, he stared at Zaytuna meaningfully.

Her face fell.

Yulduz brushed off his words with a wave of her hand. "Never home? You ask the servants in the marketplace. They know everything an' share it. I know more about the people of Baghdad than you an' that friend of yours an' I'm home plenty. That one? He should go home to his wife. I saw 'er the other day, heavy with that child in the great market in Karkh."

"What was she doing here?" Zaytuna glanced quickly at Tein.

"Looking for her husband," Tein answered.

Zaytuna addressed Yulduz, "Did you greet her?"

"Wasn't she a pale one? I said it was a surprise to see 'er here. She got some colour in 'er face with that question, claimed she wanted our famed pomegranates. You think we've better pomegranates than in

Buratha?" She offered a smile to Kamal Ali. "Excepting those from our own tree."

Saliha said, "You gossips. I'm leaving for work."

He stood by the door as she went to get her wrap.

Layla scrambled up. "I can walk with you to Uncle's. I have my Quran lesson."

"Come!" He nearly pulled the girl into an embrace. With her along, there would be no explaining his mood to Saliha. A day to clear his head and all would be well. He would take Layla to Uncle's, talk to him, then go see the mother. Later, he would let Ammar know. The man could go back to his wife, and Zaytuna would have no more reason to meet with Mustafa. Maybe by then he would know what to say to his own wife.

Saliha returned wearing the blue and white bound-dyed wrap that she had bought with her first money washing corpses. Her face was alive and open, unintimidated and unimpressed with them all. The wrap could not hide her curves and he imagined he saw her pregnancy. A sense of purpose took hold of his doubts. He gave Zaytuna a look of warning as he shut the door behind them. Since she had no restraint, he would keep her in line.

Out in the street, he took Saliha's arm to steady her should she feel faint. Yesterday morning, he had run his hand over Saliha's stomach and there was no change, but she was a woman of full-handed flesh and it may not yet show. She was nothing like his first wife, vigorous where Ayzit was delicate, but still needed watching.

Saliha pulled him close and held out her other hand for Layla. Then she leaned in, saying quietly, "One more minute with Zaytuna and there was going to be trouble. You give her whatever she needs to find out what she wants."

Tein checked to see if the girl was listening, but she was distracted. Still, he whispered, "And if she doesn't want Kamal Ali?"

"No man should want to be with a woman who does not want him the same."

His eyes flashed, fearing that she meant him.

She shook him off, saying harshly, "You're in a state. I meant her, not me. I love you."

Her tone soothed him where kind words may not have. A piece of the problem of his heart fell back into place. Everything was so easy with this woman. She was never going to put him on the spot. All she wanted was to get him out into the street and away from his sister. He drank in her warmth, the scent of rose water, and took strength from her love. But not her advice about Zaytuna.

At the entrance to the hospital, Layla ran ahead to greet Ibn Ali.

He took Saliha's hand, unwilling to let her go.

She drew close, reassuring him with one of her teases, her breath tickling his ear. "I know what will unwind that temper of yours."

"There's an alcove near here," he said, reminding them of a building they once knew in passion, pressed against walls, her head thrown back, hair loose, calling him to her and him unable to resist despite wanting her only in marriage.

She crooked one finger, drawing him away from the hospital.

Through the waves of sun and heat, the girl's voice called them back. "Ibn Ali is not in yet."

He coughed and arranged his features so the girl would not suspect.

But Saliha moved smoothly between them, giving him time to recover. "He'll miss not having seen you, I know."

"Give Ibn Ali our greetings when he arrives, then," he said to Saliha.

She turned at the door and gave him a look that promised tonight.

He took Layla's hand and they doubled back to Uncle Abu al-Qasim's home. When Tein saw his uncle's door standing open, he held her back for a moment. "I'm sorry for how I was at home."

She acknowledged it, speaking in her old voice. "I'll watch out for you."

"I don't want you watching out for me."

She looked down the road. "Auntie Zaytuna said the same thing."

"About me?" He tucked his head back.

"No, her."

So she was worried about Zaytuna, too. Of course she was. He controlled his tongue and directed her toward the door, saying, "To your Quran lesson."

Within, he found Ziri chatting with YingYue's father. "Assalamu alaykum, Ya Abu YingYue, Ya Ziri."

They turned toward him. Ziri bowed his head slightly, hand over his heart, but Abu YingYue beamed.

"Alhamdulillah, Tein. It is a beautiful day." He recited the verse, *"They plot and plan, but God is the best planner."*

"Did the shaykh put you at ease about Ibn Mujahid's men?"

Abu YingYue stared at him for a moment, then understanding crossed his face. "God forgive me, no." He grasped Tein's hands. "I mean, yes. Alhamdulillah. Yes, he did. But my joy today concerns my daughter. You will hear our good news when it can be revealed. At the moment, please forgive me for causing you any concern."

Had his uncle negotiated a reconciliation between Mustafa and YingYue? Was this why Kamal Ali was so happy? But why would Abu YingYue announce this as news? It meant something else, and Tein became convinced it meant the couple's divorce instead. What father would not be glad to see his daughter free of a man who could not love her? He feared Zaytuna's response. Saliha's admonition to let Zaytuna choose which man she wanted was going to be forced on them all.

Abu YingYue embraced him, not seeming to notice that he could not return his pleasure, then left him alone with Ziri.

Ziri shut the door and disappeared without a word, leaving Tein in the reception area consumed with worry over the misery his sister was bringing down on them.

"My son."

A hand touched his shoulder. Junayd's soothing care embraced him and he turned, taking his hand and attempting to kiss it before his uncle could pull it away.

Junayd's eyes were soft, but his expression was firm. "Son, bring us a cup of water."

Tein left him to fetch a jug set out by the pillars in the courtyard. He passed the Quran class. Adnan was reciting and Layla and the children were dutifully repeating after him. A few elders were sitting at the edge of the circle. An old Ifati woman with a soft, unlined face was listening intently. He would not have known her age if not for stray grey curls visible at the edge of her kerchief. There were two men, a regular visitor he had never met and one in a thick wool wrap pulled over his head, nearly hiding his face. But Tein knew the man by the set of his jaw. He was Ibn Ata, one of the great Sufi elders, a companion of those who would not restrain their ecstasy with sober mystical expression, and one himself. The last time he saw him, Ibn Ata was saving al-Hallaj from a riot of his own making.

Tein was surprised to find him here. The old friend of God had his own Quran commentary circle. Yet here he was attending a class meant for children. Ibn Ata pulled back his wrap and stared at Tein with shining eyes, but the light turned to shards when it reached him.

Tein took a step back, not understanding the warning, and focused on getting water into the cup, as if pouring the water just so would protect him from whatever was coming.

As he walked past the Quran class, his eyes on the cup, Adnan recited, "...*fa innama yaquluhu kun fa yakuna.*"

The old woman loudly clapped her hands.

Startled, he looked over, spilling some water. Adnan was gaping at the woman. Tein stopped to watch the scene unfold, as if this was what Ibn Ata wanted from him, but his uncle shook his head and waved him over.

He continued on, watching as the old woman raised an accusing finger. "You have one here who knows what God revealed and what our Prophet, alayhi salam, recited. It was *yakunu*, not *yakuna*! Yet, he persists in taking divine revelation from the Prophet's mouth by reciting what our beloved Muhammad did not say. You persist in leading these people astray!"

"Auntie Warda." Trembling, Adnan bowed to her, hand over his heart. "This is an accepted reading tradition. It accords with the caliph Uthman's codex and comes to us from an esteemed transmitter, Ibn Amir of Damascus."

Junayd was listening, but appearing as though his attention was held elsewhere so as not to pressure Adnan with his presence.

But Auntie Warda's focus was entirely on Adnan. "Do you repeat like a myna who steals the songs of those around them, or are you a human being with a mind? What does it mean, then, if you read it that way? You recited *God says Be, so it is*? Is that what you want?"

Adnan turned to Junayd for guidance, but he only gestured toward the elderly woman in such a way as to indicate Adnan should listen to her.

She came at him. "You need that man's approval to listen to your elder!"

"Auntie." He lowered his head. "Please help me understand."

"Should it be *fa yakuna*, 'so it is' or 'then it is'? Hmm? A something from nothing? A before and an after?"

"What do you say, Auntie, please?"

"Or *fa yakunu*, 'and it is'? Creation from God's being and in God's moment?"

Adnan waited, eyes on the old woman, not understanding.

"With *fa yakuna*, you say that God makes something from nothing. But there is no nothing to create something from. Nothing does not exist! No! Everything made is His making. There is no deficiency in His making. No recourse to nothingness! There is nothing other than God in existence, boy."

Openly confused, he looked to Junayd, who directed him to return his attention to Auntie Warda.

She gave him a wizened eye and leaned forward, gesturing at him, her palm up. "And if you say, '*Be, so it is*' what you mean, too, is that there is a before and after with God. You mean '*Be and then it is*'! There is no 'was' with respect to His being because God 'is' before creation and existence. To read otherwise is contrary to the true revelation. '*Be, and it is*'."

There was a difference, and Adnan had walked into it. The same verse. A vowel different. Two accepted reading traditions from the caliph Uthman's codex. Tein got some sense of what drove the incisive studies of men like Ibn Mujahid. It was not just fights between those who simply kept within the bounds of the codex and those who did not. There were arguments within these communities, too. And not just among the Quran scholars. Here, he saw, it mattered to his Sufi community. He supposed Baraqan, Ibn Ali, and the men who gathered to talk philosophy would have taken Adnan's side. Everyone had a stake.

The young tutor looked shocked, still not understanding. The children were even more confused, looking to Adnan for guidance. Layla looked back at Tein, but he was unsure how he would explain it to her even though he thought he knew why it mattered.

Junayd nodded with appreciation at her clarification, then said to Adnan, "Move on to the next verse," prompting, *"wa qala aladhina…"*

Adnan recovered and returned his attention to the children, reciting *wa qala aladhina*, but with a nervous eye on the old woman waiting for her to intervene again.

Tein kneeled before Junayd and carefully placed the cup of water before him.

Junayd said, "Adnan teaches the Quran at the level of the reciters, fidelity to the reading tradition he has been taught. This is good. We have asked him to teach proper recitation to those who do not have it. There are so few distinctions in these readings it hardly matters to us. But he must be corrected when the pronunciation of a vowel leads to a meaning we do not accept."

The old woman's vehemence had startled Tein, but even more so his uncle's insistence that it be corrected. Yes. Everyone had a stake. It worried him. He no longer doubted that Ibn Mujahid's men would be willing to hurt Nabil because of the mere threat to print a Quran reading tradition, whether the manuscript existed or whether it was in agreement with the caliph Uthman's codex.

But instead of making him feel an obligation to get back to the case, Tein was more certain he should abandon these people to their fighting. All of them. His aunts and uncles, too. He was done with each and every one of them. Their fighting, their wanting more than he could give. He wondered if he could flee Baghdad itself, take Saliha and the baby and start someplace new away from their games.

He stared at the water in the cup, wishing its stillness for himself, and recited a verse aloud without realizing. *"Say 'God' and leave them to their vain debates and playing."*

"Tein."

He raised his head to find his uncle giving him a look of warning, but he defied it. They all thought they drew nearer to God and the Prophet with these niceties, but they only came closer to grasping at each other's throats.

"Tein," Junayd repeated, but this time more sharply. "Our elder, Warda, gave Adnan an explanation anyone in our community could accept, but one not to be shared. And sharing knowledge with people who cannot understand it is dangerous, especially with the Quran. The Quran scholars argue on the level of language. Our understanding of revelation is more expansive than theirs. We speak from a plain of knowledge denied them. They are threatened because we have special knowledge to which they have no access. No one is playing here."

"It's that exactly. Each of you thinks you have something the other does not."

Junayd ignored him, continuing, "Adnan will be taught the other levels, not only when he is ready to understand them, but when he is ready to be quiet." He leaned in, saying categorically, "Those who are taught before they are ready need guidance and restraint."

Tein felt someone watching and looked over his shoulder. Ibn Ata was now seated nearby, his wrap pulled back from his face. The mystic clucked at him, then covered his face again.

Enough.

He would say what he came to say and leave them to their petty disputes. "Nabil has no association with al-Hallaj. The women who made the accusation should know by now and the risks of repeating it."

"Thank you for doing your part. Surely, we are in the hands of God."

He added, "It was al-Hallaj who told me Nabil was not with him."

Junayd held his hand up to silence him before he could say what else he had done.

Tein stopped, not out of respect, but because the courtyard was strangely withdrawing from view, leaving only him and his uncle. He struggled to hold on before they were lost entirely, only to see a golden veil of sand surrounding them, like dust glinting in the afternoon light, veiling them from the others. Several men appeared on either side, but their faces were in shadow. A man sat at the head. Tein gaped, astonished by his presence.

"Alayhi salam," he whispered. He was a man like no other. A man who possessed nothing and, therefore, everything. His broad forehead, the curve of his brow, the thick wave of his beard, the strength and power of his body, the intelligence of his eyes, all announced a warrior's potency. Tein would not wish to face him in battle. He would surrender before the man's sword was drawn and fall into his embrace. The Prophet Muhammad smiled gently, accepting him. Then the Beloved of God recited in a slow, melodious voice in which each word, each letter, each vowel, was a perfected articulation, *"Recite what has been revealed to you of your Lord's Book. No one can change His words."* He paused, commanding, "Recite after me, *In the name of God, the Most Merciful, the Most Compassionate. Praise belongs to God, the Lord of Worlds..."*

Like a child before his tutor, word by word, Tein recited the opening chapter of the Quran. Then, just as he appeared, the Prophet Muhammad withdrew and his companions followed. The light and glittering sand faded, the courtyard returned, and his uncle sat before him. Tein wept into an unfathomed opening in his heart, releasing all the volatile fears and resentments that threatened to kill, always, from a place of barely-held control.

Junayd spoke through Tein's astonishment. "I will tell you what I told our daughter, YingYue, when she came to me confused about God's word. Our friend, Abu Said al-Kharraz, said, 'The first degree in listening to the Quran is to listen to it as it is recited to you by the Prophet.' This now, you know. 'Then you progress to listen to the Quran as it is recited to you by the angel Gabriel. Later, you progress to listen to the Quran as it is recited by God Himself.'"

One by one, his uncle's words wrenched Tein back from the disarming presence of the Prophet and the release offered him. First, al-Hallaj, now his uncle, and the rest of that lot. They thought they had made him one of them. But all his openings were forced on him. How could these men not know him? He had walked away from the battlefields, tired of killing, tired of himself. The only thing keeping him here was this world, his love of Saliha, the promise of their child. Tein spit out what he was given and rubbed his tears away with his fists.

"Mansur al-Hallaj brought you to this. He should not have. He frightened you. The Prophet himself came to assure you. It is a promise for the future. Do not doubt. Do not fear. You are in our hands now, just as you have been in our hands since you were a boy. You cannot escape this love that binds you to us."

Junayd took his hands and released each clenched finger.

Tein stood suddenly, wresting his hand from Junayd. "What have you done to me?"

al-Hallaj's accusations swarmed around him. The only peace he had found was a lie. The only moments he did not feel death in his hands were in attachments to this world. For them, his love of family was idolatry. His need to protect them, foolishness that flaunted God's will. Fatherhood was no more than laying seed in a woman. The only choice they offered him was to leave them for God, to lie down before the Prophet, womanless, childless, alone.

A firm hand was on his shoulder. Ibn Ata's voice was in his ear. "You cannot be saved without seeing."

Junayd was standing now. He put his hand to Tein's cheek, turning his face away from Ibn Ata, then gripped a hand tightly until Tein thought the old man would break his fingers. "I would not have done it this way. You will run. But you will come back to us. We will be waiting."

"Come back?" Tein bellowed. "You all have damned me from love!"

He ran from them, not knowing if they called after him or followed. Out in the street he turned without thinking, taking one corner, then another, until he found himself in their old neighbourhood. The narrow streets, the houses mere rooms leaning on each other around tiny courtyards. Windows and roofs opening onto the lives of others, no doors to keep in secrets. Every joy or suffering was shared in a song, a laugh, a lowing, a scream, a thrusting groan of solace or fear.

He stopped in front of the passageway of their old rooms, lay his hand on the wall, letting himself feel the grain of the sun-dried mud bricks. He took the dust and grit and rubbed it on his face, a dry ablution for a living corpse, and limped as if already drunk to the small square, looking for Salman's tavern.

A shopkeeper halted a sale to watch him and reached for a bludgeon in case he wandered that way. Another came around to the front of his shop. But Salman stood and called to him.

"My brother!"

Tein headed straight for the tavern, watching the shopkeeper with one eye as he put the weapon aside and went back to his customer.

The tavern was no more than a few tables and stools set out in front. Inside was a small room with wine jars and a bedroll where Salman slept. Day after day, Salman sat on one of those stools holding court as if he were a great man, not the grandson of a disgraced scholar and purveyor of wine to drunks. Not even teaching his grandfather's hadith collection to impoverished boys with no other chance to learn could raise him in the esteem of the neighbourhood. Unashamed, he waved for all to come and visit. The drunks came and went, not one of them caring who saw their sluggish, weaving steps. And Tein was grateful for him.

"Wine," Tein hailed him. "More than a cup. Bring the jug." Tein settled uncomfortably on a stool too small for him, making him feel like a child.

Salman gestured to the wall. "Sit over there."

He moved as commanded, leaned his back against the wall and stuck his legs out.

When Salman returned with the jug and cup, Tein took the cup, holding it out to be filled. He drank the wine down in one gulp, letting the tannins pucker his cheeks and the heavy sweetness curdle on his tongue.

"Again!"

Salman poured him another. "A watchman was by here asking for you. I had to tell him you had moved. Sadly, you did not inform your old friend where, so I could not direct him."

"A watchman?" Tein looked up dizzily. He was already drunk, faster than he remembered.

Salman sat down. "Yes, he heard that you and your partner were paying watchmen to do your legwork on a case. Paying a lot."

"He wanted in."

"Yes." Salman leaned over. "He also told me that a man is missing."

"He's not missing." He held out his cup for more.

"Then you've found him! Mabruk!" Salman poured.

"All he wants is trouble." Tein drank the next in three gulps and rested his head on one hand, the wine loosening his thoughts. "Disappearing was part of his plan. He makes a threat, then another, then disappears, leaving everyone afraid of what he'll do next."

"But why, Tein, why?"

"I can only guess."

Salman smiled eagerly. "Guess away."

"I don't want to anymore." He put both hands over his face. "He's poisoned us all."

Salman was silent for too long. Tein lifted his heavy head to see if he was even still there.

"You said that he had poisoned you all?"

Like one of Salman's sopping drunks who cried their woes once deep in their cups, Tein told him everything. Mustafa showing up. Zaytuna risking her marriage to Kamal Ali. Threatening the reputation and livelihood of the printers, especially those good men, Abu YingYue and Imam Hossam. Forcing him to find al-Hallaj, who forced him to see Junayd, who forced him to see Muhammad, who forced him to see that he had no right to love in this world.

"Alayhi salam? The Prophet, alayhi salam, you saw?"

"Junayd, al-Hallaj, the lot of them, they want me to give up Saliha! My baby! They asked the Prophet to come and tell me to give up my family!"

"You are to be a father. Congratulations." Salman smiled thoughtfully, lifted his cup in cheer, but did not drink.

"Didn't you hear what I said?" Tein reached for the jug, but Salman moved it out of reach.

"Tein, I heard. You are going to be a father. The Prophet was a father. He wept when his son Ibrahim died. His daughters were the light of his eye. You have misunderstood."

"Idols. Idols. al-Hallaj told me loving my family is idolatry."

"I do not know why he would say that," Salman said. "But who is he to the Prophet?"

Tein looked at him sideways.

"What did the Prophet say to you?"

"I… He… He didn't say anything." Tein reached for the empty cup, then pulled back, empty-handed. "He recited from the opening chapter of the Quran."

Salman removed the jug of wine entirely, putting it in the back room, then sat on a stool across from Tein. "What did your uncle say to you?"

Tein did not answer. In his drunken haze, he could not recall what had happened anymore. Did his uncle tell him he must leave Saliha and his child behind for God? Did his uncle call him an animal? He could have sworn he did.

"You will be a good father."

"How can you say that?" Tein asked bitterly. "You know me for who I am."

"What could you possibly mean, man?"

"I thought churning butter. I thought I could escape that man."

Salman prodded gently, "Who was that?"

"A killer. I was a boy and pulled a man off my mother in the night. I was always watching. Always ready. I had to protect my mother and sister. On the battlefield, it was the same. I had a wife and child, then." He looked at him. "Did you know?"

Salman shook his head.

"We were killing for the caliph while soldiers snuck into the camp and killed our families. They died. My wife. My son. Then I killed to avenge them. Even here in Baghdad."

"You have killed here?"

"I have had men's necks in my hands and let them go, but within me"—he slapped his chest—"within me, I killed them all the same."

"And you thought putting down your dagger and picking up the butter staff…"

"…would make that part of me go away."

"The butter staff is still a weapon."

"My hands." Tein spread them out on the table.

Salman took Tein's hands in his own, then stood. "You have misunderstood. By God, by God, by God, you have misunderstood. My brother, leave this tavern. Do not return here again except to show me your son and to let me congratulate Saliha."

"No. You don't understand." Tein stood, holding the wall to steady himself, and stumbled into Salman's embrace. He pushed him away, leaving the tavern, the square, and their old neighbourhood behind.

He stomped and shuffled his way through back streets to Umm Nabil's house to inform her that her son was alive and reigning chaos from a hiding place of his own choosing. Tein did not know how he would get the silver case from Ammar, but he would, and he would sell it, and he would return to the woman what was hers.

Coming around from the neighbourhood behind the mosque, he could not immediately find her house and was forced to go all the way to the mosque and turn around again. Students stared at his leaning gait, his shoulders back and his chest out, a roar in his throat. They scuffled away, and he mocked them with a sneer, then turned to walk back, tracing each door on the right until he found it. He raised his fist and pounded.

Oliga opened the door and looked him up and down as if he were the filthy drunk he was and attempted to shut the door in his face. He jammed his foot in, wincing as the door pressed against his boot. She threw her body against it, screaming. Umm Nabil joined in her screams, and the pressure against the door doubled.

"Your son is alive!" he yelled through the crack. Neighbours were coming out to see what was happening. From a safe distance, one man threatened to intervene.

The women let the door go, and he stumbled inside, falling to his knees, sending stabbing pain up his thigh. Oliga yelped overhead while the mother tried to drag him by his wrap, twisting it until it was nearly wringing his neck. "My boy!"

Sitting up, Tein tore the wrap from her hands so he could breathe, then pushed himself up along the wall and went straight to the main room, sitting heavily on the couch.

"He's alive," he said, reaching up to straighten his turban and uselessly tugging at the wrap trapped beneath him. Only then did he see the old woman's silver braid had come undone and that she had uncovered herself in the effort of fending him off. He turned his head to one side to give her some privacy. Realizing, she hurried into the other room. Oliga had retreated to the courtyard and was glowering at him through the window.

He stood again, unsteadily, pulled his clothes straight and shook out his wrap.

Umm Nabil emerged, properly clothed but still in distress, and gaped at him.

"We're done," he said. "He'll be home one day when he's good and ready."

Tein left her standing there, but she followed him to the door. "This is not over until my boy is in my arms! I do not release you!"

He turned his back on her, opening the door and walking away from the house, waving his hand in farewell. He headed directly for a tavern he had seen along the road.

Umm Nabil's heavy footsteps were behind him. Tein heard her screaming, "I do not release you!"

21

"Is Tein out of his room yet?" Zaytuna asked.

"No," Yulduz said. "Want me to kick 'im awake?"

"Let him sleep." She imagined the case had pushed him too far in some way that she did not want to have to think about, not yet. Yesterday had been hard enough. Seeing Mustafa. Coming home to her husband. Let him sleep a bit more.

Always a man of few words, Qambar had only sighed sadly when Tein had come in long after midday, stumbling drunk and frantic, and led him to his room. But Qambar had words for the women when he came out. "Leave him. None of us knows what drove him to it."

Kamal Ali had returned just after, with a package under his arm, to find Qambar and Zaytuna standing in front of Tein and Saliha's closed door. "Is Tein ill?"

"He's drunk," she answered. "He's asleep now."

"Poor man. Has anything happened between him and Saliha?"

Guilt stabbed at her, and she went to him. "Maybe the case. I don't know."

"May God heal him." He held out his hands in prayer, then led her to their room. "Sit," he said, a playful smile on his lips. "I have a gift for you."

She sat on the edge of the bed as he asked, but could not smile, feeling undeserving of any kindness.

"Give me those beautiful feet." He sat on the ground, legs tucked under, and opened the package. Taking one of her long, bony feet in his hands, he slipped it into a red leather slipper lined with shearling. "You mentioned them."

They were exactly the same as those she enjoyed at Saadia's. Zaytuna did not remember what she had said, an offhand comment, more? Yet he had been listening. This man. This good, perfect man. She pulled his face to hers, kissing his lips, his cheeks, his eyes, his forehead. He withdrew only to remove his turban.

He kissed her cheek, asking for her love, and she drew him down onto the bed. Every gentle and knowing touch filled her with exquisite gratitude for the blessing of this man. When the final pleasure consumed her, she wept quietly into his neck, fearing this would be the last time he would be so openly loving.

After, she brought out the garments they wore to the bath. Kamal Ali reached for them, but she pushed his hand away and dressed him with reverence, not knowing how to make right all that she had done wrong. He tried to object, then allowed her, his eyes glistening, his cheeks still bright from their lovemaking.

"I will see you tonight at the sama, inshallah."

The door shut behind him. Zaytuna prayed, "God, lift my betrayal from him. Whatever you do to me, I deserve it. But he deserves no harm."

Once dressed for the baths, she forced a smile before opening her door.

Immediately, Layla ran to her, upset. "Uncle Tein is sick."

"Yes. He'll be all right soon," Zaytuna told her. "He just needs some sleep."

"Uncle Qambar told me I should spend the day with Rana and Sara. Auntie Yulduz is making me a bag of nuts and dates to bring."

How could she not believe something was wrong? Zaytuna wanted to give Qambar a scolding eye for scaring the girl, but he was gone. Kamal Ali, too.

"There's no need for you to fuss over him. Go to your friends."

"Layla, girl!" Yulduz called.

She did not accept Zaytuna's assurances and trudged off to the kitchen.

The door to Tein's room opened. She took a deep breath, worried about the state he would be in, but only Qambar and Kamal Ali emerged.

"How is he?" She need not have asked. Their faces said it all. She approached Kamal Ali, but he shook his head and turned toward the outer door.

Qambar stepped in and led her away. "He's still very drunk, Zaytuna, saying things he should not have. Who knows if he will remember later, but I..." He looked at her sadly. "I will try to forget."

"Forget? What has he said?" In a panic, she lunged after Kamal Ali, but he shut the door and Qambar pulled her back.

"Tell me." She grabbed his wrist.

"Tein was unkind to him. Let him go."

"What did he say?"

"Not now."

She tried to push past him to the door.

"Daughter," he said quietly. "Stop."

A true hand of fear slipped into her breast and her knees came out from underneath her.

"Auntie!" Layla ran to her and put her arm around Zaytuna, demanding of Qambar. "Is uncle dying?"

Zaytuna could barely feel the girl's arm, but answered her. "No, my sweet, no."

Yulduz's voice was behind her. "Layla."

The girl let go. Zaytuna heard footsteps. The outer door shut and then Qambar and Yulduz went to their room, leaving her alone. She forced herself up and went to her brother.

One arm thrown over his head, Tein was lying on the bed moaning. The blanket was a tangled mess around him. He was as before, a man who fought and slept drunk in cemeteries with nothing to live for but punishing himself.

"What did you tell them?"

He lifted his head, opening one eye. "You know what you did."

She sat beside the bed, distraught. "What have you done?"

"What you should have. I've been honest with your husband."

"God protect him."

If there were dirt to cast on her head, if she had the right to rend her garments, to wail, she would have, but she was bereft of grief's language by her own guilt.

Tein pushed himself up onto his elbows. "It's my fault. I left you and went to the frontier. Mustafa was all you had. I thought you had his mother, all the aunties and uncles."

"I went to Mustafa to know for certain what I wanted."

"And?" He slumped back down.

She took his hand. "I only want Kamal Ali."

But he was not listening. "I wanted to escape you and Mother. Always having to watch over you. When she died, we were ten. I wanted to leave you even then. When I ran away, I drove you to Mustafa. When I got back, I avoided you. He did what I should've. I should've protected you."

"All the aunts and uncles hoped we would marry," she protested. "What could you have saved us from? Our own unhappiness?"

"Yes! If I had not left you. If I had not left you, maybe you could have known love."

"No, Mother took that from me. Not you." She put his hand across his chest and rose unsteadily to her feet. "But today you took from me my right to tell my husband. It was not for you to say. Maybe the end would have been the same. He will leave us and he would be right to do so, but it was not for you."

He mumbled behind her, but she did not wait to hear.

Outside, Qambar and Yulduz were waiting.

"It's not true. Not like you think."

"Did you see Mustafa yesterday?"

"Yes. To release myself."

Yulduz pulled her into an embrace, but Qambar said over her

shoulder. "The truth is, daughter, you still went to him. It was for Kamal Ali to do."

"Mustafa would never have accepted it." She pulled back from Yulduz. "He would have always been there, around every corner, even if he married again."

"Then you should've asked your uncle. He could've sat with the two of you." Yulduz's voice was soft, but did not mince words. "From that first day when you chose to walk with 'im to your husband's work, you betrayed your husband."

The old woman was right. From that first moment, she had betrayed Kamal Ali. She had been making excuses all along, chasing down her sorrow. Uncle Abu al-Qasim was right, too. She should have been worried about herself, not Mustafa. But when al-Hallaj made her taste a drop of divine clarity, she knew the only way out was to go to him. Like that the first time, when she had been pushed under the divine waters, she rushed headlong into error to confront her soul.

When Mustafa had brushed her fingers with his own, instead of pleasure, revulsion had coursed through her. Junayd's warning, her true desire was laid bare. Their companionship was fed by pure waters, yet kept course with the turbulent misery of her soul. She still did not have an answer to the question she had asked herself at the beginning of her path, "Who am I, if I am not my pain?" But she knew enough now to say, "I am not that."

All was lost. Her tender Mustafa. All their years loving each other this way. He deserved something. A word of farewell. More, he deserved a hearing, but there was no way to do it. Her trusting and generous husband, so betrayed. She blamed herself and grieved them both. And these people she loved, everything she had done to these men, she had done to them, too. Mouth agape at this piercing sight of herself, she tried to speak, to say she was sorry, but none of that would ever matter. It was all too late.

"You going to the baths?" Yulduz asked, hand on her back.

"To wash away what I've done?" she scoffed.

"Wait there. I'll come with you."

She could not have moved if she wanted.

Yulduz returned and led her away.

They must have turned several corners, because they arrived at the baths. They must have entered the bath, because the heat surrounded her. The stones were warm underfoot. Water poured, cascading from taps, ringing into copper bowls, sloshing in pools. Women spoke in hushed tones or lively banter. Bathers came and went. Girls hawked fruit and cool water. A woman called to her for hair removal. Then they were in the dressing room. Hands undressed her and wrapped her in a long towel. Yulduz was beside her, a firm hand always on her back, leading her into the baths, then pulling her down to a bench.

"Say bismillah." The attendant said, leaning over her.

Zaytuna repeated it, feeling the word in her mouth like a grain of wheat.

"Wash this wrongdoing away, daughter," Yulduz prompted. "Tell God, you are going to wash it all away."

"Forgive me," she begged.

The attendant poured water over her hands, saying, "God forgive what these hands have done." Then, lifted water to her mouth, "God forgive what this tongue has spoken." Then her nose, eyes, and ears, saying, "God forgive," until the water had washed over every part of her.

Yulduz sang to her. "*Gara gozum, my black-eyed beauty*," and poured more water over her. The attendant lifted each arm, washing with a rough cloth, scrubbing, and humming along with Yulduz's song.

Gara gozum.
I'd spread my shade
on the road you walk on,
my black-eyed beauty.

It was a song Yulduz had sung before, teasing that she and Mustafa would marry someday. But Zaytuna did not stop the old woman from singing. She mourned all her ways of loving Mustafa and carried them to those pure waters and returned them to their Lord, reciting the words of loss, "*Those who, when disaster strikes them, say, we belong to God and we return to Him.*"

Water flowed over her head, washing away her tears.

"Say alhamdulilah."

She repeated it, and felt the grain of wheat reach out a first, tentative root.

When they returned to the dressing room, she began to notice the world around her again. Yulduz dressed her like a child, guiding her head and arms into her qamis, her legs through her sirwal. All the while, Zaytuna watched women dressing, undressing, sitting on benches, standing, pulling their clothes from pegs set into the tiled walls. Each glanced at her, some holding up their hands and murmuring prayers. Her wet hair bound, her clothes restored, she pulled her wrap around her and covered her face so they could no longer see her, even to pray.

In the street, the chill was bracing, waking her to her new life. She reached out for God and felt Him only at a distance, and prayed the sama would at least return Him to her.

Yulduz and Qambar offered to walk her to her uncle's, but she insisted they stay home. They had done enough. As she dressed for the sama, she thought to wake Tein and ask him to come with her, but left him to Saliha instead, praying she would forgive him.

The outer door shut behind her. She walked alone to her uncle's in careful steps. Approaching the stone-bound field of her dream, she did not understand why certainty and peace would be so disturbing once chosen, and needed the aunts and uncles to guide her through its gate. Then, she remembered Kamal Ali would be there and that cold hand on her heart returned.

Nearly there, a small hand slipped into hers.

"Auntie. I made them tell me." Layla's voice broke.

Zaytuna wondered that they would hurt her that way.

"Uncle is drunk," she said. "He told everyone you went to Mustafa."

She could only manage to say, "Don't blame him."

Ziri held open the door, his expression understanding.

The long reed mats were laid out in rows and covered with sheepskins, leaving an empty circle in the centre of the courtyard under the sky. Cut-metal lanterns hanging from the archways swayed with the slight breeze, casting moving shapes along the faces and bodies of the seekers gathered to sing songs in praise of the Prophet and God's encompassing mercy. Some would rise with the beat of the drums and, moved by the words into ecstasy, sway and dance in the centre, but at the moment they chatted, heads together here and there, waving to others in joyful expectation. She stood starkly grieving amid the joy, unable to enter the courtyard.

Layla tugged at her. "Auntie Hakima."

The old woman was coming directly at them, anger transforming her stern but always loving features.

"Go ahead." Zaytuna pushed Layla away, not wanting the girl to hear the old woman's reproaches. Kamal Ali must have already come and told them what she had done, but when she looked for him, she did not see the light of his face or the soft turn of his shoulders among the guests.

Auntie Hakima waved her off, saying as she marched past, "Go sit down!"

Zaytuna turned around sharply. Mustafa was behind her, his eyes pleading.

"Stop now!" the old woman hissed at him. "I told you to stay away until this was sorted!"

Layla pulled Zaytuna into the crowded courtyard, leading her through the seated attendees towards the kitchen.

Her uncle Abu al-Qasim was watching, his expression unreadable. His closest companion, Abu Muhammad al-Juwayri, was on one side, and on the other was Imam Abu Abdurrahman. The imam was distracted by conversation with a man on the other side of him. Zaytuna glanced back. Mustafa was still staring at her while Auntie Hakima tried to draw him away.

Layla found them a place among the old women. A man sat in the far corner, his cloak pulled over his face, but the shape was familiar enough. Uncle Ibn Ata was where he and Uncle Nuri would sit behind the women, near to the kitchen and the back door. She put her hand over her heart to greet him, but he did not seem to notice her. She longed for Uncle Nuri, wanting to fall into his lap and have him promise to set things right as he did when she was a child. The aunts returned her greetings, smiled at her tenderly, and reached for Layla to fuss over. Zaytuna took her place on the edge of a sheepskin, a bony hip feeling for the hard earth underneath her.

By then, Auntie Hakima had returned, but Mustafa had not left and was trying to find a spot to sit. There was no space near Junayd and the imam and their uncle did not signal anyone to move for him. She could not see Mustafa's face, but she knew he would feel the censure for what it was. Her heart went out to him.

The woman next to her made room so Auntie Hakima could sit. In such close quarters, her aunt's thigh rested against her own. Slowly, she felt the soothing waters flow from the old woman to her heart.

"I have you, girl," she whispered. "I have you."

By this woman's prayer, she knew God had not abandoned her and covered her face with her wrap, pressing her eyes with gratitude.

"Look." Layla nudged her, pulling one of Zaytuna's hands away from her face and gesturing to the arched entrance to the reception room.

Kamal Ali was standing at its edge, searching the women's section for only a moment before finding her. His face was a mask of pain. She willed him to feel her regret and her love. He lifted his hand to his heart, but turned from her. Abu Muhammad al-Juwayri was already beside him. They greeted each other with an embrace and he led Kamal Ali into the courtyard, seating her husband in his own honoured place directly next to Junayd.

Kamal Ali's head sank in humility at the gesture. He could not have avoided seeing Mustafa seated not far away, but Junayd had his attention, first introducing him to the imam, then speaking to him alone. As her uncle spoke in his ear, he nodded, acknowledging what was being said, then glancing quickly at Mustafa.

Mustafa's face was strangely lit with wonder and it filled her with dread that he might try to approach her husband. She prayed, *God heal his brokenness, protect him from himself, protect us all.* Turning her attention back to Junayd and Kamal Ali, she held her breath, watching, and prayed again, *God, let uncle save my marriage.*

A drum sounded, then another. A voice rose up, "Ya Allah, Ya Muhammad," and she felt herself slip away. Junayd, Layla, Kamal Ali and the rest dissolved before her into the stream of ecstasy. The last to go was the sweet pressure of Auntie Hakima's thigh. The courtyard was empty, although she could still hear the praise of God and the Prophet, but as if from another household not far away.

Auntie Hakima appeared across the courtyard, walking ahead of a tall, slim old man. "Light of my eye," she said, "look who I brought for you."

She got up and ran to him. "Uncle Nuri!"

"Zaytuna, my daughter."

She tried to kiss his hands, but he pulled her into an embrace as if she were a child again and he was assuring her that all would be right in the world. She felt loved with a love greater than herself, and wondered if she might die from it.

Then Auntie Hakima drew a woman out to stand next to him. "God has taken her from the world and accepted her."

The old woman from the graveyard stepped around from behind her. Tiny, wizened, bare-footed and draped in green light, she, too, held out her arms.

Instead of falling into her embrace, Zaytuna whimpered. "God forgive me."

Uncle Nuri took her hand, saying, "Shh, daughter."

"What is the source of love?" the old woman asked, taking her other hand.

Every muscle fell loose as an ocean current coursed through the old woman's hand and into her heart. There, it pressed against all that she had used to bind her heart to her old pains. The current lifted, crashing through her as if the whole of the ocean were behind it. The wave carried on from her heart up into her shoulders and arms and head. Her body moved with it, swaying, her head thrown back with its force. Zaytuna's eyes opened, she saw the gate of peace open before her, the bounded field, the thin wheat sheafs now bound securely, white light streaming from the pasture beyond. She drew her head down from the vision to face them.

Straight-backed and intent, she answered the old woman's question. "God."

"Who is the air that you breathe?"

"God."

"Who provides for you and your family?"

"God."

"Who loves?"

"God?"

"Who is loved?"

"God."

With that final question answered, Uncle Nuri took her hands in his own and kissed them. The old woman took her hands from her uncle and kissed them.

"Continue through the gate to the sheltered pasture and remain there until you are finished binding all the wheat, then a new door will open," she said. "This work now begins."

"Mustafa." She squeezed the woman's hands. "I was selfish. Help him."

Uncle Nuri answered, "We have him, daughter."

The old woman warned, "Do not seek what God has taken from you."

"My husband."

Auntie Hakima said, "Do not fight God's will."

The sounds of the sama returned. Her head was in someone's lap. Layla. Once up, she held the girl's cheeks and kissed one, then the other. She heard herself say, "Daughter." But she said it not as people say it, an endearment from an older woman to a younger girl, but as a mother to a child born from her womb.

Layla gazed at her devotedly.

But as Zaytuna awakened fully from her ecstasy, she feared she had done to the girl as her mother had done to her when lost in those moments, and jerked away without thinking. The girl's loving expression twisted into a frown.

"No! Duduga." Zaytuna pulled her in, calling her 'my baby' in her mother's language just as her mother had called her and Tein, 'andudugu', 'my babies' in moments of fierce embrace.

"She's only afraid she could not take care of you while she was away in ecstasy," said Auntie Hakima to Layla. "But her family will always be with her, watching over her and you."

Now fully understanding the old woman's reach, Zaytuna's fear fell away. She raised her teacher's hand to her forehead in deference and love.

Auntie Hakima pulled her hand back and waved Zaytuna off with a glittering smile.

She turned her attention to Kamal Ali, wishing she could find her way through the people to him, but could only observe him silently as the music came to an end and the last praises of the Prophet were spoken. Finally, a single, clear voice recited, *"And the retribution for an evil act is an evil one like it, but whoever pardons and makes reconciliation, his reward is from God."*

Kamal Ali swayed with the verse, the pain on his face softening, but not erased. His eyes met hers and held her with all his love. She begged his forgiveness within her and prayed for the restoration of their marriage. She chose him. She chose this community. She chose her family. She chose Yulduz, Qambar, Saliha, Tein, and finally, her daughter, Layla.

After the sama had ended and everyone lingered, chatting or retreating into a quiet place for themselves to savour what they had tasted, she, Layla, and Auntie Hakima met Kamal Ali halfway. Eyes red-rimmed and heavy, he took a deep breath and held out both hands for her and Layla to take, then said, "Let me take you home."

DAY EIGHT

22

When Ammar arrived, Zaytuna, Saliha and the others were organizing loaves of bread and sacks filled with dates into a cart held steady by Malik.

"Where's Tein."

Saliha faced him squarely, and gestured to the room, but did not try to stop him as he walked past them and opened the door.

Tein was awake, but lifted his hand to block the sunlight from the courtyard from reaching his eyes.

"I see," Ammar said. "The man of fine ethics who tells others what to do has a hangover."

Saliha's voice was loud enough for them to hear. "Let Ammar deal with him."

"You hear that? Your woman wants me to deal with you."

Tein groaned and pushed himself up, then said like a man who had been beaten, "Be quiet. I know what I've done."

"I'll be outside."

Ammar rejoined the others. Only then did he sense that their mood spoke of more than Tein coming home drunk. Zaytuna's face was drawn, with dark circles under her eyes, and her shoulders were slumped in defeat. Layla was holding onto her like a lost child. Saliha and Yulduz had the posture of women you would not cross if you wanted to live. Qambar was the only one steady among them.

"Where is Kamal Ali?"

"Butter shop," Qambar said.

"It's Friday. He should be closed. Is something wrong?"

Yulduz gave Zaytuna a hard look. "He slept there last night."

The old woman's eyes. Zaytuna's face. Tein's drinking. Kamal Ali gone. Ammar huffed, as the full force of his ire turned on Mustafa. Mustafa had interfered with Zaytuna in some way. He wanted to take him by the back of the neck. That was for Kamal Ali to do, but the man was too good for what was needed.

The door opened and Tein lumbered out. His wrap hung off one shoulder and his turban fell undone under his arm. He leaned over the basin to wash his face, and the edge of the wrap grew muddy as the water splashed onto the pounded earth. The courtyard was silent until Saliha walked heavy-footed to their room and returned with a tooth stick.

"Your breath stinks," she said, holding it out to Tein.

He nodded sheepishly. "Where did you sleep?"

"Not with you." She put out her hand again. "Give me your turban."

He handed it over, and she used it to thump his head down within reach. Instead, he kneeled before her and she placed the turban gently on his head, rewrapping where it had come loose. Then she went around behind him, smoothing the tail firmly along his back. Finished, she retreated to stand with the rest. Ammar acknowledged her mastery of the man. If Tein hoped her caring gesture meant forgiveness, he discovered he was wrong when he stood and faced her. Her expression would have told any man they were far from done.

Ammar went to the door, knowing Tein would want to leave immediately. Avoiding the looks of the others, Tein followed him into the street. No one had sent him off wishing him peace, and he kept his mouth busy with the tooth stick until they were well away, heading to Buratha.

"While you were sleeping off your drunk, I was searching for Bahr."

Tein grunted.

"I finished questioning Himmat and found out where Bahr lived. No, I didn't find him. He's moved out. The landlady has nothing to say. Turns out your sister had been by to ask, too." Ammar nearly added that the landlady said she had been crying and tried to wheedle out of him the reason why, but he decided to leave it. "Himmat says all this is about ruining Bahr because Bahr's father forced Nabil's family into financial ruin."

Tein did not reply, only leaning silently into the walk to Ammar's family home in Buratha.

Ammar looked the man up and down, shaking his head. Tein winced as he arranged his wrap so he could pull an edge over his turban to protect his eyes from the sun. After, he gripped the hilt of his dagger as if waiting for someone to attack. Whatever he had done, Ammar's mother would see it on him and forgive him. Nasifa would look the other way. But Ammar's father would not. Tein had better find a better footing before they reached the family home.

It was not until they were over the Ushnan Bridge into Buratha that he pushed Tein to speak. "What happened?"

"I got drunk."

"You've been sober a long time now."

"People want from me what I can't give."

"What's that?"

"If I knew that..."

"So that's why you slept alone and Kamal Ali didn't sleep there at all?"

Tein turned, his face broken with guilt. "He didn't sleep there?"

"You going to tell me, or do I have to play detective all day?"

"I don't remember everything." He looked away. "I know I told Kamal Ali that Zaytuna had been alone with Mustafa."

"Alone!"

"Mustafa tried to lure her."

"Did she follow?"

"No. She said she wanted to release him."

"My God, Tein, what does 'release' mean?"

"Not what you are thinking!" Tein turned on him. "For him to move on, find another woman."

"She's married! He's married. He lives with his wife's father. Even if she left Kamal Ali, is he thinking that he could bring a second wife into that home?"

"It's complicated."

"It would have to be!" He swung his head around to Tein. "And you told Kamal Ali that she betrayed him? Is he more to you than your sister?"

Tein tucked his head back at the accusation, then looked away, ashamed.

Zaytuna never should have been in on the case if this was a risk. Kamal Ali would never have stopped her, but Tein should have. And now? Knowing Kamal Ali, he suspected the man would take Zaytuna back and forgive Tein.

"You fool." Ammar tried to restrain himself, but the words came out sneering. "First, you tell me how to manage my wife. Then you betray your own sister and tell a good man what he does not need to know. You, the fine husband, a man who comes home drunk to his wife."

"It's on my head," he admitted, stricken. "Will they ever forgive me?"

"Enough of this. Pull yourself together. None of this comes out in front of my family."

They made their way off the main road, past the larger homes, to the narrow streets leading to the outer edges of the city. Tein flattened himself unnecessarily against walls as people passed, forcing Ammar to stop and wait again and again.

Close to their home, Tein said, "I should have been with you searching for Bahr."

"I had a watchman with me."

"I heard," he said guiltily. "The word is out that you are paying."

"I have as many as I need, at least until one of them gets caught using their work hours for my cases. I've got two continuing to search for Nabil in Rusafa."

"Take it out of my pay."

"I already have," he snapped.

"Maybe it's better using a watchman for the long hours?"

"You better not be suggesting that so I would have more time at home."

"No." Tein stopped short, hands up. "I mean, yes. I mean, if you don't have to wait in doorways all night or go door to door, you can be where you are needed most, at work and at home."

"You still talking about me?"

"What's left for me but working cases?"

Ammar snorted. "When you say it like that."

"Maybe there is a way to keep a family and get the work done?"

"Work on getting your family to forgive you first. Me, I wish we did not have to waste our time with this lunch at all. I can't take my mind off the case."

"It's more than that. You don't want to be home."

Ammar looked at him askance. "I left for war rather than herd goats."

"You weren't married then."

"Men leave their wives and children behind."

Tein reared up. "Then go back to the frontier, if that's what you want."

Instead of turning for a fight, Ammar remembered the feeling of his wife curled against him at night, the press of their child against his back. "It's not what I want. But I won't tend goats and I won't tolerate my father's insults.

"Does he treat Nasifa that way?"

"He dotes on her. Never a harsh word. She has a touch. He no longer snipes at my mother. Maybe he saves it all now for me and my brother, and my nephews, but my mother is free of it because of Nasifa." His voice softened. "She is a good woman and I don't deserve her."

"Now you are going to have a child."

"And what kind of father will I be?"

"You will not be your father."

"No, but my father will be the child's father unless I am home often enough to intervene."

"So be at home."

"I don't want to be at home!" he burst out without thinking. His family's house was nearby and he prayed no one heard him, including the neighbours.

Tein slowed, staring at him uncomprehendingly.

"Churning butter is killing me. Mindless work. I have no problems to think through. No questions to ask. No pressure to set things right. Just day after day of Kamal Ali's good humour and easy work, then home to my father's bitterness. This past week has been..."

"You are going to be a father," Tein interrupted, grasping his arm, his voice desperate. "Find a way to be home."

"You judge me?" Ammar pulled his arm away and strode toward the house, pushing open the gate into the front courtyard.

The gourd vines were so heavy with fruit, the trellises looked as though they might collapse under the weight. The onions and garlic were yet to be pulled, but the herbs had been harvested for drying. Since Nasifa had been here, his mother's garden had expanded. Tender greens had been planted in a new bed. A twig of an apricot tree stood with a bench positioned hopefully beside it. The promise of it all only stoked his resentment.

Instead of his mother or wife rushing to greet them, they heard the sound of the two women laughing from the back courtyard and went around to meet them.

Despite Ammar's hunger, the scent of goat fat sizzling onto a hot pan in the tannur did not whet his appetite. And Tein, always eager for his mother's cooking, did not seem to register it at all.

They found Nasifa and his mother standing hip to hip, his wife cutting an onion in her hand, laughing, their eyes watering.

"You made me cry," his mother teased Nasifa, then leaned in to kiss her on the cheek.

She smiled sweetly, her love for Ammar's mother plain on her face.

It only made Ammar feel worse. With his father's acceptance, she was in a better place than she had been with her own family. He had given her that, at least, but wished he could give her more. And when his son arrived, what then?

The women finally noticed them. Nasifa said brightly, "You are early!"

A cheerful welcome yet he had barely seen her this week. She fed him before he left, got up for him when he came home late, if he did come home, and rubbed his feet and shoulders until he fell asleep in her arms. But a rush of love slipped past his guilt. For once, he did not take her pleasure at seeing him as a reproach, and said, "Habibti."

His mother broke the moment, rushing to Tein, "My son, what is the matter?"

Ammar turned to find Tein weeping and his mother already with him, leading him away to the front courtyard. He prayed Tein would not share the details, or else his mother, for all that she loved Tein and Zaytuna as her own, would never think of them in the same way again.

Nasifa watched them walk away, wiping her hands on the old wrap she wore wound around her like an apron. "Is Saliha unwell? Zaytuna?"

"Marriage trouble. They'll sort it out." He took his wife's hands.

She jerked them away. "No. The smell."

But he took her hands again and kissed each finger until his eyes stung, thinking of the rose-scented women in the marketplace and the beautiful dishes he could not buy her.

"Oh, my sweet." She kissed his forehead. "You're home."

"I have to go back out after we eat."

"Mosque first, then eat." She put her hand on her belly. "Then we let you go." She said it as if this was their new life and all was well.

Ammar put his hand next to hers and felt their son push out a foot or an elbow. He imagined grappling with the boy at play and leaned in to kiss Nasifa's cheek.

"So! You grace us!" his father bellowed from behind them. "I have to come outside to greet my own son! Maybe Tein should have sent a note ahead that you were coming?"

Nasifa stepped back to give the men space and picked up another onion to chop.

"Assalamu alaykum, father."

"The only good thing you have ever done for this family is bring this daughter of ours to our home," he said, picking at a bit of food that had stuck to his open robe.

Ammar checked on Nasifa, but she did not look cowed, only intent on chopping the onion.

"Where's your mother?"

Nasifa answered, "Helping our brother, Tein. May I get you what you need?"

He gestured to a small pile of day-old flat bread. "Shouldn't that be in the fat of the pan already?"

"You are hungry!" she teased, cutting the last of the onion into a bowl of chopped rosemary and garlic. "These have to sizzle in the pan first. Then," she said, describing the food as if to a hungry child, "I will drag the bread through the fat and layer it to catch the rest of the drippings as the goat finishes roasting while you are at prayer."

Assuaged, he bowed his head as if she were the caliph's own daughter. "I will wait."

Muhsin and Tahira came in from the adjoining house. Their baby was cradled in Tahira's wrap and the other children rushed through around them, the boys stopping cold at the sight of their grandfather. They paused, then approached with deference to kiss his hand. He patted each on the head, then they rushed to Nasifa, looking for a snack.

"Boys!" Tahira called out and went over to help Nasifa deal with them.

Muhsin put his hand on Ammar's shoulder. "Have you thought more about what I proposed?"

Their father heard and grumbled. "Of course he has and of course he'll do nothing to lift the state of this family. He'll retreat as he always does, the coward."

Ammar wanted to remind him he was a ghazi, but there was no use in it.

"Well?" Muhsin carried on as if his father had not spoken. "I visited Kamal Ali and discussed with him what it would take for our goats to produce milk he would consider for his butter shop."

"He's not going to buy your milk."

"Yes, he explained that he does not want to grow his business any further. It would require a separate churning for goat milk alongside his sheep milk churns, twice the men, an expanded shop."

"I've given you my answer."

The brother ignored his response. "I have assured you that you would not be out in the fields with the goats. You would be running the business, selling our milk to the other butter makers. In fact, Kamal Ali advised us on how to get started."

They were trying to trap him. Ammar gestured to the hard earth beyond the house. "You see about getting that to produce the kind of pasture you would need year round to fatten the goats properly and get the quality of flavour Kamal Ali gets, then we'll talk."

His father sneered. "I wish we did not need you."

"I've already given all my savings to you. I don't need to run the business."

Muhsin stepped forward. "My sons and I will be bound up with the pasture, the goats, milking, delivering the milk. We need you. You know the world out there. Baghdad is teeming with people waiting to take advantage of us. We would be lost without you."

"You overestimate me," Ammar said. You would start small, locally, people you know. You'd catch on."

His brother gestured to Nasifa. "This is for your wife and child, too. Our families will keep growing. We have this chance to make something for them."

They were trying to push him into a corner where his only choices were to abandon his wife and child by staying or by leaving.

Ammar turned his back on them and went to stand at the low wall looking out towards the plain of Karbala in the farthest distance. The Prophet's grandson, Husayn, was a father, a husband, and a warrior. He had sacrificed everything. Husayn's family had suffered and died alongside him for the highest good. Yet, he was to remain within these walls tabulating costs and sales. When he was out, he would be charming customers into buying butter they did not need.

If he opened his own investigation business, at least there was some small justice to pursue. The money from this case would put him in a position to do some good. He would be his own man. That choice would give him some life rather than the slow death of living under his family's thumb.

Complaints were brewing behind him. Then his brother's voice reached him, purposefully loud enough for him to hear. "Father, if you want him to stay, then you must leave this to me."

Muhsin joined Ammar at the wall. "Instead of investing in the business, why don't you build a house for yourself and your wife instead?" he suggested. "Being in business with the family might seem different when you are not living under the same roof as father."

"You need that money to build the pasture and irrigation, buy more goats."

"There will be enough for both if we limit our expansion initially."

"In our parents' house. In the one next door." Ammar whispered so Nasifa would not hear. "It's all the same. I will be as trapped as I was when I was a child and escaped to the frontier. Do you want me to leave everyone behind again, but this time, a wife and child?"

"Isn't that what you are doing now with this case? Won't it be the same with every case that comes after?"

"I'll make it work." He embraced his brother. "I'll do what I can to help, but I have to find another way."

Muhsin, always the peacemaker, shocked him with a derisive laugh. "Father said you would abandon your wife and child, preferring to be out in the street threatening the poor with your sword."

Ammar tucked his thumbs into his sword belt and declared without any ground on which to stand, "I'll make it work." He left him to go find Tein in the front courtyard with his mother, ignoring his father and avoiding looking at Tahira and Nasifa, who had likely heard it all.

Tein and Ammar's mother were sitting on the bench, facing each other. His great hands were in her small ones and he looked as though his burden had been lifted.

They saw him coming and she asked him a quick question. He nodded in reply.

"Come, come," she waved him over.

Ammar crouched before them.

"Tein is to be a father. He told me that a friend of God informed him of the child," his mother said with a knowing expression.

Thank God he did not tell her about the betrayals.

"And he told me he has harmed his family."

Ammar sighed with frustration.

"You have to tell her she is with child." She patted Tein's hand. "You go to them with your cheek on the floor. The important thing is that you help to save your sister's marriage, not just your own. But I think you are correct, Kamal Ali cannot have you back. Perhaps you and Saliha will have to move away. Still, all will be well. Trust in God, my son. *It may be that you hate a thing that is good for you and love a thing that is bad for you.*"

He prayed his mother was right, and not just for Tein's sake. If there would be no more churning for Tein, then he would make investigating work for him. They could split tasks. Hire watchmen. Tein could be home as much as he liked, and Ammar could stay away. He would give Muhsin whatever money he could to get the business off the ground, then maybe, after that, he would build a separate house beside his parents.

It was a glimmer of hope. "We wanted these women, Tein. We must be responsible. You come work with me. We'll be fathers, together."

Relieved, Tein accepted the offer, but Ammar also saw the regret behind it.

His mother, her disappointment clear, "You won't stay and help the family?"

"I can't work with the family, mother, but I won't abandon you and Nasifa."

Muhsin called out, "It is time to leave for the mosque!"

Ammar turned. The whole family was approaching from behind them, Nasifa struggling to maintain her smile.

23

MEN MOVED SLOWLY out of the Shuniziyya mosque. Mustafa and Abu YingYue jostled for space to slip on their shoes before heading home to the Friday meal.

His father-in-law had been cordial to Mustafa when they left for Friday prayers, asking him along the way about his studies and teaching, but he avoided discussing the case. Mustafa had been trying to speak to him at home about the manuscript and Nabil's visit, even the threats from Ibn Mujahid's students, but his father-in-law had resisted, gently changing the subject. But with every polite inquiry during their walk to the mosque, Mustafa found himself being less than honest with Abu YingYue.

"Busy days always, as you know. My studies and daily work teaching Ibn Shahin's children."

"And the boys, how are they taking to the discussion of the Quran variants?"

"I was pleased that Ibn Shahin wanted his boys to have some small introduction to the variant reading traditions of the Quran. They will not be among those who riot in despair when they hear a change in vowel length or a grammatical difference. I hope they will find solace in the efforts of our scholars. Surely, our Book is in the best hands."

"Ibn Shahin must be pleased with your work."

"Alhamdulillah."

But after they left the mosque, Abu YingYue's demeanour changed. "I was moved by the recitation today. *Nothing good comes from their secret conversations except those encouraging charity, kindness, or reconciliation between people. Whoever does this seeking God's pleasure, We will grant them a great reward.*"

Secret conversations. Reconciliation. Knowing he meant to raise the question of his marriage to YingYue, Mustafa dove into a diversion. "Yes, it is a good reminder to us that the caliph and his people have our best interest at heart."

"Son." He stopped Mustafa and gestured to a gathering of women and children taking shares of food brought for charitable donation. Zaytuna and the women of her household were there, handing out bread and dates to those waiting their turn to eat.

He wanted to run to her, but shame turned him away, only to face the inevitable censure.

"You know my daughter has spoken to me."

Nervous sweat pricked at him, and he pulled his wrap away from his throat.

"Son," he said again, leading him along so that they were walking again and away from Zaytuna. "You remember I never wanted my daughter to marry you. I did not leave my family behind in Taraz, to carry that blessed child great distances, only to have her marry and be distracted from God. God is her true love. It is a love that took hold of her as an infant. It is no passing emotion such as young people feel for one another."

"This is my fault," Mustafa admitted, choking on the words.

"Nonsense. It is mine. I relented when our shaykh, Abu al-Qasim, insisted."

"We begged him to intervene with you. We were in love."

He tugged at Mustafa's sleeve, asking tenderly, "Is there any love left?"

"Yes."

"If you love her, then you will do the right thing and not divorce her."

"I understand *reconciliation between people*, but we are past that."

"Yes, yes." Abu YingYue became impatient. "You are not listening to me."

His voice rose, panicked and pleading. "But Auntie Hakima had said that uncle was arranging, that there was a plan."

"Your uncle has arranged this." He eyed him sharply, all tenderness gone. "You will remain married. I am here to command you do as she asks. Take in marriage the women you choose for your needs. By God, buy a woman if you prefer it. But you will not divorce YingYue. She will maintain the respect due a married woman and return to her life of worship."

The horror of it consumed him. Never had he heard Abu YingYue speak this way. Women for his use! Auntie Hakima had said they were arranging his divorce so he could marry Zaytuna. He himself saw Junayd speaking privately to Kamal Ali the night before. He watched in wonder as the man was brought to tears. Then he understood, and relief washed through him. They had convinced Zaytuna to be a second wife. A first marriage in name only. A true marriage with Zaytuna!

Waiting for his decision, Abu YingYue's expression became rigid.

Grasping his father-in-law's arm tightly, Mustafa declared, "Yes! I will!"

"Good." He pried his arm away. "No more talk. YingYue is waiting at home with our meal."

But his mind was swarming. "No. I will be home late for lunch."

"I will inform her." Abu YingYue walked away from him without a farewell.

Mustafa rushed back to the mosque. The crowds had thinned, but many remained behind for charity. Zaytuna had moved and he circled the courtyard, searching for her. There she was, with Layla pulled in close, sitting among the poor, listening to an old woman. By the cadence of her voice, the elder was reciting verses of the Quran, then pausing to speak. A discussion had opened. The women leaned into each other, asking questions, getting answers that seemed to excite or soothe them.

The old days came back to him. He and Zaytuna had sat side by side in lessons, reciting Quran and asking questions, or, in Zaytuna's case, posing problems and pushing back. Their teacher went easy on her, letting her unwind her tangled thoughts, whereas when Mustafa would do the same, he would be scolded. "Stop taking your courage from her," his mother had warned him when he complained. "When you have something to say, the teacher will listen."

He had something to say now. He loved her. They would be a family. She would bear his children. If necessary, he would go to Kamal Ali himself for her release.

Mustafa left the mosque and wandered through the narrow streets, turning over one plan after another in his mind until a small square opened ahead of him.

A small candy shop was tucked in-between a dry goods shop and a vegetable stand. He recognized it, but the rheumy-eyed shopkeeper he had known as a child was gone. Of course, the man had been old even then. Mustafa remembered when he had devised to snatch a sweet from the counter to bring to Zaytuna. They had been fighting, like they always did, and he needed it to beg her forgiveness. But the old man had caught him by the wrist and hauled him up for a slap on the head with his free hand.

He felt the slap as if the old man had him in hand again, and his hope soured. How could any plan he came up with work, when nothing had ever worked in the past?

Mustafa turned away abruptly and kept walking, eyes on his feet, barely noticing the passersby, when he ran into a man and stumbled. Grasping at the man to steady himself, instead he pulled him to the ground, losing his own turban and scattering the man's bags.

Mustafa left his turban behind to help, but the man was on his hands and knees, getting upon his own. Three bags were strewn on the street. Mustafa pulled them out of the middle of the alley as the man stood.

"My apologies. I was distracted." Mustafa reached out to hand over one of the bags. The man turned to him and Mustafa exclaimed, "Bahr!"

Bahr pulled the bag away from him in one swift move, grabbed the other two, and pushed off into a hard run down the alley. Mustafa took after him. Ahead of them was an old hawker with a small barrow of fish he was selling door-to-door. Bahr would have to upset his barrow to get past. Thwarted, he threw the bags down and faced Mustafa.

"Please, Bahr, I mean you no harm!" Mustafa approached slowly. "I only want to find Nabil!"

"I told you everything I know. Let me go, please." He looked past Mustafa for an escape, but then stood back, defeated.

"Why run from me?"

"You are with those two men!"

"No! I am alone."

"Thanks to you, everyone thinks I killed Nabil or have hidden him somewhere."

"Me?"

"You! You and those men laid suspicion on me at the mosque." He turned his head aside in shame. "Ya Rabb! The gossip!"

Mustafa wanted to object again, but Bahr was right. Rightly or wrongly, they had exposed him to suspicion until the case was solved, and after, he knew too well, there would be no controlling gossip. It would never end.

"Not just you. What does it matter? By God, Nabil already ruined me! You must understand," Bahr pleaded. "He used my stature among Ibn Mujahid's students to press his case about the manuscript. There are students of Ibn Mujahid who believe I have it. One of them even ransacked my room. Others wonder aloud if I killed him over it. What will they do if they find me?"

Mustafa hated it, but he looked down at the bags, needing to know if the manuscript was inside it.

Seeing, Bahr yanked open the bags and scattered his belongings, except a single manuscript which he held to his chest as if he feared Mustafa would take it from him. "I do not have it! Walla! I've never seen it. Nabil has concocted the manuscript out of his own greed."

"And that?"

"My personal reading tradition."

Ibn Mujahid prohibited his students from producing them, preferring they spend their time working with reading traditions that had already been transmitted. Mustafa did not believe him. "I need to see."

"Of course, you continue to suspect me." He shook his head and opened the manuscript, showing a text partially marked with dots of different colours. But there was the opening chapter of the Quran, a chapter Ibn Masud did not include in his own reading tradition.

Satisfied, Mustafa looked up from the manuscript. "Where are you going?"

"I escaped my room after one of them turned it upside down. I took only these things with me to that hostel." He indicated a building down the street. "Today, a student saw me. It took the morning to lose him then I came back for my things. I am safe nowhere!"

"Why not just show them you do not have it?"

"How would that prove anything? They would believe I had hidden it."

"Ibn Mujahid sent these men after you?"

"I cannot imagine he would," Bahr said. "He is a man of impeccable character. They must be acting on their own. The day Ibn Mujahid questioned me, he seemed satisfied with my answers but told me never to return to his classes as there could be no suspicion surrounding their work. One would think his students would agree that banishment from the learning that has been my life would be enough. Yet they come after me all the same."

"Do you know where Nabil is?"

"No." He crouched to repack his things.

Mustafa finally noticed his clothes. They were finely made, with well-wrought embellishment. Two of the bags were finely tooled leather and had beautiful copper clasps, but the third was a worn out camel sack picked up in a shop serving the poor.

Bahr looked up from his things. "If you want to do some good, expose him!"

"Fish!" The hawker was behind Bahr, calling out to get them to move aside. Bahr dragged his bags to the side of the street without looking at the man.

Mustafa found his turban, brushed off the dust and fitted it back on his head.

"I can only think Nabil is trying to sell his manuscript, sight unseen, to the highest bidder. Maybe ask those who would buy it, private collectors, the librarian at the Sharqiyya Mosque. He used me to make a case for its legitimacy. He thought people would believe he had it once my good name was attached to it."

"We heard he wants to print it."

"Print!" Bahr's face turned red. "My God, his mind is poisonous. Which of us would not pay to stop him?"

"Did you hear anything?"

"They talk like they believe it does not exist, but if that were the case, why are Ibn Mujahid's men searching my things for it?"

Mustafa stood back, speechless. Why, indeed?

Bahr carried on, eyes wide in realization. "The search must be related to Ibn Mujahid's present project. He argues there is a case for limiting the existing reading traditions. Meaning, those bounded by the caliph Uthman's codex. He fears that more and more reading traditions will be produced solely from the accepted variants."

"He what?"

"Understand. It is possible to have hundreds of readings, some differing with only one vowel or two. The elder scholars have been circumspect in their choices, but if the arrogance of my colleagues are any measure, what comes, well, it would be chaos. They talk about picking this variant reading or that as if they were assessing women slinking past the tavern doors. The community needs stability. Walla, Ibn Mujahid is right."

"Right?"

"You are not listening. He plans on limiting the acceptable reading traditions to a handful of well-established ones from different regions."

"The other scholars would never permit it!" But then Mustafa thought of the safe pastures and how Muslims were already confused when they heard even a different vowel from what they were used to in their own mosque.

"I suspect that Ibn Mujahid believes someone must act with the decisiveness of the caliph Uthman."

Mustafa wondered if Tein and Ammar were aware of Ibn Mujahid's plans. "And the manuscript?"

"Ibn Mujahid may be involved in this search. Perhaps he needs to be certain it does not exist? So he has sent them after me? He would want Ibn Masud's manuscript so he can destroy it, finally."

"But what about the manuscript of Ibn Masud in Kufa?"

"It is not an autograph, not signed by Ibn Masud himself as an accurate copy of his own personal manuscript." He looked past Mustafa again, wanting to go. "Maybe he has plans to destroy that one, too?"

If this were true, if Ibn Mujahid sought to destroy manuscripts relied on by the community of scholars, it would be his reputation that would be destroyed. He would be no better than Ibn Shanabudh to his peers. Mustafa could not believe it of him.

"What is any of that to me now? I carried my family's pride of having memorized five reading traditions of the Quran. How can I return to them having harmed our reputation?"

If there was a manuscript, Mustafa no longer believed Bahr had it or had anything to do with it. The same with Nabil's disappearance. Bahr had been ruined by circumstances beyond his control, and he had been a part of it. Tein complained that many lives were ruined in seeking justice for one. Mustafa prayed that there would be compensation. For Bahr, and for him, whose reputation had been ruined undertaking these cases. But he had done it for her. And Zaytuna would acknowledge the sacrifices he had made for her love. Then he understood. The compensation. He had been brought low to be made high.

He stared at Bahr, shocked. Him, too. For only the lowest of the low could have the strength to carry so many reading traditions of the Quran in their heart. And only the lowest of the low, the humblest, would be worthy of the love of a woman like Zaytuna.

Mustafa recited under his breath, *"God is the best of planners."*

Bahr heard it and staggered as if he had been hit. "What have I done?" Tears came to his eyes as he recited. *"And when those who disbelieved plotted against you to restrain you or kill you or evict you. They plan and God plans. And God is the best of planners."*

"My brother." Mustafa took his arm to steady him.

Bahr shook it off, distraught. "You do not understand." He crouched before his bags again, sorting through them until his manuscript and a few pieces of clothing had been placed in the bag made of camel sack. He stood, holding that one bag. "What have I done? I have turned the Quran into an idol upon which I built my reputation! God is the best of planners! God has taken my reputation from me and left only the Quran. I will leave Baghdad! I will leave Baghdad and travel to memorize more readings. I will sit at the edges of circles, not at their centres. God forgive me! My standing! God forgive me!"

He ran from Mustafa toward the square and turned out of sight.

DAY NINE

24

FOOTSTEPS WERE THUDDING in a rush outside. Someone was pounding on the outer door so that the bolt was rattling. Zaytuna sat up in a rush, and reached out to wake Kamal Ali, only to remember that he was not there, and felt sick. In the courtyard, the outer door opened and the pounding stopped. She peered out of her room. Tein spoke quietly to someone outside, then shut the door behind him.

"It was a watchman." He came to her. "They've found a body in the river."

"Where is the body now?"

"In the Round City. They've got him laid out in a cell."

"Are we going now?" she asked without thinking.

"You don't need to go."

He said it gently, but she caught herself for even asking.

Everyone was awake now, standing in their open doors, listening.

"Nothing to do about it tonight. Ammar sent the watchman to say to be ready to go in the morning."

He went back to his room, Saliha followed him in and shut the door behind them.

Zaytuna unrolled her prayer rug and sat, legs tucked underneath her, but laid her hands palm down in her lap. Prayer did not come.

Only a sickening heaviness within her belly and rushing thoughts too loud and fast to hear.

Saliha's voice awakened her. "Is she praying or asleep?"

The morning light was coming through the high window. She was still on her prayer rug, having somehow fallen asleep. Her body was twisted into kinks, her back was spasming, the back of her throat burned, and she tasted bile. Forcing herself over, she lay flat on the rug, groaning, and slowly rubbed her belly, hoping to calm its sickness.

"Zaytuna, we'll be leaving soon," Tein said through the door.

Why was he telling her?

"Zaytuna." There was a thump on the door as if he had put his head down heavily. "I want you to come."

Her back spasmed and she cried out.

The door opened. "I've hurt you," he said quietly, shutting the door behind him. Then he approached, standing over her, looking down, and she watched as his eyes welled with tears. He wiped them away with his sleeve and crumpled beside her.

She took his hand, swallowing hard. "I did it myself."

"What happened to us?"

"Too much to let us be happy."

"Maybe the baby will change us."

"Does Saliha know?"

"No," he said warily. "Not yet."

"Has she forgiven you?"

"She let me sleep in the room with her last night, but not on the bed. It will be enough for her when I beg forgiveness from you and Kamal Ali."

"And me?" She tried to smile, showing him she had forgiven him. "Will Kamal Ali ever trust me again?" Her back spasmed again. She moaned.

"Roll to your side." He helped her over and began prodding to find the sore spot.

"Down. Ah!"

He hit it straight away and began digging in, not knowing the strength of his fingers. She winced and moaned, but not long after, the spasm released. He laid his hand on her shoulder. "Can you forgive me?"

"I have already, my brother."

"Alhamdulillah." His voice caught. "Come with me today."

"I shouldn't even have asked to go last night." She let him help her up.

"He'll come back."

"I have to stay here, wait for him, prove to him he is more important than anything, even investigating." She pulled away. "What is that compared to my love for him?"

"He won't be back until this afternoon. I don't think staying here when there is no chance of seeing him would make him trust you more."

"I don't understand."

"He doesn't want your submission. But you cannot speak to Mustafa again."

"If you hadn't told him, Tein, I would not have. I admitted it to myself only last night. When I returned to my husband, certain of my love for him, not Mustafa, I didn't tell him what happened. It made me a liar. I would have lied to him for the rest of my life and made you all complicit in those lies." She took careful steps to the door. "I hate that you told him, but I'm grateful."

"I love you," he whispered.

"No more lies." She stopped, her hand on the door. "I was alone with Mustafa in public twice. The first time you know about. The second time, he touched my hand for only a moment, but I pulled back immediately. Walla. I felt it and I did not want it."

"I believe you. No need to say more."

They stood together at the closed door for a moment longer. "Tein, why did you drink?"

A shadow passed over his face. "I don't know how to explain. Not now, anyway."

She accepted it and went out into the courtyard with him. The morning light stung her eyes. Everyone was seated on the mat under the pomegranate tree, speaking quietly as they ate breakfast.

"My family." Zaytuna called them to attention.

Except for Saliha, their faces expressed the ways she had hurt them. Yulduz's resentment was plain. Qambar's disappointment was almost harder to bear than Layla's fear that her family, so recently gained, might be lost. Saliha, blaming her for nothing, standing by her without doubt, gave her the strength she needed. She did not deserve it, but she clung to it.

Tein put his arm around her. "We are going to eat, then I am taking Zaytuna with me to the police station to see about the body. Staying here won't help."

Yulduz snorted. "And if Kamal Ali comes home to talk to her?"

She pulled away. "She's right, I can't go."

"Go," Saliha said, taking a bite of food. "It's no penance for you to sit here all day to suffer. We don't even know if he is coming today."

"We are taking food to the cemetery," Qambar intervened. "Malik will be here soon. Come with us."

"Let her go," Saliha said to him.

"If you insist on going with your brother," Qambar warned, "then know I went to check on Kamal Ali yesterday at the butter shop. He said he would be here after work to speak with you."

He was coming for her. For gain or loss or something in-between, he was coming for her and she would wait. "I have hurt you all. I will tell Kamal Ali everything when he returns today," she said. "He may no longer want me. I don't know how, but I will do what I can to protect you."

Saliha sucked her teeth, started to speak, then took it back.

The door opened, and they all turned, expecting Kamal Ali.

Ammar stepped in and looked at each of them, staring. "Assalamu alaykum?"

Zaytuna grabbed a fistful of Tein's wrap. "I can't go."

"Go change." He ordered. "You are coming with me and I will tell Kamal Ali myself I took you."

Yulduz remarked savagely, "And your word matters?"

He turned on her, not in anger, but in desperation. "Let me do this my way."

The old woman gave him her back, while Zaytuna retreated to her room. There, she saw Mustafa's jug and cup in the corner and retched, holding up her wrap to her face. This whole time. The whole of her marriage. Beside their marriage bed. It was not just what she had done these past few days; it was what she had been keeping all this time. She wiped the bile from her lips and grabbed the jug, holding it to her chest like a baby. Then she took up the cup and resolutely walked out of her room, across the courtyard, past Tein and Ammar and opened the outer door. A tall, barefoot girl with long black braids hanging from her kerchief was walking by carrying a bucket of water from the fountain.

"Daughter. Take this jug and cup home. We can no longer keep it."

The girl stopped, but her bucket was full. She shrugged, not caring one way or another but seemingly not knowing how she would carry it all.

"Put the cup in the bucket." Zaytuna did it herself, not allowing the girl to object, only needing it out of her hands. "There, now the bucket in one hand and the jug in the other." She gave the jug to the girl. "Take it and pray for the one who made it."

Zaytuna hurried back in before the girl could come to her senses and object and found Layla waiting for her. She pulled the girl into her arms. "I won't let anything bad happen to you."

"Now I believe she's done with him." Yulduz was standing by the pomegranate tree. But then came the slap. "Imagine keeping that by her marriage bed."

Tein touched Zaytuna's arm. "Let's go."

"I'll be back before Kamal Ali comes home from work." She said it like a declaration, but it felt like a question. She vowed to walk away from Tein and Ammar in time to return, no matter what happened.

Yulduz called after her, "If you knew what I knew, woman, you'd not leave!"

Panicked, Zaytuna looked over her shoulder. But Tein was shutting the door behind them.

An additional worry appeared before her. As she walked between the men, Tein's arm in hers, she searched the distant faces of those coming towards them and tried to see if she could recognize Mustafa's turban and the slope of his shoulders from those walking ahead. She imagined she heard his voice and swung around to find him, but he was not there.

"I'll see him, sister."

She pulled the edge of her wrap over her face entirely, letting Tein lead her to the Round City. At first, she gripped his arm, fearing they would walk into a wall or the back of a cart, or he would let her trip over a boy running in front of them without pulling her back. The crunch and clop of a donkey cart, a boy calling out "Ho!" in warning as he came through, even the casual chat of passersby made her tense. But little by little, as they wound their way along the route that took them to the gates of the Round City, she let herself rest. One infinitesimal act of trust after another allowed her to feel the hesitations, direction and speed of his gait, but, too, the strain the walk was putting on his injury. She moved with him until she could focus on what they were about to do.

The wind whipped around her, nearly twisting her wrap about her ankles, and she heard the lap of the water against the walls. They were at the gate of the Round City. Pulling her wrap away from her face, she let go of Tein and the three walked up the ramp and past the guards at the tower gate.

At the top, she paused to look out across the city, the roofs of houses connecting to one another, courtyards open to the sky, fruit trees rising, palms towering and swaying, the warren of roads and alleyways, the palaces and estates, some abandoned for richer homes across the river. The people of Baghdad. She felt their struggles and joys as if they were her own and wanted to cry out to them. Then she took in the blue-green Tigris winding its way between the two sides, separating yet nourishing both, uniting them as one city, and she felt the first inklings that there would be peace at the end of this. If Kamal Ali left or stayed, she would find a way.

"The moment is a sword," she said into the wind.

"I remember that." Tein led her away. "One of the aunts or uncles. The moment is a sword. Whatever happens, if you accept it, the sword is gentle. If you fight, it cuts."

She wished she could remember who had said it, so she could pray for their soul and tell them that she finally understood.

Ammar grumbled, "We should have brought his mother."

"Better to see if it is him first," Tein responded.

"I'll go on and get the men to meet us." Ammar set off in a hurry.

By the time they got to the Solomon Gates, Ammar was already returning with one of the new investigators and the two were sharing a laugh. If not for the fact that Ammar no longer wore the black turban of the police, he was as easy with the man as if he were still one. Zaytuna wondered how Tein was reacting to the sight of them together.

"It might not be your man," the investigator said to Tein as they drew near. He gestured for them toward the ramp leading to the jails below.

"Shabib ibn Yunus, this is Tein's sister, Zaytuna bint al-Ashiqa as-Sawda."

The investigator smiled like one who finds laughter easy. He was young and eager, and she did not look forward to meeting him again when the job had done its work of hardening him. She nodded in greeting.

Ammar put a hand on Shabib's shoulder as they walked. The garrisons and stables were ahead. The jail to the right, then right again. They walked down a shaded path to the walls supporting the arcades and road above. An iron-barred door set into the wall was the only indication of the holding cells within. Zaytuna shivered from the chill and damp exuding from it.

Shabib yelled for the guard.

More like a bull than a man, the guard boasted a smashed nose and a breadth to him that made sheathed dagger at his belt unnecessary. He unhooked a large ring of keys from his belt, unlocked the gate, and swung it open.

"Grave Crimes," Shabib said. "We're here to see the body."

He looked Ammar and Tein up and down and cracked, "Long time. You two prisoners now?"

Shabib chuckled. "If they're not careful."

The guard locked the gate behind them, then picked up a lantern and waved for them to follow.

"If he's your man," Shabib said, "he'll need to go to the hospital to see if they can tell us how he died. Otherwise he'll go for his funeral prayer today and in a pauper's grave by nightfall."

"As long as he is out of my jail before he stinks up the place."

"If it's our man and he's been murdered," Ammar said to Shabib. "I'll give you everything we've found out so far."

Tein was noticeably silent.

"Do you hope this is your man or not?" Shabib asked, noticing Tein's silence and not understanding.

"I'd rather a man not be dead to close the case, but he's angered many people."

The guard's lantern sent flickering light along the damp walls of the hall, but it was swallowed by the surrounding darkness. The only steady light came from a turn off the hall. Zaytuna peered down the turn as they passed. Lamps burned in niches and prisoners' voices came to her as if from a distance. She took hold of Tein's arm, wishing she had not come, not wanting to think about the living or the dead trapped within these windowless walls. The guard opened a door at the end of the hallway. She flinched, remembering the bloat and stench of a body that had been pulled out of a canal by the landing boys once. Her stomach turned despite there being no scent of death yet.

The man was laid out on one of three bench tables in the centre. The guard held the lantern over the body. His clothes were in tatters, his legs and arms uncovered, his head bare. He had been in the water, but was not bloated. His fair skin was unnaturally smooth and seemingly translucent, exposing blue veins. There were small wounds everywhere and his knees had been battered. She felt she should not be looking at him but could not look away, and pressed her back against the wall, the cold seeping into her, praying, "May God have mercy on his soul."

"Amin," Shabib said, and the others repeated it.

Ammar pressed the flesh on the man's arm. "Did you puncture him, or is this it?"

"Not bloated," said Shabib.

"So he was only long enough in the water for the fish to have a few bites."

"He got caught at the edge of a reed bed just after the bridge in Rusafa. Fish could have fed on him there, birds would have got his eyes, but he was on his stomach." He pointed at his exposed knees. "He's been kneecapped. That's why we thought he might be your man."

"His height is correct," said Ammar.

"Red beard," Tein added. "We should go get his mother."

"We can send a watchman for her," Zaytuna said.

"It has to be us," Ammar told her. "That woman would refuse to leave her home, more likely to turn the watchman out onto the street, denying her son could be dead."

"Ask for Oliga to come instead." Zaytuna suggested, moving to the door.

Tein left first and she gratefully followed behind him. His leg was dragging. It wasn't too far, but he could not get to the mother's and back, then home again. And she could not go alone or with Ammar. They would need a third to chaperone. Ammar would have to go himself.

As they left, Ammar said behind her in a frustrated voice. "No stone was left unturned. I asked about him at all the gambling houses in Rusafa. The wat...," he broke off.

"Everyone knows you are hiring watchmen," Shabib remarked. "One sergeant has vowed to beat any man he catches."

Tein said, "We had evidence Nabil was alive in Rusafa six days ago."

"I'd say this one got into the river yesterday," the guard said.

They waited at the gate to be let out; Zaytuna wanting to shake the bars to get into the field and the light and air.

The guard squeezed around them to unlock it. She nearly ran past him.

Tein was not far behind. Walking with Shabib, he called out, "Ammar is going to get her, we'll wait here."

"Stop in the office," Shabib offered.

He punched out, "No."

Zaytuna stopped at the end of the path to the jail and heard the door clang shut. She looked for a bench where they could sit and turned toward the archer's barracks. Tein met her and led her in the opposite direction. Several iron banded equipment chests were along one wall.

"The time," she said, looking to the sky. She wanted to put the dead man and whatever had put his body in the river behind her, to run home and wait for her husband.

"It's still early."

They sat in silence, Zaytuna taking slow breaths to steady herself. Finally, she asked, "If Saliha had done what I have, would you forgive her?"

Tein laughed uncomfortably. "She is my Aisha bint Talha."

She shook her head.

"Aisha bint Talha was a cousin-in-law of the Prophet. Her sensuality was renowned. Men lined up for a chance to marry her. One husband even invited a poet to see her disrobed and write of her beauty."

Zaytuna saw the comparison to her friend's wild nature. "You are worthy of Saliha."

"Kamal Ali is worthy of you."

She fell against him, and he put his arm around her.

"God, leave his heart open to me," she prayed.

"His heart is open to you."

"He left me."

"You know what he did. He followed the instructions in the verse."

She had not realized it until he said it, and recited, "*If you fear licentious conduct from your wives, advise them, then abandon them to their beds…*" She did not finish the verse to the part where God gave men permission to beat their wives if the first two methods did not work.

Tein assured her, telling her what she already knew, "It's not in his nature. Kamal Ali follows the way of the Prophet. Your husband would not beat."

"I would not be beaten," she said, emptied of emotion that such words had to be said. But life was not like that. Was Saliha a woman who would be beaten? And yet her husband had beaten her and when she ran away, her family returned her to him. The verse was meant to restrain men from the wanton beatings they were used to inflicting, but all she knew was that men who beat find a way and men who do not beat do not look for one. The Prophet even tried to stop them, refusing to beat, advising against it, even jumping on a man's back once as he went after his wife. It was no wonder that God sealed every admonition directed at men with a statement of their arrogance and a threat of humiliating punishments. Men do as they like and families abet them.

"Kamal Ali knows the woman he married. You need to show him you know the man you married."

Zaytuna nodded, accepting the task.

He took a deep breath, then said, tentatively, "Zay, I did no better, trying to control you, telling Kamal Ali. Uncle Nuri taught me better than that. A man…"

"Stop. That's done now."

"Assalamu alaykum!"

Ammar had Oliga by the elbow. She was covered in a wool wrap against the chill of the morning. Her bare feet were crusted with dirt from the road. Blue veins were visible through her pale skin reminding Zaytuna of the body and her stomach turned. But Oliga's eyes were alive, intent on seeing the dead man and not hiding that she wanted it to be Nabil.

"His mother would not come?" Tein asked.

"She did not take the news well," Ammar said.

Oliga laughed as if a great joke had been told.

Zaytuna observed her, wondering if she was pregnant. If the child was born alive, Oliga and the child would be free.

As they made their way back to the jail, Tein walked ahead, while Zaytuna fell in beside Oliga, and Ammar came behind. Tein banged on the bars.

The guard walked to the door in a rolling gait, taking in Oliga as if she were meat searing on a fire. "This one is for me?"

Tein's body relaxed, his stance readying for the fight, and the guard caught it.

He opened the gate with a shrug and led them to the room where the body was being held.

Nearing the door, Oliga broke from Zaytuna's side to stand beside the body and searched his face. "It is like him. But it is not him."

Ammar gestured for the jailer to bring the lamp closer.

"I said it is not him," she snapped. She looked again, then rushed out of the room.

Zaytuna followed. Oliga was stopped at the locked gate.

"The family knows Bahr," Oliga said breathlessly. "From before."

"We know."

"She did not say how." Oliga said it like the information would somehow transform the body into Nabil and set her free.

"Tell me."

"Bahr's father took everything. Umm Nabil says that Bahr has to pay his father's debts just as they had to pay the debts for Nabil's father."

That checked with what they heard from Himmat, even Nabil demanding money from Bahr.

Ammar was right behind and asked, "What else have you heard at that house?"

Oliga and Zaytuna backed up to get out of the guard's way. Once the door was unlocked, Oliga burst out into the open field. Zaytuna ran after her.

Once there, Oliga turned, her arms outstretched and cried out, "Why not him!" Then she stopped, nearly screeching. "Debts! All they talk about is debts. I thought he would be killed for them."

"Dead men don't pay their debts," Ammar said, approaching her slowly.

She looked at him viciously. "Nabil's father did."

"Did Nabil have a debt like that?" Zaytuna asked.

"God will make him pay his debts."

Ammar and Tein drew alongside her.

"What debts?" Zaytuna asked again.

She crossed her arms, refusing to answer.

"You're angry it isn't him," Zaytuna said.

"Yes?" she said, challenging her.

"His death would not release you. Unless…"

Tein and Ammar understood the implication and stepped to either side surrounding Oliga.

The girl turned on her before she could finish. "That hag, she fingers that talisman night and day. If curses worked, I would buy one to kill them both."

Zaytuna grabbed her by the arm. "Did you kill him?"

"I should have," she said in Zaytuna's face, her teeth bared, and pulled her arm free.

"If you did, maybe you should run. Leave Baghdad now."

She turned and walked slowly away from them, saying over her shoulder, "I do not need to run."

25

IT WAS EARLY YET, but Tein understood when she said, "I have to leave."

"Maybe Yulduz and the rest are still at the cemetery. I can walk home with them."

"Go."

Zaytuna left him, arranging her wrap to cover most of her face.

Ammar sighed with frustration. "Your sister just told Oliga to run if she's guilty."

"Are you police now you should care?"

But Ammar did not take the bait. "If she killed him, I just hope she left the body someplace where we can find him."

"I wonder who it is that's dead in there?" Tein asked.

"That's not our job anymore."

"What have we got, then?" Tein held up his hand. "Don't say gambling or hostels."

"If Bahr or Oliga didn't kill him, then he's out there hiding." He paused, then added, "Gambling or in a hostel."

Tein sucked his teeth. "Look, none of what he's doing makes any sense except to cause the reaction he's getting. He had already ruined Bahr's reputation before he disappeared by forcing him in front of Ibn

Mujahid. I think Nabil's alive and out there watching Ibn Mujahid's men threaten the paper shops and laughing at them. He is enjoying every bit of this."

"Or maybe he's left Baghdad to find someone who will do the work to print it?"

"I don't think there is a manuscript to print."

"You keep saying that," Ammar said impatiently, "but I don't see the evidence either way."

Tein knew it did not exist. His uncle had confirmed it. Ibn Shanabudh's men had said Nabil was not even aware of what was in the Ibn Masud manuscript in Kufa. If he had an Ibn Masud manuscript, he would know those details. All the same, Ammar had planted a seed of doubt. He considered it. No one respected Nabil's intelligence. Maybe Nabil could not recite what was in the manuscript he claimed to have because he was never smart enough to work with these readings in the first place? What evidence did Tein himself have other than a certainty that made no sense to anyone other than the one who held it? He thought of Ammar's resentment that Seyyidina Ali's personal manuscript had not been taken as the Quran itself, and was struck by what they had never considered. "What if Nabil's sincere?"

"What do you mean?"

"He has the manuscript and wants Ibn Masud's reading to be widespread."

"Anything but Seyyidina Ali's reading for you Sunnis."

Tein ignored it, but his point was made. "We're left with Oliga or Bahr possibly wanting him dead. Ibn Mujahid's people wanting to stop him from getting the manuscript printed." Maybe the threat of block printing was enough for Ibn Mujahid's people to restrain him, beat him. But kill him? He thought of the dead man who looked like Nabil, his knees broken and thrown into the river. The knees pointed to gambling debts. But dead men don't pay their debts, right? "Look, whether the manuscript exists or not, Ibn Mujahid's people seem to think it does. What would they do to stop it from being printed?"

Ammar turned red. "Do you mean to ask if Sunnis kill for power?" He pointed toward the city of Kufa far in the distance, outside of which lay the plain where the Prophet's grandson and great grandson, the son and grandson of Seyyidina Ali, Husayn and other members of the family of the Prophet himself, were slaughtered by the caliphal forces to prevent the Prophet's family from holding power. Ammar shouted, "Karbala!"

"They might just try to scare him," Tein said, hand out. "But we have to consider the worst."

"Uff!" Ammar exclaimed. "So the body in there was a mistake?" He turned his back on Tein to pace back and forth.

While Tein waited for Ammar to walk off his temper, he thought about their next step, but that made his own temper rise. Mustafa was supposed to be searching for Bahr, and he only now realized he would use it as an excuse to go to the house to see Zaytuna. He gave Ammar a moment more, then said, "I have to find Mustafa. He may have found Bahr, and I need to get to him before he tries to speak to me at home."

Ammar directed the last of his anger toward Mustafa. "You've got to stop him! Do you know where he works?"

"Zaytuna knows, and she's left."

"You deal with that. I'll tell Shabib and Ahab what we suspect about Ibn Mujahid's men. There's nothing they can do about it until there is some evidence, but at least they'll know what we're thinking. Maybe hold off on burying the body. After that, I'll go to the mosque. Question them again."

"Curse this case." Tein's hands twitched for some way to make things right.

Ammar paced again. "I think you're right. Nabil is alive and is loving the trouble he's caused."

Trouble beyond anything Nabil could have imagined. Tein crossed his arms, trapping his hands as if Nabil were in front of him and he needed to restrain himself from laying a fist on him.

"At the mosque"—Ammar stopped pacing—"I'll poke around about Bahr, too. See if anyone knows where Mustafa works."

"Don't bother asking about that." Tein shook his head, realizing. "Abu YingYue will know. Come with me there, then we'll go to the mosque together."

"There's no need. You focus on Mustafa." He put his hand out, adding awkwardly, "I have my own personal errand to run. You'll be happy to hear, something for Nasifa. Then I'll stop by the mother's to find out if Oliga wants to admit anything."

Tein walked heavily to the market, leaving the Basra High Road as soon as he could to take back streets and alleys into the market towards the paper shops. His thigh hurt, forcing him to swing his leg so his foot did not drag. He put his hand on his dagger to feel a bit of strength, then stopped.

The stench of a Byzantine soldier on the battlefield overcame his senses. He spun around, searching for his attacker. His ears filled with metal clanging, men grunting, warning, and yelling. His body thrilled, feeling the force of his dagger's thrust and the resistance of the soldier's flesh and bone. One strangled, gasping cry and he was surrounded by the sharp rot of feces.

He howled, letting go of the hilt of his dagger as if it would consume him. The street spun around him. A woman screamed as Tein stumbled into a wall, sucking short breaths, trying to find his way back into this world.

A hand lay on his back. A man's voice. "Brother, let me help."

Tein roared up against him. He pulled the dagger from its sheath and held it out to him, hilt first. "Take it!"

The man took several quick steps back, his hands up. "God protect me!"

The woman screamed again.

He dropped the dagger and lurched away through one street after another until he came to an archway set into a wall separating the neighbourhood from the market. A tavern was in view and he clung to the wall, walking by it, head down, refusing to look, fearing he would see himself already sitting there, making his way to the bottom of a jug of wine.

Step by step he headed to the paper shops, willing himself to focus on the hard earth beneath his feet, the haggling boasts and whines of shopkeepers, the grassy scent of a laden donkey, and the dappled sunlight on the bodies streaming around him. By the time he turned the corner onto the back way to the paper shops, his waking nightmare had receded, leaving behind a strange lightness in being relieved of his dagger. He did not know what to do with the feeling, reminding himself of the weight of having hands that kill and that there was more to this than whether or not he wore a dagger at his waist.

Firdaws ibn Ali and Ahmad Baraqan were sitting outside Baraqan's shop and thick in their usual philosophical debates. He was not expecting to see them, but felt they must be meant to be there. Tein hesitated to say that God had meant them to be there for him, but he allowed it to be true without articulating it fully in thought. These elegant, educated men of African descent, who welcomed him despite his lack of schooling and social graces, seeing something in him that he did not see in himself, were there for him. For the barest moment, he saw again the shimmering golden gathering of the Prophet with his companions. He pulled himself up and approached the men.

Ibn Ali noticed him first and stood to meet him halfway, his face full of concern. He led Tein to Baraqan and the cluster of stools set out in front of the shop. "The men missed you two evenings ago, but Abu YingYue said you were on a case and not to worry."

"Yes." Tein took strength from his hand. "It's been a difficult week."

"If you wish, please tell us. Share your load."

Tein took a deep breath. He had no idea how he would find his way to telling them that his wife was pregnant, how he knew and all the rest, that he had sat with the Prophet and his companions, gotten drunk, and set his sister's marriage and their family on a terrible path. The only certainty was that he had thrown his dagger aside and was delivered into the companionship of these men, even if only for a moment. He wanted to sit the whole of the day with them, but he had to find Mustafa first.

Baraqan was standing for him, also with a worried expression, but kept his tone cheerful. "Assalamu alaykum, come sit!"

He looked down the road to Abu YingYue's shop. It was open. "I came to ask Abu YingYue how to find my cousin. I can't stop now."

Ibn Ali clucked his displeasure, sounding like an old woman. "Come back to us."

Reluctantly, Tein kept walking. Abu YingYue was in the back of the shop, leaning over the shoulder of a young man working on an open manuscript on the copyist's table. When Tein entered, he lifted his head and came to greet him.

"Assalamu alaykum." He reached out. "What has happened?"

"I wish I could walk away," he said, meaning the case and so much more.

"I wish my son-in-law would do the same."

"This will be over soon," he said, meaning not only the case but also the trouble between Mustafa and Zaytuna. "I must speak to Mustafa. He was searching for a man to interview. If he has succeeded, I want to catch him before he tries to find me at home."

Abu YingYue understood immediately. "He will be at work." He put a finger to his mouth for a moment, as if deciding to speak, then tipped up his chin. "Ibn Shahin, whose children he teaches, complained to Shaykh Abu al-Qasim that one day he walked out without a word and that he has been erratic."

"Where does Ibn Shahin live?"

Abu YingYue explained, then said, "He will eat the midday meal with them and stay for a while longer. After work, he goes to the Sharqiyya Mosque in time for the afternoon prayer. Although it won't matter soon, I do not want him to be in more trouble. Please meet him at the mosque."

"Won't matter?"

"Soon, soon," Abu YingYue said but did not elaborate. "Go to the mosque."

But he did not trust that Mustafa would not go directly to their home. "I can wait for him outside his work. I won't ask for him. Just wait for him to leave."

"Then, at least sit with me awhile. The midday prayer has not come yet."

Tein glanced back at Ibn Ali and Baraqan, who had their eyes on him. He had time for them, after all. Hand over his heart, he replied, "It would be my honour, but I must speak to Ibn Ali and Baraqan."

"Of course," Abu YingYue bowed his head slightly.

Relieved, Tein asked, "Anything more about the manuscript?"

"Only that the students continue to warn us."

"They are back?"

"The same men, the one with the severe face and the other."

Ibn Hammad. Tein put his hand on his heart again and left Abu YingYue.

Firdaws Ibn Ali asked when he returned, "Was that about the case?"

"Yes." He turned to Baraqan. "Have men been here to warn you not to copy a particular manuscript?"

"No. I do not provide copying, as you know, but I saw them."

"Is it the case you wish to discuss?" Ibn Ali prodded.

Tein did not answer, but took the stool offered by Baraqan.

They gave him a moment.

Finally, he said, "I was at my Uncle Abu al-Qasim's the other day."

"How are the great Sufis of Baghdad?" Ibn Ali asked.

Tein leaned in, not ready to share everything. He began, instead, talking around what had happened, offering a part of the story that he knew they would enjoy and would go from there if he could bear it. "One of the aunts corrected the children's Quran teacher when he recited *kun fa yakuna*, rather than *kun fa yakunu*."

"I have never heard *fa yakuna* before." Ibn Ali looked to Baraqan, who likewise shook his head.

"It is Ibn Amir's reading tradition, from Damascus, not Baghdad's Abu Amr."

"I see." Baraqan nodded expectantly.

"She explained that *yakuna* was incorrect because *kun fa yakuna* implies *Be, then it is* instead of *yakunu*, meaning, *Be and it is*."

Baraqan slapped his thigh happily. "A knotty difference!"

Tein breathed easier at his pleasure.

"Have you seen a discussion on this matter, Baraqan?" Ibn Ali asked.

"The verse, I do not know. The question, I believe al-Kindi addresses it."

"What did the woman say?" Ibn Ali brought Tein back to the conversation.

"Auntie Warda castigated him, saying '*Be, then it is*' suggests there is a before and after for God."

"Ah, Dr. ar-Razi would likely choose *yakuna*, yes?" Baraqan asked Ibn Ali, then said, "He argues, that God is one of five living eternals, along with the eternal Soul, and brings life to matter in time and place."

Ibn Ali picked up the thread. "Yes, Dr. ar-Razi emphasizes the process of creation. Not this instantaneous '*Be and it is*' from nothing that is implied in that reading of the verse. Dr. ar-Razi once described creation to me in terms of the time it takes for a child to mature from seed to birth."

Tein shook his head, not understanding.

"This may help. After he explained it to me, I considered how much it is like the verse, *We created the human being from an extraction of clay*. The clay would be akin to Dr. ar-Razi's notion of pre-existing, eternal matter from which creation is made. *Then we set the being as a drop in a firm resting place*. The resting place would be the pre-existing, eternal location from which creation springs. *Then we created from that drop a clot, then we created from that clot a lump, then we created from that lump, bones. Then we clothed those bones with flesh, thusly we produced the being as another creature*. All of which fits Dr. ar-Razi's explanation of the process of time in creation. Through the passion of the eternal soul, a creature is born. Just like the verse, it is a process, you see? So Dr. ar-Razi would argue that there is a before and after even with these eternal principles and would, I suspect, prefer *fa yakuna*. I must ask him."

Baraqan explained excitedly, "Yes! But consider it could also be read 'so that it is' and for the doctor there is no creation from nothing as that would imply."

Tein tried his best to understand and was shocked, but tried not to show it. What he had experienced at the hands of al-Hallaj during their last case, it did not feel this way. He had passed away in a moment, his existence erased, and returned to this world sensing somehow that the divine could not be bound by a time or a place or a soul demanding that it act. There was no before or after or otherwise. How could he explain? These men accepted only rational arguments and this was not that.

Hand over his mouth, he understood Auntie Warda where he had not before and said, "The elder I mentioned, I think Auntie Warda would also say that she prefers *yakunu* because she does not agree with creation from nothing, either." Then he made the connection to ar-Razi's thought. "Dr. ar-Razi prefers creation from eternal pre-existing matter, but my Sufi family prefers creation from God's eternal being. Our elder said, 'Nothing does not exist that a thing should be made from it.'"

"Fascinating! Perhaps our next conversation should be on notions of 'nothing'?" Baraqan asked, delighted with the idea. "We should begin with al-Kindi's discussion of bringing to be from non-being. I will bring the manuscript."

Ibn Ali smiled at Tein with a hint of pride in his student, and Tein revelled in it. He carried on, "My uncle Abu Bakr al-Wasiti, he said something that may be useful, but I was younger then, I did not understand." His heart eased thinking of him, broad-shouldered, dark-browed, and brooding. Uncle Abu Bakr rarely spoke, and then he was brash, saying too much. Tein suddenly remembered al-Hallaj's remonstration that he held him to an unfair comparison to some of his aunts and uncles. He was right. Tein sent al-Hallaj an apology from his heart, and immediately felt a wash of expansive, heavy life settle into him.

The men put their hands on him as he nearly slipped from the stool. "Are you faint?"

Tein shook his head anxiously, grasping onto them. The traces receding, he rushed into the story of his uncle Abu Bakr to regain control over himself. "Uncle would say extraordinary things. Shaykh Abu al-Qasim warned him against it. We heard that he was stoned out of every city where he tried to teach until he found a place in Marw."

"Why Marw?" Baraqan asked.

"One of the uncles said because they are a rough lot."

"He found his home." Ibn Ali bowed his head in respect.

"It was Abu YingYue who told me. He lived in Marw with YingYue, studying the meanings of the Quran with my uncle Abu Bakr before coming to Baghdad."

Baraqan winked. "We must ask Abu YingYue if the people of Marw are indeed uncouth!"

Tein nodded, feeling wanted. "Uncle Abu Bakr said that there is nothing in creation other than God. Existence is God's being manifest." He held his hand to his forehead, trying to remember. "Abu YingYue related something similar from him. I don't have it exactly, but this may be close. God is manifest in all of creation because when He creates, He creates through Himself. If you look carefully, you will not find anything other than God in existence."

"Bah bah," Ibn Ali said with pleasure. "You must tell us. We know they say that they arrive at these observations from direct experience." He asked, "But what of the Quran? Do they have direct experience of revelation? Do they sit at the feet of the Prophet, alayhi salam?"

Tein searched his face for any hint of mocking. If he did not know these men so well he would be afraid to speak and invite their pity for believing such foolishness. Worse, he feared opening the aunts and uncles up to their disapproval, and, given what had happened to him when he cursed al-Hallaj, open them up to God's censure. But there was no mocking. Both Ibn Ali and Ibn Baraqan waited for him to speak, but all he could say was, "I... er."

The men did not push him, but gave him time to gather his thoughts, decide for himself if he would say it. But what he wanted to say was inside a circle and there was no one spot to enter. Finally, he opened with a denial. "My aunts and uncles, I've never been one of them, like them. They taught me as they taught the other children, but they never expected me to speak like them. Be like them. Know God like them. I had no time for God and all the trouble God makes."

"What has happened?" Ibn Ali asked.

"On our last big case, al-Hallaj was involved."

Baraqan sat back.

"He did something to me, forcing me to understand God in a way I cannot explain. I left myself for a moment and returned. It changed me. The constant worry that someone was always lying in wait to attack was gone. I had a sense that all would be well. I stopped looking at the world as a curse."

"Subhanallah," sighed Baraqan.

"It faded, the overwhelming part. But I was able to settle into my work at the butter shop and my life with Saliha and the family. I was happy. Then this case happened and that easiness was lost. I saw al-Hallaj again recently, and it only made things worse. I feel like I am back where I was before." Tein crossed his arms, trapping his hands again even though there was no risk of violence. "He told me Saliha is pregnant."

Baraqan's eyes widened, but the men did not rush to congratulate him. They waited with grave expressions, understanding more was coming.

"He insulted me. I am an idolator. I give up knowledge of God for the petty things of this world, like"—he paused—"being a father."

The men shook their heads. Ibn Ali finally spoke. "That was unfair to you."

"I went to see Uncle Abu al-Qasim and he, he did something to me, too, and next thing I knew I was sitting at the feet of the Prophet, alayhi salam, surrounded by his companions and listening to him recite the opening of the Quran."

Ibn Ali became quiet, but Baraqan burst out. "I would have collapsed at his feet, then got up and run, the shame of myself before him!"

"I ran, too," Tein said, grateful for his response. Then he gave voice to his fears. "I knew my uncle and all of them wanted me to give up family too, to give up being a father. Uncle pushed me into the Prophet's circle so I could not remain an idolator. When I returned to this world, I ran to a tavern and drank until they would know that I am a father first." He spoke with a kind of desperate insistence, as if someone were lurking around a corner to take his family from him. "I am for my family first and if that makes me an idolator then bring me more wine."

Ibn Ali put a steadying hand on Tein's knee. "That cannot be what they meant. Yes, al-Hallaj, he speaks without measure, but even if he had some secret knowledge, and your uncle, these men are fathers, Tein. You grew up around your uncle's family. The Prophet was a father. You have misunderstood."

"Why then? What is this?"

"Your uncle knows you. And it seems now the Prophet and his companions know you. A piece of your mother's heart is in your own. I am not surprised. I am only sorry it was confusing for you and has come to this. When you can, ask your uncle for clarification."

He turned his face away. Something of his mother was within him. Tein clung to it and feared it, wanting to have something of her for himself and yet fearing that it would make him choose God above all else. Make him as dangerous a father to his child as she was a mother to her twins. His shoulders slumped as he pushed away the thought of wine, allowing himself to rely on them as they passed his burden between them.

Baraqan leaned in. "We are here."

"I haven't told Saliha yet. She doesn't want a child. I'm afraid of what it will do to us." He faced them. "I'm afraid she might end it."

"If you can," Ibn Ali said, "keep in mind that you may have misunderstood al-Hallaj. He speaks in riddles and taunts. She may not be pregnant."

Baraqan acknowledged Ibn Ali, but said anyway, "Just in case, you must tell the other women of the household your concerns."

Ibn Ali lowered his voice. "If she is pregnant and unwilling to bear it, and I am not convinced that she is, nor that she would be unhappy at the news, I believe she would come to me. The midwives are skilled, but it could end badly all the same and she knows this from the women she has washed. She would trust my advice."

Tein wondered, and waited for him to say he would not help her, but he did not.

"Tell the other women," Baraqan insisted. "They will help her accept it."

Ibn Ali glanced at Baraqan with a flicker of annoyance, then addressed Tein. "She is a singular woman, but you must show her that she need not fear having a child. Nor fear you being a father to your child. More, a day-to-day husband to her. Her pregnancy would transform your temporary marriages into a typical one. You need to talk to her directly."

Tein stood, and they stood alongside him. Ibn Ali pulled him into an embrace. "I trust you," he whispered. Tein fought back tears, but an involuntary shudder ran through him. Ibn Ali felt it and held him a moment longer. Baraqan put a hand on his shoulder.

He stepped back, not looking them in the eye, afraid he might weep to see their friendship on their faces. With a hand over his heart, he left them for Abu YingYue's shop to say goodbye.

Tein walked slowly, needing a moment to right himself to avoid any difficult questions from Abu YingYue, but Razba, the maker of talismans, hailed him from down the street. "Assalamu alaykum! I did not think I would find you today. I was coming to tell Abu YingYue that I found out about your talisman."

Tein stopped, not ready and not wanting to hear his news, but the man waved to Abu YingYue in his shop and hurried past to meet Tein.

"I asked my wife to question the women," he said. "Walla, the woman is a jinn. She treated my request literally only to vex me and did not ask the girls. I asked again, and this time, she found one who remembered a beautiful Slav, white hair, and wide blue eyes. The girl thought she was one of the virgins of paradise come to life in this world. Can you imagine! She did not remember any names, but said the Slav insisted her mistress wanted a curse against a whole family. The Slav must be the one you mentioned. Does the request make sense?"

It made sense and he was sorry for it. "Are you sure she said her mistress ordered the curse? She did not want it for herself?"

He shrugged. "I can only report that she told the girl it was her mistress's desire to curse a family and ordered a talisman to do the job."

"The mother was part of this all along." Tein touched his throat as if the talisman were hanging from his own neck. What had Oliga just said out in the field? "If curses worked, she would buy one to kill them both." The mother was not relying on a talisman for the protection of her son, but a curse against Bahr and his family.

"The girl assured the Slav the family would be ruined by it." His eyes glinted mischievously, "But when the girl went to the back where the block printers work, she asked for a talisman for the righting of wrongs. Even better! She asked them to add to it a handwritten curse against the mistress herself. A curse that all her ill intentions would come back to her. The girl returned with the folded talisman and told the Slav that no one should read it or the talisman would not work."

26

YULDUZ and the others had already left the cemetery. A man and his wife, their small son between them, rested against the outer wall. But as she knew too well, it was the rest that lies waiting, one eye open. At least they had eaten, Zaytuna consoled herself and prayed for Kamal Ali whose money had fed them and for her family who had brought meals to those forced to live within the cemetery walls.

An older man sitting next to his burrow smiled and bowed his head in greeting, clear-eyed and open-faced. His white turban was yellowed and stained, but otherwise clean. His clothes were well-tended, patched again and again. A whisk-broom lay against the wall beside a small pot and bricks used for a makeshift brazier. He reminded her of the old woman, who when asked if this life was enough, answered with the freedom of one for whom the world no longer matters, "Is this not plenty for someone who is dying?"

Zaytuna asked, "The auntie who lived in these walls, the one who died recently, God have mercy on her, do you know where she is buried?"

"May she be with *those brought near*. No, my daughter. She did not die with us. We didn't know she was gone until Marwa saw her in a dream asking us to divvy up her things." He shook his head. "Graves dug every day, how can we tell what body comes with the funeral procession?"

"Would you permit me to leave you something in her name?"

"For her sake, yes."

Zaytuna placed a few coins in his pot and then they both held out their hands in prayer for the old woman's soul. She withdrew, walking into the cemetery, checking for signs of a new grave, but they were many and scattered. There was no time to stop by each and ask her heart, "Is this her?"

The two palm trees over her mother's grave called to Zaytuna, but she held back. She needed to get home. Instead of going to her uncle's grave and then her mother's as she always did, she opened her hands where she stood, praying first for all their souls, then for guidance. But finding the right words, the right thing to pray for, seemed impossible. Wanting Kamal Ali's heart to be restored was more complicated than it should have been. She questioned her motives and sincerity, wanting his restoration to make what had happened go away and allow them to return to their old selves. And for Mustafa, some happiness, somehow.

She wished she had done what the old woman had told her to do nearly two years ago, throw off the chains of her sorrow and walk through the door to peace. The old mystics and their stories of hearing one word that transformed them utterly, never to return to their lives of ignorance. That was not her way; she seemed to have to circle around and back and over again to the same trouble in her soul until it wore away.

The image of standing in the stone-walled field of white wheat came back to her. The grain of wheat. The wrongdoing of Adam. The need to take responsibility for it all. The sheaves of wheat breaking their bindings because she was not stable enough to hold them. The work left ahead. The only way back in was to not turn away from what she had done. When confronted by God, Adam blamed no one else saying, *I have wronged myself.*

Sick with the force of recognition, Zaytuna held out her hands to pray. "I wronged the dignity of my own soul in running after my pain. I wronged them." She begged forgiveness, over and over again as if repetition could force God's hand, and ended with a prayer for the family. "May the way back be easy on us."

In the distance, a flash of colour caught her attention and she turned toward it. Saadia was coming towards her through the gravestones, leaning into her stride such that Zaytuna thought for a moment she was under attack and squared herself to meet it.

Then she saw the woman with Saadia, not walking alongside but trailing her in a way that could only mean they were together. She worried for them, wanting to warn them they could not hide in plain sight like this.

"What are you doing here!" Saadia demanded.

The woman came up next to Saadia and eyed Zaytuna defiantly.

Zaytuna could not answer, taken with the woman's dark-eyed beauty. Her hair was loose, flowing like a black-watered stream. Her luxuriant figure rivalled Saliha. She was the woman of Yulduz's song, a woman all would spread their shade for her to walk under. Her dun-coloured wrap had fallen open, revealing a red velvet gown beneath. Small jewels were sewn into the neckline and glittered in the sun. All this time, Zaytuna had assumed Saadia's lover was a poor woman, a plaything for her the way she used Zaytuna and the case for her own entertainment. But this was a woman of equal or greater wealth.

"What are you doing here?" Saadia demanded, again.

Unsteady, Zaytuna retorted, "I'm not asking you that question."

"No," she said derisively, "but your answer would not damn you to a life without love, so tell me what you came here to say and leave me.

It was a stab to the heart and Zaytuna had no words.

"Save that distraught look for us who are forced to marry." She waved a hand. "Now, why are you here?"

"I didn't come for you," she replied gently. "My people are here. The living and the dead." She did not say, "I may be damned, too," because she could find her way back one way or another.

Saadia reconsidered her anger, then said to her woman, "Samra, give me a moment."

Samra pulled her wrap around her, but did not wander far off and watched them warily.

"I suppose I have news, but it is not related to your case," she said as if it were no longer amusing to her.

Zaytuna started. "Something new?"

"It is gossip, of no use."

"Hurry and tell me, then. Please, I have to go."

"The women believe al-Hallaj has been arrested." She brushed it away with her hand.

"Why?" Zaytuna started.

"One of their maids, a Christian woman from Shammasiyya, heard there was a man being held by the government in a home there. So they all gasp and suppose it is al-Hallaj." She shook her head. "They have no reason to believe so. He would be held in a cell in the Round City awaiting the High Court, of course. It is nothing to be turned into something for the sake of conversation."

Saadia was right; it was not related to their case. It was not unusual for a man of privilege and respect to be held under house arrest or in a judge's cell, but someone like al-Hallaj would not be held that way. They would make an example of him.

"You see why I did not bother sending a message." Her tone changed. She even looked slightly apologetic.

"Thank you for telling me." Zaytuna said with a small bow of the head before leaving. "I must go, but perhaps one day you would introduce me to Samra."

She laughed at Zaytuna the way wealthy women do, feigning delight, but mirthless at heart. "Please bring Mustafa and your husband to see us sometime." Without a farewell, Saadia rejoined Samra, whose back was to Zaytuna, reciting a poem,

Shall I visit you or will you visit me?
My heart bows to your longing,
my mouth, a stream of clear sweet water,
my hair, leaves of dappled shade.

Zaytuna wanted to go after Saadia and tell her those days of longing for Mustafa were over, but she took the slap for what it was, a reminder of how obvious they had been to everyone but herself. She checked the sun. There was plenty of time, but she feared being late all the same, and hurried from the cemetery. It was not far, just a few turns, and she was there in her busy alley, the fountain just beyond.

She stopped at the outer door, placing her hand on the latch, eager to open it. There would be time to sit in prayer, ready herself to hear Kamal Ali and let her heart speak with no lies or evasions, but somehow do the least harm. But once she opened the latch, she heard voices within. Yulduz, Qambar, and Layla. They sounded tense, especially Layla, whose voice was high, almost crying. Zaytuna threw open the door, seeing no one but Layla and fell to her knees, taking the girl up into her arms. "My daughter. I'm here."

Layla clung to her. "Ummi, my mother."

The word slipped past everything, those surrounding her, speaking over her, gesturing. She saw none of them. Only Layla in her arms. The fawn of her dream, held close in her protection. There was nothing left of her old fear of mothering, knowing she would never have enough of giving love to this girl.

Finally, she lifted her head. Kamal Ali was before them. His tender eyes were holding her safe. She loved him so much in that moment, she barely understood the capacity of her heart. Zaytuna kissed Layla's cheek and stood, keeping the girl close to her, her hand flat on her back. Kamal Ali moved closer, standing beside them but not touching her.

Yulduz stepped harshly into her awareness. "Where were you?"

"You know," she said, uncomprehending. "I was with Tein and Ammar."

Qambar stood behind her, his face stern in a way that she had never known from him, except the one night when he had found Tein and Saliha together. "Yes, at dawn. Now the day is nearly done and you walk in alone."

Kamal Ali stiffened. "The midday prayer has not been called."

Despite everything, he protected her from their censure.

She looked between Yulduz and Qambar, shocked that they would turn on her in front of Kamal Ali. Then she realized. They were afraid of losing their home and wanted to show him they would have a hand in controlling his wife if that was necessary to keep it. Her stomach clenched at what had become of them, especially Qambar. But what had they known before this but a life of boiling the same bone over and over with greens they had plucked from the roadside? She wanted to tell Kamal Ali not to be angry with them, that she had done this to them.

"You were gone too long," Yulduz said as if Kamal Ali had not intervened.

But he responded for her, gently. "She was with her brother, please."

"Don't you 'please' me," the old woman snapped. "You need to stop being so soft with her."

Qambar put his hand on her arm but she shook it off.

Zaytuna faced Kamal Ali, pleading, "Tein knew what I would do if I stayed here waiting for you to come. My mind would go round and round and…"

"Shh," he said. "I know."

Layla did not let go of her, but turned to Yulduz. "See!"

It only spurred Yulduz on, but this time Qambar was behind her, demanding an answer. "Who are you obligated to? That missing man? This family? Us? Your husband, Kamal Ali?" Her eyes were hard as stone. The last name she threw at her was not a question but an accusation. "Mustafa."

"Come." Kamal Ali gestured toward their room, still not touching her.

She did not want to leave Layla with Yulduz and Qambar in their complaining, fearful state. "Can you go to Sara and Rana?"

Layla pulled Zaytuna's wrap around her, trying to hide within it.

"Are they home? Kamal Ali and I have to talk."

She felt a small nod against her belly and walked Layla over to the door, bent over and kissed her on the cheek. "Habibti, I'll come for you after."

The girl ran off, but looked back as Zaytuna shut the door.

Kamal Ali was waiting for her within their room. His face was drawn. He had not been sleeping. Zaytuna wanted nothing more than to sit him on the edge of the bed and take his feet in her hands, as he had done for her so many times, and massage them until his tension wore away. Instead, they sat on the floor apart from one another, him at a distance that would not allow her to reach out to touch him.

At first, neither spoke, only sharing looks of love and disaster.

His first words were a whisper, catching in his throat. "I do not want to know how far this has gone. But I cannot remain with you if you love another. You must decide for yourself."

"I want you, my love." She could not help but reach for him, but he shrank back, if only slightly. "I want you."

"First, I will leave this house today and return when we have come to a resolution on whether I will stay or go. These people are my family and I will not revoke my responsibility toward them." He raised his voice so they could hear. "This is your home. I do not want Zaytuna to choose to love me because you worry about your livelihood."

There was a sharp scuffle and cry of relief just outside the door.

"Enough," Qambar said outside, then they retreated.

She waited a moment, then said what he declared he did not want to hear. If she did not, if he returned to her without knowing, the doubt would always linger. "I did not tell you everything before. When I went to him the first time, he invited me to be alone with him. I felt a pull, but I denied him and made it clear that I loved you, my husband. The second time, he reached out for me, a brush of his finger, and I withdrew, repulsed."

She watched as relief unwound the knot of fear in him, but left a man wounded by betrayal. He remained silent and she took it as an invitation to tell him everything.

"Mustafa and I have known each other since we were children. We have always loved each other. He wanted to marry me when I was not able. I pushed him away, again and again. My heart was too broken to accept him. When he fell in love with YingYue, I was so jealous of her I could barely stand to go to Uncle's. I went to Mustafa and asked him to consider us again before it was too late. This time, he did not accept me. The propriety of it all. How could he leave her and all the promises he had made?"

Kamal Ali paled, but did not stop her.

"I left him grieving the loss of us, but I told myself that once Mustafa was married to YingYue, he and I would return to how we always were, sharing a bond that could never be severed. I saw myself alone for the rest of my life, holding onto that thread between us. Happiness was not for me."

He frowned, nearly objecting.

"Then I met you. You made me feel loved in a way I had never known. You found me beautiful when no one ever had before. You promised to love me as I was. The whole of me. I saw the man you are and I knew you were a gift given to me by God. I loved you immediately. I never knew there was a way to love the way I love you. I have never stopped loving you."

His eyes welled with tears. "Then why?"

"At his wedding. You saw. He as much as admitted that he had married the wrong woman. I was furious with him, that he had done this to all of us. I did not want him back. I only wanted you, my love. But I did not understand that while I had let go of wanting to marry him, I had not let go of the sorrow that was the mark of the love we shared." She pressed a hand to her cheek. "Our relationship had always been like this. Tears and fights. I turned to you, constant, loving."

He finally asked, "Before this case, had you approached him privately?"

"I saw him at the sama only. We would acknowledge each other, but nothing more. I was angry with him for putting us in this position, for harming YingYue, for not being as happy as I was with you."

"No, Zaytuna. You were angry with him for rejecting you."

Her eyes widened. He was right. She hated saying it, fearing once she did there would be no way back to him, but if she did not, there would be no way back to herself. "Yes."

"And when he came to you with this case?"

"I lied to myself that I felt anything more than tenderness toward the Mustafa I had grown up with, nothing toward the man who had married YingYue."

"Is it done, now?"

"Yes."

"Zaytuna, I knew about the jug and cup beside our bed, next to your mother's cherished drum. But I thought whatever love was left between you would settle into a memory only touched from a distance." He moved toward her slightly. "I have those memories, too. I understand. I remember the good love I shared with my former wives and I am not sorry for it. If I had a memento from them, I would not have given it up, either."

"The jug is gone." She put both hands on her heart. "And the cup. I put them out on the street with my old pain. Or at least, I have begun, truly."

"Part of me still believes that you could not have done this," he said. "My other wife, when I discovered it, there was no doubt that she was capable of being with another man. But you? A woman of such moral stature." He glanced down. "I still do not believe it." When he looked up, she saw a tremor of anger cross his face. He stood.

"What did uncle say to you at the sama?" she asked, standing alongside him.

"He urged me to trust that you are on a path away from your attachment to Mustafa and that I should understand I am your partner in finding peace."

There seemed to be more, but he did not say and she did not push. But she silently thanked her uncle, wondering how much of his assurance was keeping Kamal Ali there with her, rather than abandoning her for good.

Kamal Ali took his second turban off the high shelf over the pegs where he hung his cloak. Only then did she notice he had been packing to go. She clasped her hands tightly to keep from tearing the bag away from him and trying to hold him there. "Are you sleeping at the shop?"

"I was. I've moved into a hostel nearby."

"When will you come home?"

"I do not know."

"Will you come home?"

He did not answer her, but said, "Tein came to see me."

She looked surprised.

"He did not tell you? He came to apologize and to defend you. Coming home means making peace with both of you."

His bag was in one hand. The other was on the door latch. He left her, affirming to Yulduz and Qambar on the way out that they had nothing to fear, but he did not say to them that he would only be away for a time.

She went to the door of their room and watched as he shut the outer door behind him.

Yulduz came directly for her.

Zaytuna stayed, gripping the door frame to steady herself from the coming onslaught.

"You selfish woman. He was always above your station. You forget I've seen you all these years. I know your temper an' the way you tortured Mustafa until his heart was broken. Then you weep when he finds another an' rush into that good man's arms in the grief of it."

What good was there in explaining herself?

"You break this man's heart," Yulduz carried on. "If you can break his heart, you never deserved 'im. Now, he's tied to you an' what can save 'im?"

She took a moment, refusing to stare the woman down, only saddened by what she had done to put her there. "I won't fight you, Yulduz. Let me pass."

Expecting a fight, Yulduz did not know what to do with this small triumph, and stood by stunned as Zaytuna walked past her, then Qambar, into the street.

Kamal Ali was gone. She was not expecting to see him, but it hit her in the gut all the same and her stomach already in knots threatened to loosen into sick. Her only thought was to find Saliha at work, then come back for Layla. The hospital was not much farther than the cemetery, and she began to run, hoping to shake herself loose from the pain.

Out of breath, she stopped, bent over, hands on her knees. She observed their sun-marked backs, wrinkled and spotted already like an old woman. Straightening, she held her palms out before her, looking at the softer, but still calloused skin. These hands had never complained to her. They had done what was needed and they would not lie. They told her this trouble was nothing they had not seen before. But she had never known a love like this. Still, her hands objected, her own voice speaking for them. "We are strong enough for being loved. We will hold it for you when you cannot."

She hurried on to the hospital. Within, she walked past the trees, the benches and the fountain in the courtyard, past the pharmacy without looking to see if Ibn Ali was there, then the surgeries until she was at the door behind which Saliha and Shatha washed the corpses of women and children. She lay her shoulder and head against it, imagining herself on the table, hearing the kind and gentle voices of the washers reminding her of God and Prophet. Once cleansed, this world behind her and the grave before her, how would she answer for herself on that Last Day when her sight would be piercing? What lies would she still find hiding within herself?

The door opened suddenly and she stumbled in. Shatha caught and steadied her. Saliha rushed over and the two settled her on a bench.

Saliha sat with her while Shatha brought a cup of water. Saliha took the cup, saying to her, "I'll finish here. You go."

Shatha pulled on her wrap and left, mumbling a prayer.

"Tell me," Saliha said, handing her the water.

"Have you forgiven my brother?"

"I think you're too easy on him. I'm waiting for him to tell me what's been at him since this case started. It's far more than he is letting on."

Zaytuna worried how Saliha would take the news when he finally decided to tell her, but that was not for today.

"Now what about you?"

"I have wronged myself."

"And you believe you have wronged us," she said angrily.

"Yes." Zaytuna had not expected Saliha to come at her like Yulduz and readied herself for the blow.

Saliha stood, hands on hips. "You do not owe us a marriage to put food in our mouths." She held out her hands. "These hands put food in our mouths. Your hands. Your brother's hands. Not one of us needs a soft mattress or a room with a hearth. Walla, stop flattering yourself that we all depend on you alone!"

"But Yulduz…" she did not want to object, praying what Saliha said was true.

"Oh that nasty old bird. We put meat in her mouth before you met Kamal Ali, we'll do the same if he leaves us."

"He won't leave us," she said. "He promised to take care of all of us even if there is no way for him to come home."

She watched Saliha's face carefully for a sense of relief, but there was none there. It did not matter to her. It was Zaytuna who mattered.

"That's all well and good for the old people," said Saliha. "Maybe they will give you some peace." She looked at Zaytuna squarely, demanding the truth. "Now, do you want Kamal Ali to come home?"

"Yes." She gripped the cup tightly. "With all my heart. I love him without doubting I am worthy of being loved."

"You are worthy of it," she said sharply.

"But how can our love be the same as it was?"

"You should hope it's never the same. You wanting Mustafa the way you did in secret. Pray it's something new."

Zaytuna put down the cup and took her hand. "Please."

"I warned you."

"You told me I was lying to myself. I couldn't see it."

"I was wrong, too. I should have seen the risk to you. Your brother did." Saliha jabbed a finger at her. "But no matter what these people say, you cherish the sweetness you had with Mustafa. Wanting him is over for good now. I see it. But you keep that bit of good for yourself in your memory. Who are these people who think our hearts are so narrow?" Saliha sat down beside Zaytuna and put an arm around her. "Drink that water, you fool."

She took small sips, grateful for her friend. Grateful for all of it, but strangely in a way she had not yet tasted. The cup she held filled with gratitude. And as the worst of what she had done and what had been done to her rose and fell within her awareness, she sipped, observing its pattern as if she were standing on a densely woven carpet yet unable to explain the design to herself who was also caught in its threads. But each drop of gratitude soothed the burning in her belly and restored some semblance of hope.

The leaves of the pomegranate tree in the small courtyard beyond rustled and hushed. In the room, the shelves were full and orderly with folded shrouds, jars of lotus and camphor and baskets of cotton. Shining copper basins sat near the tap. A drop of water clung to its edge, then fell onto the stone counter. The scent of camphor lingered and she took deep breaths, imagining herself again as a body laid out, but it was her old life that had passed into the hands of the washers to be cleansed and prepared for the next world to come. A new world, she prayed, one that held a new love between her and Kamal Ali. A love more worthy of them.

Saliha broke through her thoughts. "I saw Kamal Ali this morning."

"Where?" Zaytuna faced her.

"He was handing out loaves of bread at the cemetery. I helped him until the sack was empty. I told him he was a good man. He looked at me, slumped over, denying it, saying the charity was nothing but selfishness."

"No, not him."

"He said he was feeding the poor instead of his anger so that his anger toward you would subside. Then he sat down in the dirt, among all those people taking their treasured bread from his hands, and wept."

27

"GOD, FREE HER."

Mustafa knocked sharply on the door to Zaytuna's home. He had itched and burned to leave during the lesson for the children, thinking only of her. During the family meal, he picked at his food, glancing at the door. They noticed his discomfort, and tried feebly to attend to him, not knowing what he needed. Sick in love, it was no lie to say he was not well and beg off their classes. There would be no more secret declarations. Today, he would ask Kamal Ali to release her.

Layla opened the door a crack and he thanked God for it. "Assalamu alaykum, is your uncle Kamal Ali in?"

But her face crumpled at the sight of him and she left him without a word, the door ajar. He took it as permission, but when he pushed against the door, Qambar pulled it wide open.

"Have you no shame?"

Zaytuna was sitting in the corner on the reed mats where they gathered for their meals. Saliha was next to her, holding her hand. Layla had rushed under Zaytuna's arm, and tucked herself in so closely she was almost sitting on her lap. Yulduz was next to her friend Marta, but the old woman was angrily pushing herself up to standing.

"Love knows no shame," he retorted, his back straight, eyes begging Zaytuna to come to him.

But Yulduz came at him instead, hand raised. The full handed slap nearly took him off his feet. He raised his arms to protect himself from another blow, but Qambar was already pulling her back as she struggled to come at him again.

"If you do not want another, then leave," Qambar said, having got Yulduz to stand back. "I cannot protect you from the women in this house."

Mustafa stayed where he was, unwilling to leave without Zaytuna. Let the women beat him. Let the men beat him. Would she come to him, then? But no one moved. He took one more step into the courtyard. "I am here to speak to Kamal Ali. Is he home?"

Zaytuna made a small choking sound.

Saliha cursed under her breath and jumped up, hand out.

Zaytuna let go of the girl and scrambled up to stop her.

"Let me!" she growled at Zaytuna.

Mustafa said past Saliha's fury, "Is he home?"

Qambar put a firm hand on him to direct him out.

She finally spoke, pleading as she held onto Saliha. "You must go."

"No more secrets, Zaytuna. You can tell them. We must tell them."

Yulduz turned on her. "What is this?"

Marta had been still with shock, but then stared at Zaytuna, expecting an answer.

"Nothing!" she snapped, letting Saliha go who stood beside her at the ready.

"There's something here, girl."

"Yes! Zaytuna, tell them. Do not be afraid." He swept off Qambar's hand and took a few more steps into the courtyard. "I am the Prophet to her Zaynab, asking Kamal Ali to divorce her for my sake. Don't you all see?"

Saliha went for him again, and he flinched. But she did not hit him, instead she presented herself as a barrier he could not pass.

"You must go," Qambar insisted.

"Let her tell me to go and I will."

"What is going on?" Tein came through the open outer door, saw Mustafa, and grabbed him by the back of the neck.

Qambar stepped out of his way.

His knees nearly buckled under Tein's grip. He tried to answer, grunting with pain. "Zaytuna…"

"Mustafa, go!" Zaytuna cried out.

"You heard her," Tein said.

"They are making her say it!"

Tein forced him out of the courtyard and into the street. The door slammed behind them.

Yulduz's voice carried over the wall. "Go with him, Zaytuna. None of us will stop you!"

Then Saliha, "Talk to her like that again, old woman, and I'll show you what a slap is."

"Please," Zaytuna cried.

He was grateful for the old woman's intervention all the same, and stared past Tein, waiting for the door to open, for Zaytuna to appear.

Tein's grip loosened, but he did not let go. Instead, he turned him around, shifting his hold to his shoulder and forcing Mustafa to look him in the eye. "My brother. It's over. She has chosen Kamal Ali. I spoke to her alone. She's under no pressure."

It would have hurt less if Tein had kicked him to the ground and beat him mercilessly. "I will not believe it."

"It's true."

Mustafa wrested himself away from Tein, but did not run away. Unable to leave her, he pressed his hands flat against the wall of the house, willing her to feel him holding her from there. But Tein pulled him loose and took him into an embrace.

"My brother. My brother." Tein's great arms around him, his body broke into falling apart. "It's over."

A whisper of what he had done spoke in his ear. He moaned, "She loves me."

"She does," Tein agreed. "She always will, but not in marriage."

"It is because of YingYue? I cannot divorce her."

"No."

Mustafa pushed Tein away and searched his face for the lie, but there was only kindness. "Why won't she come with me?"

"You know why. She clung to you because you gave her solace in her anger. You clung to her because you took strength from her."

"We need each other," he pleaded.

"You've loved the best in each other, but you need the worst in each other."

His breath became shallow and he lunged forward, but Tein took hold of him again.

"How will I live?" he begged, straining uselessly toward the door.

"You will find a way, but for now, let her live."

Tein tried to lead him away from the house, but he resisted.

"You cannot sleep here." Tein made a joke of it.

He gave in, letting Tein draw him away, but he looked back again and again until they had turned the corner.

"Let me walk you home."

There was no home for him now. He ran by a man coming toward him, made his way to a spot along the wall, and heaved. Nothing but spit came up. He heaved again. Tein's hand was on his back, comforting. He leaned into the wall, breathing into his spasming gut.

When the sickness passed, Tein waved over a water seller. The man bowed to pour from the long-spouted copper jug strapped to his back, first rinsing the cup, then pouring for him.

Mustafa wiped his mouth with his sleeve and sipped until it was all gone.

Tein passed the man his coin, then said to Mustafa, "Home."

"I cannot face her."

"Where then?"

"The Shuniziyya mosque. I'll rest there." He looked at Tein. "And pray."

"Maybe uncle's would be better?"

That, too, was more than he could bear. He had been certain his uncle had arranged for Kamal Ali to divorce Zaytuna for his sake. A thought appeared forcing, him down. He slid down the wall, and pulled his wrap up to cover his face as if it would protect him from the revelation. His uncle had instructed no such thing. Neither had Auntie Hakima. He, Mustafa, had misunderstood, hearing and seeing only what he wanted. No one had said anything outright except that he should remain married to YingYue.

Tein sat down beside him.

He heard shuffling feet, words here and there, but the street felt eerily quiet, as if the death of Mustafa's love had reached them, but the mourning had not yet begun.

"Is it true?"

"She will never forget you, but her life is with Kamal Ali now."

"How could I have been so wrong?" He felt sick again from the humiliation.

"We carry our pasts on our back." Tein leaned into him. "Too heavy to move on."

"But not you, Tein." He pulled the wrap away from his face. "You have your wife. Your family. Work you enjoy."

"I'm going to be a father."

"Mashallah. You see?" Mustafa grasped his hand. "Tein, the blessings of your life. Not like mine. I have nothing left."

"My brother, we are more alike than you think."

"Tell me. Tell me I am not alone."

Tein stopped and started, opening his mouth to say one thing, then changing his mind. Finally, he asked, "What do you think of me?"

Mustafa wondered what he wanted him to say. When he spoke, he prayed the words were right. "You remind me of the Prophet, alayhi salam. A man of great honour. A warrior. A protector. A man who respects women and watches out for the vulnerable. You will choose what is right over what is easy." He paused. "A loyal friend."

"Muhammad wasn't a killer."

He did not understand what Tein meant by it. "The Prophet killed, but he was not a killer. They were at war; he did what was required of him by God and no more."

"He left it on the battlefield."

"Yes."

"Then I am nothing like him."

Mustafa thought he understood. "There are men who speak as if there is glory in killing, even when they do not kill for their own desire. I heard it said that Seyyidina Ali himself spoke of strutting like a peacock in full feather after leaving the field of battle."

"Maybe because they could take pride in what they had done? Those battles had meaning. What I did?" Tein shook his head. "It's not the same. It's left me knowing who I am and what I am worth."

"A killer," Mustafa said softly.

"A killer." He snorted derisively. "A killer who could not protect his own wife and child from Byzantine raiders. How will I protect my wife and child now, from others, from me? How can I keep my violence from touching them?"

Mustafa felt his pain as deeply as his own, grabbed his brother's hand, and wept. Tein slumped against him. The example of Prophet Muhammad came to him. He wiped his tears and waited until Tein had quieted, then said, "I think the Prophet, alayhi salam, knew men like you, men for whom war scars in that way. It is said some soldiers came to him after battle and he told them they had come from the lesser jihad and now must enter into the greater jihad. The Prophet described that greater battle as the struggle for the soul's goodness."

"I never understood it that way," Tein said.

Mustafa thought he heard a note of ecstasy in his voice.

After a few moments, Tein straightened up, letting out a breath. "Let's go to Uncle's."

But Mustafa's heart clenched. He was not ready to hear Uncle Abu al-Qasim and Auntie Hakima say he got it all wrong and that Zaytuna was lost to him. He deflected, hoping to draw Tein away and leave him there in the street, staying as close to Zaytuna as he could, holding onto a last shred of hope. "I saw Bahr."

Tein did not react eagerly, as he had hoped. He sounded exhausted. "What happened?"

"He has left Baghdad. Nabil had so compromised his reputation that he had no other option than to leave and start again."

"You let him go?"

Tein asked it in the same tired tone of voice, leaving Mustafa feeling defensive. "I admired him. He understood that he had been memorizing the Quran for the sake of his reputation. Nabil's efforts to ruin him had freed him. He left to wander with little to his name except his adoration of God's word."

"Did he know what Nabil wanted?"

"He thought Nabil was trying to sell the manuscript, create interest until someone, a library or private collector, would buy it from him. And that he used Bahr to shore up his reputation."

"So Bahr thinks there is a manuscript."

"It seemed so, at times."

"I don't see how." Tein started to speak, but held it back.

"Tell me."

Tein looked at him for a moment first, considering. "Nabil's mother played us for fools. The talisman she had was a curse to destroy Bahr's family for what they did. She and Nabil were out to ruin Bahr. There never was a manuscript. The idea of it was enough to turn Ibn Mujahid against Bahr. And they used us to do it. With us in the mosque questioning, Bahr was tainted, along with Nabil. Oliga was the one who purchased the talisman. She had to have known all about the plan and went along with it." He paused. "I think she is happy to stand aside and damn us all to hell."

So much deception, and he had brought them all into its circle. Brought them in by means of a deception of his own. He had only gone with Ulgen to speak to Nabil's mother because he hoped to draw Zaytuna into a case. And what had come of it? He felt Yulduz and Qambar's censure. Layla's worry that first day when she took him to the butter shop; her fear just now clinging to Zaytuna. Zaytuna's shock when he touched her. Kamal Ali's desolation. Tein's grief at himself. He had disrespected YingYue from the moment they married. He admitted it all, moaning as each accusation took its place in his awareness.

"Brother, enough, let's go."

Grasping Tein's hand, he stood and pulled Tein up with him. "I want to go to the mother's house. I need to set this right."

"There's no setting this right."

"I brought you to them. It's my fault you are in the middle of this."

Tein did not disagree just to be kind, which it made it worse, but he agreed to go to Umm Nabil.

Every step along the Basra High Road was a step away from Zaytuna, and he stifled the urge to run back to her. Once they turned off toward the Sharqiyya mosque, he veered as far from the entrance as he could, drawing his wrap over his turban to cover his face.

When they neared the house, Tein pulled him back. "I was wrong. You're in no state for this. I'll tell Umm Nabil that we know everything. Please, wait outside and we'll go to Uncle's together afterwards."

"Let me do this one thing."

"It won't bring Zaytuna back to you."

He gulped at Tein, saying it so plainly, but he urged him to knock.

Oliga opened the door, looking Tein up and down with derision. "I did not run, didn't your friend tell you?"

Tein said, "No. But I didn't think you would."

Mustafa looked between them, not understanding.

"That hideous woman, the skinny crow," Oliga answered his questioning glance. "She warned me to run if I am guilty."

She meant Zaytuna. Bile bit at the back of Mustafa's throat and unthinking hate shifted his whole body forward. Tein forced him back. Only then did he realize how close he had come to spitting on her.

Oliga laughed at them both. "What do you want?"

"To talk to Umm Nabil."

"This one, will he spit on her, too? Or will you hold him back again?" She gave him a piercing look. "Do not hold him back."

Tein stepped toward the door without asking again and she led them within.

Umm Nabil must have heard them coming. She had positioned herself on the couch in an air of distress. "My son! My son!"

When she saw Tein, she sat forward, clutching one of the pillows. "Have you found him?"

"We know what you did," Tein said flatly.

Her eyes widened and she reached for the talisman around her throat, now stitched up in plain leather. "Oh, and what I have done! What have I done but paid you to find my son?"

"We know that Bahr's father impoverished you when he took repayment of your husband's debt. You wanted to bring the whole family down, starting with Bahr. We know you had that talisman made to destroy Bahr and his family." He gestured to Oliga. "We know she purchased it on your order. We know that Nabil used the manuscript or the threat of the manuscript to hurt Bahr's reputation. We know you hired us to stir things up and keep the suspicion focused on Bahr. You've succeeded. I don't know why Nabil keeps going and doesn't just come home. Mocking the rest of the scholars? Chaos? Tell your son it's over. This case is closed."

The woman heaved off the couch to confront them, drawing so near that Mustafa could smell the stench of her breath.

Mustafa watched, immobile, stunned, until the hatred he felt for Oliga turned on the mother. It was her. She was at the heart of it all. If it had not been for her, would his world have come down around him?

"Lies!" she countered. "Bahr has done something to him! Ever since we got here, Bahr lorded over Nabil his position with Ibn Mujahid's circle. If a word was said to praise Nabil, Bahr cut him off from every advantage. Then, when Nabil inherited the manuscript…"

Mustafa interrupted. "What do you mean, inherited?"

"His teacher in Basra bequeathed it to him. It arrived just a few weeks ago after the good man passed." She held up her hands. "God have mercy on his soul!"

He looked to Tein, but he was giving nothing away.

"My Nabil, such a good boy but naïve, he showed it to Bahr despite everything, asking him to accompany him to Ibn Mujahid and vouch for him. He wanted to present it to the great scholar."

Mustafa refused to believe that Bahr would lie. If this manuscript was real, he never showed it to Bahr. This horrible woman who had driven him to such shame was still lying.

Tein asked, "Why not give it to Ibn Shanabudh, his own teacher?"

"He tried!"

More lies! They knew from the students and teaching assistants at the mosque that he had refused to show it, and they refused to give him any more attention. Even Ulgen, whose word could not be challenged, said the same. Was it possible she did not know? That she had never seen it but believed her son's story? The talisman could have been for revenge, but not tied to any of this. He studied her face, the black kohl lining her eyes bleeding onto her wrinkled cheeks, the wretched downturn of her mouth. No. She did know, she had to know. And he hated her for what she had done to him.

Oliga leaned against the wall, as if she were watching a play on the streets of Baghdad. She prompted, "The dream, mistress, tell them the dream."

"Yes! Nabil had a dream, a visionary dream that proves it all!" the mother said. "There were seven circles of students seated around Ibn Mujahid. The great scholar sat at the centre with Bahr beside him. Nabil was not even in the outermost circle, but beyond them, alone. Ibn Mujahid was holding a thick wool cloak and placed it over Bahr's shoulders. Nabil ran through the circles until he was at the centre and took the cloak for himself. He stood at the centre, his rightful place." Her eyes lit up with pride. "He was triumphant! But the cloak became heavier and heavier, forcing him to the floor, until it was so heavy, he felt his bones creaking under the weight. He begged Bahr to take it from him and once released, ran from them screaming."

Mustafa had been holding his breath while she recounted the dream. He had not misjudged Bahr. He was a man worthy of carrying the weight of so many readings of the Quran, now, by God's permission, freed from the traps of scholarly arrogance. "Subhanallah," Mustafa said aloud.

"Yes!" Umm Nabil raised her hand in declaration. "They sit in their circles only to crush my baby and Bahr is at the centre of it all!"

"I spoke to Bahr. He had nothing to do with your son's disappearance. He has left Baghdad."

She leapt off the couch, grabbing fistfuls of Mustafa's robe. He stumbled back, trying to push her away. "You had the man and you let him go? You believed him!" She collapsed onto the floor. "You have cost me my son!"

Oliga smiled at the two men, gesturing toward the door. "Enough?"

Tein turned away, taking Mustafa by the elbow, but he shook off his hand and returned to watch Umm Nabil wail piteously on the floor. "You," Mustafa whispered. "You drove your son to this. All of this is, everything that has happened is on your head. I have lost my one true love because of you!"

28

TEIN GOT HIM OUTSIDE, said, "The case is over," then turned him toward their uncle's house. Mustafa wanted to break away and nurse the anger keeping his failures at bay, but Tein had his arm through his and held him firmly when he tried to yank free.

"You are going to Uncle's."

"So he can tell me whom I should marry and divorce?"

Tein did not release his grip until they arrived. He knocked hard on the door, so hard that Ziri opened it in a rush, ready to act. "What's wrong?"

"I need to deliver this one to Uncle Abu al-Qasim." Ziri looked at Mustafa, understanding. They all knew his shame.

Ziri went ahead of them. The courtyard was busy. Auntie Hakima was sitting in a group of old women in her place near the kitchen. Groups of men and women sat in small clusters, chatting, while others sat alone against the wall in quiet contemplation. None of them raised their heads to stare at him. Ziri crouched before Abu Muhammad al-Juwayri. He caught Mustafa's eye and gestured for them to come forward. The others who were waiting looked between Juwayri and Mustafa and visibly resigned themselves to waiting longer. Juwayri stood to join them. Mustafa pulled back, but again Tein was behind him.

Before they could step out of the arched entrance to the reception hall, Auntie Hakima came towards them, her stick barely touching the ground. Ibn Ata was directly behind her.

Juwayri got to him first and Tein passed Mustafa off into his care. Mustafa shrugged off Juwayri's hand on his elbow. "Am I a prisoner?"

"No brother. The shaykh only wants to speak with you."

Tein had gone ahead and was now crouching before his uncle, Shaykh Abu al-Qasim. Junayd listened, his face not betraying any emotion. Tein could only be informing his uncle of his humiliation. He pulled again on Abu Muhammad, to no avail. In a moment, he was seated before his uncle, the tap of Auntie Hakima's stick behind him. There was a groan as she sat down next to him. Ibn Ata sat next to Tein, embracing him briefly, then lowering his head.

"My son." Junayd did not reach out to greet Mustafa and Mustafa was unable to show him any respect. "My son," he said again.

The second time, he heard the words as an invitation to release his burdens.

Mustafa's head dropped so heavily he thought his turban would come away. He removed it and placed it between him and his uncle, exposing himself to everyone. A man without a turban was no man at all. Mustafa then looked among them: Junayd, Abu Muhammad, Tein, Auntie Hakima, and Ibn Ata, and the world began to spin. A hand was on his back.

"Breathe, my son," said Junayd.

"But Zaytuna is my breath."

"This is why you cannot marry her."

He let his resentments out. "I thought you were arranging for my divorce and hers. I thought you wanted us to be together."

"If I told you what we wanted, would you have listened?"

"But Auntie Hakima..."

"She was trying to keep you and Zaytuna away from each other before you made a mistake you would regret for the rest of your lives."

Mustafa looked at the old woman. "But you said they were making plans."

"They were, but no one consults me." Then she snapped at Junayd, "He never should have been left in ignorance for so long."

Junayd bowed his head to her, but not in a way that gave any ground.

"What? What is it?" He begged, praying it was a reconciliation with Zaytuna despite everything that had been said. "I live for her, her alone."

"You two gave each other strength. You inspired each other. No one can deny the good care you took of her when her brother had to leave us to defend our frontier. But there was something else."

Auntie Hakima grumbled behind him, then spat out, "This is not complicated, yet you will not get to the point!" Mustafa turned to look at her. She pointed insultingly at him. "You are like an animal who takes his will from his master. And she took up the rein because that is her sorry-hearted weakness. The two of you did this to each other! God is the Master!"

Shaking from the force of her, he saw himself standing over Nabil's mother, blaming her, angry with her, angry with Oliga. Angry with Zaytuna for not loving him the way he wanted, for YingYue not wanting a marriage with a man who could not love her the way she dreamed. Using the case to compromise a married woman and betray his own wife. He had no honour. He panicked, grasping his robe over his heart. He had lost everything.

Zaytuna.

YingYue.

Himself.

"Son," Junayd pulled his attention towards him. "Who is your breath?"

He could not answer, still only able to clutch at himself.

Junayd reached out and took his hand, holding it between his own. Calm washed through Mustafa. His shallow breaths became deeper until he saw himself as a young boy, when Zaytuna and Tein had first arrived, their regal mother holding Zaytuna's hand. Tein walking behind Uncle Nuri, who had offered the mother and her children a safe haven in the Sufi community of Baghdad. Zaytuna was frightened and defiant all at once. Thin as a reed, her narrow face, her sharp nose, her eyes aflame. She was never beautiful. But he loved her then and vowed to serve her. He followed her every command. She was better than him. He shrank in fear when she ran towards it. He made her his heart. And she took hold of his heart, depending on him as surely as he depended on her. And nothing had changed.

"Who is your breath?"

"I am my breath." It was the wrong answer for them, he knew. But he could not say God. If he could not say "Zaytuna," he would only say "I."

"Yes," Junayd agreed. "Zaytuna is not your breath."

He tried to say the right thing. "My breath serves God."

Auntie Hakima patted him on the arm as if he were a child. Junayd picked up his turban and gestured to Mustafa to lower his head, then put the turban back in place.

But all he could see was Zaytuna's horrified expression when Tein drew him away from their house that afternoon. He saw Kamal Ali's distraught face at the sama. He saw YingYue's face at their wedding. "What have I done? I have wronged them!" He faced Tein. "How did you embrace me?"

"You are my brother," Tein said softly. "I knew you would find your way."

"For your wife," Junayd said, "we ask that you respect her wishes and remain married to her."

"She wants me to marry another woman, but there is no other for me than Zaytuna."

Junayd did not address the complaint, saying only, "As for Zaytuna and Kamal Ali, you must leave them alone. For yourself, pray for God to forgive you." He paused. "Repentance means not returning to your old wrongs. Turn to God for help, not these feelings, no matter the solace they give in the moment. They are nothing but a trap laid to return you to where you lost your way."

"I do not want to forget her!" He turned his face away, tears coming again.

Junayd put his hands out in prayer. "God, may he preserve the beauty of his love for Zaytuna, but from a place of memory alone." He leaned over and whispered to Abu Muhammad, who got up and left them. Mustafa watched him go, wondering why.

"Your aunt said we had a plan for you."

He pulled his head around, staring at his uncle, terrified.

Junayd stood and the others followed suit, except Auntie Hakima, who remained seated. Mustafa hurried to his feet, looking behind him. Abu Muhammad had returned with Imam Abu Abdurrahman.

"Assalamu alaykum." He gestured widely, taking them all in, then to Mustafa. "I have been waiting to greet you!"

Mustafa blushed, not understanding why he should be so kind. Had no one told him that he had made himself unworthy?

"Come, let us all sit."

Abu Muhammad guided Imam Abu Abdurrahman to the spot next to Junayd, who forced him to sit before he did. Only after that did they all take their places.

"When I returned to Baghdad, the shaykh apprised me of your troubles. Your father-in-law even came and spoke to me at the shaykh's invitation." He bowed his head and Mustafa wished he could run. "At the mosque, the imam shared that your reputation had been unfairly marred. He feared that no accomplishments could help you repair it. He said you had been spending time in Quran classes, hoping to find another path through, but that Ibn Mujahid's representatives wanted to send you back to us hadith scholars."

Mustafa moaned, lowering his head even further.

"Look at me, son," the imam said.

He raised his head, but only at the imam's command.

"Would you like to come to Medina and study hadith under me? There is a waqf for students' living expenses. You would have no responsibility but learning."

"Me?" He stammered, not understanding, then turned toward Junayd. "I do not deserve it."

The imam ignored his protest. "It would mean studying the words of our blessed Prophet, alayhi salam, in the shadow of his tomb and, God willing, with his gracious approval."

"YingYue has agreed." Junayd interrupted. "Her father presented it to her. Her only concern is your happiness."

It was an opportunity he could have never achieved for himself, never having had the money nor the freedom from responsibility to go. But he could not leave Zaytuna's city. He may be barred from speaking to her, but no one could stop him from walking her streets to capture her footsteps, gazing at her during the sama or from a distance as she fed the poor in the cemetery.

Auntie Hakima said, "You need the distance, boy."

The imam went on, happily, "If it is not too much, I have a niece living under my protection." Junayd placed a hand on his arm to stop him, but he continued. "She was married to a cruel man who took advantage of her gentle nature. She has a young son. The man divorced her without even a thought for the child. I negotiated with him to give away his right to raise the boy. I fear a man taking advantage of her again."

Was this part of their plan? Another woman! How could they think he would agree? He tried to stand, but Tein kept him where he was.

Auntie Hakima broke in. "He's not right for a woman now! Not for a long time. For his sake and your niece, do not push them."

The imam tucked his head back at her rudeness, but Mustafa was grateful and took her hand and kissed it in thanks. The imam must not be aware of the wrongs he had committed to YingYue, to Zaytuna, to Kamal Ali, to everyone. He addressed him, his voice cracking. "I am not worthy of your attention. And I am not worthy of any woman."

"I am not offering her to you in marriage." He bowed his head slightly. "I invite you to study with me. Only that as a friend of my household, you will have the opportunity to meet her."

"Imam." He closed his eyes for a moment, insisting, "I cannot go with you to Medina. You do not know the worst of me."

The imam looked at Junayd, concerned. "What worst?"

"Our Mustafa has had to give up his childhood love."

He nodded, understanding. "His father-in-law mentioned that she was unwilling to be a second wife." He addressed Mustafa. "I assure you that my niece would not object, especially as your first marriage is chaste and kept out of respect for her worship."

Did the imam not know that Zaytuna was married?

Junayd said, "I ask you to accept that all of us here stand for Mustafa's good character, but the situation amounts to more than what you suppose. We rely on our son's honour to disclose everything at a later time. At the moment, your offer to allow him to leave Baghdad and study under you, and so close to the Prophet, alayhi salam, is a gift he will not decline. From this day forward may he live in such a way as to be worthy of the Prophet's presence."

This was what his uncle had planned, to remove him from Baghdad and Zaytuna's presence before what did happen could happen. The niece was part of the plan. Only Junayd had been too late, unable to prevent Mustafa from harming so many, and the imam did not know. Did his uncle not understand that even the chance to rectify his studies and reputation could not have kept him from her?

But now there was no refusing.

He saw himself again, following Zaytuna wherever she went. Returning to her house again and again, waiting for her until she came outside and admitted their love. It would never end.

They were right, and he hated it. It would destroy him and ruin her. "God protect me from evil things. God protect me from evil things." He whispered the desperate prayer over and over, then looked up at the imam. "I will go!" The words burst out of him, and the imam was taken aback. He corrected, thinking of Zaytuna and what she would want, and took strength from her again. "I am sorry, imam. I am honoured that you would think of me and my situation and give me a second chance. I vow that I will not give you an opportunity to regret your generosity." He rose to his knees and took the imam's hand and kissed it.

"I will be leaving soon, tomorrow or the day after. Will you be ready?"

Mustafa stared at Junayd. "Ibn Shahin."

"You are free, son. I have spoken with him already. He has already arranged for a new tutor for the children. We knew you would choose correctly."

"Now." Junayd indicated the reception area, and he turned that way.

Several people were chatting, but YingYue stood alone to one side, watching him. She raised her eyebrows as if to ask if everything had been fixed.

"Go to her."

Mustafa took his uncle's hand and tried to kiss it, but he pulled it away. Then he turned to Auntie Hakima, took her hand, but she dragged him into an awkward embrace instead. Her wrap smelled of smoke and orange flower water and he lay his cheek on her shoulder. When he raised his head, he whispered in her ear, "My mother, you saved me."

She did not object as he pulled away, instead shook her stick at him playfully. "God saved you, boy. But I'll come to Medina to clap you on the ankles again if I have to, so do not make me."

Tein had moved closer to Junayd, his head bowed, asking a question. Ibn Ata moved with him and put a hand on Tein's back.

Mustafa would thank Tein later for all he had done, too.

Walking to YingYue, she was transformed in his eyes. She was no longer a woman who thwarted him, but a woman who believed in him, his companion.

She stretched her hands out. "Husband."

"Wife." He took her hands in his own.

"Will you go to Medina?"

"Yes."

Relief settled into her face. "You will be happier there."

He did not feel it, but he nodded because it was right.

"Come home with me now. I will tell you how often I expect you to write with all your news."

DAY TEN

29

Tein had been drifting in and out of sleep, enjoying Saliha's slow breaths against his chest as she slept nestled under his arm. Out in the courtyard, The family was speaking quietly. He had more time with his beloved and fell back asleep, dreaming momentarily of her standing on a verdant plain, her hair unbound, her wrap draped over one shoulder and moving with the breeze. A baby was in her arms, suckling at her breast. She gazed at him with heavy-lidded eyes, then snorted loudly, surprising him awake. The sleeping Saliha returned to breathing gently and he touched his hand to her belly, hoping to feel some change, but there was nothing yet. The weight of his long dead infant son fell heavily against him.

All that time passed, and he could still feel little Husayn nestled on his chest, hear his quick breaths, take in the scent of him. How small he was, cupped in Tein's large hands. Soft tears spilled down his cheeks. He thought he could feel the touch of Ayzit's delicate fingers wiping them away and, for a moment, wanted to die from his inability to save them. But the aunts and uncles surrounded him after his return, soothing him, never letting him reach that place. Uncle Nuri always there, his arms out. Ammar had seen and pulled him into working in Grave Crimes. Zaytuna's own grief and anger mingled with his, fighting him back into existence. And, then, Saliha, his wild mare, loving him so freely, forcing him to abandon death all together. All of this, given to him.

His uncle had whispered in his ear yesterday, "Savour each gift."

After Mustafa had left with YingYue, he told his uncle everything; admitting his fears of what he thought the aunts and uncles expected of him, of the impossibility of protecting his family, of returning to brutality.

His uncle said, "You were born a soft-hearted boy. But you were made into a guardian of your mother and sister, the empire, then the people of this city. You have had to kill, but you are not a killer. It is that broken heart of yours that reaches out in fury. The cure is love and being loved."

As his uncle spoke, Auntie Hakima cupped her hands on his back and whispered prayers into his heart. Ibn Ata moved closer and the binds that had held him fast his whole life began to loosen.

His uncle did not tell him all these people he loved were idols. No. Each of them was to be cherished. "Sip from the cup of love held out to you," he commanded.

When Tein left these good people, he wandered the streets of Baghdad until late in the night with a new awareness, tasting life, from the birds scattering from the reed beds against a setting sun to the sound of drums and song, then the rising of the stars and flickering lamplight over the crumbling courtyard wall of a home built on the edge of a canal.

Then home.

Zaytuna was sitting in the courtyard, both hands low on her belly, her head bowed, breathing a prayer he could not hear. She lifted her face to the moonlight. Pearlescent tears sparkled on cheeks rounded from a smile that he had only ever seen in her moments of ecstasy. But she was not lost in God and she beckoned to him. He knelt before his twin sister and kissed each cheek, then her forehead, then took each hand and kissed those, too.

She held his face. "Brother, you are back so late. Go to your wife."

"Kamal Ali?"

"I'll wait here for him."

"Is he coming?"

"If God wills."

Tein left her to her prayer and waiting, not knowing if Kamal Ali would come home or not. Many men would have left for good, others stayed to do worse. If he knew the man at all from working under him and living beside him, Kamal Ali would never return to carry that burden on his back. If he came home, it would be to loving her and, he hoped, trusting him again.

He had slipped quietly into bed, slept deeply, and awoke with the dream of Saliha holding their child to her breast.

Her eyes fluttered. Tein admired her beauty even in the untidiness of sleep. Her cheek was pressed against the mattress, pushing her mouth open, and her braid had come undone. Black hair spread in messy tendrils across the pillow. Then she snorted again, gasping awake next to him. Realizing where she was, she wiped her mouth with the back of her hand, moaned sleepily, and reached her hand through the deep neckline of his nightshirt, wrapping a leg around him until her body embraced him fully. His body responded, wanting to enjoy her however she offered herself to him, but he covered her hand with his own and whispered, "Later, my love. We have not said our marriage vows."

But she lifted herself up anyway, straddling him, pulling off her nightshirt and leaning over, brushing his lips with her own. "Say that again."

"We haven't renewed our marriage." He did not want to be with her again until he had talked to her like Ibn Ali and Baraqan had urged.

"Tease," she said, lying down beside him.

"We were only sleeping. How did I tease you?"

"Your body is enough." She got up on one elbow. "Going out early on the case?"

"The case is over," he said, relieved, and tugged the blanket up over her breasts.

"What?" She pushed it away and put on her nightshirt instead.

"Ammar will be here soon. I have to be ready to explain why. He might not agree."

"You going to tell me?"

He explained, finally saying, "I think Nabil enjoyed the madness of it all. His mother is the same. Whatever their life has been, they have dug into the bitterness of it and all they want is to poison everyone with them. I told her we know everything, so she'll send word to him to come home now."

"You better not give her one fals in return from selling that silver case."

"Never fear. Ammar will not." He paused, taking a breath and deciding in the moment to talk to her now, rather than later that night. "But I've got something on my mind."

She came awake with that, sat up.

The advice had been simply to talk to her, but he did not know where to begin. He sat up and took her hand, opening her palm to him and stroking each of her fingers absentmindedly. "We have been careful, but I worry that it won't be enough. What if you became pregnant? What would you do?"

There was a long silence, long enough to make him wonder if she already knew.

"Tell me what you mean."

"I found out that if you become pregnant, our daily temporary marriages become a regular marriage and we cannot divorce until the baby is born, making the child legitimate."

She pulled her hand away. "Who told you that?"

"Ibn Ali," he lied. He had known since the days he saw it done on the frontier, but kept the truth of it from her, afraid she would never agree to even one night, hoping, but never thinking, this day would come.

Saliha remained silent, her shoulders tensed, but she did not withdraw her hand.

"It may happen. We should talk about it."

"Should we?" She looked away.

"Would you...go to a midwife for herbs or..."

Facing him again, her eyes flashed. "Do you want me to?"

He shook his head sombrely. "Never."

"Good." Her shoulders relaxed and a weight fell from him.

"Do you want to have a child with me?" he asked softly.

She reached a hand out to him. "Inshallah."

It was not a "yes" nor a "no." He took it to mean that she would not try, but would welcome what might come, and it was enough. The way she said it, though, he did not think that she knew she was already pregnant. One thing at a time. At least this conversation would prepare her.

A shadow crossed her face. "All that time with my husband before and I never came up pregnant."

He jokingly pounded his chest. "I am not him."

She half smiled, but the cloud was still there, that look behind her eyes that he read as the reason why she needed a temporary marriage rather than a full marriage. The reason she would not try for a baby. There would never be a day in which her dead husband's violence did not haunt her. When she knew, he would remind her from the birth on that they could return to their daily commitment. He leaned over and kissed her lightly. "We can face anything together."

Saliha did not reply, only slipping out of bed and pulling on her quilted sirwal and qamis. She added a wrap, turning to nag him playfully. "You. Out of bed. Breakfast."

All was well.

She looked out the door, then shut it again, whispering, "Kamal Ali is here!"

He got up quickly to dress. "Good or bad?"

Saliha smiled slyly. "They have that look on their faces, like when they try to sneak off to the public baths in the morning."

Kamal Ali had come home last night for good. Tein grinned as he pulled his clothes on, feeling his own wrongs forgiven along with Zaytuna. He took his time, letting the relief of the family back together and Saliha's acceptance settle in until he felt it quietly enough to join them without breaking into song.

Outside, everyone was sitting around food laid out, a jug of buttermilk, fresh cheese, olives, bread, and a small plate of olive oil with herbs. They hailed Tein softly as he came out. Zaytuna seemed chastened, but strangely peaceful underneath it all, as if her moonlit joy from the night before was merely behind a cloud. Kamal Ali seemed embarrassed but happy, near tears and making an effort to hold them back. Still, they sat thigh to thigh, with Layla nearly on top of him on the other side, and his arm around her. Zaytuna tore a piece of bread, dipped it in oil, then used it to take up a bit of cheese and held it out to him. He took the bite of food from her without holding back any tenderness, then gave it to Layla, who opened her mouth so he could feed her like a baby bird.

Everyone had been speaking as if a loud word would break their newly restored family into pieces. But they were not so fragile and so he returned their quiet greetings of a good morning with a boisterous, "Sabah an-nur!"

Yulduz grinned at the release of tension. She no longer seemed angry at anyone and waved him over, her voice now at her full, penetrating volume. "Come sit! You came in so late last night I could not tell you the news."

With Yulduz, this could mean anything, generally the business of one of the neighbour's men, something she thought would require his intervention and something that he would ignore. But instead of being frustrated, he was relieved. He settled on the mat, tore off a piece of bread and stuck it in his mouth, giving her a muffled, "Yes?"

"Your case." She sat back triumphantly.

Zaytuna shot him an involuntary look. She had not been told.

"I've been talking to Marta. Her old cousin, Yara, is always complaining about noise in the street." She leaned over to make a point. "That old woman can barely sleep at night if a mouse turns over a crumb!"

"What did Marta say, Yulduz?"

"Uff. I'm trying to explain why Marta ignored what 'er cousin said. Yara, her cousin, is always complaining. This, that, and the other thing. Something always. So when the woman said she heard screaming out of a house on her street, Marta ignored it. Marta only got serious when

I told 'er about your case. She went and asked Yara about the screaming and other women were there, an' they told what they knew and she told me."

Yulduz, who never had any trouble getting her point across, took her time with gossip. There was no trying to make any sense of it or forcing her along. He went back to eating, pretending he was not paying attention.

"You'll take that food out of your mouth when you hear what I have to say!"

Qambar knew better than to get involved and poured more buttermilk into the cups.

Tein took another bite, glancing at Saliha, who was stifling a laugh.

"Marta said 'er cousin Yara told 'er it was Nabil who had been dragged into a house by two government men, screaming the whole way. More screaming came out of that house, too."

"What?" Tein swallowed hard, then coughed. "How did she know? Did they say his name?"

"No. Not Nabil!" She leaned in with a look as if she had finally hooked him. "One of the government men said the name, 'Ibn Mujahid'. Now you tell me how two old Christian women would know that name. Walla, I did not know it myself until a week ago."

"Who are these women?"

"Two women from Yara's street. Marta knew the name 'Ibn Mujahid' because I mentioned it. So when they said it, she knew. That's why she knew to tell me when the other woman was complaining about crime in their neighbourhood and the watchman doing nothing about it."

"Yulduz," he said impatiently.

"Folks tried to intervene, but the watchman stood by an' did nothing." She tipped up her chin.

Zaytuna whispered to Kamal Ali, who looked at her oddly, saying, "Why won't you tell him?"

She hesitated, then said, "I saw Saadia recently. One of her friends said her Christian maid reported men from the government were holding al-Hallaj prisoner in her neighbourhood."

"If it were al-Hallaj," Tein said, "he'd be held in the Round City or a judge's cell, not someone's house in a Christian neighbourhood."

"That's what I told her. But it means someone is being held there."

"Like I said, one of them that is doing the holding said, 'Ibn Mujahid'...," Yulduz pressed.

Zaytuna and Yulduz were right. The case was still live and he did not want to admit it. Not just that, he did not care what happened to Nabil. If some of Ibn Mujahid's men had enough of him and decided to teach him a lesson, why was it his business? He huffed. "Where is this place?"

"Shammasiyya, al-Masbah, the first alley off of al-Warda. Look for a watchman standing around doing nothing," Yulduz said.

To him, it sounded like the watchman had been paid off, easy enough to do, probably both the day and night watchman. Tein glanced toward the door, wishing Ammar would get there. It was a long walk, half the morning at least. And what would they do if the watchman on the street tried to stop them from releasing Nabil? Were they going to get different watchmen to hold up their end? The only way would be to go to the Round City first and grab the men from Grave Crimes. First to the Round City, then across the bridge to Shammasiyya. It was going to be a long day, and all for a man not worth finding.

Zaytuna said something he could not hear. Kamal Ali whispered in her ear again. She faced Tein. Her skin was mottled but her eyes were clear. "When will Ammar be here?"

Yulduz glared at her, and Qambar gave her one quick exasperated look. Layla looked scared. But it was obvious Kamal Ali had encouraged her and Tein wanted to embrace him. All this and he refused to break her spirit. He had chosen to trust her, but it would be a long time until the others would. He wanted to tell them that Mustafa was leaving, she was safe to go out. But not in front of Kamal Ali, not like this. Later, he would tell Zaytuna and she would tell her husband. Only Saliha gave her friend a nod of encouragement.

"Soon," Tein answered.

Kamal Ali held Layla closer. "Your mother can fix everything. Did you not tell me that once?"

The girl forced a smile.

The outer door rattled with a hard knock and Layla jumped up to open the door.

"Assalamu alaykum," she said to them in her happy, sing-song voice, but he was not sure if she was putting on a show for them or being genuine. Once the door had opened fully, Tein saw her happiness was real. It was Ammar, and Nasifa was with him. His arm was around her, and hers around her belly. She was wearing rose attar, the warm, sweet scent making her heaviness with child even more beautiful.

"I brought Nasifa to visit while Tein and I are off at work."

Everyone got up to greet them, Yulduz clucking over her, then arranging the pillows on the reed mat for her.

Zaytuna kissed Nasifa on both cheeks.

Saliha stood back, taking her in. "Your perfume!"

"A gift from Ammar," she said with pleasure.

Nasifa took Zaytuna's hand and placed it on her belly, and the two chortled.

Saliha joined them, feeling the baby kick, then glanced at Tein with sweet longing.

His heart broke open and it took all he had not to shout, "Us too!"

Yulduz patted the pillows loudly. "Nasifa, come 'ere!"

Zaytuna led Nasifa to sit, then came to Tein and Ammar. "I'll stay home with Nasifa. We haven't had a visit from her in so long." She looked back at Layla, who was pouring a cup of buttermilk for their guest. "Right, daughter?"

Relieved, Layla handed Nasifa the cup.

Ammar grinned as if all his troubles had been resolved and Tein accepted it. It was the right thing for Zaytuna to do today, at least for Layla, and in truth, they did not need her.

"Did you find out about Bahr?" Ammar asked.

Tein slapped him on the back. "Brother, you have missed a lot."

"What?"

"I'll tell you on the way to the Round City to get some men from Grave Crimes. If the old women are right, we've found Nabil."

Ammar glanced at Nasifa, who shooed him off. "Go!"

He slapped his chest. "I wore the cuirass for a reason!"

"You wear the cuirass and sword every day," Tein said.

He laughed. "Where's that dagger of yours?"

Tein headed to his room, not saying it was gone, left in the street for another to use. But Saliha was already coming out with his belt. "Where is your dagger?"

He shrugged. She saw something in his face and did not ask, nor did she say, "Be careful." He was grateful, but he would be careful because everything mattered, not just her, but their child. Still she walked him to the door, her concern for him clear.

Only Kamal Ali stopped him. "Ya Tein, if the case is coming to a close? Will I see you back at the churn soon?"

"Yes!" he replied, hugging him hard but briefly, nearly coming to tears with gratitude, and hurried out the door.

Ammar was already in the street and Tein had almost shut the door when he heard Yulduz say, loudly, "We'll have to be propping you up with pillows before long, too."

Then he heard Saliha. "What do you mean?"

Yulduz knew. Tein nearly jumped. Do old women know everything?

He walked briskly alongside Ammar as if his leg had never hurt him and gave his friend the news.

"So, Nabil's threats to print the manuscript became more than Ibn Mujahid could bear?"

"It looks like it."

"I tell you," Ammar said, "I don't like being used, but it seems like the mother's talisman worked."

"Yes, it turned her curse back on her."

"It's a bit strange, though. What are Ibn Mujahid's men planning on doing to him?"

"Scare him?" He looked at Ammar. "Everyone insists that Ibn Mujahid would bring any complaint before the court. Maybe he couldn't get the case seen, nothing to prosecute? So he did this? I'm having a hard time believing he's behind it even if the men were using his name."

"Nabil's probably sitting in that room wondering how he got himself into this mess."

"A large part of me wants to leave him there," Tein admitted.

"It would serve him and the mother right," Ammar agreed. "But Ibn Mujahid can't just abduct people he finds a threat, and let them go when they relent."

"Maybe it's students of Ibn Mujahid acting without his knowledge?" Like Mustafa said, a scholar could not survive a bad reputation, even one of the greats. Holding a man hostage would be devastating.

"Either way, we've got to thank these old women! I'll hire one in my new agency."

"You've decided?"

"I'll have to make it work or my family will surprise me one day with a new herd of goats or sheep and I'll have no choice!" He put a hand on Tein's shoulder. "I can't go back to churning butter."

Tein nodded in understanding. "Kamal Ali is home."

"I saw. What do you think?"

"All is well, especially as Mustafa is leaving Baghdad." He wanted to say more about Saliha, but let it go for now. "And Nasifa?"

"Regular hours when I can. I'll hire watchmen to help, and," he raised his eyebrows, "maybe some old woman."

"You might try my sister." He held out a hand. "Don't say anything now."

Ammar understood. "When she's ready. After all, without you around, I'll need someone to keep me in line."

"Zaytuna can do that."

Tein wondered if it was possible that all these things could fall into place, then remembered his uncle's command to accept the good and hitched his empty belt, not missing the weight of the dagger.

They walked up the ramp to the Basra Gate. "If Shabib and Ahab are not around, you'll go in to see Ibn Marwan? Get us a few watchmen?"

"Whatever it takes," Ammar said.

They passed through Solomon's Gates. Tein hoped that this would be his last time. Soon he could return to churning butter, his small world restored to him.

As they drew near their old office, they could hear the men. Ammar strode in, but Tein waited by the door.

"We've had a credible witness tell us our man is being held captive in Shammasiyya," Ammar said. "It looks like a couple of Ibn Mujahid's men are holding him."

"Walla? Is Ibn Mujahid involved?" Ahab said, unbelieving.

"We don't know that, but the men are using his name."

Shabib said, "That kind of high-level trouble will go to Ibn Marwan to manage."

"It looks like the watchmen for that neighbourhood are on the take. The old women say at least one of them would not act when they complained."

"Maybe, maybe not." Ahab got his back up. "You were never watchmen. You don't know."

"The people spat on us," Shabib added bitterly. "An old woman like that threw dung on me. I know why he would look the other way."

Tein stepped forward. "They hated us, too, and for good reason. And the watchmen? We saw how watchmen preferred to beat men down than do any good, beat women and children, too."

Ahab tipped his chin. "Not all of us."

Tein remembered the old man on the Tigris who would not carry police in his skiff, calling every last one of them a mother's son. It wasn't an insult he cared for, but the sentiment was true enough. It did not matter if it was not all of them. He did not respond to Ahab's protest. There was no convincing them that policing would create every opportunity to draw them down into their worst selves.

"We'll have to check this with Ibn Marwan," Shabib said, walking past Tein closely enough to brush against him and have it not be an accident.

Tein rolled his eyes.

Ammar chuckled at the move. "I'm going with him."

"To see Ibn Marwan?"

"A greeting, merely." He tapped his turban with a wry smile.

Tein understood. He would tell him about the agency and Ibn Marwan would throw him cases the police would not touch, like this one had been, right up until now.

"You like this work, investigating on your own?" Ahab asked.

"No. I'm going back to churning butter."

Ahab drew back. "You can't be serious?"

"If you change your mind about policing, you'll find me in Buratha, Kamal Ali al-Fassi's butter shop, just outside the cheese market."

"That's where you work! My mother begs me for it. She doesn't live far from there."

"You walk up here every day from Buratha?" Tein felt for the man.

"No." He shook his head. "She's with my father and sisters in Karkh in the Imami neighbourhood, not far from the hospital. In any case, I've moved up here into a room with Shabib."

Moved away from family who might keep him in check, just Ahab and Shabib, working around the clock. "Come visit me sometime when you are in Buratha. We'll have butter for your mother, our gift to her."

Ammar returned. Shabib was behind him, looking unhappy. "Tein! Great news! We can have our old job backs if you like. He's not so happy with these men."

"Ibn Marwan being happy or unhappy doesn't mean much from one day to the next," Ahab complained.

Shabib said. "He's a mother's son."

30

Instead of turning to the left off the bridge over the Tigris into Rusafa, they turned right toward the Shammasiyya Gate. The walls of the Rum monastery opened up not much further to their right. Its grounds were fed by fertile land nestled in a bend of the Mahdi canal and boasted several gardens lush with fruit trees and flowering vines. Ammar fell behind for a moment, distracted by the parks busy with families, enjoying the grounds, strolling, sitting on benches, enjoying a picnic. He imagined Nasifa and the baby there with him one day soon.

"Ammar," Tein called out to him and he hurried to catch up.

They turned down several streets, then into one alley and another until they were on the street that Yulduz indicated, but were unsure which house. They presented similar fronts, a gate set into yellow brick buildings made of fired clay rather than an outer courtyard, most with two stories, and each building built onto the one beside it. Houses like this, the first floor was usually used as stables or storage for merchants. There were no watchmen on the street. They walked through slowly, listening for a man's cry, but there were no sounds other than the usual women calling to children and old men sitting in the street on stools talking. A group of well-shod boys at the end of the street were kicking a ball between themselves. They gave the men a quick look, then went back to their game.

"We better ask," Ahab said as he approached a cluster of men.

Three men in turbans and robes with rope belts watched them warily. One of them tapped the ground with his walking stick and said bitterly, "You're too late."

"Too late for what?" Ahab asked.

"The man's stopped screaming. We've been demanding help for days and you've done nothing!"

Another grumbled, "We Christians pay more in taxes than the rest of you. You should come to us first."

"Where's the watchman now?" Shabib asked. His tone told the man he agreed they had been done wrong.

"Gone. Another came running up just before you got here and they went off in a hurry."

Ahab gave Shabib an angry glance. It could only be that a watchman overheard them talking to Ibn Marwan and ran ahead to warn whoever had been taking bribes on this street.

"Where's the house?" Ammar asked.

"Two down. There." The man pointed with his stick.

Tein got there first, knocking loudly on the gate. Donkeys brayed in answer, but there was no sign someone was coming.

The man with the stick wobbled over. "That man was bound with rope and dragged in screaming. He hasn't come out. Lots of noise coming from there, agitating the donkeys."

Tein yanked on the gate, trying to force it open, but it was shut fast. He stuck his finger inside a hole used to grasp the latch, but turned to Ammar, shaking his head. He could not get to it.

"The men who put him in there," Ammar asked, "what do you know about them?"

"One wore a scholar's turban and he was fierce, the other a nervous fellow tapping his ear. A watchman we'd never seen before was with them and told us to stand back."

"We heard they mentioned a name."

"Ibn Mujahid." One of the other men joined him, while the third remained seated, looking away. "I heard it clear as day. Said he would be pleased with them."

Ibn Hammad, one of Ibn Mujahid's teaching assistants. It had to be.

"Fools or madmen," Tein said.

"What?"

"Imam Abu Abdurrahman had said only fools or madmen would consider the manuscript to be a threat."

"I don't know that Ibn Hammad is either," Ammar said.

Ahab joined Tein and the two of them got a corner of the gate pulled back enough that they were able to get a solid grasp. The latch broke with a loud crack and the gate opened.

The donkey's brays doubled.

Ahab ran in, checking the stalls, while Tein was already on the stairs going to the second level. Ammar followed, with Ahab behind him.

"Here!"

Ammar turned the corner and there he was in a dark room off a large, empty hall. Tein was already by the man's side. Ahab went around and kneeled by his head. The room stunk of feces, urine, and putrid flesh.

A red-bearded man was on his side on the floor, clothed only in sirwal, bleeding from lashed wounds on his back and feet. His lips were crusted over, dried vomit was in his beard, and his eyes were rolled back in his head. He moaned as Ahab reassured him.

Shabib appeared in the doorway and surveyed them. "There's no time to get him to the hospital across the river," he said, backing out hurriedly. "I'll get a healer."

Ammar opened a shutter, letting in air and light. The man fit Nabil's description. More, he looked like the brother of the dead man pulled out of the river. But there was no knowing for certain it was Nabil unless he could say his name.

Shabib came out in the street. Ammar watched a man lead him down the alley.

A moth-eaten blanket lay mounded in the corner by the window. Ammar lifted it, exposing a large leather bag and a few items of clothing, including the taraz-bordered red silk robe Nabil's mother described. It was Nabil. Ammar squatted and opened the flap of the leather bag. It was empty. No manuscript.

Tein came up behind him, looking over his shoulder. "Nothing?"

"Did you expect one?"

"Ibn Hammad took it?"

"I'm with you now, there never was one. It's all him."

Tein glanced at Nabil.

"A bad flogging, but they weren't trying to kill him."

"Beating him until he turned over the manuscript?" Tein asked.

"He admits there never was one, then he gets beaten more as punishment."

They heard a man's voice on the stairs. Shabib was ahead of the man, calling him "Doctor."

Tein swung his head around to look, then seemed relieved.

The doctor, wearing a yellow robe and a zunnar rope belt, put a bag down beside Nabil and spoke to him in low tones.

Ammar stood. Most of Baghdad's doctors were Christians. In one of their own neighbourhoods, it stood that a doctor would be nearer than a woman healer.

"I'm going to search the rest of the place," Tein said.

Ammar left the stink of the room and Nabil's moaning to go back down to the street. A small crowd had gathered. An old woman with a sharp eye stood out. She was holding tightly onto a small boy with a snotty nose. The woman bent over and wiped his face with a cloth from her sleeve, then waited for Ammar.

"Who owns the donkeys?"

"Mikael ibn Adi, he rents them. He's here all day, coming and going."

"How could the owner not have noticed a man screaming?"

"The men stuffed his ears with coin."

A man next to her said, "Is the man up there alive?"

"Barely. Did you hear them call him a name? A name of anyone else?"

"I heard from someone they said 'Ibn Mujahid', that's all."

A boy holding a ball, his face gravely drawn under his neatly wound turban, said, "Nabil."

Ammar clicked his tongue and smiled kindly. "How did you hear that?"

"They yelled it. Upstairs. We were down here." He gestured to his friends.

He asked the group, "I hear there were watchmen who wouldn't do anything."

"Not just that," a man said. "They threatened us."

A younger woman behind the old one, a baby strapped to her chest, her wrap loosely covering them both, said fearfully, "My man tried. He came with a bar to take the door down and one of them hit him with a staff. The other said he was coming with his torch to burn us out if we interfered."

"The two inside with the black turbans, they are from Grave Crimes. Tell them all this. Describe the watchmen."

The old woman looked him up and down. "You aren't police?"

"No, just came to help."

Shabib joined him.

"Tell this one." He pushed Shabib in front.

The crowd complained, voices rising, but he held his hands up and backed away. "One at a time!"

Ammar left him to it and met Tein as he was coming through the broken gate, shaking his head. "Nothing else there."

"It's Nabil," he said. "One of the boys out there heard them say his name. That and the robe in there are enough to prove it. The watchmen were more than derelict, they were threatening the neighbours from doing anything. It looks like the owner was taking bribes to look the other way."

Ahab was behind him, looking over at the crowd. "We'll find the watchmen and the owner. I came down to tell you they've got your man ready to go to a clinic. He could survive the flogging, the doctor said, but maybe not the infection. He'll know once they clean him out."

Tein said, "It's a grave crime now."

"If he dies, then it's murder in addition to kidnapping and torture."

Ahab grimaced. "Looking at Nabil in there, you might have been right. The dead body that washed up might have been a mistake. They look a lot alike."

And none of his business anymore. "I'll give you everything we got on the case."

Ahab nodded. "We'll take it."

"You'll find the men who did this at the Sharqiyya Mosque," Ammar said. "Look for Ibn Hammad. The other is a student of his with a nervous tic." Ammar tapped his ear.

Ahab said, "I've got to go find a pallet."

Ammar took Tein aside. "Let's get to the mosque."

"It's done, Ammar. They'll get the men later."

"I want to tell Ibn Mujahid myself. Then the mother."

Tein still resisted but in a way Ammar knew he would be coming along.

"What will you say to the mother?" Tein asked.

"Tell her that their desire for revenge may have got her son killed."

"And Ibn Mujahid?"

"Let's see what happens when we get there. I don't want Shabib and Ahab stumbling around, making accusations, and seeing their own lives ruined. It's better if Ibn Mujahid hands over Ibn Hammad and the other one without being asked."

By the look on his face, Tein still thought Ibn Mujahid had nothing to do with it, but Ammar would see if that was true or not.

As they made their way to the pontoon bridge over the Tigris, Tein's limp became more and more pronounced. Ammar slowed his pace, despite wanting to hurry. Shabib and Ahab would not go to the mosque looking for Ibn Hammad until Nabil was safely in a clinic. That gave them a bit of a lead to question Ibn Mujahid, but not as much time as he would like.

Waiting in line to get onto the bridge, Ammar could not hold back the thought any longer. "I want to see Ibn Mujahid's face."

"And if he was involved?"

They stepped out onto the bridge, getting their balance under the pressure of the pontoons holding against the swift current. Ammar stared at the multi-storied houses lining the banks of the Tigris, their balconies overlooking the water. A few people here and there leaned out or could be seen withdrawing. The glint of gold in one man's turban caught the light. "I'll make sure everyone knows it."

Tein grunted, but Ammar could not tell if it was agreement or not and he did not ask.

Off the bridge, Tein was swinging his leg in that way that said he would have to rest soon. The mosque was just ahead.

"Do you think Mustafa will be there?"

Tein shook his head. "I didn't tell you. He got an offer to study hadith in Medina under an important scholar. Might be leaving today, tomorrow."

"And YingYue?"

"Sending him off with her blessings. They'll remain married, but he's free to marry there, although…"

Ammar leaned on the wall of the mosque to pull off his boots. "…although Zaytuna."

"I can't see him marrying again for a long time."

"But all is well at home again."

Tein had the look of a man who had escaped death. Ammar was glad for him. The small world of the butter shop, along with Kamal Ali's relentless good spirit, was what his friend needed, as much as he might wish otherwise. He would have more time with Saliha and the child coming to them, and Ammar would do the same somehow for Nasifa and their child.

The study circles were busy across the mosque. Ibn Shanabudh's circles were crowded, but the scholar was nowhere to be seen. He must still be out of the city. Ibn Mujahid's circles dominated. Hundreds of students were sitting around scores of teaching assistants leading classes. Ibn Hammad was there, staring at them. Ammar did not acknowledge him, preferring to let him think they were not there for him. Tein did likewise and was already skirting the students to get to the other side where a man was sitting surrounded by a large group of eager faces.

Ibn Mujahid was humbly dressed in unadorned robes and a hooded cloak of simple wool in dark brown with muted stripes. His turban was not grandiosely wound, like some scholars Ammar had met. His expression was sharp, his attention focused on the student speaking. There were no words for Ibn Mujahid other than elegant and powerful. Ammar would call him a hard man, but there was also a clear sense of justice about him, to the point where one should fear him. He would have a man flogged or killed, but only through the courts. Ammar no longer wondered if Ibn Hammad had been acting under Ibn Mujahid's orders.

Tein took a seat near a pillar, far enough outside the circle that he could stretch out his bad leg without being rude. But Ammar went on the other side, moving in closer, and stood watching. He would have thought Ibn Mujahid would be teaching the most advanced students himself, but those around him were young and fresh-faced. By the accent of one who had just asked a question, not all were from Baghdad. That one came from parts further west.

Ibn Mujahid responded to the question, his dark eyes now sparkling, "I understand the desire for the clarity of one reading tradition, but it would not give us greater certainty. We have certainty. We have certainty that the caliph Uthman's codex comes to us without one word changed. That the variant possibilities from which our accepted readings arise have not increased nor decreased. We may argue amongst ourselves over which among those possibilities is more or less reliable, even consider some to be wrong. But we do not accept" —he glanced in the direction of Ibn Shanabudh's circle—"adding other possibilities."

The young man looked like he wanted to interject, but wisely held his tongue.

Pointing to himself, he said, "This local boy does not want a single reading chosen to be 'the Quran'." Ibn Mujahid held up his hand. "While that one reading would be a reliable account of the revelation as the Prophet, alayhi salam, recited it, we would lose the others. We need to engage ourselves in memorizing the readings that have already been established, rather than choose one reading tradition for those after us to recite."

"But, professor, you must have a personal reading of your own that you prefer."

Ibn Mujahid smiled as if he had heard this question a thousand times before. "I do not. I likewise forbid my students from doing the same."

A student in a poor man's turban, clean but worn, coughed, then spoke, his voice quavering. "We may say this in Baghdad or Kufa. But I fear for my own town where people encounter traveling scholars with recitations that confuse them. It seems each one is different in some small way. It disturbs my people and I am left to console them after these scholars leave." He bowed his head. "I have come to study the variant readings, but on my return home, I plan to share only one reading tradition with them."

"I am glad you are with us, son." He looked around the circle, then cast his eye on Ammar. "All are welcome." Returning his attention to the student, he said. "I do not disagree with you. We stand at a precipice and something must be done. How many variant readings are there from this small pool of possibilities? And as our friend from Syria reminds us, scholars may choose their own ways creating more and more."

To a one, the students were rapt, though many obviously did not understand what he meant. That included Ammar, who wished he could ask Ibn Mujahid to explain.

"Imagine a small basket before us filled with slips of paper upon which each accepted variant sustained by the caliph Uthman's codex is written." He held up his hand with an imagined slip of paper. "Each slip has written on it a long or short vowel, a verbal or nominal form, a consonant. We gather here to argue intelligently among ourselves, which is more reliable for this or that reason, which is more likely, which we think may be impossible despite it being widely-accepted. We pluck from the basket on well-reasoned bases. Our methods have guided us well, and the readings have been limited to a large degree. But it is becoming such that all scholars are not as precise with their methods, inventing rather than refining our criteria. As a result, on the basis of their novel methods, they may pull out of that basket unimagined possible combinations, resulting in untold and frivolous new readings. This is not the preservation of God's word and it must end."

Ammar bit back a question, but Ibn Mujahid saw it. "You there, who stands at our edge, you are one of us now. What do you want to ask?"

"You are saying that given old and new methods, there is a mathematical probability that the number of possible readings would increase year by year until…"

Ibn Mujahid finished his sentence, "Until all that differs between one reading tradition and another is one vowel, and another, and another, and this will lead the community into grave doubt over the reliability of these transmissions, transmissions that come to us unbroken from the community of the Prophet."

Ammar held his tongue, wanting to say it could all be solved by simply choosing Seyyidina Ali's manuscript, not caring that his own Shia Imams would have agreed with this man. But that was not why they were here and he would get to the matter of Ibn Masud's manuscript soon.

"We have gone far enough." Ibn Mujahid addressed the circle. "I suspect the best way forward would be to limit ourselves now to readings that are already well-established in different regions of the empire, excise those that are not, and add no more." He said with finality, "I, myself, would be willing to accept a variant choice with which I disagree for the sake of stabilizing the present readings."

"Such as, *kun fa yakuna* as recited by Ibn Amir of Damascus?" the first student asked.

"Yes!" Ibn Mujahid barked with pleasure, then became serious again. "It is for the sake of our community, for my love of the generations to come, for my love of the Prophet, God, and His revelation."

The student in the poor man's turban, said, "As our Prophet, alayhi salam said, 'That which is lawful is clear and that which is unlawful is clear, and between the two of them are doubtful matters about which many people do not know. Thus, he who avoids doubtful matters clears himself in regard to his religion and his honour, but he who falls into doubtful matters falls into that which is unlawful, like the shepherd who pastures around a sanctuary, all but grazing therein. Every king has a sanctuary, and God's sanctuary is His prohibitions. In the body there is a morsel of flesh, which, if it be whole, all the body is whole, and which, if it is diseased, the body is diseased. It is the heart'."

Ibn Mujahid's eyes moistened. Hand over his heart, he said, "Our prophet, alayhi salam, gave us this wisdom to find certainty in safe pastures. I will do my part."

Ammar asked. "You mean to choose them yourself?"

The other students looked at him as if he had crossed a line. And he had, there was a tone he could not hide that spoke to his resentment that it was men like this who decided.

Ibn Mujahid considered Ammar for a moment, then said, "Yes."

"The scholars who agree with you, the ones you share methods with, what will they think? Will they accept your choice?"

"If God wills. I will make my case. I believe they will, even if that time comes long after my passing."

His moment had come. "And what happens to the companion reading traditions, even what only survives in memory? Will you destroy them like the caliph Uthman tried to do? Like he tried with Ibn Masud's manuscript?" And he left unstated, "Seyyidina Ali."

Ibn Mujahid grinned. "I will ask my students to go, so that you and I can speak alone." He looked over his students' heads. "Is your partner not with you?"

Ammar nearly laughed aloud at being caught out and glanced at Tein, who was already getting up to join him.

Ibn Mujahid addressed the students. "Nothing will be destroyed. We may limit the readings for practical use across the empire, but us scholars will never be limited in our knowledge of what comes down to us, even what survives of the companions' personal manuscripts. All of them." He addressed the student in the poor man's turban. "I hope you will teach your community one reading tradition but to respect the others and not fear them. Now, all of you, carry on with your day. We will meet again tomorrow before you take your places with your teachers."

The students stood, eyeing him and Tein, some with curiosity, others with suspicion. Ammar had to control himself from checking to see if Ibn Hammad had been watching. He could only imagine he was and likely becoming more and more uncomfortable.

"Now," Ibn Mujahid said, slapping his thighs. "Do you have news of Nabil ibn al-Qays?"

Tein spoke in a low voice. "Two of your men were seen keeping him hostage in a home in Shammasiyya. They tortured him. He is near death. One of them, we are certain, is Ibn Hammad. The other is a student of his, a man with a nervous tic."

Ammar watched Ibn Mujahid carefully. As each word led into the next, Ibn Mujahid became by turns horrified and furious, but not once did he look in Ibn Hammad's direction. Instead, he waved over a teaching assistant who was standing not too far off and spoke in his ear. That one could not control himself and stared directly at Ibn Hammad.

A shout erupted across the mosque as Ibn Hammad and the other man took off in a run towards the entrance. The teaching assistant yelled to others to follow them.

Ibn Mujahid snorted angrily. "We will deliver them to the police ourselves."

"What do you know about this?" Ammar asked.

"You mean to ask me if I ordered Nabil's abduction and torture?"

"Yes," he said, even though he no longer believed it.

Instead of a flash of anger or a defensive gesture, Ibn Mujahid's face fell. "No, I did not. Not directly."

"What do you mean?" Tein asked, gently.

"I am strong in my views. There is no room for error in matters regarding the Quran or faith. Ibn Hammad was always too eager when such questions arose. Too eager to pursue error without thorough debate, examination, and proof. I should have advised him more closely." He looked between them. "In the end, these are matters for the High Court to determine on the basis of evidence, expert testimony, and witnesses. We are not animals."

"I believe you. A man whom you have censured publicly even said that you would never act outside the court," Tein said. "But the police will ask."

"I invite them. Perhaps this man will speak in my defence?"

Tein deflected. "I am sure you will have more than enough men speaking for you."

"And the manuscript?" Ammar asked. "What did you think of his claim?"

"There was no autographed copy of Ibn Masud's personal manuscript. When closely questioned, Nabil could not even give an account of the known manuscript in Kufa."

"And what if Nabil was not bright enough to know?" Tein asked.

"He was bright, but lazy. He was able to repeat the errors that are broadly known, but none of the smaller variant choices that we know through the existing texts and other reports that Ibn Masud insisted on in his reading. He could not produce the manuscript. He could not cite from it. It seems even beyond Ibn Shanabudh to have let the man sit in his circle. I told Nabil never to approach me about it again, thinking that was enough."

"It was not enough for Nabil." Ammar paused. "Do you mind me asking why you cast out your student Bahr even after he swore fealty to the caliph Uthman's codex?"

A gentle cast came over his face. "He had come to us arrogant, unworthy of God's word. I had spoken to him about his pride, but he thought his capacity to memorize was proof of God's pleasure. The young man needed to be debased before of all those whose admiration he sought. The opportunity arose when Nabil forced him in front of me to vouch for the manuscript. God provided the perfect solution. I am confident he will find his way, now a humbler man."

"And if not," Tein asked, "then he was never worthy in the first place?"

Ibn Mujahid inclined his head.

They had enough. Ibn Hammad either believed the manuscript existed and was going to be printed despite the certainty of everyone around him or he was just out to punish Nabil for causing so much trouble. Ibn Mujahid was not involved and Ammar would say so to Shabib and Ahab. Whatever Ibn Mujahid wanted, he would get but he would get it by making a legal case. In fact, he was certain one day Ibn Mujahid would have Ibn Shanabudh and those like him in the High Court, flogged and kneeling before the judge to pledge his allegiance to the caliph Uthman's codex alone. Ammar wished the Shia had a man like this on their side. He put his hand over his heart to leave, but Tein took a step closer.

"If I may. I want to make certain you know that the paper sellers sent Nabil packing. They would never print a Quran."

He nodded, but there was a quizzical look in his eyes. Ammar would swear this was the first Ibn Mujahid had heard of it.

"Also, I grew up in the Sufi community here in Baghdad," Tein continued. "I am aware of your thoughts on Mansur al-Hallaj."

Ibn Mujahid's expression hardened. "Yes?"

"Mansur al-Hallaj is not from among my Sufi family. Just as you cast out Nabil, they cast out al-Hallaj long ago."

He lifted his chin. "If your family is concerned about being swept up when—and I say when—al-Hallaj is brought before the High Court, then they should not associate with him. I can guarantee nothing when his time comes."

Ammar put a hand on Tein's arm, fearing reprisal, but Tein only nodded, frowning. "I hope you will remember me and my words when the time comes." Then he turned and walked away without farewell and Ammar followed.

Outside, there was no sign of the men who had gone after Ibn Hammad and the other one, nor of Shabib and Ahab. He wondered if they had already got hold of them and were delivering them to the Round City. Ammar pulled on his boots. "All that effort and Ibn Mujahid already had plans to ruin Bahr. Nabil didn't need to do a thing. Well, just the mother to see now."

"Fine."

"You don't have to come."

"Let's finish this. I want to put it behind me."

They went around the side of the mosque to get to Umm Nabil's home. Tein slowed his pace as they approached the door.

"You sure?" Ammar asked.

Tein gestured for him to go ahead, so he knocked. It was not long before Oliga answered it with an air of furious exhaustion. She held out her hands as if they were there to manacle her.

"We found him," Ammar said, ignoring her gesture.

"Again?"

"This time, it's him."

A blood-curdling scream came from within. Oliga flattened herself against the open door, out of the way of the mother who was hurtling herself at them. "You!" she screamed at Tein.

Tein took a step back, sighing.

"We found him," Ammar repeated. "Because of your plan, all you two concocted, because you would not quit even after Bahr's reputation was ruined, Nabil was abducted and tortured. He may not live."

This time the mother screamed in what sounded like true grief and fell to the ground, grasping at Oliga's ankles, but she jumped aside out of reach.

Oliga shouted over her wails, "Where is he?"

Ammar realized that they did not know the location of the clinic. He looked to Tein who shrugged in that way he did when he is hating his job and himself. He turned away, leaving Ammar alone in the doorway. "He's in a clinic in Shammasiyya. It's police business now. You'll have to ask them. Remember the man who was with you when we took you to view the body? Go see him. The Grave Crimes offices in the Round City."

"Give back the money she paid you." Oliga sneered. "What kind of job is this?"

"She paid us to find him," Ammar said. "And we did." He ran to catch up with Tein, the mother's wails trailing behind him.

EPILOGUE

As they turned the corner toward Tein's home, the sound of a drum and women's calls and ululations reached them over the walls.

"A wedding?" Ammar guessed.

Tein smiled. During the walk from the mother's home to their neighbourhood in Tutha, he put the case behind him. He had done all he could. Nabil was in the hands of a doctor suffering wounds of his own making. Bahr was where he should be, on a humble path in service to the Quran. Ibn Hammad and the other scholar were likely already under arrest. He wished Oliga would run, the mother would have no means to track her down, but it seemed like she and the mother were left to each other's bitter company. He still did not understand why Nabil had not given up even after Bahr had been driven out of the mosque. But he had no desire to know why. People like that, there was no use in knowing. Abu YingYue and Imam Hossam were safe from suspicion of printing the Quran. Beside passing on Ibn Mujahid's warning to his aunts and uncles, there was nothing else he could do. If the uncles like Ibn Ata would not listen to Junayd himself, what would his word mean? They knew the risks, but their loyalty to each other mattered more. Ibn Ata would never give up al-Hallaj, no matter what it meant. Tein set him aside, too. *Surely they are in God's hands.*

"Sip from the cup of love," his Uncle Abu al-Qasim said. So he sipped and clapped as they drew near their street, wishing he had his mother's drum and could join whoever it was and celebrate the beginning of new lives. He was to be a father. A family man who churns butter and raises his son in peace. As they drew closer to his home, the calls and drum only grew louder. Then they heard it.

Ammar hurried to the door, grinning. "It's your home!"

Tein burst in.

Nasifa was resting against the pillows, smiling and clapping her hands. Qambar was beating their mother's drum with joyous abandon. Kamal Ali, Zaytuna, Saliha, Layla, and even Yulduz were holding hands, dancing in a circle. Their shoulders shook up and down. Their feet stomped. Round and round they went to the sound of the drum and Nasifa's calls and whoops. Saliha raised her voice and ululated until the call was answered by neighbours. Then clapping and drumming came over their walls, returned to them as a gift for their celebration.

Saliha knew she was pregnant and had told them.

Ammar joined Nasifa, while Tein took a place between Saliha and Zaytuna, holding their hands and stomping his feet, feeling no pain in his thigh. Layla was grinning, red-faced from exertion and happiness. Kamal Ali looked as if paradise had been promised to him. But Saliha let go of Yulduz's hand and pulled Tein out, pausing the dance and the drum, although the sounds of the neighbours carried on. Then she took Zaytuna's hand and put it in Tein's.

"Go!" she said to Zaytuna, then looked at Tein with overflowing happiness. He rushed to hold her in his arms and say, "Our child," but she had them turned around and nearly out the door.

Zaytuna looked back to Kamal Ali, who came forward to embrace Tein.

"Come," Zaytuna said. She separated the two men, then pulled Tein out the door and into the street.

"They know?"

Her expression softened. "There is news and I pray you'll be happy."

Of course, he would be happy. He did not understand, but followed her as she hurried through the alleys, turning this way and that, then out onto the cemetery road.

His old injury began to ache again, and she slowed for him.

"I will tell you and mother at the same time," she promised.

"Hold on. First, I need to tell you about Mustafa."

She stopped, searching his eyes for unwelcome news.

"Imam Abu Abdurrahman has invited him to study with him in Medina. He's leaving."

"The aunts and uncles. They took care of him. Alhamdulillah." But then relief gave over into a flash of panic. "How can I say goodbye?"

"You could do it with Auntie Hakima there, or Uncle Abu al-Qasim," he offered, hoping she would not accept. Not because she could not be trusted, but because he doubted Mustafa could stand it and she would have to tell Kamal Ali.

She looked away. "Kamal Ali would urge me to go, but I won't put him through it."

"I will do it for you," he promised.

"Yes, yes! Tell him," she said, placing her hand on his arm. "Tell him that I will always cherish the good we had. That I pray for his happiness in his new life."

"Inshallah, I will." He held her, saying in her ear, "He'll come back someday. Maybe with a new family. It will be different. You can greet each other instead of saying farewell."

There were tears as she pulled away, but not the weeping he expected. "It's done. He will have a chance now. There is nothing left for him in Baghdad." She gave him half a smile and wiped her face with the edge of her wrap. "Now, come with me."

She leaned on him as they walked, finally through the gate to the cemetery, past the people resting in its walls, the families within. Some called out greetings as they passed. Zaytuna greeted them all in return, her voice bright again.

Uncle Nuri's grave was just ahead and Zaytuna stopped there for just a moment, long enough for Tein to feel the warmth of family reach him. She held up her hands in prayer for Uncle Nuri's soul, and Tein joined her. But no sooner was the "amin," out of her mouth that she was tugging him along as if they were children again towards their mother's grave.

The afternoon sun showered the low hill in warm light. Dust rising on a breeze caught the light and turned into shimmering gold. The two palms they had planted dipped over the grave as if they were bowing in respect to their mother. Zaytuna placed a hand on her palm tree, said a prayer, and sank to the ground, out of breath.

He sat beside her. "Does Saliha know? Did she tell everyone?"

"Mother," she said, placing one hand flat on the grave, then took his hand with the other. "Tein. I am pregnant. Kamal Ali and I are going to have a child."

Both women pregnant! His eyes widened, the joy of the dance returning to him. Cousins! "You, too!"

She squeezed his hand. "No. Not Saliha, me. Only me."

"How do you know not Saliha?" He pulled his hand back.

"I told Saliha that you thought it was her. She said she's been feeling her menses coming."

"That could be anything!"

"Tein, she knows what it is. I'm sorry it's not her, too."

"But al-Hallaj?"

"He said 'a woman you know'."

His gut bottomed out as if she had taken his child from him herself. Keening grief doubled into embarrassment. It was true all along. He had heard "a woman" and thought it had to be Saliha because he wanted it so badly. He lowered his head, weeping.

Zaytuna touched his chin, lifting his face to see her.

"What Saliha must think of me," he moaned.

"No. She was relieved to understand. The questions and assurances, the conversation you had about her becoming pregnant, made her feel that she could be a mother with you. It surprised her."

He held himself, grief in one hand and mortification in the other. But the light in Zaytuna's eyes beckoned and he commanded himself to sip the love that was offered to him.

He placed one hand on the grave, then the other.

Mother, help me.

His heart released, and the sound of his mother's drum beat within him.

"The night I saw you waiting for Kamal Ali in the moonlight. You knew, then."

She nodded, tears coming. "I need you."

"You have me."

"I will place my child in your hands as if he were your Husayn."

They fell into each other's arms. The drum beat within him and he felt her heart beating, too.

"She's here, Tein. She is with us."

A warmth flowed through him, thick as honey, settling him and transforming into a memory that came alive around him. He was lying across his mother's back, held against her with a wide cloth, his hand a tiny fist around one of her locks. She tugged it away, laughing, scolding him to let go. But he tried to put it in his mouth and tasted her hair and smelled the beeswax she worked into it. Then he heard Zaytuna, strapped across their mother's chest, cooing. Their mother laughed and laughed with the purest sound of love, then called out to all who might hear, "Andudugu, my babies! My babies!"

CHARACTERS

Arab Naming Conventions

Umm Marwa [Mother of Marwa] Fatima [Personal Name] bint Fahim [Daughter of Fahim] al-Jarriri [Fahim, the Potter] al-Karkhi [From Karkh]

1.Parent of Child Name: Abu (Father) or Umm (Mother) of Marwa

2.Personal Name: Fatima

3.Child of Father/Mother's Name (then often a list of ancestry, Parent Child of Grandparents's Name, and so on): ibn (Son) or bint (Daughter) of Fahim

4.Nickname or Profession Name: "al-Jarriri," The Potter.

5.Tribe Name or Neighbourhood/City/Region Name. "al-Karkhi," from Karkh

Characters are mainly referred to by their parental name or their personal names in the book. The narrator uses short forms of nicknames or profession names, Nuri rather than "an-Nuri," or "Ibn Salah" instead of "Ibn as-Salah." Shortening is an English language convention of Arab names, but Arabs do it, too, in some regional dialects.

The pronunciation guide is an approximation for North American English speakers without strong regional accents.

Main Characters

Zaytuna [zay-TOON-ah]: Our heroine, Zaytuna, is a twenty-eight-year-old clothes washer of Nubian and Arab descent. She is the daughter of a female mystic, unnamed in the story, but known as al-Ashiqa al-Sawda, the Black Lover of God.

Tein [TEEN]: Zaytuna's twin, a former frontier fighter, a ghazi. He was an investigator alongside Ammar in the Baghdadi Police's Grave Crimes section.

Mustafa [MOOS-tah-fah]: Zaytuna and Tein's childhood friend, twenty-seven years old, sometimes called a cousin or a brother to them. He is a Hanbali hadith scholar of Persian and Arab descent.

Saliha [SAH-lee-hah]: Zaytuna's best friend, neighbour and a corpse washer. She is a twenty-six-year-old Arab who comes from the countryside.

Ammar [ahm-MAAR]: Tein's old friend from his days as a ghazi, formerly, the principal investigator for the Grave Crimes Section and Tein's boss.

Recurring Characters

The Sufis

Auntie Hakima [Hah-keem-ah]: An elder female mystic, a composite character based on a number of early Sufi women. She is a teacher and a mother figure to our characters.

al-Hallaj [HAL-laj]: A controversial mystic who shared the divine secrets in public. He most famously said, "I am the Real," which people misunderstood to mean that he thought he was God. He, along with mystic **Ibn Ata**, would be executed and Ibn Mujahid would play an important role in bringing him before the court. My account of al-

Hallaj, and some of his dialogue, is taken from the works of Louis Massignon and Carl Ernst.

Junayd [joo-NAID]: This character is based on the famous historical Sufi of Baghdad, Abu al-Qasim al-Junayd ibn Muhammad ibn al-Junayd al-Khazzaz al-Qawariri. The portrayal of Junayd in *The Lover* is the most accurate historically. There, his dialogue is taken directly from early sources. As the novels go on, he becomes more of a character in my hands, but still true to what we know of him.

Nuri [NOOR-ee]: This character is also based on a famous historical Sufi, Ahmad ibn Abu al-Husayn an-Nuri. I have adopted Annemarie Schimmel's loving take on this great mystic in *The Heritage of Sufism*.

Zaytuna and Tein's mother, known as *al-Ashiqa as-Sawda* [al-AH-shee-ka as-SOW-duh]: A Nubian woman who is overcome without warning by states of ecstasy in which her ego-self dissolves into the ocean of God's love. Her character is a composite of women from the early period, but most explicitly based on Shawana, a 1st H/7th CE mystic of African descent.

The Household

Kamal Ali [kuh-MAL ah-LEE]: Zaytuna's husband. A butter dealer. He originally hails from the city of Fas (now in Morocco), but left as a boy for adventure, eventually finding his way to Buratha, a suburb city of Baghdad.

Layla [LAY-luh]: Layla, a ten-year-old Arab servant girl, indentured by her parents at a young age who now lives with Zaytuna and the rest.

Yulduz [YOOL-duhz] and Qambar [KAHM-baar]: Zaytuna and Saliha's neighbours. Yulduz is a bold Turkmen woman, wife to Qambar. Qambar is an Arab Shia who fell madly in love with Yulduz when they were young.

Other Family and Friends

Ammar's family: His parents Umm and Abu Ammar, his brother

Muhsin, his wife, Tahirah, and their three children. They live on the
edge of Buratha on the Kufa Road side.

Khalil [kha-LEEL]: A friend of Tein. A former ghazi who works as an
enforcer for a loan shark.

Marta: Yuduz's best friend, a widowed Syriac Christian.

Nasifa [nah-SI-fuh]: Ammar's wife, a Shia woman from an
impoverished and difficult family.

YingYue [ying-yway]: Mustafa's wife. YingYue is an nineteen-year-
old Chinese mystic prodigy from Taraz, a city on the edge of the
Muslim empire in the East.

Saadia bint Salah [SAA-dee-ya]: The sister of Ibn Salah. She is based
on the poet Wallada bint al-Mustakfi, who some claim was bisexual.
The "Lion" poem belongs to Wallada. Her final poem is from the work
of Hafsa bint al-Hajj al-Rukuniyya (translation adapted from Marla
Segol and Arie Schippers, see Segol, "Representing the Body in Poems
by Medieval Muslim Women").

Grave Crimes

Ibn Marwan: Tein and Ammar's former sergeant.

Shabib and Ahab: Two watchman who Ibn Marwan hired as Ammar
and Tein's replacements.

The Hospital and Paper Shops

Abu YingYue: YingYue's father. A Chinese man who ran a paper
manufacturing business in Taraz. In Baghdad, he owns a papershop
that also produces block printed prayers.

Shahta [Shaah-TAH]: A corpse washer at the Barmakid Hospital and
Saliha's boss.

Ibn Ali and Baraqan: Ibn Ali is the pharmacist at the Barmakid
Hospital where Saliha works. He and Baraqan lead a philosophy salon
of men of African descent that meet weekly at Baraqan's paper shop.

Characters in This Book

Nabil [nah-BEEL]: A young Kufan Quran scholar now living in Baghdad who claims to have a controversial manuscript of the Quran.

Bahr [BAH-r]: An accomplished Quran scholar from Kufa who grew up near Nabil, now in Baghdad.

Himmat [him-MAT]: A Nubian student of Quran.

Ibn Hammad [hahm-MAD]: One of Ibn Mujahid's teaching assistants.

Ibn Mujahid [Moo-JAH-hid]: A famous Baghdadi Quran scholar who would argue to limit the Quran variant reading traditions to seven only. He only accepted possible variants that fit with the Uthmanic Codex. See "Note on History" at the beginning of this novel for more.

Ibn Shanabudh [sha-NAH-boodh]: A rival Quran scholar who preferred companions' manuscripts to the Uthmanic codex when analyzing variants. See "Note on History" at the beginning of this novel for more.

Razba [Raz-BAH]: A Ghuraba (Roma) leader who discusses the possibility of moveable type printing with Abu YingYue. For more on the Ghuraba of the medieval Middle East, including their influence on the development of printing, see Kristina Richardson, *Roma in the Medieval Islamic World*.

GLOSSARY

Please read the "Note on History" at the start of this book for terms and people specific to Quran scholarship.

Adhan: The call to ritual prayer. See **Time**.

Alhamdulillah: "Praise God."

Ali: The cousin and son-in-law of the Prophet Muhammad, husband of Fatima, and father to Hasan, **Husayn**, and Zaynab. He is known as the inheritor of the Prophet's knowledge of God for Sunnis, Shia, and Sufis. He is also famed for his extraordinary bravery and restraint. He refused to kill a man who spit on him in battle lest he harm the man out of petty anger. He is called "The Lion."

Allahu akbar: "God is great." This can be used in times of shock or distress to say, "God is greater than whatever is happening," in times of joy, "God is amazing," and affirming a statement, "You said it," to "Wow."

Assalamu alaykum, wa alaykum assalam: It means literally "peace to you" its reply is "and on you peace" but can basically mean "hi." Arab Muslims and non-Muslims alike use it.

Bismillah: "In the name of God." Used to start any action.

Buratha: A suburb city of Baghdad, known for its large Shia population, south of Karkh in Baghdad.

Fals: The smallest denomination of money. These and other coins could be chinked, meaning hand-cut into pieces to make smaller denominations.

Ghazi: One who fought on the frontier of the empire's expansion. They are held in high respect, unlike the troops who fight internal, civil battles.

Ghuraba: The people we recognize now by the collective name "Roma," but who have always had distinct names for their individual communities. On their contributions, language, and culture see Kristina Richardson, *The Roma in the Medieval Islamic World.*

Habibi: Masculine form of "my love," or "my dear one." Feminine is "habibati, or said more colloquially, "habibti."

Hanbali: Mustafa is a follower of the Hanbali school of law. He is not a legal scholar, but a scholar of hadith. He collects, memorizes, and transmits the reports about Muhammad. But hadith scholars were asked to give legal opinions in the early days.

Hadith: These are individual reports of what Muhammad said, did, accepted, and rejected. There are major compilations of hadith. These compilations may have several similar accounts of the same event or the same saying, or even contradictory accounts. The goal of very early Muslim Sunni scholars was to collect everything, not necessarily to resolve differences.

Husayn: The grandson of the Prophet. See **Karbala**.

Imam: An uppercase "I" refers to the Shia Imams or leaders of their communities. A lowercase "i" refers to the leader of the prayer or the leader of a mosque. The term simply means leader. When used as a title in dialogue, in either case, it is capitalized.

Inshallah: "If God wills." It is used to mean "Yes," "No," and "Maybe," and "if God wills," also as a statement of humility in response to praise.

Karbala: After the third caliph, Uthman, was murdered and Ali was ultimately offered the position of caliph, several prominent companions of the Prophet, led by his wife Aisha, challenged Ali's authority. This challenge ended on the battlefield with Ali soundly defeating them. Nevertheless, his authority continued to be contested. After Ali's death, his son Hasan negotiated away his right to lead, and the caliphate came into the hands of the Umayyads under the leadership of Muawiyya. After Muawiyya's death, Ali's other son, Husayn, was encouraged by the people of Kufa to lead a rebellion against the hereditary designation of Muawiyya's son Yazid as caliph. Husayn answered the call, but before he could reach Kufa, he was met on the plain of Karbala by Umayyad forces. The people of Kufa, under threat from the Umayyads, failed to support Husayn in battle. Others argue that no rebellion was planned, and the tensions arose from Husayn's refusal to submit to Yazid at his behest. Whatever case, Husayn's party, which included many members of the Prophet's family, were brutally killed, including women and children, while survivors were marched away and taken into custody. The loss of the Prophet's family, the loss of the leadership of his family, and the sorrow of the people of Kufa haunt the Shia religious imagination, as we see Ammar often experiencing.

Karkh: A large region in Baghdad located to the south of the Round City, west of the Tigris, and north of Buratha. It was the home of wealthy merchants, caliphal administrators, and scholars, Shia and Sunni alike, as well as populations of poor to impoverished Baghdadis. Tutha is a neighbourhood where Junayd's house is and most of the Baghdadi Sufis lived, it is not far from the Shuniziyya cemetery.

Mashallah: "God willed it." It can be used to mean "Well, that's a done deal," to "wonderful," to "God willed it, so nothing can harm it."

Mastaba: A gathering place and/or a hostel used by the Ghuraba.

Mihrab: The prayer niche that indicates the direction of Mecca. Those who pray in the niche are typically leading the mosque congregation in prayer.

Nabidh: Light or hard cider made from any fruit. It was enjoyed by all, lightly fermented like kombucha or hard like an alcoholic cider.

Nahariyya: Literally a "daytime" marriage house, meaning a brothel.

Prayer: There are five required ritual prayers daily. They must be done with specified words and movements. There are many videos on youtube to look at for examples. There are other supererogatory prayers performed in the same manner that one can do if one likes. Zaytuna, like many pious folk at that time, would perform prayers such as these late into the night. There are also distinct ritual prayers for funerals, eclipses, during Ramadan, and other times. Then, there are supplicatory prayers. This is when one calls out to God in one's own words for what one needs or using well-known formulas, some from the Qur'an, others from the Prophet, and still others from respected pious-folk that have become a tradition.

Qamis: A tunic worn by men or women of different lengths over undershirts of lighter or warmer material depending on the season. It was typically covered by a robe or a wrap, or both, in the case of men and women, according to season and depending on wealth.

Qarmatis: A controversial Shia community who threatened the Abbasid caliphate. At the beginning, they held almost communist values of equality and income distribution. They felt that the end of time had come and ritual practices were thus transformed.

Quran: For Muslims, the Qur'an is the word of God in the Arabic language, as received by Muhammad through the angel Gabriel over 23 years. See "A Note on History."

Sama: A Sufi ritual involving music, recitation of prayers remembering God, praise of the Prophet, and meant to induce ecstasy.

Sayyid/Sayyida: Master or Mistress, in the vein of Lord or Lady, typically used to refer to the Prophet and his family by Shia and some Sunni Muslims. Sayyidi means "My Master." Versions of this can also be used as the equivalent of sir or ma'am, as well.

Shaykh: It can refer to any teacher of any sort, with or without credentials, then and now. In these books, I use it to refer *only* to an established Sufi guide. It was not used by Sufis at this time, but since it is the accepted term later and now, I use it.

Shia: Those who would come to be known as Shia were those who believed that the Prophet and God, as articulated in certain verses of the Qur'an, had designated, Ali, his cousin and son-in-law to be his successor rather than Abu Bakr. Although Shia did not use the name at the time of the book, I use it for clarity's sake. Most believe that true

MORE FROM LAURY SILVERS

Available Now

The Sufi Mysteries Quartet: The Lover, The Jealous, The Unseen, and The Peace

Rat City, published in *Revenge in Three*: Three novellas written by three Muslim authors in three genres, inspired by The Count of Monte Cristo.

Coming Soon
Contemporary Thrillers set in Toronto. ***Disgraced*** in 2024 and ***Darling*** in 2025.
Ghazi Ammar's Agency of Investigation and Implementation in 2027.

Social Media

www.llsilvers.com
Bluesky and Meta: @laurylsilvers • Twitter: @waraqamusa

www.ingramcontent.com/pod-product-compliance
Lightning Source LLC
Chambersburg PA